RAGS and OLD IRON

ALSO BY
LORELEI SHANNON

Vermifuge and Other Toxic Cocktails: A Collection

RAGS and OLD IRON

Lorelei Shannon

JUNO

Rags and Old Iron

ISBN-13: 978-0-8095-5624-3
ISBN-10: 0-8095-5624-3
Library of Congress Control Number: 2006937385

Cover art copyright © 2007 by Timothy Lantz
www.stygiandarkness.com

Cover design © 2007 by Stephen H. Segal

Juno Books
Rockville, MD
www.juno-books.com

For more information, contact Juno Books
info@juno-books.com

To the VAAMPS:
For hauling me out of my shell,
For getting me in and out of trouble,
For teaching me to drink and cuss and be a lady,
For high drama and low humor,
For listening,
For trusting,   -
For getting me through high school alive.
Some of us have grown apart (and some haven't),
but what we had was as real as it gets.
And somewhere, in this world or that, we are
Girlfriends Forever.

Thanks, as always, to my family: my infinitely patient husband Daniel, my gorgeous boys, Orion and Fenris, and my mom Fran, the Deadliest Proofreader in the West. Thanks to Bridget McKenna, Mike Marano, and Tia V. Travis for reading this fractured fairy tale and helping me whip it into shape. Huge thanks to Oscar Brown Jr. for giving me permission to use the lyrics of his haunting classic, "Rags and Old Iron." And thanks to Bear Peters, who's been saving me a spot on his shelf for years.

With Love,
Lorelei

ᘉᘍᘉ

PROLOGUE

Amy steps through the door. She sees nothing but spots as her eyes adjust from banana-colored sunlight to sodden blackness. Her lungs fill with stale, bitter air and another more corrupt odor. The little girl takes a step back. Her green eyes go wide with confusion. She reaches out her hand, but she is suddenly afraid. He's still my friend, isn't he? *She tries to smile.* "Ruh—Rags?" *she says in a tiny voice. The fetid air snatches her voice from her lips, chokes it wetly and drops it to the ground, unheard.*

She looks around. She hates it when he hides from her. She hates it when he pops out and scares her. She opens her mouth to call to him, louder this time.

"Rags!"

Her voice is squeaky with fear.

"Yes, baby," he says from the darkness. She frowns. His voice sounds funny, like he has a mouthful of oatmeal.

"Yes, my angel, my precious."

He steps liquidly from a shadow, and she can see him kneel down and open his arms to her. It's all right. He still loves me. He does.

She runs to him. "Baby!" he laughs. "Oh little love . . . " He brushes the hair from her face, cupping her cheek in his hand, and his skin feels slimy. Her insides squirm. He must have been playing in the pool again. Yucchy. *She pulls back and tries to look into his eyes. They are flat and cold, like the eyes of the sharks at Sea World.*

That's 'cause it's so dark. He doesn't look like that.

7

He is picking her up, holding her way up in the air so she can fly, and a pale ray of light from the filthy window strikes his face.

She screams. She begins to struggle, pounding at his hands with her tiny fists.

"It's true! It's true! It's true!" she cries, her voice thin and high. "What Virginia said is true! You're not real! You're a monster!"

His body is shaking. He's crying. I made Rags cry. Amy goes limp, suddenly unsure. She bites her lower lip, tentatively puts her small, pink hand on his chest. "I'm sorry, Rags, I didn't mean . . . "

He spins her around, tossing her in the air, and light gleams on his long pointed teeth as he silently laughs.

"I am real, angel. I'm more real than Virginia or anyone else you know. You're going to be real, too, my sweet one, my baby bride . . . "

And his face is shifting, moving sluggishly like the scum on the surface of the pool, and the little girl's soft features twist in fear because his mouth is too big, and something moves inside it like worms and his fingers are growing longer, flowing through the pink chiffon of her Sunday dress and gripping her skin like the spongy pads of a tree frog—

With a squeal, she kicks out wildly with her hard black little Mary Jane shoes. They connect with Rags' face and sink in, and it feels like stepping in deep, cold mud. He shrieks and drops her.

She is running. She slips on the black mold that feeds on the ancient carpet and falls to one knee. Squish. Cold wet seeps through her pretty dress and her white tights and onto her shivering skin. She scrabbles desperately for a moment, the slick soles of her shoes refusing to grip. She can hear him right behind her.

She is on her feet again, running, running. Tears stream down Amy's face as she tries to find the door. She blinks and wipes her eyes. It is so dark. Wet moss brushes her neck and she yelps and jerks away, hitting her head on a wall. She can smell him. Sobbing, she ducks around a corner and runs down the hall. Her heart leaps. Ahead of her the room widens, she can see the looming twist of the staircase. The red stained glass in the front door winks at her like a dragon's eye. She runs as fast as her short legs will carry her. She is going to make it.

He laughs right next to her ear.

Suddenly she realizes that he is playing a game with her, that he can catch her any time.

Her shoe strikes something hard. She pitches forward, grabbing at the banister of the spiral staircase. Her fist closes on moss and she lands heavily on her chest. Squish. *Gasping, she rolls over and scoots backwards across the slimy floor. Her back presses against the door. She grabs for the doorknob and twists, but her hands are wet with slime and she just can't grip it and he is right behind her* right behind her. *She turns and looks up at him. Laughing softly, he reaches for her with long, ropy arms. Her bladder lets go. She doesn't want to see him any more, so she covers her eyes as he bends over her.*

It has to be a bad dream oh please it just has to.

Whether or not it happened that way, that was the way she remembered it, but only in her darkest nightmares. Mercifully, she didn't remember the rest.

After a while, she didn't remember it at all.

ONE

Amelia stood at the mouth of the long, dark hallway, one slender hand clutching at her heaving breast. Her other hand held a small, baroque— no, Gothic—candelabra. The bodice of her ivory lace nightgown was soaked with sweat. Her pale skin glowed, bathed in the cold moonlight streaming in through one narrow window. She breathed in, gathering up her courage. She took one tiny step, then another. Nothing happened. Emboldened, she walked on. Her bare feet were cold on the stone floor.

Her pretty mouth turned down as she brushed away a thick dusty curtain of spiderweb. A fat hairy spider dropped down—no way I hate spiders—A bat flew past with a silken rustle, its wingtip grazing her cheek. Amelia threw up her tiny hands with a stifled scream. She sagged against the rough stone wall, close to tears. She couldn't take one more shock. Not one more. Feeling a vapor coming on, she closed her emerald eyes against the world.

She couldn't escape. Images of dinner with her host flickered across her eyelids like the moving pictures of the cinematograph. She covered her face with her hands. Her mind wanted to dismiss it as a nightmare. But it hadn't been.

She could picture Lord Gareth with perfect clarity, looking at her across the table with burning black eyes. Her heart had pounded so, she could hardly finish her meal. She hadn't found it terribly unusual that he wasn't eating. He had told her that he ate only a very special diet, and she considered it just another of his rather charming eccentricities. She wouldn't have expected less of a real European nobleman.

Amelia opened her eyes, and a single tear slipped diamondlike down her heart-shaped face. Little fool!

When the strange, silent Gypsy servant woman had cleared the table and given Amelia a snifter of lovely apricot brandy, she had felt like a princess. And then, when Lord Gareth had offered his arm and escorted her to her chamber, well . . .

Amelia imagined him as he had been just a few hours earlier, stroking her hair and confessing his love for her. He had bent to kiss her, and his lips had been soft and insistent and . . . cold. But that was not so strange, was it? After all, it was cold in the castle. Central heating hadn't been invented yet.

Then she had glanced up and looked into the tiny antique mirror she had brought with her and hung on the wall, and saw she was alone. Her arms were draped around empty air. She watched in terror at the tiny depressions that appeared in her throat as he passionately kissed her there.

She had fainted. When she had awakened, she lay in the elaborate canopied bed, and he was gone. Amelia knew then what he was, just as she knew she had to get away. Hurriedly lighting the little candelabra—with gargoyles on it, gargoyles are cool—she had crept from her room to search for a way out of the castle. When she found it, she meant to pack her few possessions and leave at first light, before the servants were awake.

She shuddered. When the dawn came, he would sleep, and she would be safe.

A sudden cold wind blew out the candles. Amelia started, and whirled around. He stood behind her, a smile on his cruel, sensual lips. She cried out softly as he seized her around the slender waist and pulled her to him. The candelabra clattered to the floor. His strong, lean body was cold and strangely exciting. His eyes blazed into hers, and she knew what he was going to do.

She wanted him to.

He was so beautiful. He looked just like Frank Langella—no wait, Gary Oldman—He ran his tongue slowly along her neck, and it felt like velvet. She felt herself giving in to him. Her arms slipped around his neck and clutched his spiky blond hair because he—looked like Kiefer

Sutherland—*Her fingers gripped his back as she felt his teeth pressing into her throat.* "Yesss," *she sighed.*

—Thud—

—Thud—

Amy's eyes popped open. Sarah kicked her chair again and grinned at her like a cherubic hyena. Bleary-eyed, Amy looked around, hoping she hadn't been drooling in her sleep. Satisfied no one was staring, she yawned hugely behind her textbook and winced as her jaw gave an audible pop.

Sarah suppressed a snort of laughter, scribbled on a scrap of paper, then tossed it onto Amy's desk. Amy looked at her friend fuzzily for a moment, then read it. "Does that ever happen when you're sucking face?" it said in Sarah's bizarre, backslanted handwriting. Amy grinned and wrote back "Yes, but only when I really like the guy." Sarah smiled lazily and passed Amy the bag of M&Ms.

Aah. Chocolate in the morning. Amy took a generous handful. A crunch, a burst of sweetness, and she was finally awake.

Munching, Amy looked up at Professor Winterbrook. He was looking back at her, his gray eyes twinkling with amusement.

"So our four heroes have gotten themselves into a rather nasty situation, ay, Miss Sullivan?"

"Um, yes indeed," said Amy, blushing. There was a ripple of laughter through the classroom.

With a half-smile on his thin face, the professor continued. "They thought to ambush Dracula, but he slipped easily through their fingers and ridiculed them into the bargain. Would you be so kind as to read what he says to them?"

"Certainly," said Amy, swallowing her chocolate. She flipped through the book looking for the right page, angry with herself for not paying attention. *Good job, girl. Let's just show our favorite professor what an airhead we are, shall we?* But all wasn't lost, because after an agonizing few moments, she found it. *Thank God.*

Amy didn't look over at Sarah, because she would be wearing that "What a feeb" expression that always made Amy crack up. Instead she coughed once, and began to read.

"You think to baffle me, you—with your pale faces all in a row, like sheep in a butcher's."

Amy's voice cracked, and Sarah snickered.

"You shall be sorry yet, each one of you! You think you have left me without a place to rest; but I have more. My revenge is just begun! I spread it over centuries, and time is on my side."

Amy frowned. Her skin had begun to feel prickly and hot, and her stomach felt cold and heavy. She deeply regretted eating three greasy doughnuts for breakfast. She wiped her forehead and continued.

"Your girls that you all love are mine already; and through them you and others shall yet be mine—my creatures, to do my bidding and to be my jackals when I want to feed."

Amy squeezed her eyes shut as a wave of nausea hit her hard. She felt dizzy, and she gripped the sides of her desk.

"Didn't you forget something?" Amy opened her eyes, and the room lurched. Professor Winterbrook was looking at her.

"What?" she said, too loudly.

He smiled. "'Bah!' You forgot Dracula's 'Bah!'"

The class exploded with laughter. Amy's skin cooled as if washed by water. The nausea was receding as quickly as it had come. She laughed too, just a little shakily. She pushed shaggy blonde hair from her eyes and sat up straight in her chair.

"Now Doctor Van Helsing concludes from this episode that Dracula is frightened," said the Professor, fixing her with his pale eyes. "Do you agree with him, Amy?"

Yes. I get to impress him. "No," she said without hesitation.

Professor Winterbrook had come around the podium and was standing in front of Amy's desk. "Would you like to tell us why?"

"Well," she said, "Just losing a little money and a free shot at Mina wouldn't make someone like Dracula afraid. Just pis— um, irritated. How could four Victorian geeks frighten someone who's immortal? This was a man who once commanded huge armies. I think—" Amy's throat went dry. *Oh shit.* She was queasy again. "I think Dracula thought they were pathetic."

The professor smiled. "I would tend to agree with you. However, I did not notice Jonathan Harker or Quincy Morris eating live chickens."

14

The roar of laughter from the class hurt Amy's head. Sarah held up a note that said *Van Helsing Would!* in huge letters. Her grin faded as she saw Amy's pale face.

Amy lurched to her feet just as the bell rang. Her chest was tight, and her breath was coming in shallow gasps. The room turned amber, and Amy pitched forward. Then Sarah was there, helping her out the door and into the cool hallway. Amy slumped against a Coke machine, fighting the urge to vomit.

Professor Winterbrook peered out the door, his wide, pale forehead lined with concern. "Are you ill, Miss Sullivan?"

Amy mustered a smile. "Just something I ate, Professor."

He scowled. "Stay out of the Student Union Building, Miss Sullivan. Some of that food was fresh when Dracula was a first edition."

Sarah laughed. "Don't worry, Professor, I'll take her home and bleed her." She wrapped her arm firmly around Amy's waist and pulled her away from the machine. "Come on, spewpuppy."

They lurched across campus, their arms around each other like children. Sarah had a deadly look for anyone who stared or laughed.

Amy's mouth was watering with nausea. *Droolin' like a dog. How very charming.* The warmth of the day was making it worse; making Amy feel like she was submerged in water *or something else* the temperature of her own body. Amy squeezed her eyes shut, trusting Sarah not to run her into a tree. She felt a little less sick hiding behind her own eyelids.

About halfway to the parking lot, Amy began to breathe more easily. She felt a wave of cool pass over her like a kiss. Her stomach unclenched, and it was pure heaven.

Sarah took her by the shoulders and looked her in the eyes. Amy smiled. Sarah looked like a worried Muppet. Amy touched the sleeve of Sarah's worn Social Distortion T-shirt. Her arm and side were drenched with Amy's sweat. *Goddam Arizona weather. It's fall, for shit's sake.*

Sarah's eyes never left her face. "You OK, woman?" she asked quietly.

Amy grinned with clenched teeth, feeling like she needed a double shot of Pepto. "Yeah, I'll live. Can we sit down for a minute?"

Sarah guided her to the edge of the huge, pink, ugly fountain in the plaza; the centerpiece of Arizona State University's doubtful landscaping. They sat on one of the low concrete benches, and Amy let out a shuddering breath. She looked at her feet for a moment, considering hanging her head between her knees. *Nah. Salvage whatever tiny shred of dignity you have left, babe.*

Amy raised her head and turned to smile at Sarah. Sarah's mobile cherub-face was solemn as she continued to scan Amy's face. The expression made her look like somebody else.

Amy leaned in nose to nose with her and copied Sarah's expression. "Lighten up, silly, I'll live. It's just a massive breakfast rebellion." *I hope. Damn, I really don't need a case of the stomach flu right now.*

Sarah laughed and pushed her away. "Anytime you're ready, mutant," she said, dipping her cheap imitation Wayfarers in the fountain and cleaning them on the dry side of her T-shirt.

Amy looked over her shoulder at the enormous circular pool with its pathetic spurt of water in the middle. Much ridiculed and frequently vandalized, it was a favorite meeting place of the students. She remembered seeing it full of sky-blue suds one morning last year and smiled.

Her eyes narrowed. There was something dark in the water, right behind Sarah. *God knows what it is,* she thought. *People throw all sorts of crap in here.*

She watched the thing as it rose to the surface. It was a large chunk of sickly gray-green algae, probably dislodged from the pipes beneath the fountain. Amy grimaced, thinking of water gushing through corroded, slimy piping and being pumped into the fountain. People were always playing in it, cooling their feet and even their heads. Was there algae like that in the drinking fountain pipes? The lump of green bobbed in the water, bumping against the fountain wall.

Something squirmed inside it.

Amy hung her head between her legs and was suddenly and violently sick.

❧

She sat in her room, staring at the red stain on the baby-shit orange carpet. *Kool-Aid,* she thought. *Or tomato juice. Or blood. They just better not try to make us pay for it when we move out.* Once, in a fit of perversity, she had drawn the outline of a body around it in purple chalk, with the stain where the heart would be. *Morbid bitch.*

Amy snorted. *What the hell was wrong with me today?* She shook her head. *At least I feel all right now. More or less.*

It had taken her an hour to convince Sarah that she really was OK. The girl had been about to cancel her date with Mick, for God's sake. *Just what I need,* Amy had told her. *A bored and horny woman staring at me and thinking about her boyfriend's butt.* Sarah had finally relented, but not before taking Amy's temperature (which was normal), fixing her some Tummy Mint tea and clucking over her like a curly-haired Italian chicken.

Amy closed her eyes and leaned back on the pillows. Guiltily, she wished that she had let Sarah stay. *Yeah, right. What's the matter, you wuss? Scared a big bad lump of pond scum's gonna getcha? Better stay away from the complex pool.* Amy started to laugh, but then she pictured the tiny pool with its gray water and occasional green foliage, and her stomach flip-flopped.

"Dammit!" Amy slammed the side of her fist into the wall. Tears of pain stung her eyes. "What's wrong with me?" she hissed. Cradling her throbbing hand against her breast, she curled up into a tight little ball. Eventually, she slept.

* * *

. . . Running through the *swamp. The ground sinks beneath her feet. Panic. She struggles onto a mangrove root. She slips. Skins her knees. She stands up, steadies herself on the slippery tree trunk. She wipes her hands on her pink party dress and runs. The swamp is hot, fetid. It smells like Grandma's compost heap. Something wet and soft strikes her face, covering her eyes. She shrieks and claws at it, but the moss curls around her head like the tentacles of a squid. She pitches forward. She lands face down in the rancid water, instantly thrashing like a grounded fish. She struggles to get up, but something warm and heavy presses on the back of her head, forcing her down. As her lungs begin to burn and heave, the moss slowly and insistently wriggles into her mouth and nose . . .*

* * *

Amy's screams echoed through the empty apartment, her fists entwined in the sweat-soaked sheets.

TWO

Amy stared into her own bloodshot eyes. She gingerly touched the purplish bags under them, deciding that they clashed with the green irises. After a thoroughly horrible night, she had almost decided to skip her morning Anthro class. If only she hadn't skipped the last two to have breakfast with Sarah, she could still be in bed. She brushed the knots out of her hair, and shambled into the shower stall.

The water sputtered weakly for a few moments before blasting out in a nuclear-hot gush. Amy swore and jumped out of the way, hurriedly adjusting the corroded knob. The guy upstairs must have flushed again. He got her almost every morning. Once the water was tolerable, she began to shampoo her hair, silently vowing not to be lead astray so easily. She smiled, thinking of Sarah's wicked brown eyes.

"We're ten minutes late, Ame. You don't want to walk in late again, dooo youuu?" Lured away by ham-and-egg croissants one more time.

Amy wiped the suds from her face and opened her eyes a little, steeling her nerves to stick her head under the malevolent and unpredictable stream of water.

Something large and brown moved in the drain between her feet. As she bent down to look, the enormous sewer roach ran onto her foot and up her leg.

Amy screamed. She slapped the roach from her leg, leaving a red welt behind. It hit the stained porcelain and headed straight for her again. She leapt clumsily from the tub, striking her head on the towel rack. Cursing loudly, she threw open the bathroom door and staggered out into the hallway.

Sarah looked around the corner, eyes wide in her sleep-swollen face. Amy stood naked and shivering in the hall, dripping water and soap. Sarah started to laugh, until she saw the look on Amy's face. She frowned. "What's the matter, hon?"

Amy was suddenly very embarrassed. "There's a big old monster cockroach in the shower," she said, looking at the water puddling around her feet. "It jumped me."

Sarah held up a forefinger, the corners of her mouth twitching, then disappeared into her room. A not so stifled burst of laughter came from behind the door. Amy smiled and wrapped her arms around herself as she felt her face grow hot. A moment later, Sarah returned wearing an oversized Nine Inch Nails T-shirt and her black leather, spike heel, bad-girl boots. Without a word, she marched into the bathroom.

The stomping and swearing was terrible.

The toilet flushed, and Sarah emerged triumphant.

"OK, Toots," she said. "The world is safe for democracy once more." Sarah's full mouth pulled into an evil grin. "Better get back in the shower before you freeze those itty-bitty titties clean off."

Amy made a face, realizing her dignity was beyond saving, and slunk back into the bathroom to rinse the soap out of her hair.

❧

Amy and Sarah walked into Cultural Anthropology ten minutes late. As usual. Professor Hurley made a show of staring, her icy blue eyes boring into Amy's back as she made her way to the last row. Amy slumped down as low as possible, vanishing behind the simian athlete in front of her. She didn't want to have to look at the Hurl Monster today. *Bitch.*

Sarah sat down beside her and rummaged in her mangy backpack for her notebook. Hurley began droning on about complex social structures and ritual warfare.

Amy half-heartedly took notes, missing a good bit of what was said. Her eyes were itchy and tired. She glanced over at Sarah, who was slumped down in her chair nursing a Coke and rubbing her bloodshot eyes, and snickered. *She looks as bad as I do,* Amy thought. *At least she got laid. All I got was bad dreams.* She shuddered.

Amy stretched, shifted positions in her seat. The room was awfully warm. Chin in hand, she wrote down facts about the family life of the Yanomamo. *Beat their kids. Beat their wives. Snort mushrooms. Off each other three a week. Oughta be nuked off the face of the Earth.*

Amy's eyes narrowed. Hurley was getting excited, waving her arms around like a buzzard with a brain tumor. Amy could just picture the little gobs of spit that were forming at the corners of her mouth. Thank God she was too far away to see them today.

Amy slid down even further in her chair, feeling like she was melting in the hot, stifling room. *Why are there no windows in here, anyway?* The air felt thin in her lungs, and she could barely keep her eyes open.

Hurley threw her arms up into the air, and the ceiling cracked.

With a tremendous crash, it broke open. The headhunters dropped in one at a time, landing with catlike agility. They glared around with fierce black eyes, struck their naked chests and snarled. They raised their spears and howled. Professor Hurley was explaining that they were a tribe from New Guinea when the spear split her scrawny throat. Her cold eyes bulged angrily as the warriors parted her head from her body and tossed it around like a basketball, whooping and laughing. Then they had the bitchy blonde in the front row by her mousse-infested mane, and she barely had time to scream before her head joined the game. They were dragging a frat boy around by his heels, remarking with interest at his crew cut when Professor Hurley's head spoke.

Amy's head snapped up from her chest.

"This film," said the professor, "is called *Dead Birds*. It is most pertinent to today's lecture on ritual warfare."

Amy wiped her sticky eyes. No longer headless, Hurley was at the back of the lecture hall operating the projector. Amy smiled. *She would have made such a good ghost, carrying her wailing head under her arm and walking the halls of the anthro building late at night. She scared the Hell out of the grad students now. Imagine how much better she could do if she were dead!*

Sarah passed Amy a note featuring drawings of birds meeting their doom in exotic ways. One was spiked midair by an arrow, and one was frying on a power line (it even had a little bird skeleton inside), and one just blew up. Feathers everywhere. Amy was about to add to it when the lights went out.

The film seemed to be about little kids who played with pigs and ate nature's roadkill while their parents figured out new and different ways to murder each other. Amy rested her head on her desk and watched with half closed eyes. *Who cares.* It didn't seem real to her, like some low-budget docudrama on A&E. Then one of the kids was caught by the rival tribe and stabbed with sharpened sticks.

His folks put him in a cold stream so dying would hurt a little less. His tiny, skinny limbs jerked as his life washed away.

There was a lump forming in Amy's throat. *Poor little guy. He didn't do anything. He's just a little boy, for Christ's sake . . .*

Now they had his stiff little body in some kind of throne, vowing revenge. Tomorrow, they would go out and murder someone from the other tribe in the little guy's name. Then the other guys would want revenge. And so on. And so on. Amy dry-heaved.

The jock in front of her turned around and stared, ready to fake right or left. Sarah gripped Amy's arm. The people on either side of them gave Amy sidelong glances, hoping for a show. Amy stood up unsteadily. Sarah started to follow, but Amy quietly asked her to stay and take notes. Reluctantly, Sarah agreed. Amy's stomach lurched again. She grabbed her books and ran from the room.

⚬⚬⚬

The late morning sunlight, white and brutal, hurt Amy's eyes. The temperature was already in the eighties, and she found the warmth sickening, feverish. Zombie-like, she walked without thinking, then when her knees went weak, she slumped against the wall of the Communications building. Amy laughed, a dry and hollow sound. She began walking toward the portable snack bar, shuffling like a very old woman. She bought a cold orange soda and wandered away without her change. Amy laughed again. She took a large drink of her soda, dribbling some on her grungy pink Reebok.

Her mind was strangely distant. *What's the matter with me?* She wondered, but her thoughts were abstract and disjointed. She couldn't seem to focus. *Maybe I should see a doctor.*

Amy put on her round-lensed purple shades, then ventured out onto the mall once more. She felt slow, weighted, as if she were moving underwater. *I'm nineteen, for Christ's sake. I'm not supposed to feel like this.* Again, she considered getting a check-up. *Yeah, right, the Student Health butchers will make it fine and dandy. Besides, they can't do anything for the flu. If that's what it is. It's probably just a delayed reaction to getting dumped.*

She thought of Jay, with his phony smile and wandering crotch. An overripe orange dropped wetly from one of the ratty ornamental trees lining the walkway and rolled in front of her. Amy kicked it, and dark juice splattered her shoe. *How could I have been so stupid. So totally wrong about somebody. Yeah, that's enough to make anybody want to puke.*

Or maybe it's just Ebola.

Her shoe struck cement. Amy was standing at the fountain. She cringed, remembering her humiliating experience of the day before. But her favorite bench was open, the one under the huge, furry evergreen with the branches that seemed to spiral around its massive trunk. There it was, all shadow and dappled light, calling her name. *Aaamyy! Siiiit on me, Aaamyy!*

She grinned and threw her book bag down. She lay on her back on the warm cement, looking up into the tree. Amy couldn't see into the deceptive water, the wall of the fountain was too high from here. She was absurdly glad. Amy closed her eyes, her mind wandering. She remembered looking into another tree, a long long time ago. Drifting, she smiled.

⌘

Little Amy, six years old, pressed her hands to the hotel window and looked up. The almond tree was enormous and exotic, with long leaves and huge, dangly green pods. Could they be the almonds? Amy thought they must weigh a pound each. Did they shrink later, when they're put into the little packages they give you on the plane? Amy liked the smoke flavored ones, but they made her mouth dry. Then you had to drink a whole lot of soda pop, and then you had to pee, and there was nothing worse than having to pee in the scary, noisy airplane bathroom. Amy was certain that the toilet was going to suck her right out of the plane along with the toilet paper and blue water when she flushed it, so she usually saved her plane almonds until they were on the ground.

Her train of thought was broken when a red squirrel ran up the trunk of the tree and started bustling around, jumping from branch to branch. Amy held her breath as it skittered closer to her. There it was, just outside the window. She was sure the squirrel was looking at her with its bright little eyes. She wished she had some of those smoky, salty almonds to give it.

"Amy!"

She jumped, bumping her forehead on the window. The squirrel was gone in a flash of red fur. She sighed regretfully.

"Yes, Mama?"

Her mother stood in the doorway, smiling at her. "It's time to get ready, honey. You're going to meet your Florida grandma and grandpa tonight."

Amy looked up into her mother's pretty, round face.

"Mama, where do squirrels go at night?"

Mandy Sullivan smiled. "They live in trees, Amy. They have little homes in the trees."

"Mama?"

"Yes?"

"Do squirrels have nightmares?"

Mandy frowned, just a little. "I don't really know, Pumpkin. Do little girls have nightmares?"

Amy hesitated, not wanting to answer. Only babies had bad dreams about the Boogeyman. She was a big girl, and knew there was no such thing.

"Aha! I found my girls!" Tom Sullivan strode across the room and scooped Amy up in his arms. Her real father had died when she was an infant, and her mother had married Tom when she was three. Amy knew all this, because they had been careful to explain it to her. ("No secrets in this family," Mandy had said with a smile.) Amy didn't care. Tom was her daddy. The other man was just a handsome stranger in glossy black and white pictures, somehow pretend like an actor in an old movie with no sound.

Amy giggled and squirmed as Tom blew a "blowfish" on her cheek. "Gross, Daddy!"

"You'll get another one, Mophead, if you're not in that pretty yellow party dress in five minutes!" he scowled down at her, eyes twinkling. "I'm going to set my stopwatch—now!" With a shriek of laughter, Amy seized the dress up from the bed and ran into the bathroom.

⁂

She admired herself in the mirror. She looked pretty, like a lady. The dress was all frothy, crinkly stuff (a lot like the foam on a root beer float, only pink) and soft yellow lace, with a big pink rose at the waist. She couldn't zip it up herself, but Mama would do it for her. She smoothed the layers of the skirt, turning this way and that.

Amy stopped. She heard something above her; a dry scrabbling sound, barely there at all. She looked up.

The sewer roach dropped from the ceiling onto the front of her dress.

Amy screamed. The thing on her chest waved its antennae and ran up under her hair. Amy's hands spasmed into claws, and she ran from the bathroom shrieking.

Her mother bolted to her feet as Amy burst into the living room, hot tears spilling down her cheeks. She wanted to scream "Help me, mama!" But nothing would come out of her twisting, gasping mouth. Mandy grabbed her by the shoulders. "What is it, baby? My God, what is it?"

Her mother's touch unlocked Amy's throat, and she started to shriek. "Mama! Mama, get it off me!"

Mandy grew frantic. "What? Get what off you?" The roach slunk out of Amy's hair, perching on her shoulder and waving its thick front legs. Amy froze, petrified. She felt like she might throw up. *Oh no, please don't let it get on my face please please please*—

With a cry of disgust, Mandy slapped it from her shoulder.

Tom threw open the bedroom door, his black tie half-knotted. "What the hell?"

The roach rustled its wing cases and ran between Mandy's feet, heading straight for Tom. He raised one newly polished shoe and ground it into the banana-yellow carpeting.

24

Sobbing, Amy fell into her mother's arms. Mandy stroked her hair. "Hush, baby, it was just an old cockroach. It can't get you anymore, Daddy killed it."

Tom knelt down and encircled them both in his arms. "Was all that over one silly roach? They don't even bite, Mophead!"

Amy's voice quavered, her face buried in her mother's blue silky blouse. "They're disgusting. And—and dirty!"

Tom laughed. "So is Foot, but you love him anyway!"

Amy giggled, thinking of her sweet old yellow-brown mutt waiting for her back home back home in Arizona.

"Know what?" asked Tom, petting his daughter's head.

"What?"

"That wasn't a cockroach anyway."

Amy looked up at him, ready to smile even though her eyes stung from crying. "No, ma'am. This is Palm Beach. Rich people don't have roaches. That was a palmetto beetle."

Amy chuckled. "Come on, Daddy!"

"No, that's really what they call them. Y'know, rich people don't even fart. They break wind!"

"Tom!" Mandy scolded, trying not to smile as Amy collapsed into giggles. "Go fix your tie while Amy and I give the 'palmetto beetle' a burial at sea."

❧

Hours later, staring into the faces of all the old people at her grandparents' party, Amy believed that they didn't have roaches, and they certainly didn't fart. The men were dressed in fancy-looking three piece suits, the women covered with glittering, sparkling jewelry. She wished she could try some of it on. She wished there was another little girl to play with. And she wished the food weren't so gross.

She had been given lamb, which was greasy and smelled funny. She took one bite, then thought of sweet little fluffy lambs romping and playing and put down her fork. Next they gave her caviar, which was like little bags of fishy salt. She gave up when Mr. Iris gave her a sip of something called "cold duck."

Amy took it warily, hoping it wasn't a little white duck that had been squished into juice like Mama did with oranges. It didn't have any feathers in it, but it tasted like the worst cough medicine in the world. She spit it into a potted plant when no one was looking, and wiped her tongue on her napkin.

Now she was standing in a corner, watching everybody, just trying to stay out of the way. Amy's new grandmother slipped out of the crowd and walked up to her.

"I can't get over how lovely you are!" She gently touched Amy's cheek.

"Thank you, Grandma," said Amy, smiling. She liked her new grandmother. She was tall and slim and fancy like a movie star, but she had a sweet face. She wasn't as neat as Grandma back home, who raised dogs and chickens and ducks (not cold ones) and took Amy for rides in her Mustang, but she was pretty neat anyway.

Amy liked her new Grandpa, too. She didn't have one of those in Arizona, but she figured they were all pretty much the same. He liked to tease her in a nice sort of way that made her laugh, but he didn't hear very well and you kind of had to yell at him sometimes. She wondered why Palm Beach Grandma called him an "Old Goat." He didn't look at all like SharaLee or Boiler, her other Grandma's goats.

Amy wandered through the enormous apartment, looking at all the pretty things. Everything was white and gold and looked really really breakable. Her mother said it was French Pro-vench-all, whatever that meant. Amy wanted to touch the gleaming teapot on the cherub-covered wood cabinets, or pick up the little gold dog on the glass endtable, but she didn't. She was afraid to even sit on the furniture. She suspected it would stain just by coming close to little girls.

"Hi, little doll!"

Amy jumped. A lady with lots of shiny black hair was smiling at her. Another lady wearing too many pearls sat next to that one. Amy noted with interest that they were eating sandwiches from a silver tray. Normal food!

"Hi," said Amy, trying not to stare at the sandwiches.

The black-haired lady was smiling more widely. "I noticed you didn't eat much, honey. Are you hungry?"

"Yes!" said Amy loudly. She blushed. "I mean, yes, Ma'am."

The ladies laughed. "Well, here, angel," said the one with the pearls as she lifted a sandwich from the tray. Her nails were long and red, denting the white bread like teeth. She handed the sandwich to Amy, smiling.

"Thank you, Ma'am," said Amy gratefully, before taking a huge bite. The meat was tough and cold and tasted like nothing much at all. Amy chewed and chewed, finally swallowing the dry, sticky mouthful.

"Do you like it?" said the black-haired lady, smoothing Amy's hair.

She didn't like it, and she didn't like the lady touching her, but her Mama and Daddy had raised her to Always Be Polite. "Yes," she said, with a little smile. "It's good. What kind of sandwich is it?"

"It's tongue, sweetheart."

"What?" asked Amy, barely able to make the word squeak out of her mouth.

Both the ladies were smiling. "Tongue, dearest. Beef tongue." The Pearl Lady tugged on the pink rose on Amy's dress with her long long nails.

"Oh," said Amy, staring at them. "I've never had tongue before. Thank you. I think I'll go see Grandma now." Amy backed up, wearing her pretend smile like when she went to Olan Mills to get her picture taken. She turned and scurried off. She could hear the ladies laughing.

Amy ducked around the corner into the hallway, then slipped into the bathroom. Cautiously, she lifted the white bread and peeked. She made a face. The meat was gray and stringy. Were those taste buds on the side? She stuck out her own tongue and inspected it in the mirror. Yup. Taste buds. She fled into the hallway and jammed the sandwich between the stalks of a big potted rubber plant, then looked around, feeling guilty.

Virginia, her Grandma's maid, was peering at her from the kitchen. Amy gasped.

Virginia raised a finger to her lips. Her chocolate-colored cheeks dimpled as she grinned at Amy. Amy smiled back. Virginia motioned for her to come into the kitchen. Amy took two steps forward and was lifted off her feet from behind.

"There you are!" boomed Mr. Iris. Amy flinched. *Don't touch me!* she thought. *Don't touch me, I don't like you!* He spun Amy around, bringing her face up to his. She stared into his round, spooky blue eyes. She hadn't liked Mr. Iris from the moment she met him. He was too loud, and he was always touching her; messing up her hair, pinching her cheek till it hurt.

He grinned, showing huge, yellow teeth like a horse's. "We've missed you, little lady!" He had bad breath.

Amy looked over his shoulder at Virginia as he carried her into the living room. Virginia made a funny "sad face" at her. Amy giggled.

"Oh," said Mr. Iris. "You like to fly, do you?" He let her slide in his grip until he held her by the wrists. With a painful jerk he began to swing her around. He was a big, strong old man, a lot bigger than her Daddy, even, and he swung Amy faster and faster until she thought her arms would pull right out of her shoulders. *What if I break something? What if he* drops *me?* She wanted to ask him to stop, but she couldn't get her breath. She was glad she hadn't eaten more than a bite of the terrible tongue sandwich.

"Ted! Put that child down this minute!"

It was Mrs. Iris' voice. Amy tried to look at her, but she was just a blur. Suddenly, Mr. Iris set her on her feet. Amy swayed. The room spun. Mrs. Iris grabbed her around the shoulders. "Poor baby," she crooned. "Did bad old Teddy scare you?"

"No, Ma'am," Amy lied.

"Of course I didn't," Mr. Iris bellowed. "Little children are tough customers. People are just too soft on them nowadays." He edged his wife aside and squatted down, pulling Amy close to him.

"Did you know, little lady, that children your age used to work in the salt mines?"

"No, Mr. Iris," said Amy, squirming in his grasp.

"Well they did. They also worked as blacksmith's apprentices. They carried the iron back and forth and kept the fire hot. Sometimes they got hit by those big hammers, though, and got their little arms and legs flattened." He grinned. Amy flinched. *His teeth are too big.* A word popped into her head. *Ogre. He looks like an ogre from my fairy tale book.* She shivered.

Mr. Iris was still talking. "Sometimes they got too close to the furnace, and got all burned up!"

Amy stared at him. *You are a very bad man. Yes you are.*

"Ted!" said Mrs. Iris. "Be nice." She clucked her disapproval and strolled off to the bar.

"People used to treat little children just like grown-ups," he continued. "They worked, begged, and got thrown in prison along with the grown-ups. They even got tried as witches. Are you a witch, Amy?"

She shook her head, wishing Mama or Daddy or anyone who wasn't scary would come and save her.

Mr. Iris leaned in close. "They burned some witches at the stake. But they usually didn't burn little girls, Amy. Do you know what they did to little girls? They squished them between two big rocks. Splat! Just like cockroaches!"

Amy felt her mouth start to tremble. Her throat hurt from trying not to cry. Mr. Iris laughed. "Do you know what it looks like when somebody gets squished? Just like a giant smear of strawberry jam. You can't imagine how much blood is inside you, Amy. You just wouldn't believe how much!"

She twisted away from Mr. Iris and ran. His wheezing laugh followed her down the hall.

Amy burst into the kitchen. Virginia jumped, looking up from the sauce she was stirring. Amy looked up at her, and felt the tears in her eyes spill over.

"Amy, honey," said Virginia, "What's the matter?"

Amy let out a sob. "Mr. Iris," she said. *Just like a giant smear of strawberry jam . . .*

"Oh, baby!" Virginia said, rushing over to her. She took Amy in her arms.

Amy had just met her an hour ago, but she instantly liked Virginia. She put her arms around the woman's neck and hid her face in the folds of her white cotton blouse. She smelled good, like cinnamon, and other spices Amy had never smelled before.

There was a little portable radio on the counter, turned on very softly, and Virginia rocked Amy in time to the music. It was a pretty, sad song, a man's voice singing as if his heart were about to break.

> *"I heard an old ragman out making his rounds*
> *Coming right down my alley with sorrowful sounds*

*Crying rags and old iron and pulling his cart
I asked what he'd give me for my broken heart . . . "*

"Just never you mind him, Amy," said Virginia, stroking her hair. "He won't hurt you. He's just a crazy old fart." Amy let out an involuntary snort of laughter. The radio sang to her, soothed her.

*"Rags and old iron, rags and old iron,
All he was buyin' was just rags and old iron . . . "*

"That's better," said Virginia, still holding Amy close to her.

"What's that music?" asked Amy, wiping her eyes.

"That's Oscar Brown Junior, honey, singin' from the bottom of his soul. Doesn't his voice sound just like black velvet?"

"I guess," said Amy, not really sure how somebody's voice could sound like cloth. "I like the way he sings."

"Well, you've got good taste for such a little girl. Now how about a ham and cheese sandwich and then some ice cream with blueberries?"

"All right!" said Amy. "I mean, yes, please!"

Virginia laughed and kissed her forehead.

❧

"Wake up, sleeping beastie!"

"Huh?" said Amy, opening her eyes. Xavier kissed her forehead again. A wicked grin split his broad Yaqui features.

"I said, go back to sleep, Tootsie Pop, so I can take advantage of your cute little bod."

"Oh, piss off," said Amy with a smile. "As if you would."

"Well, aren't we foul today?" said Xavier, giving her his strong, brown hand. She heaved herself up. "Would some Chinese food help?"

Amy rubbed her eyes. She was amazed to find herself hungry. "Oh, I guess so. If you're buying."

Xavier sighed deeply. "You take shameless advantage of me, Amelia. You know I can refuse you nothing."

"B.S. artist," she muttered, as they walked away arm in arm.

30

THREE

"Aaah," Amy sighed as she slid into the corner booth and stretched out. "It's cool in here."

"Wuss." Xavier picked up a menu. "It's October. You've been whining about the heat since March."

"I was born here. I'm allowed to whine." Amy scanned the lunch menu. Cheap prices and plentiful food made the Plum Tree a favorite of hers. Her stomach growled pleasantly. *At least it's not heaving!*

Amy picked out Braised Bean Curd and closed her menu. She looked up at Xavier, who was looking right back at her. His dark eyes sparkled.

"You're not gonna spew across the table, are you?"

Amy grimaced. "So Sarah told you, huh?"

"Everybody knows. It's posted on all the kiosks. It's coming out in the campus rag tomorrow."

"Yeah, yeah, yeah. Well, I feel a lot better now."

Before Xavier could whip out another smartass comment, the slender waitress came up to take their orders. Xavier winked at her shamelessly. She raised an eyebrow and ignored him, scribbling on her order pad in Chinese before bustling back to the kitchen.

"Why do you torture hapless women like that?" said Amy, shaking her head and grinning. "You know you wouldn't touch her with a ten-foot pole."

"Flirting makes the world go round." Xavier grabbed her hand. "You could try to convert me, sweetie."

"Yeah, right. Johnny would break both my legs and use me for a basketball."

Xavier's grin slipped, just a little. Amy touched his bronze, rounded cheek.

"No! No no no! Don't tell me you broke up with him!"

Xavier sighed. "Nope. He broke up with me. He said I was too spacey. Too weird. What could I say? I can't argue with that." He tried to laugh.

Amy squeezed his hand. "I'm so sorry. I thought you guys would last forever. You seemed so perfect for each other."

For a moment, Xavier's black eyes reflected sharp, cutting pain like the glint of silver at the bottom of a deep, dark well. Then the grin was back.

"Oh well. I guess I'm just not the marryin' kind. Now tell me about this honking spree. You're not contagious, are you? Eeeow!" He yanked his hand away from Amy's. She noticed it had become damp in the past few moments.

She couldn't think of anything else to say about Johnny, so she didn't. *What a shame. What a damn, damn shame.* Amy put her own grin back on. "Nah," she said, "I don't think so. I think it was just a bad case of Donut World's Revenge." Amy was immediately stung with guilt. *No, I don't, actually. Why am I lying?*

Xavier hung his pointed tongue out. "Bleh! Have you no respect for your body? That's disgusting, girl." He shook his head.

"What? No shamanic cure?"

"Sure. Don't eat at Donut World ever again. Booga booga booga."

"Gee, thanks, Oh Mighty Witch Doctor."

Xavier laughed. The waitress came back, setting their food on the table with brisk efficiency.

Amy breathed in the smell of the spicy tofu and veggies. She looked down at her plate, aiming with her chopsticks, and for the briefest of moments, saw something move in the rich brown sauce. Amy shivered to the bone, closing her eyes. When she opened them again, and there was nothing in her plate but food.

Xavier, of course, saw her. *He never misses a damn thing, does he.* Amy tried not to look at him, but she could feel his eyes on her, and she couldn't resist. His handsome face was solemn.

"Talk to me, girl. What's really wrong?"

Amy speared a cube of bean curd with a ruthless thrust of her chopstick. She turned it over and over above her plate. "Hell, I don't know. I keep having these weird dreams."

He smiled gently, drawing her out. "You always have weird dreams. Remember the one you told me about, with the pirate captain and the silk ropes?"

She blushed. "Oh, shut up. Not dreams like that. Just—weird ones. I don't want to talk about it, okay?" *Because I think they have something to do with my barfing. Because I feel like my soul is sick. And I want to know why, but I don't, because I'm so very afraid . . .*

Xavier reached across the table and slipped his hand behind her neck. He rubbed, ever so gently. Amy closed her eyes. "Okay," she heard him say in his mellow, soothing voice. "Talk to me whenever you're ready. In the meantime . . . "

Xavier's hand slipped away from Amy's neck, and he reached into one of the pockets of his black leather vest. He pulled out a tiny silver fetish and pressed it into Amy's palm. It was warm, from being next to his skin.

Amy examined the tiny thing. It was a perfect, beautiful little lizard. Xavier's work was gorgeous—Amy could tell it was a Desert Banded Gecko, with its humanlike hands and silky skin. He had even included the little lizard's stripes, defining them with dusky bands of oxidation. Its tiny head was tilted up, looking back at her with hooded eyes of silver.

"Put him by your nightstand," Xavier explained. "He'll carry your bad dreams out the window."

"Is this traditional Yaqui magic?" Amy rubbed the back of the minute lizard, enchanted.

"Nah." Xavier laughed. "It's my own idea. But it works for me. I made this one just for you. A little bat told me you were having bad dreams."

Amy stood up and leaned across the table to kiss his cheek, dunking her T-shirt into her plate.

FOUR

Friday night. Oh Boy. Biiig fun. Amy lay on her stomach on the bed, staring at her biology textbook. She tried to focus on the human digestive system. *Gross.* Once again, her eyes wandered off the page and up the wall to her *Lost Boys* poster. *Kiefer, baby. Are you a shallow little shit like Jay? What's that? You say you can't help it? It's your testicles?*

Her eyes wandered back to the book, to the Pepto-pink twists of intestine. In a shaded box next to the illustration was a list of human parasites. Tapeworms. Flatworms. Roundworms. Little monsters all. Amy could practically feel their eager little barbed heads rooting greedily into her guts, their hard, segmented bodies shifting, stretching, making themselves comfortable, filling her up like a big Italian dinner.

Could that be my problem? Her entire skin rippled with horror, as if it wanted to leave her potentially infested body.

Yeah, right. Where would I pick up a weird fucking parasite in Tempe, Arizona? The food on campus sucks, but I doubt if it's that bad.

Amy slammed the book shut. Without warning, she was hit with a wall of fear so strong it was paralyzing. She was pinned, skewered to the bed by the trip-hammer in her chest, deafened by the roar of blood in her ears. Amy knew she would do anything, anything in the world, just to make it stop. Then it was gone.

Fuck this! Amy's fists clenched. She was trembling all over. *What. Is. Wrong. With. Me.*

It just didn't seem possible, that she could be so fucked up. It seemed like the horror didn't belong to her, it couldn't, because shit like that didn't happen to Amy. *Not to me. Not to me.*

Unless I'm somebody else.

Is this some goddam Audrey Rose trip? Did I die of dysentery in a former life?

Or was I just insane?

Am I insane?

No. No. I don't want to think about this.

She rolled onto her back, pulling her purple sweat-suited legs into her chest. She wrapped her arms around them and rocked gently, determined not to think about anything for a few minutes. *Oo mou mou, papa oo mou mou . . .*

"Amy?" Sarah's voice was soft, which was unusual, for her. She knocked on the door. "Amy, can we come in?"

"We?" said Amy. "We? If you mean you and Trent Reznor, by all means. If you mean you and Mick, not a chance." She rolled over and sat up on the edge of the bed.

Sarah opened the door a crack and peeked in, grinning. "I guess that means yes, huh?" Amy grunted noncommittally. Sarah came in, pulling Mick behind her.

"Hi, Ame," said Mick, in his unhurried way. Amy glanced up at his honey-brown eyes, his mop of brown hair that always hung in his face, the good-natured curve of his lips. *Nice catch, Sarah,* she thought wistfully. *Cute* and *sweet. Un-fucking-believable.*

He reached into the pocket of his photographer's vest and pulled something out. "Here, this is for you."

Amy took it. It was a rubber finger puppet, a little blue animal with big ears and glasses. "Gee, thanks," she said, smiling in spite of herself. "I'm touched."

"It's 'Batly', from *Eureeka's Castle,*" Sarah explained. "Mick got it for you at Pizza Hut, because he thinks you're batshit." Amy laughed.

"Hey!" Mick hollered. "I never said—"

"Now wait a minute!" Amy stuck the little creature on her forefinger and looked into its silly face. "You mean you watch Nick? Mick digs Nick?" The bat gave a solemn nod. Mick turned red and mumbled something, tugged at his small silver Celtic cross pendant.

"What's your favorite? No, really, is it Dobie Gillis? Donna Reed? I know, Patty Duke!" Amy, Sarah and Batly laughed wildly.

Mick turned even redder. "Real Monsters," he muttered, peeking out from under his hair.

"So, Toots." Sarah sat on the bed next to Amy. "After you're done torturing my boyfriend, what'cha doin' tonight?"

"Why?" said Amy suspiciously.

"Well, You see, I met this guy in Art History the other day, and he's really—"

"Oh, God!" yelled Amy. She fell over sideways, lying dejectedly on the bed like a poodle slapped with a newspaper.

"Amy!" Sarah pleaded. "It's not that bad! In fact it's good! He's really cute. He's one of those artpunk types you like, y'know? He's tall and pale, with lots of spiky black hair and his name is Shane and he's pretty smart . . . Amy? Are you in there?"

"No. I'm dead. Go now, before I start to smell."

Sarah shot a desperate look at Mick, who was looking at Amy's bookshelf and pretending to be invisible. She turned back to Amy. "Listen," she said. "You've been vegetating for almost three months. Jay just isn't worth it! C'mon, Amy it's no big deal. It's a double date, so if you don't like him, you can talk to me."

Sarah grinned. "He's got a great back, Ame. We're talking a major set of shoulders here."

Amy looked up. "Yeah?"

"Yeah. And, he wears motorcycle boots. I know you have a fetish for them."

"I do not," grumbled Amy, shoving her face into the blanket.

"Yes you do." Sarah fell over onto Amy, squashing her. "So babe, will you give him a try?"

"Get off me!" Amy laughed.

"Will you?"

"All right, just get off me, you pervert!"

Sarah sighed heavily, then stood up. "I'm hurt," she said. "It was a deeply moving experience for me. I thought it meant something to you, too. Now I realize you just used me." She crossed the tiny bedroom and hooked her arm through Mick's. "Come, dear boy. We're not wanted here."

Amy watched her friend's exit, not really believing what she had just agreed to. She shook her head. *If I didn't love her, I'd have to kill her.*

Sarah paused at the door. She favored Amy with a toothy smile. "By the way, he'll be here at eight."

"Eight!" shrieked Amy. "Eight! That's in half an hour! You little—"
The door slammed shut. Amy dropped her head into her hands.
I can't believe she set me up with someone named Shane.

⟳

The stereo was blasting a Black Crowes tape, the ancient speakers straining to carry the heavy electric bass: *"Boys will come a dime by the dozen, that ain't nothin' but ten cent lovin' . . . "*

Amy boogied and shook as she looked at herself in the mirror. She smiled. In a fit of sheer perversity, she had dressed to kill. It felt wonderful. In her silver brocade bustier and long, black-velvet-and-lace skirt, Amy decided that she did, indeed, look devastating. She inspected her makeup as she wove tiny silver beads into a thin braid at her temple. Perfect.

Black liner and silvery-blue shadow made her eyes look exotically feline. She wore her favorite shade of lipstick, a deep red which made her mouth look full and sensual. Or wanton and trashy, as Sarah put it. Amy laughed softly. She groped in her overcrowded makeup case for a moment, then pulled out her bottle of Dark Musk essential oil. She rubbed the wild, heavy scent into the skin of her throat, wrists, and, as an afterthought, her belly. *Okay, Shane ol' bud, get ready to be knocked on your ass.*

"Pretty little thang, lemme light your candle 'cause Mama I'm sho' hard to handle now yes r'am!"

Looking at her silver Art Deco watch, Amy reached for the door-knob. She paused. It was eight-fifteen. She wondered if The Mystery Artpunk had arrived yet.

Amy turned off the stereo and listened. She heard Sarah's throaty laugh, and Mick quietly and earnestly swearing that Amy hadn't really crawled out of her bedroom window and run down the street screaming. Someone laughed. It was a low chuckle, rich and sexy. *Hmm*.

Amy pressed her ear to the door.

"I wouldn't blame her if she did," Shane was saying. "She probably expects me to look like Peter Lorre."

"She'd probably like that," Sarah said wickedly. "Amy just loves old movies."

Again, the devastating chuckle. "A woman after my own black heart."

Amy bit her lip. His voice was deep and velvety, the kind that always made the hair stand up on the back of her neck. *Don't get your hopes up, Toots. He could still be an asshole.*

"Oh!" squeaked Sarah excitedly. "Oh! Do you like old scary movies too? *M* is one of her favorites. She's seen every Todd Browning film ever made. Have you ever seen *Freaks?*"

Amy took a deep breath and flung the door open. Her eyes slid over Sarah and Mick and landed squarely on Shane's back. He was tall, almost as tall as Mick, and beneath his black leather duster, his shoulders were just as fine as Sarah had promised. His hair came back in glossy black hedgehog spikes, ending in a foot-long braided tail. *Oooh my.*

"Amy!" cried Sarah. "How kind of you to join us."

Shane turned around and smiled. *Ooooooh my.* His eyes were dark blue, the color of the sky just before a thunderstorm. His face was thin and feral. Amy thought of deep midnight woods, of satyrs and wild faeries. She swallowed hard.

"No problem. The window was stuck."

Shane laughed his sexy laugh, and walked over to her. He picked up Amy's hand in his, and raised it to his lips. The tip of his tongue flicked the back of her hand almost imperceptibly. He smiled at her over her knuckles. "When Sarah showed me your picture yesterday, I nailed that window shut. Hello, lovely Amelia. I'm Shane Matthews."

Amy matched his intimate stare with one of her own. "Hello, lovely Shane." She grinned at him. *Oh God, he has dimples!*

"Well, well," said Sarah, squeezing Mick. "I think the children like each other."

"Amy looks like she's going to bite him," said Mick matter-of-factly. Amy glared.

Shane touched Amy's face. "She's probably just hungry. Didn't you say our reservations were for eight-thirty?"

"Yup," said Sarah. "Black Angus waits for no one."

"Let's go, then," said Shane, offering Amy his arm. She took it, resting her hand lightly on the petal-soft leather.

His eyes locked with hers. He grinned. "I'm absolutely starved."

⌘

Nine twenty-five. Plates were pushed to the center of the table, littered with fat and baked potato scraps and bloody juice. Amy took another sip of her white wine and glanced at Shane. He was looking at her, smiling. His leg pressed lightly against hers. She smiled back.

"Aw, aren't they cute!" Sarah beamed at them.

"Precious," said Mick. For a moment, it looked like he was trying to control a sneer. "I want cheesecake."

"Mmmmm! I want *chocolate* cheesecake!" Sarah began scanning the room for their waiter. "Garçon! Oh Garçon! Get your butt over here!"

Shane pushed the hair out of Amy's eyes. "How about you, Pretty? Are you up for dessert?"

Amy squirmed under the weight of his stare. "Um, I think I want to dance."

"Anything you want," he murmured. He slid out of the booth, then helped Amy up.

"We'll be right there," said Sarah, waving frantically in the general direction of the waiter.

Mick was irritably creating a sculpture out of his leftover horseradish and parsley. His brow was knit beneath the curtain of his hair. For some reason, he didn't seem to like Shane very much.

Shane . . .

Amy momentarily found herself staring at Shane's lean chest, displayed nicely under his thin, black, silk shirt. His shiny motorcycle boots reflected blue in the soft light. *Yum.*

They reached the tiny dance floor. Something by Paula Abduhl hammered through the speakers, its homogenized beat nearly deafening at close range. Shane turned around and leaned toward Amy, as if to tell her something. She moved her hair aside and cocked her head. He bit her neck.

Amy pulled back, not sure if she were angry or not.

The sound of a six-gun shot whizzed through the speakers. *Wild Wild West* by the Escape Club. She smirked. *If I had half the memory for textbooks that I did for music, I'd be Einstein-ette.*

Shane grabbed her wrist, pulling her to him. Amy stared at him coldly.

He grinned and lowered his head, then looked up at her shyly, mouthing the word, "Sorry."

Oh, shit. The dimples again. Amy tried to maintain her glare, but her mouth betrayed her by slipping into a smile. *Oh, what the hell.*

She rested her hand lightly on his waist, and they began to dance.

Shane was a good dancer. He held her waist in a gentle but firm grip, and they moved together, bodies almost touching. They gathered a few stares from the other couples on the floor who were dancing apart, preening for each other. Amy wrinkled up her nose and grinned her biggest, silliest grin at them.

Shane laughed, whispering, "All right!" loudly in her ear.

It felt good dancing with him. Amy felt her muscles loosen up as she bumped and swung. She watched the lights play on the sharp planes of his face. He gave her a sexy, hooded snake-look that made her feel squirmy inside.

"Wild West" ended, and something by The B-52s began. They danced straight through, this time backing apart to show off for each other. Amy danced her best, spinning and strutting and tossing her hair. Shane tried to match her, move for move. He almost succeeded. When the song was over, they were laughing and out of breath.

Arms around each other, they strolled to the bar. Shane gallantly bought their rum-and-cokes.

They barely had time to finish the drinks before Amy spotted Sarah's voluptuous red-dressed form bounding through the crowd, towing Mick behind her. Sarah grinned and pulled Amy onto the dance floor as an old Adam Ant song boomed out over the bar. The two young women danced together for a moment before allowing the guys to cut in.

After untold dances and too many rum-and-cokes, Amy realized that the room had become unfocused. The evening became a sweaty, sexy blur. Flashes of red; Sarah's lipstick and dress. Flashes of black. Shane's shirt. Shane's boots. Black looks between Mick and Shane.

A slow Depeche Mode song started up, and Amy slipped her arms around Shane's neck as if she had been doing it all her life. Her head buzzed pleasantly as she leaned against him.

His arms slipped around her waist, pulling her in even tighter. He buried his face in her neck and began to nibble and lick. Amy giggled. His hand moved slowly up her side, stroking her breast through lamé and boning. He insinuated his leg in between her knees, pressing the top of his thigh against the warmth between her legs. A shock of pleasure went through her like a thunderbolt.

Amy stiffened, and pulled away.

She stared at Shane for a moment, wishing she could focus enough to read the expression in his eyes. In the darkness of the dance floor, they looked black, opaque.

Amy grinned weakly. "Um, 'scuse me," she said and fled to the ladies' room.

She paused at the door wishing Sarah would come in with her, but her friend was in a liplock with Mick and she didn't appear likely to come up for air any time soon. With an inebriated shrug, Amy went in.

Oh, God. Don't we just look like the Whore of Babylon. Amy sorrowfully regarded her smudgy makeup and wild hair in the bathroom mirror. She noted with embarrassment that her bustier had slipped down to quite a revealing level. *Another inch and, poit! Nipple City.* She hiked the offending garment up to a semi-modest level and began to rummage in her tiny clutch bag for her eye shadow. *Mm hmm. Just moving a little fast there, Shane, baby. Taking your hip-grinding a little too seriously . . . Gotcha!* She whipped out the little plastic case and opened it, dropping the applicator in the sink. *Shit.* She retrieved it and dried it on a paper towel, then leaned in to the mirror and tried to line up her eyelid with the tiny sponge-on-a-stick.

Amy looked into her own eyes, and frowned. They looked darker than they should.

She looked closer. No, the mirror was dark. Maybe the stuff on the back was wearing off, or—

Amy's mouth dropped open. The mirror was getting darker by the second. She shook her head slowly. *Oh, no. No. I can't take any more weird shit.* But now the mirror was almost black.

Amy began to back away. She felt something in her head, something cold, something alien. Something trying to come to the surface. She hit the wall of the bathroom, thumping her head. She didn't feel it.

Amy's brain screamed at her eyes to look away, to shut out the mirror, but they refused. *It wouldn't help anyway. It's in my head, in my head . . .*

Amy pressed her fists to her mouth. Something in the mirror was moving. Something undulated, snakelike. Something twitched like an electrocuted sewer roach.

No.

I'm passing out, she told herself. *I got too drunk, that's all. I'm gonna puke or something . . .*

On cue, Amy's stomach lurched. Her head spun, and her vision narrowed down further and further until all she could see was the mirror, where darkness whirled and seethed . . .

❧

Amy kicked a green coconut into the lake. It made a satisfying splash. She giggled, and bent down to pick up another one. The smooth little nut felt good in her hand, just right for throwing. She lifted it to her nose and breathed in the green, milky smell, so different from anything back home.

She hauled back and threw it. The coconut landed in the water and disappeared, then popped back up in a surge of dark water. Slowly, it sank back down. Amy watched the water rings.

The warm wind picked up, rustling the palms in front of the hotel. Amy looked up at the shivering clumps of fronds, then beyond them into the darkening sky. The clouds in Florida always seemed to move so fast. They twisted and changed, almost too fast to find animals in them.

She decided to try anyway. Amy was watching a mouse change into a pointy-nosed dog when a green coconut hit the ground next to her with a startling thud. Amy trotted several steps back, out from under the trees and onto the sidewalk. *Geez, I coulda been conked.* She stared at the tree suspiciously.

Another coconut hit the ground, this time from a tree about ten feet down the sidewalk. With a sudden rush of daring, Amy darted down the walk and grabbed the coconut. She skittered backwards, fully expecting to be beaned for her foolishness. When nothing fell on her, she grinned and tossed her prize into the air, catching it with first one hand, then the other.

The wind blew harder, whipping the trees and Amy's hair. She breathed in deeply, loving the smell of rain. She made a disgusted face when the wind shifted and blew a stale breath of Lake Worth into her nose.

Amy clutched her coconut, knowing she should go back to her hotel. She was supposed to stay right in front, where her parents could see her from the window. She sighed.

Amy was turning around when another, bigger coconut fell, further down the sidewalk.

She couldn't resist. After all, the big ones floated. She trotted down the sidewalk. She had almost reached the tree when another nut fell, further down the walk, and then another.

Amy stopped and thought for a moment. Something wanted her to follow the coconuts. That was pretty obvious. But what could it be? A fairy? A Cheshire cat? Amy scratched her nose and stared up at the palms, puzzled.

Of course! It was dropping stuff out of trees. It had to be a dryad. She knew all about dryads. Her daddy told her. They were the reason you knocked on wood, and the reason you never, never, carved your initials in a tree. They looked like beautiful ladies, only skinny, and with leaves in their hair. But did they live in palm trees?

Her answer was another coconut, then two more. Amy shrugged her shoulders, then set off down the sidewalk. Why shouldn't dryads live in palm trees?

The coconuts were falling regularly now, just a few feet ahead of her. Amy laughed, then began skipping. "Follow the coconut road," she sang. "Follow the coconut road. Follow, follow, follow, follow . . ."

Past the big houses with the high hedges, past the laundry and the Burger Heaven, around the corner . . .

"Oh my gosh!"

Amy stopped. Her mouth dropped open, and she stared at the gigantic structure looming in front of her. It was the biggest, oldest, neatest building that Amy had ever seen.

She set her coconut on the ground and rested her hands on the cool wrought-iron fence that surrounded it, looking up. The building was white, but red rust-stuff from the roof had stained the top part of it, and vines crept up the sides like long green cutworms. There was a sign along the top of the building. "Hotel Mar-tin-ee-cue," Amy whispered. Broken neon tubes stuck out of the shattered red plastic letters like chicken bones.

Amy carefully counted the floors; six. The bottom three had boarded-up windows, but the top three were uncovered. The windows were black, and Amy couldn't see into them at all. Some of them were cracked, and one on the top floor was shattered. Amy wondered if anyone really could throw a rock that high. The wind whipped her hair into her eyes. Impatiently, she pushed it away.

The back door was big and heavy-looking, made from dark wood. It was swollen and blistered, and hung crooked on its hinges, creating a wedge of blackness at the top of the doorframe. The whole thing seemed to bulge slightly outward.

Amy shivered with delight. It looked just like one of the things in the Haunted Mansion at Disneyland. Deciding to go around and look at the front door, Amy let go of the fence and started to turn away. She hesitated, looking back at the hotel grounds.

How had she missed it? Just a few feet past the fence was a little swimming pool. How cool! It wasn't full all the way, and the sides were black and green with mold. Amy couldn't see the actual water, because it was totally covered with thick, green, scummy stuff. It looked solid, like you could walk right across it. A tall, skinny palm tree, bent in the middle, hung directly over the pool like a green-haired buzzard. Amy wondered if tree frogs used it for a diving board. The whole thing smelled kind of bad, like Grandma's duck ponds in the summer, only worse.

A gust of wind tossed the bent palm tree, shaking a little green nut loose. It plunged into the slime-covered pool. When it hit, the scummy stuff stretched down, like when Daddy set his bowling ball on the bed. Then the coconut popped through with a gross sucking sound. The scum closed over, and it was gone.

"Neat-o," Amy breathed, eyes wide with horror and excitement. The wind stopped, and the tree was still for a moment. Another coconut fell from it, hitting the scum with a yucchy plop. Then another fell, sitting on the surface for a moment before going under.

Amy gaped. Could the dryad be trying to tell her something?

She bent down and picked up her own abandoned nut. She weighed it in her hand for a moment, then tossed it into the pool. It slipped through the surface of the scum and disappeared. Amy saw it bobbing under the carpet of goop like a kitten playing under a sheet.

It popped back up. Amy blinked her eyes. Her coconut was sitting on the scum carpet, rolling gently over the surface.

—Glorp—

It was sucked under.

Amy started to back away. With a wet pop, her coconut came flying out of the pool. It hit the weeds just behind the wrought iron fence, and rolled out onto the sidewalk. It left a thin trail of water and scum as it rolled toward her feet.

Amy ran.

She ran all the way back to her hotel, where her parents were out looking for her. She heard them calling her name before she saw them. It started to rain as she ran to her mother.

"Amy!" Mama looked half happy, half mad. "Amy, where were you?"

Her daddy's face, squished up with worry, was inches from hers. "Amy, honey, what happened? What happened?"

"Amy! Amy, what happened?" Amy squinted and blinked repeatedly, her head tossing back and forth.

"Amelia! Say something to me. Now!" Amy tried to twist away from the loud voice in her head. Small hands held her fast. She opened her eyes, and for a flickering second she didn't recognize the face in front of her. When she did, she sagged with relief.

"Sarah . . . "

"Damn straight. Now, do you know who you are?" Sarah's cherub face was squinched up with worry. She looked just like a Muppet. Amy smiled.

"Amelia Sullivan. Excuse me please, I'm gonna puke."

Sarah helped Amy into a stall, then waited outside. When it was over, she watched Amy intently as she washed her face and rinsed out her mouth.

"So," said Sarah cautiously, "What happened to you? You didn't—take something, did you?"

"Take what?" said Amy irritably. "Crack? LSD? Liquid Sky? Oh, yes, Sarah, all of the above. I've joined the Heroin Generation."

Sarah pulled out her compact and began to powder Amy's pale face. "Now don't get bitchy, or I'll tell Shane you just barfed your heels. But you didn't take one of those bargain basement 'ludes that Jay gave you, did you, sweetie?"

"No, no," said Amy, closing her eyes. "I flushed them down the toilet that very night, remember? Sarah, you know I don't do anything anymore. I get asthma if I try to smoke pot, for Chrissakes."

"I know, I know." Sarah was trying to fix Amy's eye makeup, which was beyond repair. "But you didn't even see me when I came in, Amy. I think you were hallucinating."

"Bullshit," said Amy. "I was just spaced out. I think I hit my head. I think I'm getting the flu."

"I think you're lying," said Sarah, "But I'm not gonna push it. Now let's get you home."

Amy didn't say anything.

She hardly said a word on the short ride home. She was concentrating on not thinking about what happened in the restaurant's bathroom.

She did a pretty good job, managing to empty her head by counting streetlights.

Shane was quietly solicitous, squeezing her hand and pressing her head to his shoulder. He wrapped his arm around her protectively as he walked her up to the door.

"May I see you again?" he asked, taking both her hands in his.

"Yes," said Amy in a small voice, with a little smile.

"I'll call you later in the week, then?"

Amy was suddenly angry with herself. This was such a fantastic date, and she had ruined the whole thing. She looked Shane straight in the eye. "How about tomorrow night?"

He looked surprised. "Amy, do you think you'll be feeling—"

"Yes," she said firmly. He smiled and took her face in his hands. It was a long, soft, sweet kiss.

❧

Later, curled up under the covers in her Grimm the Dog nightshirt, Amy could smell Shane's almost-animal scent on her skin. She smiled, and closed her eyes.

FIVE

"TAKE IT, take another little piece of my heart now baby . . . "

Amy grimaced in her sleep. Her arm flailed out at the nightstand, landing heavily on the old radio alarm clock. Her fingers groped for the snooze button, but Janis Joplin wouldn't shut up. Amy's unwilling consciousness was wrenched to the surface of her rum-soaked brain.

Amy's eyes opened, just a slit. She heaved herself up to her elbows. Yellow late-morning sunlight filtered in through the cheap curtains and blasted her in the face. Hissing in pain, she squeezed her eyes shut again.

Slowly, slowly, Amy rolled over on her side and turned off the alarm clock. Janis was silenced, mid-scream. Amy fell back on the pillows with a sigh of relief. She wriggled deeper into the sheets, anticipating another hour or three of uninterrupted sleep.

Her eyes popped open. *Damn. I have to pee.*

Amy rolled onto her stomach, allowing one leg to drop off the side of the bed. *Doing good, doing good. Just one more.* She heaved herself sideways, and her other leg dropped. *How dignified.*

Amy slid down until she was on her knees, like a little girl saying her bedtime prayers. Using the bed for leverage, she pulled herself wobbily to her feet, and shuffled toward the bathroom.

Red eyes stared at her from the mirror. *Oh, what a beauty.* Amy gingerly splashed warm water on her face. Her flesh felt oily and swollen, and her joints creaked, stiff and sore. She felt like she had a skull full of broken glass. Amy turned her head from side to side, trying to crack her aching neck. It just made it hurt worse.

She frowned. *Ugh. Feels like tiny cats had a party in my mouth.*

Amy stuck her tongue out, to see if it were really as fuzzy as it felt. *No, just kind of gray.* She took her toothbrush from the medicine cabinet and overloaded it with peppermint-flavored Tom's Natural Toothpaste. Her jaw popped painfully as she opened her mouth. Amy winced, then prepared to depilitate her tongue.

Something moved in the back of her throat.

Amy stared at her reflection, not believing. Something squirmed, barely visible. It waved slender tentacles as it crawled up from her stomach.

She screamed and dropped the toothbrush, clawing at her throat. Frantically, she grabbed for the bottle of mouthwash. Amy poured the pungent green liquid into her mouth and gargled ferociously. *Die, you little bastard,* she thought crazily.

She spit into the sink. Nothing came out but Lavoris and a bit of chive from her baked potato. Amy grabbed for the mouthwash again, and knocked it over. It gushed from the bottle in a noxious green tide, splashing her feet. Amy opened her mouth to scream in rage and frustration. She caught a glimpse of her gaping reflection and paused.

Cautiously, she stared into the mirror.

Her throat was pink from its recent chemical assault. Her tonsils were whole and healthy, as usual. No stomach-squid in evidence.

Amy sank down to the floor, next to the green pool of mouthwash. She sat on the cool tiles, knees pulled up to her chest. She lowered her head, tapping her forehead on her knees. *Idiot. Moron. Feeb.* Amy gathered herself into as tight a ball as she could, and was still, inside and out.

After a while, perhaps a long while, Amy wearily cleaned up the mouthwash with a wad of toilet paper. She rescued her toothbrush from the linoleum. There was a dust bunny stuck in the toothpaste.

Yup. Its gonna be a wonderful day.

After an excessively long, hot shower, Amy felt like she might live through the morning. In baggy blue sweat pants and an old Bill the Cat T-shirt, she ventured into the living room. Sarah wasn't there.

Amy padded into the tiny kitchen. There was a shockingly cheerful note on the refrigerator. Oh yeah, right. Sarah went to the swap meet with Mick. She'll probably bring home a moose head.

Amy opened the door, in search of something to hydrate her ill-used body. She wrinkled her nose at the sight of an open container of leftover Thai food, then pulled out the last can of Coke. *Fend for yourself, roomie,* she thought crankily.

Amy shut the door and set her Coke on the counter to open it. She took long, cold swallows before the carbonation made her slow down. *Aah. Caffeine and sugar. Yes.* Her stomach gurgled angrily. Amy opened the refrigerator again, this time foraging for munchies.

The mangy Thai food was the first thing to greet her. "Oh, God," Amy growled. "That is so disgusting." She took the container by the corner of the lid, and lifted it out. Whatever it had been, it was no longer recognizable. Lips pulled back in disgust, Amy found the longest iced tea spoon in the apartment and began to dig. The crusty brown mass refused to move. Cursing, Amy pried harder. With a revolting plop, half of it landed in the sink.

Bloated white maggots writhed in the glop as it slid lazily down the garbage disposal.

Amy's stomach heaved. She ran into the bathroom and dove for the toilet bowl. Her stomach heaved again. *No. No, God damn it, I'm not going to puke again.* She swallowed hard, fighting it down. At last, her stomach settled.

Amy stood up slowly, taking deep breaths. She narrowed her eyes and walked back to the kitchen.

The Thai food was right where she left it. Wilted sprouts and shriveled chicken poked obnoxiously from the garbage disposal. No maggots.

Amy scowled. She braced herself, and looked into the container. Disgusting, revolting, but no wildlife. *Of course, no maggots. How the fuck would flies get into the refrigerator?*

Amy laughed. She picked up her Coke and wandered into the living room. She sat on the sofa, and laughed some more. "Idiot." She whispered. "Butthead. Wacko."

A sewer roach the size of a baby rat crept out from beneath the TV stand. Amy stared at it in horror. *Bold little fucker, aren't you.*

It charged her.

"Get away from me!" Amy shrieked, so loud it hurt her throat.

The roach froze in its tracks. It whirled around and ran back under the TV.

Amy's face crumpled, and she began to cry.

Oh God. Oh shit. What's happening to me?

Amy's mind began to race, skipping and shuddering from one horrible possibility to another.

Insanity was the most obvious. I*t's possible, isn't it? Why not? People with schizophrenia start getting sick at about my age. I remember from that special on HBO.*

Amy sobbed.

It's even in the family. She thought of Quinn, her mother's uncle, who was sweet and funny and checked himself into the hospital for electroshock about twice a year.

She shook her head so hard that tears flew from her face like sweat. *No. That can't be. I won't let it. It has to be something else.*

Again, reincarnation entered her mind. But that was just stupid. Something from the holographic covers of 1980s horror novels. Besides, the dreams were about her, about Amy as a little girl, not somebody else.

But that doesn't mean any of it really happened. Amy cringed away from thoughts of insanity as they rose up once more. *I'm not crazy. Maybe I'm sick. It's definitely not the flu. Maybe I have a brain tumor. I'm forgetting stuff all over the place lately. And I've always had those headaches . . .*

Oh, fuck. There's a happy thought. Amy shuddered and touched her forehead. Something could be in there, nestled in her brain all warm and cozy like a monstrous embryo. Something that was stretching, growing, shoving her brain aside to make way for insanity and agonizing death. Or maybe it would never get that far. *Didn't that Texas Tower guy have a brain tumor?*

Amy forced her thoughts to move on, before she could envision herself on top of the Math building with a high-powered rifle.

Amy rubbed her face, chewed the short nail of her forefinger. She was running out of options, and she grasped like a drowning swimmer at anything that popped into her head. Any explanation would be better than none. Wouldn't it?

Some kind of curse? Amy winced, immediately embarrassed at the thought. It was even more ridiculous than reincarnation. *Besides, I've never met any gypsies, so I couldn't have possibly pissed one off. So what the fuck? What?*

It's a repressed memory.

The thought was so forceful it was startling. *Why didn't I think of that before?*

Because you didn't want to, replied another part of her brain, a part that was small and cowering and frightened. *Because you might find out something bad. Something really, really bad. About someone you thought loved you.*

No. I won't go there. Nowhere near it. Amy curled up on her side on the couch, filling her mind with white noise, shoving aside the flashes of nightmare that cropped up from time to time.

Eventually, she got up. In slow motion, Amy put on her dirty red tennis shoes. She wandered the apartment until she found her keys and sunglasses. Numb, Amy opened the door.

She stared out at the belligerently bright sunshine for a moment or two, then slammed the door behind her and started down the sidewalk.

❧

The fifteen minutes Amy spent walking to Xavier's apartment were a blur. What she may have been thinking or feeling was lost to her forever in a haze of pain and confusion. All she could feel was the heat of the sun, warm as blood, pressing against her face, her eyes, her dry, cracked lips.

Amy watched her own small fist as it raised up to knock on the warped screen door. After a moment, the inner door opened with a creak that Xavier had carefully cultivated by squirting salt water into the hinges. Waves of sweet, musky incense poured through the screen.

He smiled at her from the darkened living room. Invading sunlight illuminated points of gold in his black eyes. "Hi baby," he said softly. "I thought you might be coming."

Wordlessly, Amy opened the screen door and slipped in. She looked up at Xavier's elemental face, searching. He pulled her to him, and she began to sob.

Quietly, she cried for awhile. When it was over, he sat her down on his dilapidated red velvet couch. Amy sank deep into the soft cushions, and Xavier knelt down in front of her, taking her hands.

No. Not yet. I'm not ready just yet.

Amy looked over his head, restless eyes sliding around his tiny, one-bedroom apartment, looking for something new. It was bristling with artwork and magic, like the nest of a mystical magpie. Japanese watercolor prints hung alongside plaster gargoyles, African rattles, illusion posters from the mall, and Mexican milagros. Beautiful chaos. Amy always considered it a game to try and find something new; a recently acquired Tibetan mask, a fancy new jeweler's tool, a print by an obscure Gothic painter. Not today. Same cluttered workbench. Same prints, masks, and stolen road signs on the walls. Same rough-hewn table with its eternally smoking censor.

Nothing new today. Nothing other than my recently diseased brain. Amy's eyes drifted down to Xavier's nut-brown face.

Amy opened her mouth, wanting to talk to him, then shut it again. She stared at the flickering orange of an oxygen torch, abandoned in its holder. Xavier followed her line of sight, and got up to turn it off.

He leaned against his jeweler's bench and fixed Amy with an intense stare. His usually animated face was as still as stone. "How can I help you, sweet girl?" he asked finally.

Amy took a deep, deep breath.

"Well. I've been having these . . . really bad dreams. You know, like I told you before." Her voice quavered. Xavier nodded, calm and reassuring. Another deep breath.

"But it's more than just dreams. I know it. Sometimes they're almost like visions. We went out the other night, and I got really drunk, and I went in the bathroom and when I looked in the mirror I saw—I saw—"

A sob escaped from her mouth, and she bit her lip to stop the one behind it. Xavier crossed the room and sat on the couch next to her. His thick, warm arms slid around her, and she gratefully lay her head on his chest. Amy's breath hitched a few times, and then she started talking again.

"I had a vision, Xavier. I think I was remembering something from my childhood. Something really horrible, you know?" Amy forced a laugh. "Like I was kidnapped by aliens or something. And another thing. Since I've been having these dreams, I keep getting sick. I mean, I hurl if you look at me wrong." She tried to laugh, and sobbed instead. Xavier began to stroke her hair, and she closed her eyes. One hand was balled into a fist, the other clenched and unclenched on the couch, squeezing the flattened, threadbare velvet.

"I don't know what's wrong with me," she whispered. "I think I might be going crazy."

Xavier pulled back from her, holding her at arm's length. Amy looked into his eyes, and saw worry. More than worry. Fear.

Oh God Oh Jesus he thinks I'm crazy too—

"Amelia. You are NOT crazy. I think you were right the first time; you're starting to remember a suppressed memory. I think someone hurt you once, very badly."

Amy sagged. "Oh shit. You think I'm another of those people who's going to suddenly accuse my parents of renting me to a Satanic cult in exchange for timeshare on a condo in the Bahamas or something?"

Xavier didn't smile. "No. But Amy ... do you think your father might have hurt you?"

"NO!" Amy put her hand to her mouth. She didn't mean to shout. But the thought of Tom, the only father she had ever known, hurting her in some way was unbearable. No. Impossible. She trusted her daddy with her life, and always would. She *knew* he hadn't hurt her. But just as surely, she suddenly knew that someone close to her, someone she loved, had betrayed her in the worst possible way. The revelation hit her so hard it was physical. She shivered from the inside out.

" ... Amy?" Xavier was staring at her, face sick with worry.

"What? Oh—my dad. No. Absolutely not. It was someone else. Someone really ... different."

Xavier's brow was furrowed with concern. He opened his mouth as if to say something, then shut it again.

"Xavier? Do you think you could find out what's wrong?"

Nervously, he twisted the amethyst and silver ring on his left forefinger. His eyes grew large. "Amy . . . you should get professional help. I'm not a psychologist. I'm not qualified—"

A quick flash of fear grabbed Amy in the guts, followed by a hot stab of anger. "Bullshit!" She snarled. "You know me better than any stupid shrink. I don't want someone I don't know poking around in my head. I— I—" *No not more goddam fucking tears no no—* But they couldn't be stopped, although Amy's chest ached like pneumonia from trying. She groaned miserably, her face hot and wet. "Please . . . "

Xavier tugged at the long, beaded braid next to his ear. "I can try, Amy," he said quietly. "I haven't done it in a long time, but I'll give it a shot."

Amy swallowed hard, and wiped her eyes with the backs of her fists like a child. She smiled at Xavier, and took his hand.

"Now, remember," he said quickly, "I'm not a full shaman. I'm a dropout, Amy."

"I know," she said. "I haven't forgotten. The blood magic . . . "

"Was too much for me. I couldn't kill." He sat down next to her, drawing her head down to his shoulder. "But I can heal. And I can interpret, sometimes. Now shut your eyes, Amy."

She lowered her lids, staring at the curl of incense rising up from the brass burner. Xavier's blunt fingers brushed against her lashes, and she closed her eyes. He massaged her temples, and the back of her neck. Amy sighed, relaxing against him. "That's it," he whispered, his breath stirring her hair. "That's it, baby."

Amy felt warm and safe. Xavier's blunt fingers stroked her cheekbones and throat. His touch grew increasingly light and delicate. Amy felt as if she were floating. Everything bad seemed far, far away. His hands on her face felt like feathers, like a gentle breeze on a warm spring night . . .

⚶

Amy stood pressed to the wrought-iron fence, staring in at the pool. In the bright moonlight, the scummy stuff on the water was the color of her mother's turquoise Squash Blossom necklace. Amy couldn't believe that something so gross could look so pretty. *By the light of the silvery moon, the moon, by the light of the silvery moon . . .*

It had rained the past few nights (fat, heavy drops as warm as tears which Amy loved to catch in her cupped hands) and the scum-coated water was almost up to the rotten pool decking. A warm gust of wind lifted her hair and tickled the back of her neck. She whirled around, expecting at the very least a ravening werewolf, or perhaps a mummy. There was nothing but the empty street.

She breathed in a deep sigh of relief. She was, after all, being a Bad Girl. Monsters always looked for Bad Girls. Amy wrapped her arms around herself. She still could not believe that she had actually sneaked out of her room, through the living room, and out the door. She had walked down the long, dark hallway by herself, and gone out into the night.

I had to, she told herself. *The Dryad was calling me.*

So where was that Dryad, anyway? Amy frowned. She had answered the magical, whispering dreamvoice when it awakened her in the night like a kiss on the cheek, and had done a Very Bad Thing because it asked her to. *You will see something wonderfuuulllll . . .* That's exactly what it said. So here she was, waiting.

A big, hairy cockroach skittered across the sidewalk and dived down the storm drain.

"That's not wonderful," Amy whispered. "And I'm going home." She took a step back, still facing the pool.

And there it was. The Wonderful Thing. A beautiful green firefly, Just like the ones in Aunt Carolyn's yard in New Hampshire, dancing over the pool. *Tinkerbell!* Amy clasped her hands in excitement. The firefly circled the scum-covered water lazily, reflecting against the algae in shimmering blues and greens. Amy gasped. The colors were as pretty as an Arizona sunset, and her daddy always told her that Arizona sunsets were the prettiest things on Earth. The firefly swung back and forth like the metronome on Amy's piano. Amy swung her head back and forth too, watching, delighted. The firefly began to grow.

At first Amy thought another firefly had come to play with it, but there was still just one. It became as bright as three fireflies, then four, then five. Then it didn't look like a firefly at all. It looked like a beautiful green jewel, the size of Amy's four-square ball. Amy's mouth dropped open, and she stared. The glowing ball was as bright as a streetlight. She held up her hands, and they were as green as a kitty's eyes in the magical light.

Silently, the light-ball plunged into the pool. Amy could see it glowing beneath the surface of the algae like a light bulb under a green blanket. Slowly, it sank, the spot of light getting smaller and smaller. Then the pool was black.

Amy clasped her hands, bouncing on the balls of her feet. What a great show! Much better than the Ice Capades. "Thank you," she breathed. "Thank you, Dryad."

"Aaaaamy . . . "

The voice rustled like the wind in the palm fronds. It was quiet and small, a voice that might belong to a little mouse. Amy squeezed her head through the bars of the fence, trying to see who could have made it.

"Aaaaamy. Help. me. Help meeee . . . ."

The voice was coming from the pool. Amy frowned. What could it be? Then it dawned on her. "Oh, no!" she squeaked. Tinkerbell was drowning!

Amy wriggled through the bars frantically, tearing the hem of her sundress. She wiggled harder, pushing herself forward, and all of a sudden she was stuck. The bars pinched her chest like bony fingers, and Amy couldn't move. Her wiggling turned to thrashing. She sucked in air to scream for help, and the bars felt even tighter.

Mica!

Amy suddenly remembered her Arizona grandma laughing, telling stories about her bad old fat horse Mica. "If you weren't careful, Amy, that wicked horse would swell up with air when you were trying to put on his saddle. Then once you were on him, he'd let it all out. Whoosh! I tell you, honey, that saddle would slip, and you'd fall right on your head!"

The saddle would slip. Amy held perfectly still. She let out all her air, breathing out until her lungs felt as flat as paper. Then she pushed herself toward the pool.

Sure enough, she popped out on the other side of the fence. She staggered in the squishy, weeded grass. She stepped onto the slimy pool decking, regained her footing—and then she hesitated. The pool was black, black, like an open mouth.

"Amy," whispered the voice. "Oh, please . . . "

Cautiously, Amy sidled up to the edge of the pool. Her foot slipped on the algae growing on the rotted deck. She gave a little scream and sat down hard. Amy's hands touched the cold, slimy cement. *Oh, yucchy, yucchy!* She yanked them away and wiped them violently on her dress, leaving a nasty green smear on the pretty fabric. Her feet hung over the side, almost touching the surface of the water.

Amy scrambled to get up, and slipped again. She was suddenly very frightened. "Hello!" she cried, her throat tight. "Dryad! Are you there?"

The surface of the pool began to glow.

" . . . Amy? . . . "

"Yeh, uh, yes," she whispered, torn between wanting to see the dryad and wanting to run like heck. The algae in the pool rippled with light. A small bulge appeared next to the edge, by Amy's feet. With a gasp she yanked them away.

The bulge stretched up to meet her like the big, fat, waving earthworms she found digging in her back yard at home. Amy stared, fascinated, too afraid to move. The skin of the algae split open. A tiny pink hand, the size of Amy's own, opened and closed on the air.

The hand waved around, as if it were looking for something. It reached toward Amy, right at her! She skittered backwards, whimpering, confused.

Another hand burst from the pool, reaching, reaching. The little hands opened and closed frantically, then began to sink.

It's going to die Tinkerbell is going to die in cold cold water—

"No!" Amy shouted. With a burst of courage she didn't know she had, Amy leaned out and grabbed for the hands.

They locked onto hers, gripping with strong, warm little fingers. Amy was jerked forward, toward the water. Instinctively she heaved back with all her might.

A child's head and shoulders surfaced with a squishy splash. He sputtered and coughed, holding tight to Amy's hands. A little boy! He opened his eyes, and they were the darkest, deepest green in the world.

"You're not Tinkerbell," said Amy.

The boy grinned. His teeth were little and sharp, like a kitten's. "I'm not a dryad either. I'm . . . Rags!" It was a little kid's voice, all right, but somehow different. Different from anybody's voice she knew. It was almost like he was purring when he talked. It was kind of cool. But kind of spooky, too.

"That's a dog name," said Amy, trying to get her hands back.

"It's my name," he said. "Help me out, Amy. I'm cold."

She looked at the boy carefully. She hadn't caught Tinkerbell. She had caught Peter Pan himself. As she pulled him out, she looked at his gold colored skin, dripping with slime, and his forest eyes and his sharp teeth and thought he was the most magical creature in the world. He was so . . .

Evil . . .

❧

"Evil . . ."

"Evil!" shouted Xavier. "Evil! Why didn't you see that it was so evil so evil so . . . " His eyes rolled up in his head.

Amy screamed and grabbed him by the shoulders. "Xavier!" she yelled into his face. She shook him. "Xavier!"

He moaned. His head rolled back and forth. Finally, he slumped forward.

"Xavier?" Amy asked fearfully.

He raised his head. His black eyes were haunted and tired. "Amy . . . Amy, you're in deep. That was real. That really happened to you."

"No," she protested. "It couldn't possibly . . . "

"Listen to me, my girl. It did. Whatever that was, it's real. And it's following you." The weight of his stare was almost unbearable. "I don't know what it wants, Amy. But you don't want it to get you. It's going to—do something." Xavier shuddered violently. Covering his mouth, he heaved once.

"Can you help me?" Amy asked in a small voice. She felt numb, so strange.

Xavier's look was full of pain. "I don't think so, Amy. It's too alien. It's a different kind of . . . of magic. I don't know how to deal with it. I don't even know what it is." He rubbed his eyes. "There's something I can try, but it may not do any good. Do you understand?"

"Yes." Her voice was as brittle as dry leaves.

"I'm going to walk you home, Amelia. I don't want you go out tonight, okay?"

"Okay."

"I have to talk to some people. In the meantime, lock your door tonight, sweet girl."

"Xavier?"

"Yes, Amy?"

She felt her face crumple like an old newspaper. "Xavier . . . why me? What did I do?"

He took her small, pale hands in his strong brown ones, and brought them to his chest.

"Amy . . . I don't really know. It could be that you're sensitive to magic, and that thing was drawn to you. It could have been your age. Six-year-olds will accept things that would drive an adult around the bend. It could have been as simple as the fact that you were close and convenient. You may never find out."

Her head shook violently back and forth. "No. No. I can't live with that."

He kissed her hands, first the right, then the left. "But you have to. You have to live. No matter what. Just understand that you didn't do anything wrong. Whatever the reason you were picked . . . it wasn't because you were bad, or marked, or cursed, or any silly crap like that. Okay?"

Amy stared at his chest, feeling a million miles away.

"Say 'okay', Amy."

She let out a shuddering sigh. "Okay."

Xavier leaned close, his face inches from hers. "You didn't do anything wrong. That has to be enough."

She smiled, feeling vague, feeling drained. She kissed him on the cheek, and tasted a salty tear.

❧

Two children, one pale pink, one pale green, stood close together, nose to nose, arms around each other.

"I love you, Amy."

"I love you too, Rags."

She touched his nose with her finger. "Why do you change colors?"

"'Cause I can. Wouldn't you?"

"Sure."

Amy looked into the little boy's eyes and smiled. He smiled back, his little pointed teeth glittering. He squeezed her tight, making his arms really long like goose necks, and she giggled.

"You're a silly-billy."

"Nuh-uh."

"Uh-huh."

"Oh yeah? Well, if I'm such a silly-billy, could I do this?" Rags let go of her and took a step back. His forehead wrinkled up like he was thinking really hard. He stood on his toes and looked up at the ceiling.

"Hmmph." said Amy. "I can do that."

He shot her an indignant look, and started to stretch. First his neck got longer, and then his chest. Finally his legs went too, stretching up like bubblegum stuck to the bottom of a sneaker. Rags' pants fell down as he grinned at Amy from on high, weaving like a charmed cobra. "Pretty cool, huh?"

"Yeah," she said, impressed. "You got no petey."

"What?"

"You got no petey. You're smooth down there, like a Ken doll. Are you sure you're a boy?"

Rags collapsed in a rubbery heap, looking like a plate of noodles in that weird green pesto stuff that Mama liked. He pulled himself back to normal faster than even Gumby could and jumped to his feet, already in his pants. He looked down at his bare toes, spread over the slimy hotel floor like the feet of a tree frog. "Course I'm a boy. I just . . . I don't really need one right now, that's all."

Amy took Rags' hand. It was cool and just a little sticky. "'M sorry, Rags. I didn't mean to hurt your feelings. You're just really . . . different, you know?"

"Yeah. I know." He stared at the floor for a little while longer, then his head snapped up. His green eyes met hers, and sparkled with mischief. "That's why I can do THIS!" His tongue shot out of his mouth and licked Amy's nose from eight inches away.

"Hey!" she squealed, giggling. She tried to lick his nose back, but he was already running.

"I'm gonna get you!" She shouted to him, charging through the darkness, fearless and happy.

❧

Amy smiled in her sleep, a Kathe Koja paperback open on her chest. "Rags", she whispered.

She had called off her date with Shane, pleading illness. He was sweet and worried and offered to bring her tea or orange juice.

Still smiling, her dream forgotten, Shane stood in the fog of her sleep like a 1930s detective beneath a streetlight. Murmuring, she rolled over.

There was something in the apartment. She heard it come in. It crept down the hallway, stopping at Amy's door. She could hear it breathing. It brushed against the door, soft as a moth at the window.

Amy's mind screamed at her to get up, to run, but her body was paralyzed. Caught in the terrifying, helpless spot between sleep and wakefulness, she could only wait. Could it hear her breathing?

It stood in the hallway for what seemed like hours. Amy thought she heard a low chuckle. The thing moved, shifting back and forth. Again, it brushed against the door. Amy pried her eyes open and stared into the darkness. She whined, low in her throat.

Stealthily, it passed by. Amy heard it opening Sarah's door, ever so slowly.

Oh God, Oh, no! Sarah, get out! Sweat rolled down Amy's face and into her half-closed eyes.

There was an eternity of silence. Then there was some scrabbling, and a dull thump. Amy thought she heard a strangled scream. Her breathing was frantic and ragged, but she still couldn't move. *Sarah!*

Amy heard the other girl's voice, pleading. Sarah whimpered, then she screamed.

"Aaaah! Oh, please! Please, God . . . ."

Amy tried to scream out Sarah's name.

"Uuhhnnn!"

The sound that came out of her mouth was frightening, inhuman. It was the sound of an animal caught in a trap. Terrified, Amy raised her hand to her throat. With a sudden burst of adrenaline, she realized that she could move!

Amy wrenched herself up, falling heavily out of bed. She grabbed the baseball bat she kept under the bed and crawled toward the door.

Sarah screamed again.

" . . . Aaaah! Oh God! Mick! Mick, oh pleeease! Oh! Oh, yesss! Yesss . . . "

Amy dropped the baseball bat. Amy dropped herself. Face on the floor, she groaned. "You're flaking out, woman."

After awhile, she went back to bed, but she could not sleep. Her mind replayed the evening over and over. Every time she closed her eyes, she saw the fear in Xavier's.

A monster is after me. That's basically what he told me, wasn't it? She turned her face to the wall, staring at a poster of Kurt Cobain. *Of course, maybe I'm as crazy and fucked up as you were, huh?* The room seemed to flood with brilliant light for a moment. Kurt Cobain's eyes flashed cobalt. Then it was black again. Amy squeezed her eyes shut. *Uh huh. Maybe my brain just manufactured it all for Xavier's viewing pleasure. Maybe there's no monster after me. Maybe I'm just bugfuck.*

Which is worse?

She tried to make her brain go blank, to fill it with white noise, but music wailed behind her shuttered eyelids.

Where do bad folks go when they die?
They don't go to heaven where the angels fly.
Go to a lake of fire and fry, see 'em again on the fourth of July . . .

The tune changed, morphed, shifted into something older but still so filled with pain.

. . . I asked that old ragman how much he would pay
for a heart that was broken when you went away,
or a burned out old lovelight that no longer beams,
and a couple of slightly used second-hand dreams.
Rags and old iron, rags and old iron . . .

Amy opened her eyes again, just a slit.

Flash.

Kiefer Sutherland's sullen face on the ceiling, lit as if by daylight. Then it was dark again.

Amy reached over and picked up the tiny, perfect lizard Xavier had given her. She squeezed it in her fist, holding it close to her heart.

The room flashed again, and Amy pressed her fists to her eyes and swallowed a desperate scream.

Eventually, Amy slipped into a black, dreamless sleep as Xavier's silver lizard sang to her fevered brain.

SIX

He stared in the window, his dull green eyes unblinking. He blended himself in with the bushes a little more. Spiky green vines undulated slowly against his scalp.

The Brown Man was rubbing the amulet with a rag. Every now and then, he held it up to the light for inspection. The silver winked softly. The purple crystal at the bottom seemed to glow.

Pretty.

He yawned. He really didn't need to, but he knew that was what humans did when they were tired and bored. He had been watching for a long time.

At first he found the Brown Man's actions to be fascinating. The cutting of the silver, The blessing of the stone, and the beautiful, frightening torch. The incantations that the Brown Man performed amused him. Every time the Brown Man scattered purple dust or gestured with a feather, he felt the little tug inside of himself that had drawn him here in the first place. It was kind of like the tug that lead him to Amy, but not nearly so strong or so sweet.

But now he grew impatient. The amulet was done. The Brown Man was raising it to his lips. His mouth formed the words, "Protect her," and he kissed his creation. He clutched it tightly in his fist, and strode into the bedroom.

Rags frowned. His green leaf-skin make soft crinkling noises. *What should I do?* He thought. *What, what?*

The Brown Man returned from the bedroom. He was wrapping the jewel in a silken bit of cloth.

Rags put his hand to the glass. He made the fingertips wide and porous, like the hand of a tree frog. He pulled it away with a wet, sucking sound.

The Brown Man turned immediately to the window.

But he won't see me. Because I'm already gone.

Rags sauntered around the side of the apartment to the front door. He saw the Brown Man's puzzled face in the window. Rags smiled.

He carefully pulled in the vines from his scalp, and formed his hand like a human's again. He adjusted his color until he was a rosy pink, like Amy's face when she was laughing. He hiked up his stolen blue jeans and knocked on the door.

He waited for what seemed like a long time. He was bouncing on his toes when the door finally opened.

The Brown Man's brown eyes looked out suspiciously at him. Rags stopped bouncing. He smiled. *Damn. My teeth are still pointy.* He closed his mouth. His teeth slid up into his gums, and when they came down again, they were blunt and squared.

"Begone!" hissed the Brown Man. He held the amulet up to the crack in the door. "I command you to leave this place." His hand was shaking.

Rags rolled his eyes. "Puh-leez. Speak English, man. Let me in." He grinned widely. "If you don't, I'll just come in under the door."

The Brown Man took in a sharp breath. He opened the door a little wider, and looked at Rags. Rags added some dimples to his most charming grin. Finally, the Brown Man stepped back and let the door swing wide.

"Nice place, Brown Man," said Rags, looking around. "But do you have to burn that incense all the time? It dries out my sinuses."

The Brown Man scowled. He still clutched the amulet. "What do you want from me?" he asked. "What do you want from Amy?"

"I don't really have sinuses," said Rags. "And there's nothing I want from you, Brown Man. You called me with your little magic spells."

The human took a step back. He looked very angry. "My name," he said, "is Xavier. And I did not call you."

"You did, Hav-Yaer. When you tried to repel me with magic, it tickled and tickled until I had to come see what you were up to. Nice ring."

Xavier looked down at his hand self-consciously. He was wearing a ring of chunky silver in the shape of a bat with tiny cabochon ruby eyes, the wings wrapped around his finger. Rags guessed the Brown Man had made it himself. *Talented little monkey.* Rags grinned and hooked his thumbs together, flapping his hands like batwings. Xavier shoved his hand into the pocket of his baggy jeans.

Rags sat down heavily on the threadbare sofa. "Now what are we going to do about this?"

Xavier's eyes were narrowed down to black slits. "I don't know what you are. But I will not let you hurt Amy."

Rags pulled on the back of his hair, making it inches longer. "Of course you don't know what I am. I was born in the swamps. Voodoo and Santeria and black Bayou water flow through my veins. I have nothing to do with your aboriginal dirt-magic." Rags smiled. He was delighted with his own eloquence. He made his teeth pointy again. "I am a mystery to you." He sneered like Christopher Lee.

Xavier started to say something, but Rags cut him off. "You have no right to keep me away from Amy. She is my intended. My baby bride. My Tootsie Pop. We were meant for each other."

Rags stood up. He drew himself up six inches taller. His jeans started to slip, and he caught them with one hand before they could fall down. He made a little tendril come out of his back and wrap around one of the belt loops. "Who are you, little human, to try to keep me from her? And why do you think I would hurt her? I love her."

Xavier was edging toward the door. "Stop," said Rags quietly. "Or I'll hurt you."

Xavier was shaking. His fists were clenched and he stared at Rags with a mixture of defiance and terror that Rags found absolutely fascinating. The Brown Man spoke. "You love nothing. You are evil. I feel it."

"You feel it?" shouted Rags. He made his voice deeper. "Well who the hell asked you, bubba?" Rags pushed his cheekbones up a little higher so he would look more like Christopher Lee. "I do love her. It is my fondest dream to hold her in my arms and kiss her golden hair and her creamy skin and taste her lips and her—" He brought himself up short. Had he been about to say, "Her blood?" His mouth was watering. Once again, he had begun to confuse Love and Hunger. Being human was so hard.

Rags was suddenly furious. He closed the space between himself and Xavier in a heartbeat. He stared down at the human, who seemed rooted to the spot in terror. *Alllll right!*

"My Amelia likes you. She listens to you and trusts you. You must not poison her mind against me. You must not!" He grabbed Xavier by the arms, making his fingers a little longer to go all the way around the man's thick biceps. He could feel the warm, solid flesh quivering with fear. It nearly drove him wild. "I could smell you on her as I stood by her bedroom window tonight. You touched her." Rags made his teeth longer. Xavier's face twisted in disgust. Rags shook him.

"Every time I touch Amy's mind she tries to push me away. She's making herself sick trying to get away from me. Did you cause this, human? Did you?!"

Xavier suddenly twisted away, Rags' fingers tearing bloody furrows in his flesh. He reared back, and struck Rags in the face.

Rags fell to his knees. He raised his hands to his face, and felt that it was pulled badly out of shape. He started to fix it when Xavier kicked him in the stomach.

Rags pulled Xavier's foot deep into his body, clasping it in his cool flesh. Xavier fell.

Rags let the man's foot loose. He leapt like a spider, landing heavily on Xavier's stomach. He made a fist, hard and gnarled like a weather-beaten oak. He slammed it into Xavier's jaw, like they did on TV. It felt so good.

The human's jaw made a wonderful snapping sound. Blood dripped from his slack mouth. Rags decided to try it again, but this time he made little rose-thorns come up on his knuckles. He liked the way Xavier's flesh tore, the oh-so-soft ripping noise it made.

Rags pulled back. Something was wrong here. He frowned, thinking, sitting astride the bleeding and gasping Brown Man. Rags got it in a minute or two. Xavier was no longer FightingLike a Man.

Rags stood up, and pulled the compact little man to his feet. Xavier's eyes rolled as he tried to focus. Rags held him up by the hair and slammed his thorny fist into Xavier's stomach.

The human's knees buckled. *Well, this is not much fun, thought Rags.* He decided to slam Xavier against the wall.

The noise was great.

Xavier lay in a crumpled heap on the carpet. Rags knelt down next to him. He opened Xavier's fist, and took the amulet. He felt a mildly unpleasant pulsing in his head. He closed his own hand around the amulet and was distracted by the deep red of the blood on his thorns. By the time he opened his hand again, the pulsing was gone.

Rags laughed. He inspected the pretty object in his hand. It was a little silver disc, with a tiny black stone set in the center of it and a small purple crystal that swung freely at the bottom. A hooked wire went through a little hole at the top. "Oh," said Rags. "An earring."

He held it up to his left ear and made a quarter-inch hole in his lobe. He put the earring through. He felt the hole in his ear thoughtfully, and decided it was too big. He closed it until it was snug around the wire.

He studied Xavier's still features. Slowly, Rags adjusted his skin color until it was the same as Xavier's. He took a step back, wondering if he should make his features like the Brown Man's.

Rags screamed. The little jeweler's torch, sitting in its holder, had burned his arm badly. The stench of burning vegetation filled his sensitive nose. *That's me. That's my flesh!*

He kicked Xavier's quiet form angrily. The human rolled bonelessly onto his back. *Neat!*

"Owwww," Rags whined. His arm hurt. He touched it gingerly. The burned spot was hard. He squeezed his eyes shut and did what he had to do. It hurt a lot.

The burned section was tough to get out. He peeled it loose, like thick bark from a tree. The scab ripped free, but his flesh hung tenaciously on to it by thin green stringers of living tissue. Rags whimpered. He made his arm long and thin, bringing it within reach of his mouth. With razored teeth he severed the last of the emerald threads.

Rags held the burnscab his palm. *Damn it.* He threw it on the floor. Concentrating, he grew a little pad to fill the hole. He rubbed his arm, smoothing down the little bump. *There. Good as new. Better.*

He narrowed his eyes at Xavier, enjoying the way the blood on the Brown Man's mouth made frothy little bubbles. His eyes strayed to Xavier's bat ring. The little bat's eyes looked just like tiny blood bubbles. *That is so cool.* Rags knelt by Xavier and grasped the ring. He pulled hard, once, twice. It wouldn't budge. Rags stood up and thought for a moment. Then he picked up the tinsnips from Xavier's bench, and bent over the man's beaten form. In a few moments, he stood up with his prizes.

Rags strolled out into the cool night, Xavier's braid woven into his hair, the thing in his pocket blossoming red on the blue denim. He walked down the street, headed for Amy's apartment. He knew he wouldn't have the courage to go to her tonight. Not yet. But he would sit beneath her window and breathe in her sweet scent, and dream of her.

SEVEN

Amy shrieked. "Did you see that? That was excellent! I wish I could do that". She sat up higher on the couch, setting her sketchbook aside. Her eyes were locked onto the TV screen, a grin of genuine enjoyment (and just a little malice) lighting her face.

She had awakened this morning with Xavier's little lizard still in her hand, and a velvety feeling of calm in her mind. She vaguely remembered another dream, about a sweet little boy who loved her, and kissed her with cool, soft lips. The night terrors, the panic, the weird flashes in the dark had all faded away to fantasy, quirks of her exhausted imagination. They were no more real than the monsters on the videotape. *And these monsters are a hell of a lot more fun.*

Sarah lay on her stomach on the floor, drawing intently. "You wish you could shoot rednecks with porcupine quills?" She looked up from her drawing. "I guess that would be kind of cool. You'd have to run around naked all the time though."

"Sshhh!" said Mick. "This is a good movie." Sarah rolled partway over and started to say something snide, but Mick rubbed her back harder and she sank contentedly down again.

Amy looked at her own drawing and frowned. *It just doesn't look right.* She and Sarah were violating the sanctity of Couch Potato Sunday Afternoon at the Videos by working on their Halloween costume designs.

And the God of Laziness is getting his revenge. Her semi-punk Mad Maxette sketches looked uninspired and lame. *Too much tit. Too little originality. Every boring geekchick who's ever gone to a SciFi convention has one of these in her closet.* She stared at the sketches for a moment longer, then turned to a clean page. *No, dear. You don't want to look like a twenty-dollar hooker. A three-hundred dollar hooker, maybe.*

Amy watched the end of *Nightbreed* with half an eye as she started a new design.

"Excellent movie," said Mick in his unhurried way. "What's next, *Grim Prairie Tales* or *Hard Rock Zombies?*"

"Zombies, Zombies!" screamed Amy and Sarah. Mick winced at the noise as he popped *Nightbreed* back into its case.

Amy slid off the couch and flopped down next to Sarah. "What 'choo got, woman?" she asked, reaching for Sarah's notebook.

"Loook," said Sarah, turning her drawing the right way. "Cleavage!"

"Mmmm. Victorian ball gown?"

"Yup."

"Black velvet?"

"Black satin. What's yours, Amy? Postnuclear belly dancer?"

"Nope," said Amy, opening her book. "Eighteenth-century harlot."

"Cool," said Sarah. "You get cleavage too!" She examined the drawing. "That's gonna be hard, girl. You'd better get started soon."

"True. We could go to the fabric store today," said Amy, studying her sketch. "I want black and red velvet."

Sarah looked up at her with half-closed eyes. "Yes, we could," she said. "But then we'd miss *Hard Rock Zombies*. And popcorn. And margaritas."

"Yum!" said Amy. "Go make it. I'm still convalescing."

Sarah rolled over on her stomach and gazed at Mick with huge brown puppy eyes. "Miiiick, Hoooneeey, Would you? Could you?"

Mick regarded her with hooded eyes. "Hell no."

Sarah made a silly 'shocked' face. "Mick! Shame on you! A good Catholic boy like you shouldn't be saying words like that!"

"If I were a good Catholic boy, I'd be in church today, not hanging out with you chicks."

Sarah's smile was evil. "Come to think of it, if you were a *good* Catholic, you wouldn't be bangin' me, honey-babe."

Mick turned crimson. "To hell, ah said *hay-el,* with this abuse! I'll go make the *damned* popcorn!" He high-tailed it for the kitchen.

"Ooooooo!" the girls shouted after him.

When she got through laughing, Amy took Sarah's drawing and started adding little bows to the skirt. Sarah busied herself with adding lace to Amy's collar.

Amy looked whimsically at the Victorian dress with no one inside it. Sarah never bothered to start with a body. She just drew the dress. Amy closed her eyes and saw beautiful, empty Victorian dresses spinning across a dance floor with fine gentlemen's suits. *Wonder what Xavier would say that means. It's probably symptomatic of an empty head.*

Amy took the black banana clip out of her hair and tossed it on the couch. She rested her head on her arms. *I wonder why he hasn't called.* She rolled over on her back. *Because Xavier's flaky, that's why. And we really had each other going last night with all that dream shit.* Amy snorted softly. Xavier had been known to disappear for weeks at a time. She had learned to stop worrying about him long ago.

Amy smiled against her forearm. Even the way she had met Xavier was weird.

Amy and Sarah had been hiking on Superstition Mountain on an acetylene blue spring day. Neither of them were experienced hikers, but they liked to go stomping around in the desert on weekends just the same. Sarah loved looking for birds and wildlife, and Amy just enjoyed getting the hell away from everybody.

On this particular outing they had spotted a dust-brown desert fox, a lanky, slightly ratty jackrabbit, several hawks, and something that Sarah insisted was a mountain lion, but Amy suspected of being a big orange tomcat. It had been so far away it was impossible to determine.

"I'm tellin' ya," said Sarah, a little out of breath from the uphill climb, "That thing was a cougar. We were lucky to get away with our lives."

Amy, slightly ahead of her, turned back and raised a skeptical eyebrow. "Sarah, that thing could have been anything. It could have been a poodle, for all we know! It was barely a speck on the horizon." She paused to pick a large pebble out of the tread of her hiking boot.

Taking a deep breath of the warm, sweet desert air, she looked out across the mountain. God, it was gorgeous up here. Some people looked at the sand and dusty, scrubby plantlife and rugged rock formations and saw only ugliness. Amy saw nature at its most resourceful. And the colors at sunset, the way the sky lit up in bands of purple and pink, pale jade green and celestial blue, the way the desert turned to gold and glowing rust, that was magic. She smiled.

"Oh, sure, you mock me now, but you'd be singing a different tune if that beast had come this way and decided to take a bite out of your ass. And it was NOT a poodle. Poodles don't slink like that." Sarah crossed her arms defiantly.

"Okay, it was a weasel." Amy picked up a sparkling piece of rose quartz and dropped it into her pocket.

"Hey!" yelled Sarah, pushing up her sunglasses with her forefinger. "A cave!"

"Where?" Amy glanced around.

"Right there, dorko." Sarah was pointing at what Amy had first taken to be a shadow on a jagged, head-high rock formation. "See?"

"Oh, yeah." Amy narrowed her eyes at it. "Cool!"

"Well, what are you waiting for? Let's go in!" Sarah was trotting toward the crack in the rocks, kicking up dust in her enthusiasm.

"Wait a minute." Amy grabbed Sarah's arm. "My mom told me rattlesnakes sometimes hang out in caves during the day. And we don't have a flashlight or anything."

"I have a lighter," said Sarah. "See?"

"Oh, great. I don't know . . . "

"Don't be such a WUSS!" Sarah looked around her, then picked up a long piece of jumping cactus branch. Long dead, the dried-out branch looked like a hollow pipe full of Swiss-cheese holes. "Here. I'll poke this along the floor in front of us. We'll be fine."

"Sarah, I really don't think—" but her friend was already squeezing her curvaceous form through the opening in the rocks. Just like that, she was gone.

"If you get killed, I'm not carrying your dead ass out," Amy muttered as she followed close behind.

Sarah flicked on the lighter. It cast a little light, revealing a dusty crevasse that went deeper into the mountain than Amy would have thought. She didn't see any rattlesnakes, but she still followed close behind Sarah, who was sweeping in front of her with the cactus branch like a blind woman with a red-tipped cane.

The lighter went out. "Dammit, muttered Sarah, still walking and sweeping through the darkness. Amy heard her flicking it a few times, then it came on again.

The meager light revealed nothing spectacular. A narrow passage with granite walls, dirt-covered floor, a beer can or two in the corners. They were obviously not the first people to brave this cavern.

"Okay, what a thrill. Now let's go." Amy was still nervous. She didn't like the deep shadows that could be hiding almost anything, from Charles Manson to a rabid coyote.

"But we haven't seen it all! Look, it goes around the corner!"

Amy looked at the yawning darkness Sarah was pointing out, and felt a stab of panic. *Stay out of the dark there are bad things in the dark bad things—*

—Where the fuck did that come from?

"Fine. Let's go," said Amy, angry at herself.

Sarah crept around the corner, holding the lighter out in front of her, scraping the ground with her cactus branch. "Ooo!" she said over her shoulder, grinning like a loon. "It's a scaaaaary one!"

Just then, the lighter went out.

"Shit." Amy heard Sarah flicking it again and again. She also heard something else.

"Quiet!" she hissed.

"What?" Sarah paused, and the little cave was still for a moment.

Amy's heart kick-started and thrummed in her chest like a hummingbird. "There's something breathing! Something's in here with us!"

"Shit!" Sarah began flicking the lighter doubletime.

"Don't, it'll see us—" gasped Amy, but it was too late. The lighter was on.

There was a man sitting on a rock directly in front of them, mouth slack, eyes rolled up in his head.

Dead.

Amy and Sarah shrieked.

So did the man on the rock, right before he fell off of it. Backwards.

"Omigod!" shrieked Sarah. She tossed the cactus branch aside and crouched down, crabwalking toward him, still holding the lighter. "Are you all right, mister?"

All Amy could see of the man was his hiking boots, sticking up behind the rock. With a grunt, he heaved himself upright. His round, brown face hovered over the rock like a full harvest moon.

He grinned. "I'm not sure. To the best of my knowledge, my family doesn't have a heart condition, but you never know . . . "

"What were you doing?" asked Amy, offering him her hand. He took it and she helped him to his feet. He was short, compact, and muscular, dressed in a Cramps T-shirt and hiking shorts.

"What did it look like? I was meditating." The man, whom Amy could now see was about her age, began to briskly dust off his butt. "I was seeking a dream. It's what we Indian-types do, don't-cha know."

The lighter went out. After a bit of flicking and cursing, Sarah had it back on. "You were on a dreamquest? Cool. But aren't you supposed to do that naked?"

"Ever get jumping cactus in your ass?" The man unhooked a flashlight from his belt. "Here, use this. It'll work a lot better."

Blushing, Sarah put away her lighter as the beam of the flashlight pierced the darkness. "Sorry. We'll let you get back to your meditating now."

"It's too late. My concentration is utterly broken." He smiled again, an open, charming yet slightly mischievous expression that made Amy like him instantly. "So, you ladies wanna go to Denny's?"

And so they did, after the introductions. They spent hours and hours drinking coffee and talking about all manner of things, from the X-Men (Sarah loved Xavier's name) to Yaqui mysticism. When they finally said goodnight, they had become good friends.

That had been a little more than a year ago. Sarah loved Xavier, but it was Amy who connected with him most profoundly. He had become a kind of spiritual counselor to her as well as a friend. In return, she gave him (usually unwanted) advice on his love life and brought him fresh fruit once a week, to make sure he ate right. He was special to her in a way she couldn't verbally express, didn't really understand herself.

And I really, really wish he'd call me.

"So how'd you sleep?" Sarah was studying Amy's face.

Amy blushed. "Well, I, um, had another nightmare, but after that I went right to sleep. I felt just a little sick when I woke up, but I'm fine now. In fact, I'M HUNGRY!" She bellowed the last two words in the general direction of the kitchen. A wet paper towel came flying out, but missed her by several feet.

"Sick in the morning, huh?" said Sarah, her eyes sparkling. "Are we going to pop a puppy?"

"NO!" Amy laughed. "Not unless it's another immaculate conception."

"You and Shane didn't look so immaculate on the dance floor the other night."

Amy raised up on her elbow. "The last time I checked, you still couldn't get pregnant from somebody's knee."

Sarah laughed. "You look better today, Amy."

"I feel better. I also feel stupid."

"Why?" Sarah asked. She raised her head. "I hear popcorn. I smell popcorn!"

"Oh, you know. All those stupid dreams. And my spazzy behavior." Amy massaged her own temples. "I think I've just been under a lot of stress, with school and Jay and everything."

"Stress, my butt." said Sarah. "It's all those horror novels you read. They're rotting your brain."

"Could be," Amy mused. "Did you ever read *The Light at the End*?"

"No! And I don't want to! Amy, why *do* you read all that crap, anyway? What is the deal with you and monsters?" Sarah's look was half-serious.

"You should talk, honey. You're the one who picked out *Hard Rock Zombies*."

Sarah grinned. "Yeah, I know, but I don't always watch horror movies. And I read stuff other than horror novels. I mean, when was the last time you read a mystery, or a book of essays, or a fantasy?"

"What are you, my mama? I don't read nothin' with no fooking elves, chica." Amy rolled on her back and stretched.

"Okay, all right. It just seems like . . . " Sarah's dark brows knitted together, making her look like a worried Botticelli. "It seems like it wouldn't be healthy to spend all you time playing with monsters."

Amy laughed. "I've always played with monsters."

Amy's smile dropped off her face. Her words hung in the air so heavily that she could almost see them. *It might be true, really really true . . .*

Nope. That's a big hunk of bullshit. No monsters. I'm gonna wake up one day soon and remember some long-forgotten "uncle" did some vile, nasty little thing to me, and I'll cry and scream and go to therapy for a few months, and then it'll all be over. Over.

The doorbell rang. Sarah rolled up to her feet. Amy grimaced as her friend threw open the door without looking through the peephole. It was the one habit of Sarah's that Amy truly couldn't stand.

Shane grinned at her over Sarah's head. "How is my poor wilted rose today?"

Amy breathed in sharply. Her hands flew to her face, which was bare of makeup and more than a little pale. She thought of her uncombed hair as she looked down at her baggy T-shirt and holey cut-offs. Amy grinned weakly.

"Much better, thank you." She sat up, trying to retain a few scraps of dignity.

"I can tell," he said, grinning. "both you ladies look radiant today." He stepped in, and Sarah shut the door behind him. He was wearing his leather longcoat and carrying two sacks under his arms.

"Cut the bullshit, babe," said Sarah. "We look like dishrags. What did you bring us?"

"Japanese food." He set the bags down on the couch and knelt down by Amy. He brushed the hair out of her eyes. "Its good for the constitution."

Mick came out from the kitchen with a huge bowl of popcorn and a barely concealed sneer. *What is his fucking problem? Amy thought, irritated. Probably some Alpha-male-dog territorial pissing thing.*

"Hey, Mick," said Shane affably. "You like Shumai?"

Mick smiled tightly. "Sure."

"Well, all right then!" Shane slid out of his coat and slung it over the back of the couch. He looked beautiful in baggy black pants and a torn red T-shirt. "What a feast. Teriyaki and popcorn."

"And margaritas!" added Sarah happily.

Amy watched Shane as he carried the bags to the kitchen. His easy grace made her smile. *My God,* she thought. *How'd I get so lucky?*

EIGHT

He slammed his fists into the tree again and again. He lifted his face to the night sky and howled. Rags leaned his head against the treetrunk and sobbed.

"How could she?" he moaned. He hit the tree. "How could she? She's supposed to be mine!" "It's My Party and I'll Cry if I Want To" popped absurdly into his head, making him angrier. He pounded the tree to the rhythm of his anguish.

That. Boy. That. Shane. Went. In. And. Didn't. Come. Out!

Rags howled. He ran across the campus, green water streaming from his eyes as he compressed the tissues in his face, forcing it out like juice from an overripe melon. Crying seemed like the thing to do when it hurt this bad.

He kept coming across traces of her aura. It was a gentle lavender glow, distinctively Amy's, and it was all over the campus. In most spots it had faded down to almost nothing, but her favorite bench by the fountain was bathed in her light. He could smell her. He bit through his own lip, nearly severed it.

He kissed her! I saw him kiss her! She wanted him to! He tried and tried to erase the memory of what he had seen, but every time he closed his eyes, he saw Amy's arms sliding up Shane's back. He saw her hands sinking into his hair. He saw Shane nibbling on Amy's neck, and Amy's sweet face with her eyes closed and her head thrown back . . .

Rags opened his mouth to howl again.

He didn't.

A young girl came around the side of the library, looking nervously around her, holding her head up high like an antelope scenting for danger.

Rags smiled. He faded back into the shadow of the trees, camouflaging himself in its color and texture. He waited. His chest heaved as what passed for lungs filled and emptied, as they sometimes did when he was excited. His mouth began to water.

The girl carried a book under one arm, and what looked like a rolled up poster in her other hand. Her gait was brisk and businesslike.

Did your Mama tell you not to look like a victim, honey?

Rags stared at her. She was taller than Amy, and her hair was brown, not blond. But it waved just like Amy's, and Rags was sure he could smell Dragon Tree shampoo, just like Amy used. If her hair were a little shorter, she would be almost perfect . . .

She was directly across from him, walking down the center of the mall. Rags flattened out, thinner and thinner against the wall. One with the vines, he slid along the wall. His clothes caught in the bushes and slipped from his body His eyes never left her. He felt something. Love. *No, love is only for Amy. Then what is it, what is it?*

Hunger.

He flowed around the corner of the building, into the narrow corridor between the library and one of the old dorms. He stretched his mind toward her and pushed, prying out what he needed to know.

Rosy.

"Rosy," he called softly.

She stopped. She turned toward him, squinting into the darkness. Slowly, he formed himself back into humanshape. He stepped forward, barely allowing his shadow to be seen.

"Rosy, please . . . "

"Xavier?" she called tentatively.

Well ain't it a fuckin' small world. He adjusted his voice so it would sound more like the Brown Man's.

"Rosy, I think I hurt myself . . . " He sank down to his knees.

Rosy gasped, and ran to him. He crept back further into the darkness, collapsing on the sidewalk.

She paused at the mouth of the corridor. "Xavier . . ." she whispered. Her eyes were blue, and bright with fear. She crept forward.

Closer, closer, baby . . .

He chuckled. She froze.

"Silly Rosy," he breathed. "This is how Ted Bundy did it . . . "

Rosy dropped her calculus book and the poster from the animation festival. Her smooth, oval face went from open-mouthed disbelief *she thinks it can't happen to her, silly Rosy* to a cramping grimace of terror in a single heartbeat.

Rosy turned to run.

Incredibly fast, impossibly fast, Rags shot along the concrete and threw himself across the opening of the corridor in a slimy webbing of vines.

Rosy, entangled, started to scream. Her mouth was instantly filled with leaves.

He bound her wrists with tendrils from his body, and slowly drew himself around behind her. He solidified into a manshape, tall and slim.

Rosy struggled. Her sweat stung him, and filled his head like opium. He wrapped his arms around her and pulled her tight against him. He licked her neck.

Rags made his teeth long and sharp, like razors. He bit Rosy's hair off at the shoulder. Her hair fluttered to the ground, the wings of dead butterflies shaken from a spider's web. Fascinated, Rags watched Rosy's back tremble and twitch as her body spasmed in animal terror. She looked good from the back, slim of waist, curving hips. She tossed her head, and her hair looked just like Amy's when she was laughing.

Yes, it does make her more like Amy, But I can't see her face.

"Show me your eyes, Rosy," he whispered into her ear. He bit her earlobe lightly, drawing a bead of blood. He greedily licked it away.

Rosy whimpered. Rags could hear her chewing at the leaves in her mouth. He ran his hands up her body, pausing to stroke her breasts. Bigger than Amy's, more full.

He gripped her shoulders, and turned her around.

Rosy's blue eyes grew huge, glazing with terror. She squeezed them shut. A low animal moan came up from somewhere deep inside her. Tears trickled silently down her face.

"Oh, honey," Rags whispered. "Oh, honey, baby, lamb heart, don't cry." He reached into her mind and made her stop. He kissed her tears away, voicelessly ordering her to be silent.

He took the leaves from her mouth one at a time, until they were all gone. Her face was twisted in horror at the sight of him, and it irritated him that he couldn't get her to smile. He changed his face to look like Shane's, pulling in his long teeth, and smiled at her.

Rosy's mouth opened in a silent scream.

Rags saw that there were still bits of leaf in her mouth. He bent down, pressing his lips to hers, and began to clean them out.

NINE

Sarah and Amy walked faster, spilling their Pepsis on their shoes and leaving a trail of French fries behind them. They were late.

"Tell me," said Sarah, grinning.

"Nothing to tell," said Amy, trying to keep a straight face.

"Oh, bull-double-leaping-shit. You and Shane went into your room at nine, and he didn't leave until after midnight. You gonna tell me you were playing tiddly-winks?"

"Yup."

"Amelia! Don't you trust me?" Sarah danced in front of Amy, trying to make puppy eyes over her sunglasses. She succeeded only in spilling the rest of the French fries.

Amy stopped, heaving a great sigh. "Of course I do. I wouldn't live with someone as warped as you are if I didn't trust you."

"Then tell me aaaaallll about it." Sarah grinned into Amy's face.

"We talked. We looked at my Art History books."

"Did you show him your etchings?" Sarah leered.

Amy ignored her. "We listened to music, and we necked until our eyes bugged out. No, we didn't 'do it'."

"Why not?" Sarah sounded disappointed.

Amy rolled her eyes. "Because the last time I got 'intimately involved' with someone, all it got me was a broken heart and the occasional urinary infection."

"Yeah, but Jay didn't look like Shane. Not even close. God, girl, how did you resist?"

Amy laughed. "It was tough. But I want to get to know him first, Sarah. I just don't . . . "

"I understand," her friend said quietly. "I'm sorry I bugged you about it."

"No you're not, you little shit," said Amy, grinning, "and now we're ten minutes late instead of five."

"Oh, crap!" Sarah squeaked. They ran for the English building, pausing to slam-dunk their sticky paper cups into a garbage can.

The two slunk into class, their hands wet from the water fountain in the hall. Amy had insisted that they stop, since she was unable to learn with Pepsi between her fingers. She wiped her hands nervously on her jeans, smiling at Professor Winterbrook, as she and Sarah crept to their seats in the back of the room.

He smiled back. "Thank you for joining us, ladies," he said, without a trace of sarcasm.

Amy lowered her eyes, blushing.

"We were just discussing the significance of the group of men who formed Mina's would-be saviors. Obviously, we have the father figure, in Van Helsing." He smiled, his gray eyes sparkling. "Not at all an impotent father figure, if you look at the staking of Dracula's three brides on page three hundred and seventy-five."

Sarah laughed, flipping through her book. Amy was already there. "But let us discuss the significance of Quincy Morris. He and Arthur Holmwood, both suitors for Lucy's hand, represent opposite kinds of values . . . "

Sarah was trying to pass Amy a note. Amy glared at her, pointing at her book. Sarah grinned, and when Professor Winterbrook looked down at his copy of *Dracula*, she slapped the note onto Amy's desk.

"So when are you seeing him again?" it said in splotchy blue ink.

Amy sighed. "Tonight," she wrote back. "We're going to the movies. A retro showing of *Silence of the Lambs* at the Varsity. Believe it or not, I've never seen it."

Sarah grinned even more extravagantly. She leaned over and wrote, "Ooooo! You'll love it! It's a total make-out flick, if you're a cannibal!" across the paper. Amy shot her a mock-disapproving look, and folded up the note. Sarah stuck out her lower lip and reluctantly went back to her book.

Amy started to follow along, but she found she couldn't concentrate. Her thoughts kept drifting back to Shane. She thought she could see his eyes behind the words, hidden within the pages. Amy smiled. She picked up her pen. It hovered over the surface of her notebook for a moment, and then she began to sketch.

But it wasn't Shane. The young man in the drawing had the perfect shape of his face, but the eyes were solid black, and long incisors showed just behind his slightly parted lips. Embarrassed, Amy flipped the drawing over. She looked at Sarah, who was staring raptly at the Professor as he discussed Lucy's desire for sexual freedom. Once again, Amy looked at her book, but the words wouldn't hold still for her. She pulled out her paper and started to write.

Her eyes wandered up the wall to the window, high above the ground. It was narrow and dusty, but—

It was her only chance. Amelia clutched a handful of her white cotton nightgown, and set her resolve. She would escape from here. Her bare feet were cold on the stone floor as she padded across the room to the window.

Her emerald green eyes filled with despair. It was so high up. She could never jump that high, and the wall was just smooth enough that she couldn't get a toehold. Her delicate hand flew to her brow as she sunk to the floor.

Foolish girl! Will you just lie there and wait? For him? *Her eyes flew open. No, she would rather die than submit. She glanced desperately around the room for something to end her life.*

She gasped. It was there, all along! In a flurry of golden hair, she leapt to her feet and seized the giant brass candelabra. It tilted, and molten wax spilled onto the alabaster skin of her hand.

Amelia cried out, pressing her hand to her mouth. Did he hear me? I must act quickly! One by one, she pulled the candles from their sockets and cast them to the damp stone floor, where they sizzled and died. It was difficult work, for the candelabra was taller than she was, but soon she was down to the last one.

She held the still-lit candle in her left hand, and seized the candelabra *with her right. She pulled.*

Try as she might, she couldn't move the great metal thing with one hand.

Amelia's eyes flashed angrily. "In darkness, then," she breathed. She cast the last candle aside. The room was black. The moon shone dully through the dirty glass of the window as she seized the massive candelabra in both tiny hands, and dragged it to the wall.

Her creamy skin shone with perspiration. Her breasts heaved as she caught her breath. Setting her jaw, she grabbed the baroque scrolling of the metal branches and catlike, swung herself up.

The candelabra teetered dangerously for a moment, but then righted itself. Carefully, Amelia placed her small feet on the branches of the candelabra, and slowly she stood. She could see out the window!

I have done it! *she thought triumphantly. The metal cut into her feet cruelly, but she ignored the pain. She knew she was about to experience much worse. She made a fist, and drew it back to shatter the window.*

The heavy iron door swung open with a crash. He stood in the doorway.

Lord Jay of Carillon smiled evilly, his simian features creasing into a parody of mirth. He crossed the room in a few strides and plucked the screaming Amelia from the candelabra like a succulent fruit from a tree.

He crushed her flailing body against himself, breathing his rank breath into her face.

"So, little one, you thought to escape me? I think I shall have you right here—"

The window exploded, glass flying, lead bent inward like the branches of a wind-whipped tree. Tiny shards of glass glittered against the orange moon before raining to the floor with a delicate tinkle.

A man leapt in at an impossible angle, landing lightly on his feet.

No, not a man, *thought Amelia. For the stranger had black and leathern wings. In fact, his entire body was black, and glistened like finest jet. His eyes blazed scarlet, and when he opened his mouth, he had fangs like a beast. Amelia felt herself growing faint.*

Lord Jay loosened his grip on her, and she slid to the floor. Through half-closed eyes, she saw the stranger lift Carillon off his feet, and fling him against the wall. She lost consciousness.

When she awoke, she was in the stranger's arms, atop the castle battlements. Amelia bit her knuckle in terror, before she remembered her manners.

"Thank you, kind sir, for saving me from that beast."

His scarlet eyes studied her beneath inky lashes. His onyx hair fell in loose curls over his forehead. He smiled, showing his beautiful, terrifying teeth.

"How could I do otherwise," he whispered. "I love you, Amelia."

His breath was sweet, like orange blossoms on a summer night. He bent to kiss her, and demon or no, Amelia kissed him back. She slid her hand up his back, and toyed with his braid . . .

"Amy!"

"Amy! Amy!" Sarah was hissing at her, brown eyes wide. Amy gasped. Sarah was staring at her. Professor Winterbrook was staring at her. The whole class was staring at her.

"Miss Sullivan, are you still ill?" The Professor was approaching her, concern in his eyes.

Amy slid her paper under her notebook. "Um, a little bit, yes." She tried to smile at him.

"I was asking which of Lucy's suitors you might have picked."

Amy breathed in deeply. "Well, I always have been a sucker for a Texas accent," she said. The class laughed. "But I think I would have dumped all three of them and taken Dracula. Bad breath or no, eternal life is hard to pass up."

The Professor smiled. "Indeed. But poor Lucy's choice was made for her." He turned and walked back to the front of the class. "It is fairly obvious that Dracula represents unbridled sexual freedom." Again, the class laughed. Amy blushed. "But were his attacks on Lucy, and her ultimate demise, meant as a cautionary tale, or a comment on the repressive Victorian society? Mr. Chessex?"

Sarah was shoving a note at Amy. "What the hell were you doing, girl?"

"Spacing out," Amy wrote back.

Suddenly, Sarah grabbed the paper from beneath Amy's notebook. She looked at the Shane-with-fangs drawing, rolled her eyes, then flipped the paper over. Her eyes widened.

Oh, God, she's reading it! Amy dropped her head to her arms as Sarah read the poem.

Finally, her friend grinned like a Cheshire cat and handed the paper back. Amy studied her own words for a moment, her cheeks burning.

> My love has wings of leather
> They beat across the midnight skies
> Dark, they chill my velvet soul,
> Reflected in my moonlit eyes.
>
> My lover's smile is cold and sweet
> His teeth, like wolves', gleam sharp and white
> Shivering, I wait for him,
> Sweat glistens in the candlelight.
>
> I know tonight he'll come for me
> I feel him in my veins
> He'll drink my flesh and blood like wine
> 'Til nothing else remains.
>
> My love has eyes of scarlet
> My love has skin of blackest coal
> He'll wrap me in his silken wings
> And swallow up my virgin soul.
>
> I lift my hand up to my throat
> I turn my face up to the moon
> He spirals through her silver rays
> I'll know his hungry kisses soon.

Not bad, not bad, Amy thought, smiling. Then she saw the note at the bottom, in Sarah's spiky handwriting.

"My God, woman! You are horny as a toad!"

Suppressing an attack of the giggles, Amy shoved the paper into her notebook. She avoided looking at Sarah for the rest of the period, because she knew they would crack each other up.

Class was over. Sarah and Amy walked laughing across the mall to their favorite bench. Amy didn't notice the poem slip from her notebook as they settled down in the shade.

They talked together, easily, happily, as real friends do. They talked about the time in high school when they toilet papered the principal's house and got chased for seven blocks. They talked about their first boyfriends. They remembered their first day in college, when they had been utterly lost and scared and excited and had wandered the campus in big circles looking for the library. They talked of sleepovers, and high school feuds, and movies, and chocolate cheesecake. They avoided speaking of the future, and grades, and careers. The present was more fun, and the past was so much safer.

When Amy and Sarah finally got up from the bench with elaborate groans and stretching, it was late afternoon. Walking together with her best friend toward the parking lot, Amy smiled, capturing their light conversation in a crystalline photograph in her mind. She would one day look back on this moment, and realize why it was so special. It was her last day of true innocence.

The sun was low in the sky when the young women reached the dusty parking lot. They were both surprised to find Mick sitting on the hood of Sarah's battered Mustang.

"Hey, babe," said Sarah, insinuating herself between his knees, "What are you doing here? Don't you have Econ right about now?"

"I left early," Mick said. His eyes were clouded, and his mouth was tight with worry. "Did you two hear about Rosy?"

"Rosy?" asked Sarah. "Who . . . ?"

"Oh!" said Amy. "You mean tall Rosy, the girl who hangs around with Xavier sometimes? Bio major, isn't she?"

Mick's eyes were focused on the asphalt.

"What about her?" Sarah asked quietly.

90

He looked up at her. "Campus security found her sometime after three AM." He rubbed his forehead. "She was raped."

"Jesus," said Sarah. "Jesus."

The pit of Amy's stomach grew cold and hard. Mick's voice continued, grating in her ears, which continued to hear him even though she didn't want them to.

"That's not all. You know my friend Sally? Her mom works at the hospital. She said that Rosy had . . . " Mick swallowed hard, mouth turning down in disgust. "Rosy had some kind of . . . vegetable matter inside of her. In her mouth. And in her—everywhere."

Amy leaned against the old car heavily. Her head was buzzing, like static on the radio. Her stomach clenched down, tighter and tighter.

"Sally's mom said that Rosy was totally freaked. She wouldn't stop screaming at first, and then she wouldn't say anything at all, she just tried to bite. They had to put her in restraints."

Amy slid down the side of the Mustang. She squatted by the tire, stomach heaving. Her head was spinning, and suddenly the whole parking lot was the color of summer wheat. Sarah was down beside her in a moment, and she managed to catch Amy in her arms before the lights went out.

TEN

Blackness. Heat.

Heat and steam and rank decay assaulted her senses as she stumbled through the ruin of the old hotel. The whole thing was black and slimy and pulsing with heat. It was, in some perverse way, alive.

She ran, hands outstretched, sometimes colliding with things she was glad not to see. She was certain that some of them clutched at her, tried to hold her there. She twisted away and ran, trying to wipe the slime from her hands. She only made it worse. Her clothes were heavy with it.

Her own breath hung in the air in front of her, trapped in the foul, stagnant air. It caressed her face as she ran past.

She could barely hear it. A faint slither, like a wet rope being dragged through mud. She knew it was there. She knew he was there.

Her breath caught in her throat, and she choked. That was all he needed. The noises became louder. He was coming for her.

She whimpered, turning her head to look. Her eyes bulged into the darkness. Something slapped against her face, and she screamed. She clutched at it. It was only a wet, dripping curtain, rank with mildew. Desperately, she pushed past it.

Something glinted in the darkness ahead. A candle. A mirror. Or maybe a crack in the wall, or maybe the door . . .

She cried out hoarsely and ran for the light.

The floor collapsed. She plunged into the gut of the hotel.

Filthy, stinking, oily water closed over her head and filled her mouth. It choked her as she tried to scream. Little tendrils of some cancerous water weed twisted around her arms and legs, crisscrossing her face like a slippery spiderweb. She clawed them from her eyes. As her nails drew bloody furrows across her forehead, she saw that the glimmering light was not the door or a candle.

It was his eyes.

⤬

Amy thrashed and rolled onto her stomach, suffocating her screams in the pillow.

She threw her head back, mouth gasping for air, and opened her eyes. She was staring at her stuffed toy buffalo.

Amy sank back down into the sheets. She rolled over and looked at the digital clock. Six forty-five PM.

Shit. She jumped out of bed and switched her light on. Amy stretched, rubbing her face. She bent over and shook her hair out.

Something caught her eye.

Xavier's silver lizard lay next to her alarm clock, tinged red by the digital glow. There was something wrong with it. Amy bent down closer to see.

The tiny lizard had split in half, right down the center. The silver eyes stared at her from separate halves of the little creature, looking isolated and strangely miserable.

No.

No. I cannot fucking deal with this. No way.

Amy opened her nightstand drawer and swept the pieces of the lizard into it. She slammed the drawer and took a step back, wiping her hands on her thighs.

Amy blinked. Once. Twice. She shook her head. She looked at the alarm clock once again. Six forty-seven.

I have forty-three minutes to become a love goddess.

Amy pulled off her They Might Be Giants T-shirt and padded over to the closet. She rubbed her eyes, and started pawing through her clothes.

Rosy.

Amy grimaced. The girl's name resonated through her mind. Thoughts of Rosy's anguish, along with Sarah's nagging, had driven her to her bed hours earlier.

93

But I'll be damned if it ruins tonight. Amy grabbed her long black cotton skirt and her red poet's blouse, and yanked them off their hangers.. She slammed the closet door, stalking across the room in search of earrings.

She was ready in thirty minutes. She greeted Shane with a smile and a kiss. He told her she was beautiful, and her smile became real.

Yes. tonight will be good.

⤬

It was nearly one AM when Shane's black Barracuda rolled into the parking lot of Amy's apartment complex. Amy yawned and snuggled against Shane's arm as he coasted into an empty space beneath a jacaranda tree. He cut the Barracuda's engine, and the night was very quiet.

He smiled down at Amy. "Did you have fun?" he asked, playing with a strand of her hair.

"Absolutely. Couldn't you tell by the way I clutched your arm and screamed all the way through the movie?"

His brow creased. "Did it really bother you?"

Amy laughed and beeped him on the nose. "Of course not. I love scary movies. Especially ones with face-eating psychiatrists and transsexual wanna-bes who skin people."

"I thought so." He grinned.

Amy gently touched his face. "Shane, I want to thank you. Really. Dinner was wonderful, the movie was great, and I had lots of fun beating you at pinball."

He laughed softly. Amy tugged at the lapel of his jacket. "I thought I would never meet someone like you."

He put his arms around her and pulled her close. "Am I everything you hoped I would be?"

Amy tried to look into his eyes, but they were in shadow. "What a strange way to put it." She leaned her head against him. "Yes, you are."

"Good." He tipped her chin up and kissed her. Amy kissed back, loving his scent.

They kissed for what seemed like a long, long time. His mouth was warm and sweet. His lips were soft, but she could feel just a hint of

9 4

stubble from time to time, male and electrifying. She felt like kissing him all night.

Finally, reluctantly, Amy pulled back and smiled. "I'd better go. I have Algebra in the morning." She made a face.

"No you don't." he kissed her again. She laughed and pulled away.

"Really, Shane. I'll be worthless if I don't get some sleep."

"You'll be fine." His voice was rough, edgy. He pulled Amy closer, slipping his hand under her blouse.

She gasped, grabbing his hand. "Shane, cut it out!" She tried to turn away and open the door.

He grabbed her wrist and held it behind her. He bit her neck, pushing his hand up under her skirt.

She hit him. Her eyes widened as her fist solidly connected with his cheekbone. It didn't seem like it was really her hand, really hitting Shane.

He laughed, and hit her back. Only a slap, really, but it snapped her head around, and her eyes filled with tears of pain. She squeezed them shut, and the tears spilled down onto her face and neck. She sobbed. The pain spread from her face to her throat, and down into her heart.

"Shane, why?" Her anguish poured over her in a black wave. Her voice cracked. "I don't understand . . . "

"The hell you don't," he hissed. "Do you think I'm stupid? I could see it in your eyes the first time I met you. You're hungry, Amy. I'm going to feed you." His fingers curled around the waistband of her panties.

Her eyes widened, and she wordlessly shook her head no. He ripped her panties away. The fabric burned as it gave way, digging into her skin.

He was touching her. He was touching her inside.

Amy started to scream, and he clapped his hand over her mouth. She tried to bite him, but he pressed down until her lips were bleeding. He shoved her against the door. Almost effortlessly, he pulled her hand over her head. She tried to pry his fingers away with her free hand, and he immediately captured her other wrist.

His leg was between hers. Slowly, grinning, he forced her thighs wide apart. His knee pressed painfully into her leg, pinning it against the dashboard. He knelt down in the floorboards and shoved his body against hers.

"Be quiet, now," he breathed into her ear. "We don't want to wake the neighbors." He took his hand from her mouth and started to unzip his pants.

Amy filled her lungs for a desperate scream.

He saw it coming. His fist slammed into the side of her face. Her head snapped back, striking the glass.

Amy's eyes were filled with darkness, and little spots of light. Her head rolled as she fought to keep her consciousness. She heard his zipper open. She felt him pressing against her inner thigh. No . . .

"Open up, baby. Yum, yum . . . "

Amy spit in his face. Shane grinned, a savage, mirthless grimace. He drew his fist back.

The car door flew open behind him. Someone grabbed his fist. *Mick?* Amy thought. *Sarah?* Amy heard a strange sound, like popcorn popping underwater. A trickle of blood squeezed between the stranger's fingers, and down Shane's wrist.

Shane took in air with a great shuddering gasp, and started to shriek. Another hand closed over his mouth and jerked him out of the car.

Amy leaned forward, trying to see, and her head whirled. She grabbed the dashboard for support. Something was happening on the pavement, just outside the car. Wet thumping sounds. Bodies flailing. Shane's head was jerked into view, then back down with a sickening thud. It happened again. And again. Someone's hand was tangled in his hair. Amy could hear Shane breathing, a gurgling rasp. His head turned toward her, and his eyes stared from a bloody, shapeless mass.

Amy tried to scream, but nothing came out but a thin wheeze. She heaved herself around and yanked at the door handle.

Someone's hands were on her shoulders. Someone was in the car with her.

"Don't run," he whispered. His voice was distantly familiar.

Amy yanked at the door handle again. Locked. She grabbed for the button.

"Amy, please, I had to. You don't belong to him."

Amy recognized the voice. Her eyes opened wide. Her heart jumped in her chest like a frightened rabbit. Even before he turned her around, she could see his dead green eyes in her mind.

His face was inches from hers. Movie-star perfect, splattered with Shane's blood, it was smiling. It bent down closer, until Amy could feel its cold breath.

"You belong to me." He caressed her face with long, white fingers, smearing her skin with cooling blood.

Amy started screaming. She was still screaming when the lights came on in the apartment building, and when the thing in the car with her slipped noiselessly away. She was still screaming when Mick and Sarah burst from the building doors, wearing only their robes. She was still screaming when the ambulance came.

ELEVEN

Bent over, he ran through the parking lot, arms wrapped protectively around his middle. He protected something else, a long jacket of soft black leather, which he cradled against himself. The salty, coppery smell of blood was all over him, but he didn't have time to clean up. He ran.

He tried to make himself cry, but he was too angry. Amy, his love and his life, had screamed in horror when she saw him.

Wasn't I pretty enough? he asked himself. Of course he was. He had taken the face from TV. A toothpaste ad, as a matter of fact. *Of course I was.*

Oh, how his heart pounded when she recognized him! He had felt so good when her beautiful eyes had opened wide in understanding. And then she screamed. At me.

His lips peeled back in a furious grimace. He made his mouth and nose stretch into a snout full of long, long teeth. He wished he had someone to bite. It wasn't just fear he saw in her eyes, it was disgust. He threw back his head and howled.

A dog answered him, far away. Rags wished it were closer. Close enough to get.

Red thoughts were filling his head, making it hard to think. He crossed the street, and ran across the lawn of the university music library. He trotted into the shadows beneath a huge evergreen, and stopped.

The sirens wailed through the night. *They're taking her away.* He could feel Amy getting farther and farther from him, until she was just a little throb in his stomach. It just wasn't supposed to go like that. She was supposed to be surprised (Not terrified, no!), maybe even faint. He'd catch her in his arms, carry her away. Maybe up on a rooftop. When she awakened, her lovely eyes would get huge, he'd feel her heart pounding against him like a hummingbird—and then she'd smile at him. "Oh, Rags," she's whisper. Then he'd kiss her there under the stars, over and over, until she was delirious with love for him. The TV told him it would happen that way. Watching from his prison of glass, he saw beautiful humans enacting it many, many times.

Yes. It *would* happen.

I just have to keep trying. That's all. I have to find out what she really, really wants, and do it for her. Be *it for her.*

He bent over, breathing hard, because it felt interesting when he did so. People did it when they ran a long way, didn't they? He briefly wondered what it was like to be "out of breath."

Shane is out of breath. Rags smiled. Totally out. He laughed. He had a pretty good grasp of humor, he decided.

Grinning, he looked at his hands. Red, red, red. He licked, experimentally. "Gooooood," he whispered. Silently, Rags cleaned himself, and then the jacket he had peeled from Shane's limp body.

He slipped the jacket on. It hung on his narrow shoulders, so he widened them a bit until the fit was just perfect. He breathed in the smell of cowhide and chemicals with pleasure.

Rags sprinted across the campus, trying to clear his head. *I am excited,* he thought. *Excited!* He was getting better at emotion. He thought of Amy. The anger was there; he was quite good at anger. Along with it was something else. Jealousy? *No, I already know that one.* This was a complex emotion, involving want, sorrow, and a fierce affection.

He imagined himself squeezing her the way Shane had done, tighter and tighter. Again, his thoughts turned to kisses. Kisses hadn't been much fun with Rosy. Her mouth was slack, and much too wet. He grinned, remembering her soft body. He wanted to give to Amy, the way he had given to Rosy. Rags shuddered with pleasure, remembering the way Rosy thrashed. A word popped into his mind.

Murder.

He gasped. "No!" he shouted. "No!" I never, never, never think that about Amy. Not ever. He hit himself in the face a few times, to make sure he got the point. Uninvited, a vision of Shane's head slamming into the asphalt filled his eyes. He shivered. It felt soooo good.

Against his wishes, Rags felt a smile creeping over his muzzle. *Oops.* He pulled it back in, reforming his face into a young man's. He played with his skin color as he walked, going from pitch black to porcelain white. He wished he could change his eye color, but that seemed to be impossible.

His eyes narrowed. He spotted Amy's most recent "trail," glowing like fine amethyst. He decided to follow it to her favorite bench, because he knew that was where it would lead. He could think better there, basking in her light.

It was so beautiful. The bench radiated Amy. Little sparks of her hung like fireflies in the tree, and sharp, glittering spikes shot out from underneath the cement. With a sigh, he sat down. *Tell me what to do, my love,* he thought. *Tell me how to make you love me.* He hung his head.

His eyes followed the path of the spikes of light. He had never seen Amy's aura looking like that before. He bent down for a closer look. The spikes seemed to converge beneath the bench. Rags elongated his neck, and looked between his own legs.

And there it was. A sheet of purple fire, emanating her heavenly scent. Cautiously, reverently, he reached for it. Rags held the paper delicately, as though it might shatter or disintegrate under his touch. Pulling his neck back in, he narrowed his eyes against the terrible beauty of the light, and began to read.

My love has wings of leather . . .

He closed his eyes, shivering in ecstasy. *She has told me what she wants. It was my fault, I did it wrong. Oh, Amy . . .* He read the poem again and again, burning it into his heart. He stared deep into the face of the drawing, until he had memorized every line. Then, worshipfully, he ate the piece of paper. Amy's aura was warm and sweet and juicy in his mouth.

Rags stood up and stretched. *Thank you, Amy. Thank you.* With a lazy smile, he grew thorns on his shoulder blades. They pushed up easily through the back of Shane's jacket, then traveled down. When he was finished, two parallel slits gaped in the leather, exposing Rags' back to the warm breeze. He closed his eyes to concentrate. *Damn eyes, can't do anything about the damn eyes.* He sighed. But the teeth and the hair and the face were easy. He spread his legs to steady himself, and started on the hard part.

His body shrank a little as he extruded the wings, but he fought to keep himself pleasingly proportionate. It took longer than he had expected. He tried to remember the bone structure of the last bat he had eaten.

When it was done, he was almost afraid to look. He brought one of the wings forward. It was long and leathery and wet, and quite, quite beautiful. He flexed it. Strange. He flexed the other one. Nice. He paused to adjust his color to a velvety black, and then walked out into the grass of the commons.

Rags fanned his wings gently, drying them. He stretched them wide. Taking a running start, He beat the air.

Rags rose up a few feet above the ground. He almost screamed with delight, but then he was plunging down into the wet turf, face first.

He stood up, angry, pulling his face back into shape from the grass-coated anvil it had become. Unconsciously he made his teeth a little longer. He snapped his jaws open and shut in frustration. He enlarged the muscles in his back, and steeled himself to try again.

This time he got almost to the top of the dwarf orange trees before he dropped like a rock into the fountain.

"Shit!" he screamed. "God damn sonofabitch shit!" Rags shook out his wings, and his new long hair. He knew there were better cursewords in the English language, but he was too angry to care. He also knew that someone may have heard him, and deep inside he hoped that someone had.

He was going to practice all night, if he had to. Tomorrow night he would rescue his lady. He turned his face up toward the stars. He sniffed the air. There was something on the breeze. Something warm and soft and vulnerable. One of the many stray cats that prowled the campus at night, looking for dropped bits of hotdog and maybe a little kindness.

I must learn to fly this night.

And I'll need a little something to keep up my strength.

TWELVE

The screams ripped out of her, one after another. Amy knew her throat was bleeding. She could feel the warm trickle of blood running down her esophagus, all the way into her stomach. Somewhere in the sane heart of her mind, she wanted to stop. But the frightened animal had won.

A hand passed in front of her face, and she snapped at it. Someone's face bent down over her. It smiled, and the mouth split all the way across the face in a bloody, open gash.

"Yur ull riiite nowww," the bleeding mouth said. With a snarl, Amy lashed her fist at it. Her knuckle hit something, because when she looked at it, there was blood. *Blood. All over Shane. All over me. All over . . . him.* Amy thrashed and bucked on the gurney, looking desperately for a face she didn't want to see. The thing with the mouth was just a woman, now, holding her hand over her bleeding lip.

"Gohhd dam it, restraaaaane hur", said the voice, sounding like it were under a layer of mud. Someone grabbed Amy's arms. Someone grabbed her legs. Amy's screams rose in pitch, and her struggling was savage.

"No!" she shrieked. "Let go of me you bastard, you rotten bastard!" Shane's face loomed over hers, grinning. As she watched, it swelled up, purple and red bruises blooming like roses on the pale skin. It dripped cool blood onto her face, into her mouth.

Amy couldn't move. "O shit, therz bluud on hur lips," said the mudvoice. Amy spit, unwilling to ingest any part of Shane. "She bit hurselffff," said another, from far away. Amy tried to look at them. All she saw were dim, hunched shapes, huddled over her like pallbearers.

Amy squeezed her eyes shut. Tears joined the bloody spit on her face, washing some of it away. Someone jabbed a needle into her arm. Amy let out one last despairing wail before a black, heavy blanket of sleep covered her face.

☙❧

Amy rubbed the tears from her face, then realized she was smearing dirt on her cheeks, and cried even harder. Rags had his arms around her, pressing his cool cheek to hers. He made her feel better, and her sobs subsided. She wiped her face on his shoulder like a nuzzling kitten.

"It's not so bad, is it Ame?" he asked, face crinkled up with worry.

"No," she sniffed, holding up her bloody thumb for him to inspect. "I jus' cut it on glass from the window."

"Awww," he said, sympathetically. He took her thumb gently into his mouth, sucking the blood away. Amy watched him, feeling a little squirmy inside.

"All better," he said, dim light making his toothy grin sparkle. "I'll clean up the glass so it can't hurt you again."

He stood up and stretched. His body was long and skinny, and Amy was sure that he was taller. In fact, he looked about as tall as her cousin Billy, who was almost nine. She smiled. *He's magic.*

Amy watched him as he gathered the glass fragments in his hands. She knew he wouldn't get cut. He could make his skin really tough, when he wanted to.

She arranged the blanket that covered the mangy chair she was sitting in, so it covered all the mildew spots. It wasn't so bad, really. Amy had just about gotten used to the smell and the damp of the old hotel. Anyway, it was worth it, to be with Rags.

He was looking at her, his eyes shining. Amy looked harder. She thought his eyes were a little duller than the first time she had seen them, like they had faded or something. *Nah.* She shook her head.

He grinned. "Whatcha thinkin' about, pipsqueak?"

"Rags," she said, "How come your name is Rags?"

He lowered his eyes. "It's 'cause I'm patched together from . . . a bunch of stuff. I wasn't born, Ame. I was kinda pulled together."

"How do you know?"

"I just do." he looked around, as though he were embarrassed. "A voice told me so."

"Whose voice?" Amy asked. "God's?"

Rags looked up nervously. "Gosh, I don't know. Maybe. Just somebody. They were kinda mean, and they laughed at me a lot. Anyway, they're the one who told me my name is Rags."

He doesn't have a mama or daddy, Amy thought. *That's sad. Poor Rags.*

He kicked at a patch of rotten rug. "Let's play!"

"Okay!" said Amy. She got up and walked to him. Her shoes went squish on the old carpet. "Play what?"

"Big Bad Wolf!" he shouted. It was his favorite game, since Amy told him the story of Little Red Riding Hood. Rags grabbed his nose and pulled. His face came out into a long muzzle, and his ears became tall and pointed. He sprouted hair. Amy thought it would be rude to point out that wolves aren't green, so she didn't.

"Grrraaarrrr!!" he shouted. With a happy squeal, Amy ran.

He chased her around and around the huge lobby. Just when Amy was sure he was about to catch her, he'd pretend to trip or stub his paw. While he rolled around on the floor howling, she'd run shrieking with laughter. Finally, he chased her into a corner. Amy giggled wildly.

"Rrraaah!" he growled. "Grrrr!" Rags opened his mouth. It was black, and full of long, sharp teeth. It opened wider, until it was larger than Amy's head. He bent down over her.

And just like that, she was afraid of him. Terrified. She wouldn't remember later, but it wasn't the teeth that really frightened her, or the black, pulsing throat. It was his eyes, narrowed and dull and suddenly vicious, that bathed her heart in ice.

"Rags!" she shrilled. "Rags stop it, I'm scaaaared!" Amy stared into that horrible mouth, at those horrible eyes, and they got a little closer. "Noooo!" she screamed. Amy started to cry.

Rags pulled his muzzle into his face. A moment later, he was kneeling by Amy, kissing her cheeks, saying he was sorry.

Amy looked at him, still nervous, heart still pounding like mad. "I never want to play 'Big Bad Wolf' again," she said quietly.

"All right, he whispered. "All right, Amy. We'll never play that again." He stroked her hair.

Amy giggled. "You forgot your ears!" She pointed.

Rags felt of his head. Sure enough, he still had big green wolf ears. With a grin, he pulled them back into little round child's ears. He adjusted his skin color from brown to gold to white, and Amy laughed in delight. Then she thought of something. Something that bothered her a lot, although she wasn't sure why. Amy bit her lip.

"What is it, Ame?" he asked.

"Rags, since you can make all those faces . . . " her voice trailed off, and she looked at the floor. *I sure don't want to hurt his feelings.*

"Tell me," he said, his voice gentle.

"How do you know which one is really yours?"

For a horrible moment, she thought he would cry. Then she remembered that he didn't know how.

"I don't," he said shortly. Silence. Then he was lifting her up, kissing her head. "Do you know what time it is?" he asked

"No," said Amy into his shoulder. He set her down.

"It's time for the bugdance!"

Amy squealed, jumping up and down. Rags folded his arms, lowered his eyelids. Amy thought he looked like a genie. A moment later, fat, shiny beetles were pouring out of the walls. They all went to the middle of the room and lined up in rows, like people in a parade. Then they reared up on their back four legs and began to dance. They made lines and circles, climbing over each other, moving all together like the dancing poodles in the circus.

Amy stared, amazed, delighted. Rags scowled and waved his hands. The beetles scuttled away. Amy started to protest, but, smiling, he put a finger to his lips. "That was kid stuff," he said. "Watch this."

Rats. Rats came up from the floor, out of the walls, in through the windows.

"Ooooh," said Amy, eyes wide. She liked rats. Her cousin Billy had a big fat rat named Charlie, who liked candy circus peanuts and had little people hands with no thumbs and sometimes tickled Amy's cheek with his soft, twitching whiskers.

The rats stood on their back legs. They made two lines, joining paws. It was so cute! They waddled like tiny penguins, two by two, across the room. Then they began to leap and dance.

Amy clapped her hands with joy. She crept closer and closer to the dancing rats. She had never seen anything so wonderful in her life. She imagined them in little ball gowns and tuxedos, whirling around a tiny, rat-sized ballroom. She crept closer still.

When she was close enough to touch them, she noticed the way their bodies shook, and the way they panted. Their little black eyes bulged. Some of them squeaked under their breath; pitiful little breathy peeps. They sounded afraid, like the baby birds her Grandma's gray tomcat sometimes caught and carried in his mouth. They sounded like they were hurt.

Amy frowned. "Rags!" she called. "Rags, I, I think they're scared. Maybe we oughta leave 'em alone."

"They're not scared," he said, sounding a little mean. The rats scrambled away, apparently as fast as their short rat legs would carry them. "Dammit!" he hissed. "I lost 'em." Amy turned to look at him. There was something in his face she didn't like much at all.

"I wish I had a dog," he said. "Then you'd really see something."

"Rags . . . " said Amy, not sure what to do. "Rags, maybe you shouldn't—" He grinned hugely. His eyes locked with hers. Suddenly her muscles were moving without her, jerking her back and forth, making her feet step up and down. She felt her arms raise over her head, and wave around, like she was trying to scare off a cloud of mosquitoes. Her head bobbed as if someone were shaking her.

It was the most horrible thing she'd ever felt. Worse than a shot at the doctor's. Worse than the flu. It felt like he had his hand in her brain. Amy would have screamed, if she could.

Rags spun her around, and she almost fell. He twisted her body to catch her balance, and pain shot down her back.

Amy managed to force out a terrified whine. Rags let her go almost immediately.

She fell to the slimy floor. Amy sprang to her feet, feeling her face get hotter and hotter, feeling like she would explode and blow Rags and the whole ugly rotten hotel to pieces.

"Dammit!" she shouted. "Dammit!" she knew it was a Bad Word, but Amy didn't care. She stomped her feet, screaming, "Don't you ever do that to me again!" Amy stared into Rags' face, wishing her eyes could burn holes in him. He stared back, still as a statue. She couldn't tell what was behind his filmy green eyes. It looked like nothing at all. She stamped her foot again, whirled around and started for the door.

Rags caught her, and she kicked him in the shin. She glared up at him, furious, her stomach twisting in a way it never had before.

"I'm sorry," he whispered. "I didn't mean to—"

"Yes you did!" she shouted.

He set her gently on the floor, his hands resting on her shoulders. Amy wanted to run, but those hands seemed to weigh a thousand pounds each.

"I meant, I didn't mean to scare you. I'd never hurt you, Amy. Never." He knelt down beside her, looking up into her face. "I love you, Amy. I'm sorry."

She looked into his eyes, and they really were sorry. They were all scrunched and wet, like he might start crying any minute. "Okay," she whispered. "But never do that again."

"I won't," he said. She put her arms around him, and felt his body shaking.

⟨∾⟩

Amy twisted against her bonds, her body entwining with the white sheets. She groaned in her sleep.

THIRTEEN

Amy groaned again, extravagantly, for her mother's benefit. "Mama, I don't WANT to go to play group. I WANT to go with you."

Mandy smoothed her daughter's hair out of her eyes and smiled. "I know, sweetie. But once in a while your daddy and I like to go out together, just the two of us, and get all romantic and mushy. You'd get bored."

Amy tried to keep her sulky face, but a giggle got out anyway. "You mean like a date?" she asked.

"Yup", said her mother. "Exactly like a date."

"Are you gonna kiss and stuff?"

"Uh-huh. I'm afraid so."

"Maybe playgroup won't be so bad."

It wasn't. Playgroup was at a pretty little stone cottage, with a green, wild, tangly yard that reminded Amy of her Arizona Grandma's house. The teacher *(play leader, that's what she said we should call her)* was really nice. Her name was Miss Rice and she wore a long floaty blue dress and had a pink flower in her hair. She said it was a hi-biscuit flower, and she told Amy she was a lovely little girl. Amy liked that.

She was introduced to the other children in the group; quiet Jerry, big, scary Sandra, giggly Tony, friendly Janet. "And where could Louis be?" Miss Rice asked, looking around. "Playing out back again, I'll bet. Louis! Louis! Come meet our new friend!"

A little boy with skin the color of a Hershey bar, big, pretty eyes and a cute pointed chin slipped around the corner of the house. He looked at Amy and smiled, then looked down at his red Buster Brown sneakers. *He's shy,* thought Amy. *I like his face. He looks like an elf.*

"Amy, this is someone you should know", said Miss Rice, smiling. This is Louis Bouvier, your friend Virginia's son. Say hi, kids."

"Hi, Louis," said Amy, smiling at him. "You don't look like Virginia very much."

"Hi, Amy." Louis took Amy's hand in his and shook it, just like a grown-up gentleman. "Everyone says I have Mom's cheekbones. You're pretty."

Amy grinned. "Thanks!"

"Well!" cried Miss Rice, clapping her hands. "It's time for a story!"

The story was a chapter from a book called The Phantom Tollbooth, and Amy liked it very much. It was about a little boy who goes to a magical place, where all sorts of weird things happened. There was a really neat dog in it, too. Dogs always made stories better.

After that there was a snack of fig bars and milk, followed by Free Play Time. Amy and the other children came pouring out of the little house, laughing and talking, and spread around the yard in all directions. Miss Rice said they could play anywhere they wanted!

"Amy," asked Louis, sounding all serious, "Would you like to see where I go to play?"

"Sure," said Amy, thinking Louis was probably the cutest, nicest boy in the world.

He took her by the hand, and they walked around behind the house, to a huge, furry pepper tree. Louis slipped through the branches like a ground squirrel in tall grass, and Amy ducked in after him.

They were underneath the tree, in what Amy thought must be a magical room. The pepper tree surrounded their little hiding space, draping around it in velvety green curtains. Tiny leaves coated the ground, making a soft, spongy carpet, which the two settled down on as if it were a picnic blanket. The sun coming through the branches made little spots and stripes of light on everything, even Louis.

Amy looked around, enchanted, half expecting fairies. Louis smiled, just a little bit.

"You like it, huh."

"I sure do. It's pretty." Amy put her hand up in front of her face, turning it around, watching the light on her fingers. "Miss Rice is nice, isn't she."

"Yup. You made a rhyme. Nice Miss Rice!"

Amy giggled. "Is scared of mice!"

Louis grinned. He had dimples on his cheeks.

"And big fat lice!"

Amy and Louis dissolved into giggles. *This isn't so bad,* thought Amy. *I'm gonna have fun here.*

Amy and Louis stayed in their hideaway, talking and giggling and inspecting bugs (Amy liked bugs, as long as they weren't roaches) until Miss Rice called everybody inside for a nap.

They were supposed to sleep on little cots, lined up side by side in one of the cottage's bedrooms. Amy fluffed up her tiny pillow and stretched out, enjoying the cool breeze from the ceiling fan. She liked the tropical wallpaper. The little red frogs perched on fat, green leaves looked real enough to jump off the wall.

Louis had taken the cot next to hers, jumping right in front of Janet so he could. Amy liked that. When she rolled over to look at him, he was already asleep, lips parted, hands laced together like he was saying a prayer. *He has the longest eyelashes in the world,* Amy thought. On impulse, she leaned over and kissed his cheek. She wasn't sure, but she thought he might have smiled, just a tiny bit.

Amy didn't go see Rags at all that day. She thought about him, of course. *But Grandma and mama always say it's good to have lots of friends.* He wouldn't mind if she played with Louis sometimes, too. Why would he?

Her parents came home from their date happy and cuddling with each other. That made Amy feel happy, too.

"Did you have fun in playgroup, honey?" Mandy asked her.

"Yes!" answered Amy, without a moment's hesitation.

"Would you like to go back, Amy?" Tom knelt down next to her, stroking her hair. "We worry about you having to hang around with us and all the other old farts all day long."

Amy giggled. "That'd be fun!"

"All right, then!" Tom kissed her cheek. "It wouldn't be all day, just in the morning. And, of course, we'll take you with us whenever we do something cool."

Amy kissed him back. "It's a deal, daddy."

☙❧

Amy smiled in her sleep. Louis was a calming presence in her mind, a shining reminder of joy and innocence. She could see him in the drugged haze of her dreams; a slender, handsome little boy with dark, serious, loving eyes. She could almost touch him, feel his smooth, peach-fuzz cheek against her lips. And she wasn't ready to leave him. Not yet.

☙❧

Another day at playgroup, and the kids were making books of heavy drawing paper. Amy thought about making her book about Rags, but decided, for some reason, that he wouldn't like it. She drew a story about a black dog named Lucy instead.

"What's yours about?" she asked Louis, who was drawing so intently his tongue was poking out. He suddenly became shy.

"A princess," he muttered.

"Can I see?" Amy reached for his book. He hesitated, then pushed it across the child-sized table.

The princess had yellow hair and green eyes. She had on a pale blue dress, and was riding a horse.

"She's beautiful!" said Amy. "What's her name?"

Louis smiled and looked down at the crayon in his hand.

"Amy."

☙❧

Amy's head rocked back and forth, and she muttered under her breath. The days of her memory were flickering by, faster and faster, like film in an antique projector.

☙❧

Day after sunny, golden day, Amy and Louis played and pretended and had fun together. Amy played with the other kids during games of hide-and-go-seek and tag, but what she liked best was spending time with Louis. He was so smart and funny. He knew the names of all kinds of bugs and flowers. He was always nice to Amy, and was as polite as a grown-up. She had never met anybody else like him.

Amy sneaked out to see Rags once or twice. He was sulky, wanting to know why she hadn't been around as much, but she didn't tell him about playgroup or her other friend. She didn't know why, exactly, but a little voice inside her thought it wasn't a good idea. It was the same little voice that told her to stand perfectly still when her cousin Billy's new dog started growling at her, fur bristling, tail held low and twitching.

⁂

Where was he? Where was Louis? Eyes rolling beneath sticky lids, Amy's hand groped the air above her head. She whimpered. There. There. She could see him, but he was getting farther away. There he was, waving to her, but he was slowly being obscured by a curtain of thick, green, twisting vines.

⁂

On the last day Amy would ever spend at playgroup, she and Louis were the pepper tree hideout, sitting side by side. Louis had caught a Bahaman curly-tailed lizard, and he was holding it, ever so gently, so that Amy could stroke its tiny back.

The lizard felt warm and just a little bit rough. Its chubby sides went in and out as it breathed, and it cocked its head to look at Amy as she touched it. It didn't like being held, she could tell. Who could blame it! But it seemed more cranky than scared.

"It's so cute!" she exclaimed.

"Yup," said Louis. "Are you all done looking at it?"

"I guess," said Amy, stroking its curly tail with her forefinger. The lizard tightened its tail even more, until it was like a little cinnamon roll, making Amy laugh.

Louis opened his hand, and the little creature scampered away into the bushes.

Amy was surprised. "How come you didn't keep it?"

"'Cause it would be sad if I did."

112

Amy thought that was so nice that she gave Louis a kiss on the cheek. He grinned and blushed. Suddenly, he leaned over and kissed her back. The children burst into giggles.

...Amy...

Amy stopped giggling and looked around. Someone was calling her name.

...Amy, let's go play!

Amy gasped. It was Rags! Talking to her in her head! Her mouth dropped open. Louis tilted his head and looked at her. "What is it, Amy?"

"Did you hear that?" Amy asked.

Louis shook his head. "Hear what?"

"It was my friend! My friend Ra—"

Louis jerked. His back went stiff and his eyes glazed over, like when Daddy was spaced out in front of the TV. Amy yelped and scooted backwards. "Louis!" she whispered. "Louis, are you okay?"

The little boy didn't move. He just stared straight ahead, with his back stiff and straight like the Nutcracker on Amy's shelf at home. Amy's stomach began to grow cold.

What if he's ... dead? Oh no ...

Amy reached her hand toward Louis' face, ever so slowly. She waved her fingers in front of his eyes. He didn't move. She reached out to touch his cheek.

"Boo!"

Rags' grinning face appeared over Louis' shoulder. Amy let out a little shriek, and Rags laughed.

"What did you do to him?" Amy asked, half indignant, half scared.

"Nothin' much. Don't tell people my name, Amy. They wouldn't understand about me. 'Kay?" Rags poked Louis on the shoulder. "Pretty neat, huh?"

"What's wrong with him?" The chill in Amy's stomach was creeping up her back.

"Nothin'! He's just sorta frozen. He'll be okay as soon as we leave. C'mon, let's go play!" Rags grabbed Amy's hand and started to pull her through the wall of the pepper tree's branches.

"No!" squeaked Amy. "I mean, I can't! Miss Rice will find out I'm gone and then she'll call Mama and Daddy and I'll be in a whole lot of trouble!"

Rags giggled and kissed her on the cheek. "She won't find out you're gone. I told her brain that your Mommy picked you up. No one'll find out! We can play every time you come here, Amy! Won't that be great?"

"Well . . . I don't know . . . "

Rags scowled. "What do you mean, you don't know?"

Amy looked at Louis, silent as a statue. She really wished he'd move, just a little. "Can't Louis come too?"

"No!"

Amy pulled back. For just a second, Rags sounded really, really mad. Then he smiled. "Geez, Amy, he'd tell somebody."

Amy stuck her lower lip out. "He would not."

"Yes he would. And besides, he's just a plain old boy. He can't do stuff like I can."

"Yeah, but—"

"Come on, Amy. I'm all alone in that big old hotel. Louis can play with the other kids. I don't have anybody but you." Rags bit his lower lip and looked at Amy with big, sad eyes.

Rags is special, Amy thought. *Really, really special.* He could do things Amy had only ever heard of in books. He could do things she'd never heard of at all. And she had saved his life once, and he loved her, just like Peter Pan and Wendy.

"Well . . . okay."

Amy crawled through the branches of the pepper tree with her special friend.

"I'll meet you at the hotel, Amy," Rags whispered. "It's just down the street, that way." He pointed. "See, the sun makes me kinda sick."

"Okay, I guess." Amy felt funny about going alone. She felt funny about going at all.

Rags ducked into the bushes. Amy wasn't totally sure, but she thought he sank into the ground, like rainwater on sand. She shook her head, amazed again.

As she crept away through the garden, Amy thought she heard Louis gasp. She looked over her shoulder, and saw through a narrow split in the branches that he was staring after her, a terrible look of confusion in his dark eyes.

◦◦◦

Amy fought against her restraints, trying to cover her sleeping eyes with her hands so she wouldn't have to see. *Louis! I'm sorry, Louis.* Then the pepper tree curtain closed, and it was dark, dark, and Amy slid deeper into sleep. Anyone walking past her would say that she was sleeping peacefully, but inside her mind was a droning, an irritating buzz that wouldn't leave her alone. Amy's brow knit, just a little.

FOURTEEN

"Oh, yes," Mrs. Iris was saying. "I find Marie's people to be incredibly loyal and hardworking. If it were up to me, they could live in the city if they wanted to."

Amy watched curiously as her parents squirmed in their seats. They exchanged a look, a lot like the look they got when Amy said something embarrassing. She sighed and looked at her shiny black Mary Janes. At least she knew she wasn't the one in trouble. She hadn't said a word for ages. Mrs. Iris talked too much.

The old lady finally paused, took a deep breath and a big drink out of her glass of purple wine. *Okay!* thought Amy. *I'm gonna ask if I can go outside!* She smiled and opened her mouth.

Darn, too late. Waving her hands like Tweety Bird spotting the biggest putty tat on Earth, Mrs. Iris was talking again.

"Of course, its not like there are laws against their staying here overnight, of course not! But it does make a lot of people uncomfortable. After all, how would you feel if you saw a colored man walking past your window late at night?"

Amy started to say that she always saw a black man walking past her window at night, and she liked Officer Chenowyth very much, but Mr. Iris stopped sniffing the apple-juice colored stuff in the bottom of his great big glass and started talking, too.

"Frightened!" he bellowed. "As well they should be! Oh, there are a few good eggs, but most of 'em are allergic to work, and sticky-fingered to boot. And we all know what a threat they can be to our women." He cleared his throat and glared at Amy's Daddy. Mr. Iris looked like he was mad, for some reason.

Amy watched with interest as her Daddy's face turned red. Her mother squeezed his arm, looking at him with her special "Honey, please don't" eyes. Amy thought for a minute that Daddy was going to hit Mr. Iris. Then he glanced over at Mandy, and smiled tightly. Mandy seemed to be trying to think of what to say.

"Mama," said Amy into the silence, "Can I go play in the yard?" She tugged at the hem of her lavender sundress, then wrapped her arms around herself. The Irises kept their house as cold as the Arizona winter. Amy wondered if the Irises would go bad, like milk left in the fridge too long, if they let their house get any warmer.

Her mother smiled widely. Amy thought she looked relieved, like when Daddy got home during a bad thunderstorm. Mandy winked at her. "May I, Amelia. Why don't you ask Mrs. Iris?"

Amy stood up hopefully. "Mrs. Iris, may I please go play in the yard?"

"Oooooh!" Mrs. Iris squealed. "Aren't you just the perfect little lady! Of course you may." Amy started for the French doors. "But first, can your Auntie Estelle have a widdle bitty kiss?"

Barf, barf, barf! Amy walked stiffly over to the woman, who squeezed her cheeks painfully, and kissed her right on the lips. *Blech!* Amy practically ran to the door.

"Outside, outside, thank God I'm outside," Amy chanted under her breath. She wandered along the flagstone path, looking up at the towering hedge that hid the street. In some places, the hedges formed walls along the path, and Amy imagined she was in a forest. Other parts of the garden were open, decorated with a brilliant explosion of flowers. Smiling, she breathed in the scents of a hundred blooms. Amy named them off in her head; snapdragons, pansies, violas, sweet peas, iris. She made a face, and wondered how such icky people got named for such pretty flowers.

She knelt down next to the snapdragons, and squeezed a big pink one to make it "talk." "Hello, Amy," it said, in Amy's deepest voice. "If you kiss me, I'll turn into a real dragon. Then you can have three wishes."

"All right," said Amy. Checking it carefully for bugs first, she gave the flower a little kiss. Unfortunately, it didn't become a dragon. *Darn. I was gonna wish it would eat Mr. Iris.*

Amy brushed off a flagstone and sat down by the flowers. So many colors. She wondered why Mrs. Iris called black people "colored." *Isn't everybody colored?* She looked at her own forearm. Sure enough, it was kind of pinkish, and the little hairs on it were gold. Those are colors. Amy tried to imagine uncolored people. They'd have to be clear, she decided, like jellyfish. *Gross. Then everybody could see your guts.*

Amy touched the face of a pansy. She knew that some white people didn't like black people, or brown people, or any kind of people who didn't look like them. She frowned. Once she had asked her grandma back home about that. Grandma had said that some folks are narrow-minded, and Amy shouldn't pay any attention to them at all.

Amy touched her forehead. She wondered it you were born being narrow-minded. She wondered if it hurt.

Amy remembered her Grandma smiling at her, blue eyes bright in the Arizona sun. "It's like saying, 'I love tabby cats and torty cats, but I hate Siamese cats and orange cats.' Doesn't make much sense, does it, honey."

It sure doesn't. Amy rubbed her eyes, because they suddenly burned. She missed Grandma a lot. *And she would be so ashamed of me.*

Amy looked guiltily around the hedge. Her parents and Mrs. Iris were talking. Mr. Iris wasn't there. Amy bit her lip. She had been lying.

She told her parents that she was playing with Louis every time they dropped her off at Playgroup. The truth was, she hadn't seen him since the day Rags came to get her. She never went into Miss Rice's nice little house again. Miss Rice would meet Amy and her parents at the garden gate, then her parents would drive off and Miss Rice would get all stiff and Amy would go sneaking off just like a rat to play with Rags. Amy's chin quivered, just a little. Her throat hurt.

She missed Louis. She missed the way he laughed, and the way he looked so serious when he showed her a bug or a bird. She loved his eyes, as big and soft as Bambi's. She loved how his hands were dark on the back but pink on the palms, as pink as she was. She remembered holding his hand, so soft and warm. *I thought we were gonna be friends forever.* Amy's eyes were hot, filling up with tears.

I will not cry! She thought fiercely. *I will not cry!* Amy was suddenly very ashamed of herself. She had been lying to her parents, for the very first time in her short life, so she could go visit Rags.

She hadn't wanted to. But he made her promise not to tell anyone about him. "Amy," he had said, staring into her eyes, "If anyone knew about me, they'd kill me."

"Not my Mama and Daddy," she protested.

"Yes!" he insisted. "Even them. Especially them."

Amy wasn't sure what he meant by that, but she knew her heart would break if anything happened to Rags.

So I lied. I did.

She kicked a stray pebble savagely, and ran down the path. It snaked around the side of the house, passing flowerbeds and those ornamental trees with the tiny little plums that looked good, but tasted awful and bitter. The path ended on the far side of the house, by the kitchen window.

Amy looked in. She could see Marie, the Iris's cook and housekeeper. She was a thin little lady who always looked kind of worried. But she always had a smile for Amy, and Amy liked her. Not quite as much as Virginia, but an awful lot.

Amy waved, but Marie didn't see her. She was doing something at the sink. Amy turned around and started to head the other way, when something caught her eye. It was a little circle of stones and seashells, just big enough for a child to sit in. With a smile, Amy went over to investigate.

She squatted down by the circle. Amy remembered something her mother had told her, about fairy rings. But they were just in the forest, weren't they? Amy couldn't quite remember. The inside of the circle was filled with shiny black pebbles, like smooth river rocks. Amy decided not to sit in the ring after all, because she didn't want to disturb the pebbles. She ran her finger across one. It was warm and smooth, and a little slick.

Some of the center stones looked extra-shiny. Amy reached into the middle of the circle, and touched one. It was wet. She quickly withdrew her hand, and looked at it.

Her fingers were red.

Blood! Amy gasped, starting to wipe her hand on her dress. *No, not on my pretty dress, not on me!* She wiped her fingers in the grass instead. She scrubbed and scrubbed, until the blood was all gone.

It was time to go back in. Amy stood up and backed away from the circle of stones, not wanting to take her eyes off of it. She wished that someone were with her. Amy glanced up at the kitchen window to see if Marie was still there.

She wasn't, but Mr. Iris was. He grinned at her hugely. Amy made herself smile back. He was holding something up, and Amy couldn't quite see what it was. She took a few steps forward.

Mr. Iris was holding a headless black chicken by the feet. Blood dripped slowly from the severed neck.

Amy screamed, a piercing shrill. She turned and ran down the path, past the flowers and the hedges, and threw open the French doors. She flung herself into her mother's arms, and began to sob.

"Baby!" her mother was saying. "Honey, what's wrong? Did you hurt yourself? Amy, tell me what's wrong!"

Amy just squeezed her tighter, trying to bury her head under Mandy's arm.

❧

"Hey!" the voice was saying. "Hey nurse, get this kid offa me!"

Amy squeezed her mother tighter.

"OW!" the orderly yelped. "She has some grip!" She tried to pry Amy's arms away from her waist. Amy sobbed once, and pushed her face against the woman's stomach.

"Aw", said the orderly, "Aw, you'll be okay, sweetheart." She stroked Amy's hair gently. Amy knew it wasn't her mother. She didn't care. She hung on.

"What is she, an overdose?" said the orderly. "I saw her in restraints earlier."

"No, no, assault victim," said another voice. "And don't talk about her like she isn't here. She can probably hear you."

Amy felt her arm being swabbed with alcohol. She tried to open her eyes, to beg them not to put her back to sleep, but her mouth wouldn't work, and her arms wouldn't let go of the orderly. As the needle slid in, a single tear squeezed from Amy's eye, and soaked into the orderly's white shirt.

FIFTEEN

"Rags?" called Amy, into the darkness. "Rags, are you here?" She walked cautiously into the ballroom, brushing aside the thick, white spiderwebs that had grown across the hallway. She wasn't afraid of the spiders. Rags had told them not to bite her, and they never did. But just the other day, her foot had sunk into the floor up to the ankle, covering it with thick gray mold. She wasn't so sure that running and playing in the old hotel was as much fun as she thought it was. "Rags? Hello?" she called again, louder this time. She squinted into the dark, waiting for her eyes to adjust.

"Over here, Ame," he called softly. She looked around in time to see him doing something in the far corner, by a broken waterpipe. His body looked very strange for a moment, long and thin and wiggly, like a snake's. Amy was suddenly certain that he had just slithered out of that pipe. Involuntarily, she shuddered.

He was walking toward her, all slow and loose. Amy's dad would have called it a saunter, but to Amy it looked more like Rags was gliding. Like the skaters at the Ice Capades. Amy shivered again, suddenly remembering something she had forgotten.

The first time her parents had taken her to the Ice Capades, she was just four. Amy loved it. The skaters had just finished "Little Red Riding Hood." As the lights came up for the intermission, Amy was babbling excitedly about the "Big Bad Wuf." Suddenly, she realized she had to go to the bathroom. Right now!

"I wonder why," Tom said, grinning at her empty Coke and Slurpee cups. He kissed Mandy lightly on the lips. "Better take her, babe. There'd be quite a ruckus if I took her into the ladies room."

Amy giggled, thinking of ladies screaming and running.

Mama lead her down the worn linoleum halls of the coliseum. There was a long line at the bathroom. They had to wait and wait, and when it was finally Amy's turn to go, she was standing with her legs crossed, and intermission was almost over.

"Let's go, Balloon Girl. Your eyes are turning yellow."

Amy giggled, making it suddenly harder to hold it in. She dashed for the open stall.

Mandy had her by the hand, walking her back to the main floor, when the lights in the hallway went down. "Hurry, baby," said Mandy. "They're getting ready to start!" Amy made her short legs hustle.

A door opened, right next to her, and out came the Big Bad Wuf. Amy froze. He bent over her, teeth sparkling, tongue lolling. "Hi, little girl!" He said cheerfully. "Grrrrrr!"

Amy screamed. The wolf pulled back, but Amy was already running down the corridor. Mama was right behind her, calling her name, but Amy didn't dare stop. *The Big Bad Wuf!* Amy ducked into a doorway and cowered, crying. *He's gonna eat me! He's gonna eat me!*

To Amy's surprise, the wolf took off his head and walked toward her. His curly hair and milk-chocolate skin was shiny with sweat, and his black eyes looked worried.

Just a man, thought Amy. *Not the Big Bad Wuf.* She slowly stood up. *I knew that.*

The man with the Big Bad Wolf head under his arm smiled. "I'm sorry, sweetheart. I didn't mean to scare you. It's just rubber and foam, see?" He held out the wolf head for Amy's inspection.

She twanged on a tooth cautiously. It was rubber. She pulled gently on the foam tongue. Amy giggled. The man grinned, looking relieved.

"Honest, I'm sorry, Ma'am," He said to Mandy. "I didn't mean to frighten the little girl."

"It's all right," said Mandy, smiling at him. "She loved you in the show."

"I'm honored," he said, and kissed Amy's hand.

She blushed. "I wasn't really scared," she said, chin high. The young man laughed, and Amy laughed with him.

Just a man, she thought, watching Rags approach. *Just a man in a wolf head. And Rags was just a Rags in a wolf head.*

But what's under Rags' head?

Amy suddenly had the urge to run, to charge down the slimy hallways and through the lobby and out into the good, clean sun. But then Rags was there, grinning his happy, friendly Rags grin at her as he reached out to tweak her nose.

"Hiya, Shorty," he said.

Amy's mouth dropped open. He was much taller. His waist was narrow, and his shoulders were wide, like Daddy's, only smaller. Rags was a Big Boy.

"Shut your trap, Ame, you're gonna catch a fly," he said, grinning broadly. "What do ya think?" He made a skinny muscle.

"Amazin'," she said.

He laughed. "So how old do I look? Thirteen? Fourteen?"

"I guess so," said Amy, nodding slowly.

He hiked up his trousers, which were a little loose. He had started wearing clothes all the time after Amy saw his pants fall down. He took them off when he was in the pool, which was a lot, but he was really sneaky about it and he never let her see him naked again. "You're a lady," he had said. "A gentleman simply does not disrobe in front of a lady." She wondered where he heard that. She wondered, for that matter, where he got his clothes.

"What'cha starin' at, Tootsie Pop?" he asked her, smiling. Amy jumped.

"Just you, Rags. You really are amazin'." He laughed, looking pleased.

He knelt down beside her. "What do you want to play today, Amy? How 'bout Peter Pan? Or *Jungle Book?* I make a great Shere Khan." He growled loudly.

"Noooo," she said, thinking.

"What, then? Want me to make the rats dance for you?"

"No!" she shouted. "I never want you to do that again! Poor ratties!" He looked hurt.

Amy sighed. "I mean, no, why don't we play Robin Hood?" *And how did you know about the* Jungle Book, *anyway? I never brought you that book.*

"Great!" he said. "Fair Marion, Sherwood Forest awaits!"

Twenty minutes later, after saving a deer (played by Rags) from the snares of a poacher, being captured by the evil Sheriff of Nottingham (also played by Rags), Amy/Maid Marion stood on the rotting, cracked oak bar, waiting for Robin (Rags again) to come and rescue her from the tower. She stared up at the ceiling, at the big old chandelier, and the big, black chain that held it up. It winked at her, crystal peeking out from under the dust and mold. Amy wondered if it would fall some day. *It would squash me flat,* she thought. Amy sighed.

"Thwap! Thwap! Two more of the Sheriff's men fall dead!" Rags cried, pulling an invisible bow. "Thwap, got another one! Right in the eye!"

Gross, thought Amy. She wished he would go ahead and rescue her. She was getting tired of standing on the bar.

"Oh, no!" Rags bellowed. "I'm out of arrows!" He threw his invisible bow away with a flourish, and drew his imaginary sword. Rags began an athletic shadow duel, thrusting and slashing at his enemy. "Ha!" he shouted. "I have you now!"

Good, thought Amy.

"Scoundrel!" Rags snarled. "Can't handle me by yourself, ay?" He sprang up onto the bar, apparently flat footed. Amy jumped, startled. "I'll save you, my lady! Never fear!" He fought his invisible foes savagely. Finally he made one last sweeping slash through the air.

"I got both of them! Chopped their heads right off, with one blow! They fall down, blood gushing from their necks. Their legs are twitching, like chickens'!"

"Cut it out!" Amy yelled, covering her ears. "I don't want to hear about chickens with no heads!"

Rags froze. He turned his head to look at her. His Errol Flynn face didn't match his skinny boy body. "Why not?" he said.

"Because it's gross, that's why." Amy hung her head, studying her shoes. She could feel Rags staring at her, staring holes in her with his green eyes. "Because Mr. Iris scared me with one, that's why," she muttered.

To her surprise, Rags laughed. She started to glare at him indignantly. He pulled his face back into the one she thought was his real one, the forest-boy face. He reached down and stroked her hair. "You shouldn't be afraid of Mr. Iris, Amy. He's a good guy."

Amy stared. "You know Mr. Iris?" The back of her neck felt suddenly cold.

"I sure do. I wasn't supposed to tell you just yet, but I guess I let the cat out of the bag." Rags hunkered down beside her, looking up into her eyes. "He can feel magic, Amy. He's, how'd he put it—sensitive. He came looking for me not long after you first pulled me out of the pool."

"He did?" Amy asked, horrified. *What does that awful man want with Rags?*

"He sure did, Ame. And he's been real nice to me. He takes me to his house, to watch TV. And he even takes me to the movies sometimes, at night."

Without me? Amy thought jealously. *He went to the movies without me?* Then she thought about going with Mr. Iris, and decided she didn't really mind being left out. *That's how he knew about* Jungle Book.

Rags locked eyes with Amy, and she got a little worried. *It's only Rags,* she told herself.

"Amy," he said quietly, "Mr. Iris has been teaching me stuff. Important stuff. I'm learning how to use my powers better, and how to change better. His face split into a grin that was way too big, his teeth hanging out like a happy dog's. "Amy, he told me where I came from! I know why I was—was born!"

"Why?" said Amy quietly. Somewhere in the back of her mind, she knew she didn't really want to know.

"Do you know what a religion is, Amy?"

"Course I do. Religion is where you believe in God and go to church and stuff."

"Do you believe in God, Amy?" She frowned. "I guess so," she said.

"Well, not everyone believes in the same God you do, love." He was staring at her so hard she started squirming.

"Gee whiz,", said Amy, "I know that. Everybody knows that. Frankie Baar at school is Jewish, and Pragna is Boo-Dist. I know that."

"Good," said Rags, smiling gently. "Then you might understand what I'm gonna tell you." He took a deep breath. Amy suspected he really didn't need to breathe at all, but she didn't say so. "There are a lot of different religions in Florida. Old religions. A lot of people believe in one called Santeria, and a lot of people believe in Voodoo."

Amy knew about Voodoo. She had seen those movies where people made dolls of other people and stuck pins in them. She tried it once with her Barbie, but snotty old Chelsea Brenner still came to school the next day.

Rags was still talking. "Mr. Iris believes in Voodoo. I guess it's Voodoo, anyway. He's kinda like a sorcerer. He calls himself a Bocor."

A sorcerer! Amy didn't like the sound of that, not at all. She remembered the sorcerer from *Fantasia*. He had those big, mean, bulgy eyes, like wet boiled eggs. Amy thought of Mr. Iris's eyes, all round and glittery, when he was telling her scary stories. She bit her lip.

Rags didn't seem to notice. "Of course, a lot of people believe in Christianity. 'Specially fundamental Christianity." Amy frowned, not sure what he meant. "You know," he said. "Like those guys on TV. Hay-el awaits the sinner, brothers and sisters!"

"Oh," said Amy. "Those guys."

"On top of all that, lots of people believe in Satanism. Devil worship."

"Yikes," said Amy. She was trying to put everything together, to understand what he was really saying to her.

"Well, anyway," Rags said, "this hotel, it's kind of like a magnet. A magic magnet."

"Why?" said Amy.

"Because it's so old, and so many things have happened here."

Bad things, thought Amy, not really knowing why.

"So, when all this Voodoo and Santeria and Satanism and Holy Roller stuff was going on, it kind of spilled over."

Holy Roller? Amy thought, picturing a rolling pin made of Swiss cheese.

"All that magic, from all those sacrifices and praying and dancing and stuff just kind of spilled over, and the hotel pulled it in. Mr. Iris said it made kind of a whirlpool." He paused to grin at her. "It got all mixed together, like a cake mix. But instead of a cake, it made me!"

"He told you that?" said Amy softly. She didn't like this. Not at all. No matter what Rags said, Mr. Iris was bad. "How did he know?" she asked, frowning a little.

Rags sighed, like a teacher trying to be patient. "After he found me, Mr. Iris and his friends had a seance. That's where you sit in a circle, and talk to spirits. A spirit told him all about me."

"What kind of spirit?" Amy's stomach felt all twitchy.

"Oh, I dunno. Just a spirit."

Just a spirit. The Holy Spirit? The Spirit of Christmas Future? The Spirit of St. Louis? Aren't spirits the same as . . . ghosts? Amy felt her mouth turn down at the corners. She was about to cry, although she was fighting it with all she had.

"Amy?" Rags said excitedly. "Since I've told you everything anyway, there's something I want to show you. Something really important."

I don't want to see it, she thought. She opened her mouth, but nothing came out. Rags jumped down from the bar, then lifted her down like she was as light as a feather. He took her by the hand.

"Come on!" he whispered. His eyes were shining. He smiled down at Amy and she knew he loved her. *It's okay. It's okay.* She squeezed his hand tightly.

Rags stopped in the middle of the ballroom. He dropped her hand and bent down to the floor. He touched on a small crack in the wooden floor and started to work his fingers into it. Amy saw he had to stretch them out and make them skinnier to do it. When he was in up to his palm, he gave a small grunt, and lifted.

A big square piece of floor came up in his hand. He tossed in aside. "Look," he whispered.

Amy was looking. There was a green thing the size of a football in the hole, and it was all green and slippery looking and alive. It was beating like a heart; at least that's what Amy thought it was doing. Or maybe it was breathing. Amy bent over, looking more closely. The thing in the hole was clutching a big old rusty pipe with lots and lots of little green octopus-tentacles that moved and twisted all by themselves. The football-thing was covered with bulging, pale-green veins. Something goopy was moving through them. The whole thing was glowing green, like the biggest firefly in the world.

Fascinated and horrified, Amy bent down even closer. The thing twitched. Amy jumped back with a little squeak.

Rags laughed loudly. "Don't be afraid, my Amy. It loves you. That's my heart!"

Amy stared at him. "Your heart! Why isn't it inside you?"

"I don't know," Rags said, looking a little irritated. "It just isn't. It used to be in the pool, but it came in here. Through the pipes."

"But," said Amy, "But it's not red! It's green! What is it made of?"

He hesitated. Amy tilted her head to the side. "Rags, what are you made of?"

He scowled. "'M not gonna tell you," he muttered.

Amy looked up into his face. "Why, Rags?" she asked. She took his hand.

He looked at her for a long, long time. "Amy," he said, "I'm not just made of magic. Magic has no substance, by itself. The magic put me together out of what was around. What was available." His eyes were locked with hers. "I'm made of algae. And water. And . . . stuff."

Amy smiled. "Neat," she said. "Like Swamp Thing."

He looked at her with his mouth hanging open, then burst out laughing. "Yeah," he said, "Kinda." He set the piece of floor back into place.

"Your heart's kinda neat, Rags," said Amy, as he tamped the old boards down.

He lifted her up, under the arms, and brought her face close to his. "It beats only for you, Amelia. Only for you."

Amy's eyes widened in surprise as he kissed her tenderly on the mouth. Not even Mama and Daddy kissed her on the mouth! Rags set her down. Amy looked up at him, wondering what he was thinking. He grinned at her.

"C'mon, blondie. Let's play Godzilla!"

"Raaaah!" she shouted gleefully.

As Rags set up a green coconut Tokyo in the corner, Amy decided that his secrets weren't so bad, after all.

∽∾∽

Amy's body rested, held fast by heavy chemical chains. Her mind twisted and writhed. She managed to open her eyes, just for a moment. Someone stood by the door, watching her. *It's him,* she thought, and tried to struggle awake. She only managed to clench her hands and moan. He came closer.

"Hush, now," he said, softly, brushing her forehead. He bent down over her. She whined like an animal.

But it wasn't him, wasn't Rags. This man looked at her with chestnut-colored eyes, not algae green. And his skin, the color of boiling fudge, was warm.

Stay with me, Amy wanted to say. Please, please don't go. But her mouth wouldn't work, and her eyelids were heavy. The man smiled at her.

"That's right, pretty lady," he whispered. "Go back to sleep." His gentle eyes were the last thing she saw before the tide pulled her under again.

SIXTEEN

"So, what do you think, Mand, has someone been pretty good lately?"

"Ooooh, pretty good, I suppose. Other than putting treefrogs in the bathtub."

"Good enough for . . . a trip to Disneyworld?"

"Well, I don't know about that . . . "

Amy heard her parents' voices, and somewhere in her mind, what they said was being registered. *Disneyworld!* a little mouse-voice in the back of Amy's head was saying excitedly. She stood on the balcony of her grandmother's condo, looking out over the mango orchard. Looking at the old hotel. Amy opened her mouth, wanting to shout *Yes, I'm a good girl and I want to go to Disneyworld!* She squeezed her eyes shut.

But I'm not *a good girl. I don't deserve* anything.

"Amy? Sweetheart? Is anybody home in there?" Mandy was peering around the bone-colored French curtains, smiling at her.

Slowly, Amy turned away from the hotel, from Rags. She made herself smile, and it felt tight and funny on her lips. "I'm right here, Mama. I can't go anywhere else. I'd have to fly."

"Smartypants. Come on in, baby, it's getting dark out there. Don't want the mosquitoes to bite you."

"Chomp, chomp, chomp," said Tom with a grin.

Amy followed her mother inside, then sat down on the very edge of one of Grandma's pretty white chairs. She sighed.

Mandy knelt down next to her. "Amy," she said, "Did you hear what your father and I were talking about a minute ago?"

"No, Mama," Amy said. *I just lied again. Because I'm bad.*

"Well, we were thinking that maybe we'd leave Palm Beach a little early, and go to—" Her mother paused, waggling her eyebrows in a way that usually made Amy laugh. "Disneyworld!"

No! gibbered Amy's brain. *No, no, no, I can't leave Rags!* Amy looked into her mother's face. "That would be neat," she said.

Tom had joined Mandy, folding his long legs under him to be more on Amy's level. "Are you okay, Mophead?" he asked, gently tugging on a lock of Amy's hair. "I think you've been traveling on that midnight train!"

Amy's heart leaped like a frightened fieldmouse, pounding frantically inside her ribs. *They know, they know!*

"Yup," Tom said, "With all those bags you have under your eyes, I figured you must have been traveling."

Amy's eyes widened. She was sure that her parents could hear the pounding of her heart. "Daddy, I haven't been anywhere!" She was about to cry.

Mandy laughed gently. "Relax, Pumpkin. Daddy's only teasing you." She brushed Amy's cheek with her fingers. Mandy frowned, ever so slightly. "Have you been feeling all right, honey? You do look a little peaked." she felt Amy's forehead.

"I feel just fine, Mama." Amy looked anxiously at her father, who was looking anxiously back. Maybe he didn't know, after all. "Can, um, can I go watch Virginia bake muffins?" Amy mustered a big smile. *Fake, fake, fake!*

Her mother smiled back, looking relieved. "Sure, sweetie. But don't get dirty, because we're going out to dinner with your Grandma, as soon as she gets back."

Tom chuckled. "What your mother means is, don't get all blue from the berries you're gonna bum off of Virginia!"

Amy let go a little burst of involuntary laughter. "I promise," she said, then slipped around the corner.

She didn't go straight to the kitchen. She waited in the hall, listening.

"What a fey little creature she is sometimes," Tom was saying in a low voice. "She wasn't half as excited about Disneyworld as I thought she would be."

"It probably just hasn't sunk in yet. She'll be bouncing off the walls tomorrow."

Soft laughter. Amy waited for five seconds, ten, twenty. She was about to head for the kitchen when Mandy whispered, "I just hope she's okay. She's been a little distant lately."

Tom's voice again. "Maybe she's in love. Virginia's boy Louis is an awfully charming little character."

A stab of guilt pierced Amy's heart. She turned and ran to the kitchen. It was bright and warm, as usual. Virginia was stirring a big bowl of batter, her face turned to the window. She noticed Amy and smiled.

"Hi, sweet pea," she said. "What are you up to today?"

"Oh, nothin'," said Amy, happy to be near her. There was something warm and strong and good about Virginia, she knew. Amy couldn't begin to put it into words, but it drew her like honey. She smiled up into Virginia's pretty chocolate face.

"Why, you're gettin' a tan, little lady. If you stay out in the sun, you'll be as dark as I am!"

Amy giggled, imagining her blonde hair against black skin.

Virginia laughed too. "Why, then I could adopt you. Louie always did want a little sister."

Amy fell silent. The cold, relentless grip of guilt was squeezing her heart again. She looked into Virginia's eyes. *Virginia knows.* This time Amy was certain. She felt her heart sink to her stomach in a ball of ice.

Virginia cupped Amy's chin in her hand. "He really wishes that you would come back to playgroup and see him. He likes you a lot, Amelia. He misses you."

Louis's face flashed through Amy's mind, with his pixie grin and his dancing brown eyes. Amy looked at the floor.

Virginia set down the mixing bowl and lifted Amy easily onto the kitchen counter. She brushed the hair out of Amy's face. Amy felt her lip starting to tremble.

"Where do you go, Amy, after your mama drops you off? Louie says you never come in. He says you slip around the back and leave. Where do you go?" Virginia's dark eyes were locked with Amy's, and she couldn't look away.

Amy's mind raced wildly, leaping from one lie to another. She felt like there was someone squeezing her chest. "There's, there's this little girl, and she lives right next door . . . " Amy's voice trailed off. Virginia's eyes were seeing right through her. She could tell. Amy shut her mouth. Tears began to flow silently down her cheeks.

"You've been to the Martinique. You've been to the old hotel, haven't you, child."

"Yes." It was not so much a word as a stifled sob.

"Why, Amy? Why do you want to go to an awful old place like that?" Virginia's face was gentle, not mad at all. But there was something else there, too. She was wearing another expression under that one, almost like the gentle, worried face was a clear mask. Amy stared, trying to decide what that other expression was. All at once, she knew.

Fear.

Amy's heart pounded so hard she though it would pop. She tried to look away, and found that she couldn't. Amy looked into Virginia's round, smooth face and knew that she could no more lie to her than she could sprout wings and fly. *How come?* Amy wondered, as her tongue betrayed her and she started to speak.

"My friend lives there," she said, in a voice that was no more than a whisper.

"Your friend?" Virginia's voice was shaking a little. "What friend, honey?"

"He told me not to tell," Amy mumbled.

"It's okay, sweet pea. It'll be our secret." Virginia smiled. It was a sweet smile, a smile that made Amy want to trust her. Amy noticed that Virginia's teeth were white and beautifully even. She thought of Rags, making his teeth longer and sharper . . .

"His name is Rags," Amy whispered. Suddenly she felt as if a huge weight were lifted from her thin chest. She bit her lip to stop it, but the words came pouring out in a flood.

"His name is Rags and he's magic. He can do tricks. He can turn into all sorts of things and he can make rats dance, but they don't like it. He lives in the hotel somewhere. He came out of the pool—"

134

Amy cut herself off. And he'd be so mad if he knew! She looked down at Virginia's blueberry spotted apron. *Rags and old iron,* she thought. *Rags and old iron. All he was buyin' was just rags and old iron.* "He's my best friend," Amy said quietly.

Virginia breathed in sharply, like she had burned herself on the stove. "Amy," she said, "I want you to listen to me for a minute, okay, child?"

Amy nodded. Virginia put her hands on Amy's arms, staring into her eyes. "Are you listening, Amelia?"

Mama calls me Amelia when she's mad. "Yes, Virginia. I'm listening."

"That hotel is a bad place. It's a very bad place, Amy. Terrible things used to happen in there."

"What kind of things?"

Virginia's lip curled up, like she smelled something rotten. "Never mind, Amy. Just terrible things. And now, bad . . . people sometimes go there. It's not a safe place for little girls to go. Do you understand me?"

Amy frowned. "I understand. But Rags would protect me from bad people. He said he'd never let anyone hurt me. Never, never, never."

Virginia stared into Amy's face until she began to squirm.

"Amy." Her voice sounded scared and funny, making Amy shiver. "Amy, your friend Rags . . . he may not be what you think he is. He may be something bad, honey."

"He's not bad," Amy said indignantly. *Is he?*

"You don't know that!" Virginia sounded so upset it was scary. Amy cringed. The woman suddenly looked a lot older than she had a minute ago. "You don't know what he is, little girl. I want you to stay away from him."

Amy felt her face crumple like paper. *Not see Rags?* "Noooo," she whined.

"Hush, now, hush." Virginia's voice was gentle again. "Not forever. Just tomorrow, all right? Just tomorrow." She smiled at Amy.

"Okay," said Amy, wiping her eyes. *I guess.*

Virginia picked her up and hugged her. Amy gave a surprised laugh. Virginia set her down, taking her hands, winking at her. "Now how about some blueberries, you little magpie?"

"Yeah!" Amy chirped. "I mean, yes, please!" Amy heard the apartment door open, then close.

"Amy!" called her mother. "Your grandma's back! Let's go, honey!"

"Here, child," said Virginia, her eyes twinkling as she gave Amy a handful of blueberries. "Try not to squish them in your Grandma's Continental!"

"Thanks," said Amy, standing on her tiptoes to give her friend a kiss. Virginia gave a happy little laugh. Amy ran for the hallway. She stopped to smile at Virginia over her shoulder. Amy's stomach clenched. Virginia looked really mad, and sort of sick. Then Virginia was smiling at her again.

Clutching her blueberries, Amy ran to her mother.

Amy moaned softly in her sleep. She rolled over onto her back. Some part of her brain felt her hand being gently squeezed and stroked. "Sleep, pretty Amy," said a voice, rich and resonant. Amy smiled, ever so faintly. Then she plunged back into the icy waters of her dreams.

SEVENTEEN

Amy walked slowly, feeling like there were heavy chains wrapped all around her. She stared down at the sidewalk, at the straggly weeds that poked their heads through the cracks. Once in awhile, a hot tear slid down her face and hit the sidewalk, sinking into the concrete or trembling on a tall blade of grass. Amy had thought she felt just as bad as she possibly could when she lied to her mother. She was wrong.

Amy was going to the Martinique hotel, to see Rags.

I promised Virginia, her tormented young mind railed at her. *I promised!* But her feet kept walking. *He'll be so sad if I don't come. And he loves me.* She scowled. *Doesn't he?* Amy kicked a green coconut, sending it spinning down the walk. She no longer bothered to toss them into the lake. She had better things to do. Like playing with Rags.

She slunk through the overgrown bushes, as she always did, checking around for anyone who might be watching. She hesitated, staring at the bulging, warped hotel door.

"Come in," Rags called from somewhere deep inside the building. Amy jumped. *How did he know I was here?* After a few moments, she pushed the door open with her foot, because the wood always felt slimy. She crept in, feeling, for some reason, like she needed to be very, very careful.

A blast of music came from the ballroom. Amy let out a little shriek and took a step back. "Rags?" she called over the howling guitars. "Rags, turn it off! I hate it!" The music got a little louder. Suddenly angry, Amy turned to leave.

The music stopped. Rags chuckled. *His voice is deeper,* Amy thought. "C'mon in, little love. I'll leave the radio off."

"Well, okay," Amy called uncertainly. She wove her way through the back corridors, through the old kitchen, and into the ballroom. Rags stood by the overgrown window, dancing. *He's so tall!* Amy stared. Rags kept dancing, even though the horrible music was gone. He didn't turn around and look at her, which Amy thought was terribly rude.

A pile of books lay on the floor, next to one of the chairs. Curious, Amy picked one up and read the title. "*The Monk,*" she said aloud. She opened it. No pictures. She picked up the next one. "*The Lust-full Turk,*" she said. "Rags! What's *lust-full?*"

He laughed. *Why does he sound so nasty?* He kept dancing. Amy shrugged and picked up the next book. "*Dracula.* I saw that on TV." It had been so scary that she couldn't sleep without a nightlight for two weeks. Amy shivered and put it down. The last book was thick, and had a pretty cover.

"*Jus-teen,*" Amy said, opening it. This one did have pictures. Awful, fascinating pictures of people, sometimes naked people, getting hurt. Amy's mouth dropped open as she turned from one picture to the next.

A hand rested heavily on her shoulder. "Do you like that?" Rags asked, very close to her ear.

Amy dropped the book. "No!" she said loudly.

Rags laughed. "Mr. Iris gave it to me. And the radio, too. We've been spending a lot of time together."

He started dancing again. *Why is he doing that?* Amy wondered. He spun around just like he was in the Ice Capades, and a shaft of light from a broken window lit of his face.

"Shit!" he screamed. Rags scuttled backwards like a cockroach. "Fucking sun. I need some shades, man!"

"Rags! Those are Bad Words!" Just hearing them made Amy feel funny, like she needed a bath.

"Lighten up, baby!" He grinned down at her.

Amy looked up into his smiling face. He was tall and slim, probably as old as her Aunt Bess, who was almost seventeen. He looked like he did the first day she saw him, only a lot more grownup. His ears were pointed today, and so were his white teeth. Amy didn't think he looked like Peter Pan so much any more. *He kinda looks like Dracula.* Amy jumped when Rags reached out and ruffled her hair.

"Mr. Iris introduced me to his friends last night. They're really neat-o." His grin became wider. "They like me a lot. They think I'm really special." He puffed up, widening his shoulders. "They call me all sorts of cool names. Mr. Iris says that I'm going to get an extra-special present tonight." He looked down at her. "A sacrifice, Amy. Just for me."

Amy felt her mouth turn down, her throat tighten. She wasn't sure what a sacrifice was, but she was pretty sure that it wasn't very nice. And she knew that Mr. Iris wasn't very nice. In fact, he was awful. "You, you jerk!" she shouted. "You like Mr. Iris better than me. Him and his nasty old friends."

Rags' mouth dropped open, wider than it should have, showing off his teeth to the back of his head. He started to say something, but Amy didn't want to hear it.

"D'you know what Virginia says?" she shouted, trembling. "She says this hotel is a bad place, and only bad things live here! She says you're bad, Rags. Bad! Bad! Bad!"

And then she was off the ground, stale air in her nose as Rags yanked her off her feet. He held her face just inches from his, eyes narrowed down to muddy green slits. Amy gave a whooping gasp, getting ready to cry. "Shut up," he hissed into her face. "Just shut up, you little bitch." His breath smelled like the hotel pool on a warm day. Amy sobbed, and Rags shook her.

"You betrayed me," he snarled. "You told about me."

Amy shook her head, trying to say that she didn't mean to, and Virginia said she wouldn't tell. Nothing would come out of her mouth.

"Listen to me, little girl. You will do what I say. You belong to me."

"Do not!" Amy squeaked.

He shook her again, harder. "You do. You are going to be my bride, Amy. You've been promised to me." A sneaky look crept over Rags' face. "You're mine, Amy. We're gonna be married. Mr. Iris is gonna to join your heart and my heart together. Forever."

Amy thought of the terrible, pulsing green thing under the floor, and screamed.

"Stop it," Rags was shouting. "Stop it!" His face was suddenly worried. "Don't scream, Amy, it's gonna be beautiful!" She screamed again.

"Amy!" he moaned. "Please don't. When our hearts are joined, you'll be able to do everything I can do! Wouldn't you like that?"

"Nuh, No," Amy gasped between sobs.

"C'mon, baby, wouldn't you like to turn into animals?"

Amy paused. She pictured herself as a dog loping through a meadow full of wildflowers. Then she thought of the heart again and began to cry.

Rags' face was trembling. At first Amy thought he was going to turn into something else, but he didn't. Amy wondered if he were crying, in his own way.

"I'll show ya," he said softly. "I'll show ya." A thorn pushed up from his collarbone, ripping his shirt. Shifting his grip on her easily to one hand, he ran his other palm across the thorn. Rags' blood welled up thin and green in the cut. Then he was pulling Amy closer and closer to him. She felt the thorn pressing against her chest and screamed. Then it was cutting her. Amy struggled, crying against his neck.

Rags held her away from him, looking into her eyes, then pressed his cut palm against her bleeding chest.

Amy gasped and shuddered. She could feel his blood oozing into her. It was weird and tingly, making her skin prickle and ache like she had the flu. She wanted to fight, but she couldn't seem to move. She was cold, so very cold. Amy's eyes rolled up into her head as she lost consciousness.

When she woke up, she was in Rag's arms. Amy flinched as something wet struck her nose, like a raindrop. Then another landed on her chin. Amy opened her eyes a crack, and peeked. The ballroom was bathed in soft light. Rags was holding her, crouching on the floor. Another of his tears struck her cheek and rolled into her ear.

"Are they real?" she asked, touching his face.

Rags choked, eyes wide, then a huge grin split his face. Amy noticed that his teeth were square.

"Oh, Amy," he said, beaming at her. "Amy, I was so afraid I hurt you." Big green tears rolled down his face.

"Are they real?" Amy asked again. "Are you really crying?"

Rags' smile slipped a little. "I don't know," he said. "I guess I am."

She somehow knew he was lying.

He touched her cheek. "I love you, Amy."

"You hurt me," she said, glaring at him. She touched the hole in her dress. Amy gasped. The hole in the fabric was still there, but the hole in her flesh was not. It didn't even hurt. She felt okay, too. Her skin was warm, and the flu-like feeling was gone.

"I know I did," said Rags, looking away from her. "And I'm sorry. I fixed you, though, see?"

"Yeah," said Amy, looking around. She realized that the room wasn't lighted up after all. She was just seeing in the dark. *Neato.*

"I'll never hurt you again, Amelia, I promise. I'm so, so sorry." He bent over her and kissed her forehead.

"You promise?" said Amy. "You swear?"

"I promise, little love, I promise," he said, his face buried in her blonde curls. He raised his head and looked down at her, his clouded emerald eyes shining with love. "I'm your slave, Amy." He smiled. "Command me."

No, he definitely didn't look like Peter Pan any more. Or Dracula. Good, good, good! He looked like Prince Charming. Amy smiled back. "Can we play Wolf Rider?" she asked.

"Your wish is my command, Amelia," he murmured. Soon Amy was shrieking with delight, galloping around the room on a huge, floppy wolf with green fur.

"I do love you," it said, in its growly wolf-voice.

"I love you too," said Amy, stroking its ears.

❦

That night, Amy's parents went On A Date. That meant Amy got to spend the night at Grandma's.

"Be good," Mandy said, kissing Amy on the cheek.

"And don't sit on the furniture," whispered Tom with a wink and a kiss on the head.

Amy smiled, kissed them back, and began to worry. All evening she watched Virginia, just waiting for the woman to confront her. Amy had broken her promise, after all. She slunk about the elegant apartment feeling jumpy as a poodle, but all Virginia had for her were smiles and a big gingerbread cookie. She stayed late, it seemed, just to be with Amy. Her heart was leaden with guilt.

But nothing bad happened, and just before bedtime, playing one last game of Go Fish with Grandma, Amy finally began to relax.

"Well, you beat me again," Grandma said, her pale gray eyes sparkling. "You're just too good for me, kid. I give up."

Amy smiled and began neatly stacking the cards. She suspected that Grandma had let her win the last three games, but grownups seemed to like to do that. Amy didn't mind.

Grandma winked at her over her mother-of-pearl reading glasses. "How about some scones and a glass of milk before bed?"

"Yes, thank you," Amy answered, putting the cards back into the box. Virginia came in a minute later with a tray. She smiled.

"Is there anything else I can do for you, Mrs. Sullivan?"

"No, thank you, Virginia. Do kiss that sweet little boy of yours for me."

"I sure will." Virginia bent to kiss Amy's head. "We'll see you tomorrow, little Goldilocks."

A few moments later, the front door shut. Amy breathed a sigh of relief. She ate her scones slowly, savoring the buttery flavor. She brushed her teeth like a good girl, and said her prayers with Grandma, who knelt right next to her. Amy silently added a "God bless Rags."

Snuggled up in the big fluffy daybed, Amy quickly got sleepy. She could still see in the dark. She liked that, because now monsters couldn't sneak up on her. Her eyelids started to close.

Something moved on the floor. Amy's eyes flew open. It was a huge cockroach, and it was headed straight for the bed. Amy whimpered under her breath. She wanted to call Grandma, but Daddy made her promise to let the old lady sleep. Amy bit her lip. "Go away!" she whispered desperately.

The roach stiffened. It jerked like it just ran into something hot, then turned around and scuttled the other way. Amy stared at the ugly brown bug. *Did I do that? Did I make it run?*

"Stop," she told the roach uncertainly. It ran across the snowy carpet. "Stop!" said Amy firmly. It did. The cockroach froze. It sat so still that it looked like a little statue.

Oh my gosh, thought Amy. *Oh my gosh.* Her concentration slipped, and the roach wheeled and charged the daybed.

"Drop dead," Amy hissed.

Twitching like it had been sprayed with Black Flag, the roach flipped onto its back. Its hairy little legs pulled in tight to its body, it shuddered, and then was still.

Amy stared at it for a long, long time. After awhile, she felt a tiny smile creep over her face. "All *right!*" she breathed. She lay her head down on the pillow. *That yucchy old roach won't get* me! *No sir!* Amy was asleep in minutes.

❧

Someone was shaking her. Caught in the grip of a nightmare, Amy groaned.

"Amy!" Virginia whispered. "Amy, wake up, child. Wake up!"

Amy's eyes popped open, her heart pounding. Her hands clutched at her chest. She had dreamt of her heart, red and beating and bloody, lying under the floor next to Rags' heart. The green tendrils wrapped tighter and tighter around her heart until she could feel it, a terrible, crushing pain in her chest. But when she had touched herself, she had found only a big hole where her heart should be . . .

But her chest was all in one piece, and Virginia was shaking her gently. Amy opened her mouth to speak, but Virginia lay her finger across it. The woman's face was strained, her lips compressed into a straight line. Her eyes were huge, round and shiny as pie plates.

"Hush, now, child," she said. "Hush and listen. I've been to see it. I've been to see that Rags."

"What?—" Amy started to say.

"Quiet!" said Virginia sharply. "I'm tellin' you something important, little girl. More important than anything else you ever heard."

Her eyes locked with Amy's. She tried to look away, to look at anything, even the dead roach, but she just couldn't. No matter what.

"That Rags is evil, Amy. It is an unnatural thing created from the worst parts of people's souls. It can never do anyone any good, because it is made of bad things."

Oh I never should have told I never should have "Nooo!" Amy moaned. "He loves me. Rags is good." *But he hurt me, though, he hurt me—*

"He does not love you, Amy." Virginia's voice sounded strong as an oak tree. "He does not love anyone. Not even himself. He isn't capable of it. And if he tries to love you, little girl, he'll end up killing you."

Amy was shook her head violently. She started to shout *No, no, he'd never kill me,* but Virginia's strong hand clamped over her mouth, and Amy was suddenly afraid. The woman's face was gentle again.

"Be still, now, little one. You don't want to wake your Grandma." She reached into her apron and pulled out something; a strange, colorful little ball. Virginia leaned over Amy with a sad little smile. "You'd best forget all about that Rags, Amy. He is an evil thing and has no place on this Earth."

Amy wanted to say something, to defend her best friend, but Virginia's hand wouldn't budge.

"I know you don't understand," the woman said quietly. "But Rags is an imbalance in the natural way of things. Your life will never be right while he's alive."

She's going to kill him! thought Amy wildly. *Virginia's going to kill Rags!* She started to thrash in the covers.

Virginia held the ball over Amy's face, and she could see it was made of colored feathers. "Sleep, little girl." She rolled the ball over Amy's eyes, over the bridge of her nose, back and forth. It tickled and felt cool on her skin at the same time. Amy discovered she couldn't open her eyes. She felt herself sinking into sleep.

"When you wake up, you won't have to worry about that swamp demon any more. Not ever again."

A tear squeezed from beneath Amy's eyelid, and she felt it swept away by the feather ball. Virginia lifted her hand from Amy's mouth, but for some reason she still couldn't talk. She couldn't even move her lips. *Please, please don't kill Rags,* her mind cried out again and again. But all that escaped her lips was a low moan. She felt like she was floating in warm water, drifting, sinking. She could hear her own heartbeat in her ears, soft and soothing.

Please . . .

Amy slept.

EIGHTEEN

Amy stood alone in a vast, black desert landscape, screaming, screaming. The hot, dry wind made Rags swing back and forth at the end of the hangman's rope, his green eyes bulging, naked body gently thumping against the towering saguaro cactus from which he was hung. The needles made a thousand cuts in his pale skin. Green fluid oozed down his back and legs, pooling under his dangling feet. Virginia stood by, laughing. Amy covered her head and threw herself to the ground, but she could still hear, beneath the shrieks of laughter, the sound of Rags' blood dripping, Rags' flesh tearing softly on the hooked needles . . .

With a shuddering gasp, Amy woke up.

She jerked, hitting her head on the hardwood rail of the daybed. Clutching the covers to her chin, lips trembling, Amy looked around for her Grandma. The big, fancy room was empty. The light coming through the curtains was pale and washed-out. Amy realized that it was very early, and her Grandma was not awake yet. Then it all came back to her. Virginia staring into her eyes . . . *You won't have to worry about that swamp demon. Not ever again.* Amy's throat constricted painfully, and tears boiled up in her eyes and spilled down her cheeks. She killed him. *Virginia killed Rags, killed my best friend.*

Amy curled up into a little sobbing ball, pain chewing at her heart. *Oh, oh, I'll never see him again . . .* She buried her face in the pillow, and wished she hadn't woke up.

. . . But Rags is different, isn't he? Amy paused, thinking of her friend's flexible body. She thought carefully and hard about the way

146

his face and body changed. *Like water.* Amy thought of the hole in her dress, but not in her skin. *Maybe Rags wasn't dead, after all.* Amy pondered some more. *Maybe no one can kill him. Like Godzilla.*

She slid silently out of bed, careful not to catch her feet in her pink cotton nightie. She opened the cedar clothing chest under the bed frame, and scowled. It was Sunday. She took out the frilly dress Mandy had sent with her, then dropped it. She wanted her shorts and Cookie Monster T-shirt. Amy began to look around.

"Oh, no!" she whispered. She had changed into her pajamas in her Grandma's room. She rubbed her puffy eyelids, thinking about sneaking in.

No. She'll catch me and then poor Rags! A few moments later, she was creeping out the apartment door, wearing her Sunday best.

It was a long, scary walk. The light she had seen through the curtains was what Mandy called false dawn. The sun wasn't up yet, the streets were dark, but the air was warm. Amy was shivering anyway. She walked fast, and the click of her heels on the sidewalk was loud in her ears. She looked around constantly for cars. Her stomach hurt, like she had to go to the bathroom.

There was a sweet, slightly yuchy smell, so strong Amy could taste it, coming from the mango grove that stood between her grandparents' hotel and the Martinique. Rotting fruit lay all over the ground. Most of the fallen mangoes had been chewed by something; red squirrels and birds and bugs, Amy guessed. A huge mango lay on the edge of the sidewalk, blown open by the heat, like the figs in Arizona did sometimes. A string of orange goop dripped from the fruit to the ground. Amy looked more closely. The mango looked like—a heart—

A fat beetle burst out of the orange glop, and Amy skittered backwards, to the other end of the sidewalk. A coconut dropped to the ground next to her with a meaty thud, and she let out a little shriek. She started running toward the hotel.

⊷∽⊶

She leaned against the doorframe, panting. She didn't want to go in. She had to. Squinching up her face, she pulled at the swollen door until it popped open with a stale breath of air. Amy crept inside.

147

She moved silently through the kitchen, silently through the halls. She could see clearly, although the sun had just barely peeked up over the horizon. Amy was afraid to call out for Rags. She was afraid he wouldn't answer. Couldn't answer, and then she'd have to go find his body, find him all dead on the floor. Amy remembered the way her pet hamster Huey had looked dead, with his stiff legs and swollen body and sticky, half-closed eyes. Her empty stomach heaved.

Amy stopped. Heavy black velvet curtains hung across the doorway into the ballroom. She reached out for them, not really wanting to touch. They were wet. *Oh, icky.* Amy slowly pulled them aside and peeked in. She couldn't see Rags. She ducked past the sour fabric and into the ballroom. It stunk worse than usual. It always smelled like Daddy's socks when they'd been in the hamper too long, but today there was something else; something really, really gross. She tried to remember what it was, and saw dead Huey in her mind. Amy's nerve broke. She turned to run.

"Amelia."

The word hissed through the air, deep and whispery. Amy shivered from her head to her heels. It was Rags' voice, but different. Scary. Amy's heart lurched, pounding wildly.

He rose up from behind the bar like a rattlesnake. Amy couldn't see his face. He slipped around the bar, but Amy had trouble seeing him; he stayed in the blackest, oiliest shadows.

Suddenly he was right in front of her. Amy took a step back, confused. She started to reach out her hand, but she was suddenly very afraid. He's still my friend, isn't he? She tried to smile. "R-Rags?" she said in a tiny voice.

"Yes, baby," he said. Amy frowned. His voice sounded funny, like he had a mouthful of oatmeal. He was bigger, as big as a man, like her daddy.

"Yes my angel, my precious." In the darkness, he knelt down and held his arms out to her.

Amy's fear drained out of her in a warm rush. She felt an overwhelming surge of love. He's still alive! Rags is alive! She ran to him.

"Baby!" he laughed. "You look so beautiful. Oh, little love . . . " He brushed the hair from her face and cupped her cheek in his hand. His skin felt slimy. *He must have been playing in the pool,* Amy thought. *Yucchy.* She pulled back, smiling into his eyes. They looked flat and faded, like the plastic eyes of an old, cracked doll. *Because it's so dark,* she thought firmly. Then he was picking he up, holding her way up in the air so she could fly, and the light from the filthy window caught his eyes and Amy screamed.

They boiled like thunderclouds over the Arizona desert. Amy looked into their depths, and saw something terrible, something that looked like it wanted to get her, to hurt her, to eat her all up until nothing was left.

She began to struggle, pounding at his hands with her fists. "It's true it's true it's true!" she shrieked. "What Virginia said is true! You're not real! You're a monster!"

His body began shaking. Amy stopped fighting, wondering if she had made him cry. She was suddenly very confused. She touched his chest, petted the soft, black material of his shirt. "I'm sorry, Rags, I didn't mean . . . "

He spun her around, tossing her in the air, and light gleamed on his long, pointed teeth as he laughed silently. "I am real, angel. I'm more real than Virginia, or anyone else you know. You're going to be real, too, my sweet one, my baby bride . . . " And then his features were shifting, moving slowly like the scum on the surface of the pool, and Rags showed Amy his Real Face.

Amy shrieked. She began to writhe frantically, desperate to get away. Rags' fingers grew longer, flowing through the pink chiffon of her Sunday dress and gripping her skin like the spongy pads of a tree frog.

With a squeal, she kicked out wildly. Her hard, black little Mary Jane shoes connected solidly with Rag's face, and sunk in. He yelped and dropped her.

Amy was running. She slipped on the black mold growing on the carpet, falling to one knee, the cold slime soaking through her white tights. She thrashed, trying to get to her feet, shoes slipping in sludge. She could hear him right behind her. Then she was on her feet again, running as fast as she could.

Tears streamed down her face as she ran for the door. Wet moss brushed her neck and Amy flinched, hitting her head on the wall. Her nose wrinkled. She could smell him. Sobbing, she ducked around a corner and ran.

Her heart leapt. Down the hall, the red stained glass in the front door winked at her like a dragon's eye. She ran, panting, sobbing.

She heard him laugh right next to her ear. Suddenly, she realized he was playing a game with her, that he could catch her any time he wanted to.

Her shoe struck something hard. Amy pitched forward, grasping at the banister of the spiral staircase. Her fist closed on moss and she landed heavily on her chest. Gasping, she rolled over and scooted backwards across the slimy floor. Her back pressed against the door.

Amy looked up at Rags. Laughing softly, he reached for her with long, ropy arms. Her bladder let go. She didn't want to see him anymore, so she covered her eyes as he bent over.

The door was flung open behind her with a thick groan. Amy fell over backwards, and looked straight up at the towering figure of Virginia. The woman's eyes, locked on Rags, were slitted and furious. She reached down and hauled Amy to her feet.

"Run home now, baby girl," said Virginia. Her gaze was unwavering.

Rags' mouth twisted down, making him look like and ugly fish. "I don't think so, bitch." He held his hand out. The fingers were long and thin and bony. He closed them in a sudden movement, and the door slammed shut.

Swearing under her breath, Virginia set down the huge shoulder bag she carried. Rags watched, a little smile on his quivering face.

"What do you think you're doing here, blackie?" he asked. He made his voice sound nice, but his eyes were angry. Crazy.

In a blur of motion, Virginia drew in the air with her finger, and with her other hand, threw something at Rags. Amy watched it fly, incredibly fast, but somehow she could tell it was a colored feather ball. It struck Rags in the chest and bounced off.

He laughed and took a step forward.

His flesh began to run from his body. Strings of green dripped from his face and hands. Rags screamed. He flattened out on the carpet like a cat hunting sparrows, and slithered out of his clothes. He shot across the floor, into a dark corner of the room.

Amy stood with her back to the door, shivering. *I don't want to see this. No, no, no.* Virginia grabbed her shoulder bag and strode across the room toward Rags.

Amy could see her, standing over the writhing puddle that could only be her best friend. Virginia was drawing patterns in the air again. Amy was certain that she could see them hanging there, faint lines of peach-colored light. The woman drew her palms together, and the light became brighter.

Amy saw Rags flowing toward Virginia's feet and looked away, sobbing. *I don't want to see I don't want to see!*

Virginia shouted, a hoarse cry of surprise. She pitched back, one of Rags' tendrils wrapped around her ankle. She landed heavily on her backside and immediately reached for the thin green tentacle, but it was gone. Rags melted through the carpet and into the wood flooring.

Virginia stood up, silent and fierce. She began slowly stalking across the room, hands outstretched like a blind woman. She reached the center of the ballroom and hesitated.

You're standing by his heart, Amy wanted to scream. Nothing came out but a faint whimper. The carpeting in front of Virginia's feet began to bulge. *Can't you see it? Amy moaned.*

The carpeting split like the skin of an overripe plum. Rags burst from the floor in a shower of rotted wood and moss. Green light from his pulsing heart streamed up in a column from beneath the floor. Rags stretched higher and higher, a deadly green snake with a mouth full of knitting needles. Virginia took a step back, making a sweeping gesture with her hands. Trails of pale light hung in the air before her. With an alien howl, Rags darted forward and wrapped his writhing body around her.

He squeezed viciously. Virginia's mouth hung open, her eyes bulged. A pitiful, wracking wheeze passed through her lips.

"Rags, don't!" Amy screamed. The snake-head swiveled toward her. Confusion flashed over his weird, stretched-out face. "Please," Amy said. She was shaking so hard her teeth knocked together.

He stared at her for a moment. Then he snarled. Rags' snake-body snapped like a whip, and Virginia was flying through the air. She landed against the bar with a wet thump, and lay still.

Rags pulled the rest of himself violently up from beneath the floor. His lower body ended in a tangled mass of hairy, jointed roachlike legs, jerking and twitching, trying to get a grip on the floor. Something was caught in them.

A limp body was pulled up from beneath the boards with a shuddering jerk. Marie! The Iris's cook and housekeeper—The thin old woman's eyes were rolled up in her head. A huge, red hole gaped in her chest. Red stained the front of her yellow flowered frock.

Amy started screaming. Her own voice rang in her ears, but she couldn't stop. Her stomach heaved again and again, but there was nothing to throw up but bitter bile.

Rags froze. His green headlight eyes stared at Amy. "I didn't do it," he whispered around a mouthful of nightmarish teeth. He edged toward her.

Amy's screams rose in pitch, hurting her ears and her throat. She collapsed to the floor, covering her head with her arms.

"Amy, honest," he said. He was shrinking. Stagnant, dirty water ran from him in streams. "It wasn't me."

Amy screamed and screamed.

Rags was a man again, a tall, muscular man with a thin, handsome face. He took a step toward her, lines of fear crossing his perfect forehead. "Amy, please! It wasn't me, it was Mr. Iris. She was the sacrifice. He said it would make me strong, so you and I could be together. I just watched, Amy, I didn't do it. I didn't do it!" His voice was quivering.

Amy looked at him through slitted eyes. The screams were still coming from her mouth by themselves. Rags cautiously approached her. The light from his heart pulsed and throbbed.

Virginia charged. She screamed as she ran, holding a broken piece of ornamental iron from the front of the bar high over her head. It had once been beautiful, a twisted vine of Art Nouveau roses. Now it was rusted, jagged and deadly. Blood ran down her arms as the metal flowers cut into her palms.

Amy looked up in time to see her running past Rags. Virginia was headed straight for the hole in the floor. She leapt over Marie's body. Amy watched, saucer-eyed, as Virginia caught her foot on Marie's torn dress. Just like that, Virginia was falling. The two women, one living, one dead, were plunging into the pit.

Virginia twisted in midair, aiming the iron vine with deadly accuracy. It pierced the green heart, with Virginia's full weight behind it. Thick fluid sprayed in every direction.

Virginia lay sprawled on the muddy foundation of the hotel, Marie's dead face just inches from her own.

Rags screamed, just once. He fell in a boneless heap.

Rags, Amy thought. *He's just Rags.* Her mindless shrieks filled the big room. She felt like she was sinking into herself.

Virginia rose from the pit like an avenging demon. Bloody and silent, she crossed the room and reached into her shoulder bag. Virginia pulled out a propane torch.

"No," Rags whispered. His eyes rolled at her. Water ran from his every pore. He seemed to be flattening out.

Virginia lit the torch with a flint striker, and it hissed like a furious snake. She bent over Rags' motionless form.

"Please," he breathed.

She put the torch to his face.

His screams joined Amy's for a moment, then hers fell silent as her brain lost the ability to deal with what she was seeing.

His went on for a long, long time.

NINETEEN

Amy's hands were over her ears as she desperately tried to block out Rags' screaming. Her eyes were squeezed shut, her face twisting at the sound of his tortured voice.

Someone was touching her, talking to her. Gentle hands tried to pry her palms from the sides of her head. Amy struggled for a moment, then slowly opened her eyes.

A concerned young face was looking into hers. A very familiar face. His chocolate skin was smooth and warm-looking, and his eyes wide with worry. There was something about the pointed chin, the curved, almost beautiful mouth—

Louis. Louis, all grown up. Amy goggled. Her hands dropped away from her ears, and he folded them in his own. *I'm all grown up too, she thought. I'm all grown up, and Rags is dead.* She rubbed her eyes wearily, relaxing. Then her heart jumped. *But Rags isn't dead, because he—*

"Louis?" she asked tentatively, still not believing. Her voice was rough, her throat raw from screaming.

He smiled. "Amy." His lips still had the same puckish bow.

Amy threw her arms around him and hugged fiercely, almost pulling him off his feet. Louis held her, murmuring words Amy couldn't quite understand but which made her feel better anyway. She only relaxed her grip when her strength failed her, She sank back down on the bed, drinking in his face.

"You were talking in your sleep for hours, Amy," he whispered. "You told me a story."

Amy flushed. "It's true," she said flatly. "It's not a story."

Louis stroked her hand. "I know that, Amy. My mother told me."

"Oh!" Amy cried. "Virginia! How is she, Louis?"

He took in a deep shuddering breath. "Mama died last year. Her heart."

"Oh, oh . . . " Amy's eyes filled with tears. "I'm sorry, Louis. Your mother was my . . . my friend . . . " She cut herself off before she could break into tears. Virginia had been her friend. And her savior. And the murderer of her childhood playmate, her first love . . .

Amy shuddered violently. "Don't cry, sweet girl," Louis soothed. "Mama liked you. She wouldn't have wanted you to be sad over her. Come, let's walk."

Amy sat up shakily in bed. She tried to run her fingers through her hair, and discovered a rat's nest. She rubbed her eyes, and they felt puffy and tender. *God,* she thought. *What a sight I must be.* She grinned.

Louis reached out for her, and she noticed his hospital name tag. Suspicion clutched at Amy's stomach. She pulled back. "Louis?" she asked.

"Hmm?" His head was cocked, and he looked uncannily like he was reading her face like a book.

"What do you do here, at the hospital?" Amy's eyes narrowed. *It's not Rags. His eyes are brown, not green.*

But who says swamp monsters can't buy colored contacts?

He smiled, looking like he knew exactly what she was thinking. "I'm a crisis counselor in training, Amy. I'm here to assist trauma cases, like you. Actually, I wasn't assigned to you, but how could I stay away?" His eyes sparkled.

Amy's heart was pounding. He was so charming, so sweet. What if—

"How did you know it was me? How did you know where to find me? Louis, why do you live in Arizona now?"

His mouth turned up, mahogany eyes looking down almost shyly. "I moved to Arizona last year, because I knew you would need me."

Amy stared at him, hostility welling up in her. *Who the hell are you, anyway?*

His eyes seized hers, like Virginia's had done so long ago. She couldn't look away.

"I'm not kidding, Amy. I'm my mother's son. I'm an apprentice houngan." He smiled, a quirky little twitch. "A Vaudun priest."

Amy continued to stare. "Vaudun? Like Voodoo?"

"Yes."

"You're shittin' me."

Louis let out a spontaneous, husky chortle that made Amy want to laugh, too. "Now why would I do that?"

She smiled in spite of herself, staring down at the sheets. "I dunno. So, Virginia was, like a Voodoo Queen?"

That laugh again. "A Voodoo Queen. She would have gotten a kick out of that. Mama was a mambo, a priestess. One of the most powerful I've ever seen. She told me all about you. She was horribly afraid that she hadn't killed that thing, that it would come back for you. She loved you, Amy. She always wanted a daughter."

Amy twisted the sheets in her hands. "I loved her too. But, Louis— Voodoo—Vaudun—whatever it is, that's kind of a lot to swallow, you know?"

"Oh, and a shape-shifting slime-monster isn't?"

Amy let out an involuntary snort of laughter. "You've got a point."

Louis's smile was gentle. "Besides, you saw, Amy. You remember what she did. To Rags."

She nodded slowly. Amy felt herself relaxing, wanting to believe him. She refused. Her mouth tightened. "But how did you know—?"

His face was pained, his high forehead deeply lined. "On her deathbed, Mama sat up, grabbed my face, and told me to go to you. She said you would die if I didn't."

"And then she died?" Amy whispered.

Louis' eyes were strange and haunted. "She was already dead, Amy. For half an hour."

No. Now way. No fucking way.

Amy's mouth filled with bile and panic. She tried to swing her legs off the bed to run, but they wouldn't hold her up. Her head pounded dull, angry pain, and her vision swam. She slipped. Louis caught her around the waist, reaching for her face. With a strangled scream, Amy caught his wrist.

Louis lifted her easily back onto the bed. He wrapped his hand around her fingers, which were still gripping his wrist. His eyes burned into hers. *Just like the rats,* Amy thought. *I'm mesmerized, just like those poor little rats.*

His hand closed tighter and tighter around her fingers. She could feel her nails digging into his wrist. He smiled as a trickle of warm blood squeezed out beneath their hands and ran down his arm.

"See?" he said, his face just inches from hers. "It's red."

She watched as one, two, three drops landed on the beige linoleum. He stroked her forehead, ever so gently, and the pain ebbed away to nothing.

"Okay," Amy whispered.

He helped her to her feet. She blushed, trying to pull her hospital gown around her back as tightly as it would go. "I don't suppose my clothes are in here?" she asked sheepishly.

Louis rubbed his wide, straight nose. "Your clothes were, um, soiled, Amy. I brought you some new ones." He opened the nightstand drawer.

"Thank you," said Amy. She felt numb from one end to the other. "Could you—?"

"Certainly," said Louis. He turned and left the room, closing the door behind him.

Amy felt like was drowning in a sea of unreality. "Too bizarre, too bizarre," she muttered. Taking out the clothes, she discovered pink cotton panties, soft bluejeans, and a purple Rude Dog T-shirt. No bra, thought Amy. She looked down at her chest. *Don't need one anyhow.* She bit back the gale of hysterical laughter that threatened to burst out, and dropped the odious hospital gown to the floor. Under the bed she found her own ratty Reeboks, and a fresh pair of ankle-high, P.E. gray running socks rolled up in them.

The jeans fit perfectly; just loose enough to be comfortable. The T-shirt smelled nice, and was wonderfully soft. "Oooo, Voodoo," Amy whispered, then giggled maniacally. She looked further into the drawer, and found a hairbrush and a Ghirardelli chocolate bar. She was chomping the candy and struggling with the knots in her hair when Louis knocked softly.

"Come in," Amy called around a mouthful of chocolate. The door opened a little, and Louis ducked in. Amy smiled at him. "How do I look?" she asked.

"Ravishing. Are you ready?"

"For a walk?"

"To leave the hospital, Amy. You're not safe here."

Amy felt a chill. "Uh, yeah, just a minute. I want to wash my face." She went into the bathroom and scrubbed her skin pink with the gritty institutional soap. She peeled off the T-shirt and washed her armpits with a washcloth, although she didn't smell bad to herself. *They must have given me a bath while I was out.* Amy grimaced. The idea was creepy. She inspected her reflection. Her skin was pink and shiny, like a rubber ball. Her eyelids were puffy and a little purple. "Ravishing indeed," she told herself. Her hand crept down between her legs. It doesn't hurt or anything. He must not have—

Amy winced, her eyes squeezing shut involuntarily. *Don't think about him, stupid. Don't think about either one of the scum-sucking—*

"Amy? You OK in there?"

"Just fine," she called back softly. Amy took another moment to compose herself, then opened the bathroom door. She took two steps forward, and stumbled.

Louis was there immediately, his arm catching her gently around the waist. "I seem to be making a habit of this," he smiled.

"Sorry," Amy muttered, starting to blush.

"My pleasure."

She laughed. Slowly, they walked out the door.

The hospital corridors were brightly lit, and Amy squinted as they walked slowly along. Louis' arm was strong and warm around her waist. She liked it there. She looked down at the worn, faded carpeting with its garish Southwestern pattern, and decided not to think anymore. Instead, she looked out the huge plate glass windows into the darkness.

"Amy . . ."

The voice was weak and hoarse. The back of Amy's neck prickled. She froze.

Louis let go of her and looked around, eyes alert and bright as those of a cat about to pounce.

"Amy . . ."

The voice was close. Very close. Amy closed her eyes, and could hear raspy breathing.

"Amy, please . . ."

It was coming from room 253, directly in front of her. Suddenly, Amy knew without a doubt whose voice she was hearing. She lunged forward and threw the door open.

"Amy!" shouted Louis. "Amy, don't!"

She didn't hear him. Her eyes were fixed on the tortured frame of Xavier on the bed.

Both of Xavier's legs and one arm were in casts. His ribs were wrapped, and yellowish-red fluid had seeped into the bandages. His face was swollen and discolored. His handsome Yaqui nose had been broken: The white tape stood out against his dark skin. He smiled, then winced. His front two teeth were missing.

"Amy. You heard me."

She rushed to him, taking his hand in both of hers. Her eyes clouded with tears. "Xavier," she whispered. "Xavier, my friend . . ."

"No," he said firmly. "None of that." He reached out to pat her cheek, and that's when she saw.

The ring finger on his right hand was gone. The hand was wrapped in new cotton bandages, but a tiny flower of red blossomed where his finger should be. Amy sobbed, once.

"Oh, no. Oh, no."

"Now don't get all worked up." He grinned, showing the gap in his swollen gums. "It's only my ring finger. I can still pick my nose and flip people off." He brushed a tear off her nose. "I'm all right. Just a little uglier."

She touched his bruised cheek softly. "Nah, you're as gorgeous as ever."

"Flatter me all you want, blondie. I still won't marry you. Now listen up. You have to get out of here. That thing's coming for you."

Amy stroked Xavier's coarse black hair. "I know that, all-seeing shaman. My ass is headed for the door."

Louis slowly approached, standing behind Amy protectively.

"I don't believe we've been introduced," said Xavier, with a strange expression that wasn't quite a smile.

"I'm Louis. Nice to meet you, medicine man. You look like shit."

"So do you, Voodoo man, but I've got an excuse."

How did they know? she thought. *How did they know about each other?* Amy looked at the two men. Her skin was crawling. Louis and Xavier had locked eyes with one another, taking each other's measure in some way that was more than the obvious.

Louis grinned. "Don't worry. I'll take care of her."

Xavier's smile was sad, almost bitter. "Let's hope you do better than I did. I couldn't even take care of myself. Get her away from here, Louis. Now."

"Hey," said Amy. "Stop talking about me like I'm not even here, you macho assholes. Xavier, you'd better come with us."

"Okay," he said, "Just let me jump into some Levi's and I'll just jog behind the car." He snorted. "Look at me, Amy, I can't go anywhere."

She squeezed his hand. "You have to. What if—what if he comes back here?"

Xavier shook his head slowly. "He won't bother with me, Ame, he wants you." His dark eyes narrowed. "Besides, if he does, I have a little surprise for him. I have one for you too, Amy." He reached under his pillow with his good arm, and withdrew something in his closed fist.

"Here," he said, pressing it into her hand.

Amy held it up to the light. It was a bracelet, intricately woven in white string.

"Put it on," said Xavier. "Now, Amy. You don't have time to waste."

She held her wrist out to Louis. He started when he touched the bracelet, smiled as he tied it on. "Nice piece of work," he said. "Where'd you get the string, X-Man?"

"I batted my eyes at a nurse. Do you feel it, Amy?"

"I fee—something. What is it, Xavier? Will it protect me?"

"No." He looked down at his fractured legs, his face lined and worried. "It will help you focus your concentration, Amy. It will help you save yourself." He closed his eyes.

Amy looked at the long, silky lashes. *He looks like a little boy. How can I leave him here?*

Xavier smiled up at her, and for a moment, she thought he had read her mind. "Now go. Get out of here, Amy, while you still can. Don't worry about me. I'll be fine, I promise."

"But Xavier, you—"

"Beat it, blondie. I need my beauty sleep." He looked at Louis. "Let the Bayou King here look out for you, Ame. He's a good man."

She squeezed Xavier's hand one more time. "Okay," she whispered. "See you soon?"

"You bet." Xavier pressed her hand to his swollen lips.

Amy couldn't look back as they left the room.

Amy swallowed hard, trying not to cry. Louis started to say something, then stopped. They walked in silence for awhile.

The first glow of the rising sun was touching the outside windows, pink and pale.

"Look. We're safe," Amy whispered. "We're safe until dark."

"You're sure?" Louis looked at her intently.

"Yes. He hates sunlight. He got more sensitive to it as he got older."

"Okay. Good. We have time to make plans." Louis still walked quickly, as if something were behind him.

"Wait." He touched her arm. "Look." They had reached a corner. The hallway bent around, forming the walls of a V-shaped outdoor courtyard. Beyond the floor-to-ceiling windows, tall trees stood backlit by the sun's first feeble rays.

A figure came around the corner to join them in the hallway. Amy squeaked and took a step backwards. But it wasn't him. Was it? *It doesn't look like him but that doesn't mean anything, doesn't mean anything at all.* It was an old man, lean body once tall, now hunched over a walker. With one hand he pulled a rolling I.V. stand with him, clear fluid dripping into his ropy arm. He paused when he saw Amy and Louis, then smiled, nodded cordially.

Louis didn't seem to notice him. Amy's mouth went dry. She fought the urge to run shrieking down the corridor. He could be anywhere. Look like anyone. The old man's hand reached up to his forehead, as if to tip a hat. Instead, he brushed fine white bangs away from his milky gray eyes, and turned to watch the window.

Gray eyes. Thank God. Thank God.

"Watch this, Amy," Louis whispered, grinning, face upturned toward the big windows.

A bird flew soundlessly from the tree. Then two flew out in opposite directions. Five or six birds took off from the treetop at once.

"Wow," said Amy. "Do they do that every morning?" Louis laughed.

The tree exploded with life. Birds rose from it in a dark cloud, spiraling up and out and away. Sparrows and starlings flew side by side, straight up like little rockets. They chirped and sang and cursed each other, their wings making a sound like river rapids. They reached the top of the hospital walls and spread out like smoke.

"Oh. Wow." Amy grinned, holding onto Louis' arm. She glanced over at the old man. He was smiling like a little boy, long-fingered hands outspread on the glass.

"They come in every night, too," said Louis. "Look, here come some bats."

Amy giggled as the little creatures made their way through the wave of birds, hitting the upper walls of the hospital and crawling under a wide drain gutter.

"Jeez. You'd think they'd splatter when they hit the wall like that." Amy watched as another of the bats struck the wall, grabbing onto the coarse stucco with his tiny claws.

"Not something I'd care to do." Louis' face was turned up to the sky. The morning sun made his skin look like cinnamon.

"Do they ever crash?" Amy asked. "Do the birds run into each other? Or the walls? Or the bats?"

"Not that I've ever seen. The bats have their sonar. They don't run into anything. I think it's dumb luck with the birds."

"Ah, the wonders of nature." Amy laughed.

"Look," said Louis, pointing. "Here come a whole bunch of bats. I've never seen so many bats—"

He stopped. Amy gasped, choked, her throat suddenly dry. They weren't looking at a cloud of bats. They were looking at one big one.

But it's not a bat, stupid. It's him. What made me think he couldn't come for me in daylight? He's not fucking Dracula. He's—

Louis grabbed her, backpedaling. The creature, Rags, was dropping like a missile, his huge wings folded. Louis turned to run, yanking Amy's arm. Amy stood transfixed.

There was a thin wheezing sound, a rattling intake of breath as the man with the walker started backing down the corridor.

Rags crashed through the trees, sending birds flying wildly away. He spread his wings wide and swung around. His boots smashed through the window. Flying shards of glass winked gold in the early morning sunlight.

Amy ran. She crashed into Louis, and they both hit the ground.

Rags was on her in a heartbeat.

He pulled her up by the back of her T-shirt, then spun her around to face him.

He was huge. His chest was bare. His shoulders were broad, and heavily muscled to support the folded wings which jutted up from behind his back. His face was the face she remembered, pointed ears, pointed teeth. Only it was harder. Thinner. Angrier. She trembled uncontrollably as he lifted her off the ground by her wrists.

"Amy." He said, his lips curving into a bitter smile. "What's the matter, aren't you going to scream?" He extruded a thin tendril from his stomach and waved it in front of her face. "Go on, my love. I'll get over it."

A cold splash of anger welled up in Amy's gut. "Fuck you," she hissed.

"You will." He grinned. His teeth lengthened. "In every way possible, baby bride." The tendril slipped under her shirt, cold against her skin, and caressed her belly.

She aimed a kick at the crotch of his black jeans. He deflected it with his knee, laughing.

Louis. Where the hell is Louis. She looked over her shoulder.

Louis knelt on the floor. He held something in one hand, and was doing something to his other palm with it.

"Louis!" called Rags in a high voice. "Louis! Hayelp! Save, me Louis!" He flipped Amy around and caught her under one arm like a sack of flour. Rags ambled toward the broken window, singing softly. "Louie Louie, oh no, me gotta go now . . . "

Amy shrieked and kicked her legs and pounded with her fists. Her head whipped back and forth. *No no no no no . . .*

The old man collapsed within the frame of the walker. He sank down like a heat-blasted vine, clutching, moaning. The I.V. line came down with a clatter. His eyes were wet saucers in his bluing face. Rags paused to point and let out a melodious, movie-star laugh.

Louis leapt up and charged. He grabbed Rags' shoulder and yanked him around.

"Okay," said Rags with an amiable smile. "You asked for it, little man."

Louis slapped him across the face.

Rags screamed. He dropped Amy. She scrambled across the floor, standing up as soon as she was away from the thrashing Rags.

Rags threw back his head and howled. His face was smoking. A round, red welt of blood was burning on his cheek. *Red? Rags' blood is green, what—* But it wasn't just a welt, it was some kind of complex pattern, and it was burning its way into Rags' face like acid.

Rags clawed at his face, green spit drooling from the corner of his mouth. He rubbed the spot, then started to tear at it.

A heavyset blond nurse and a painfully young security guard rounded the corner, nearly tripping over the shuddering body of the old man.

"Mr. Katz!" shouted the nurse, kneeling down next to him. She hadn't even looked at Rags.

The security guard had. His head jerked back and forth between the shattered window and the winged demon, face twisted in disbelief and terror. He clawed for his gun and yanked it from the holster.

Rags snarled at him, showing teeth like steak knives. With a high-pitched shriek, the guard started pumping rounds into him.

Louis hit the floor, dragging Amy with him. She covered her ears and screamed.

"Motherfucker!" screamed Rags. A tendril shot from the center of his chest like a lightening strike. The knotted end of it struck the guard in the nose with a loud, wet crunch. He flew backwards in a spray of blood.

The nurse was trying to pull Mr. Katz away, her arms wrapped around his chest, but his legs were tangled in the walker. She was sobbing silently, mouth open screamlike, when Rags turned his attention to her.

He cocked his head, as if trying to decide what to do. His fist shot out, quick as a snake, and clipped her in the temple. She dropped heavily across the old man. He twitched feebly beneath her, gasping for breath. Rags started to laugh again, one hand pressed to his cheek. He rocked back on his heels, admiring his handiwork.

Amy started to crawl past Rags, toward the elevators, but Louis stopped her, silently motioning for her to go the other way. She decided not to argue. Louis and Amy scrambled to their feet and ran.

They darted around the corner, running down the hallway toward Xavier's room. Amy could hear Rags as he started to run down the corridor after them. He wasn't right behind them, but he was close enough. *Close enough.*

They reached room 253, and Louis stopped suddenly. Amy barely missed running into him a second time.

"Are you crazy?" she snarled. She pointed at Xavier's door. "We can't lead him here. He'll kill Xavier. Come on!"

Louis held his ground. "Don't underestimate him, Amy." He smiled tightly. "Besides, it's too late."

"You bastard." Amy wasn't sure if she were talking to Louis, or to the monster who trotted down the hall toward her as if he were half-heartedly trying to catch a bus. She took a deep breath and backed up a little.

Rags stopped a few feet in front of her and Louis. "Ready to go now?" he asked with a winning smile. A sizable chunk of his cheek was missing. The glistening flesh was green and pulpy.

Amy wrapped her hand around her braceleted wrist. "Come get me, asshole."

"With pleasure. But first, I think I'll pause to rip your friend Louis' arms and legs off. Do you mind?" He cocked his head, like he did so long ago.

"Just try it," said Louis. His voice was shaking. A siren began howling in the distance, getting closer. Another one joined it, then another.

Something was coming out from beneath Xavier's door. It was water, rolling over the carpet as if it were greased. Amy stared.

Rags followed her stare. "Oh, come on," he said, still smiling. "What the hell is this. Do I have to finish you off too, Geronimo?" He reached for the door.

The water leaped. It launched into the air, taking shape as it flew. When it hit Rags in the chest, it was a shimmering coyote, the size of a small German shepherd.

Rags gasped, and staggered back. The coyote bit into his throat with its ephemeral jaws. Rags screamed. The water coyote became tinted with his green blood.

Rags clawed at it, but his hands just passed through the coyote as if it weren't there. He gagged. The coyote shook its improbable head. Rags wailed, staggering back further.

Amy launched herself at him. Her hand passed through the coyote. *It's cool,* she thought, *Cool and warm both.* She straight-armed Rags in the chest. She watched, feeling strangely distanced as Rags crashed backwards through the window and plunged screaming down and down.

Howling, Rags opened his wings and pulled himself up just before he hit the ground. His wings pounded the air and he climbed, still fighting the coyote. He soared over the hospital walls, and was gone.

Amy threw open the door of Xavier's room.

He was unconscious, his skin grayish and clammy. His black hair was lank with sweat.

Amy grabbed his hand and patted it. "Xavier! Xavier, wake up!"

"No." Louis gently took her wrist. "He'll be all right. He just needs to sleep."

Xavier began to convulse.

"Shit!" Louis hit the call button. "We have to go. Someone will be here in a minute."

"No!" Amy yelled. "I won't leave him like this!"

Louis' eyes burned into hers. "Rags is following you, Amy. He has your scent. He's going to come looking for you. We don't know if that will be five minutes from now or five hours or what. If he comes back here, he'll kill Xavier for sure. And anybody else who gets in his way. We have to go. Now."

Xavier had stopped convulsing, and was trembling like a fever dreamer. Then there were running feet in the hallway, shouts of alarm and confusion. The sirens outside wailed like banshees arriving at a deathwatch.

Amy sobbed, and pushed the button again. Louis grabbed her hand, and they ran for the elevator.

TWENTY

Amy couldn't stop shivering. She sat in Louis's tiny Metro, knees pulled up to her chin, hands wrapped around her legs, and shook.

He's real. He's real. He's real.

She had known before. Of course she had; Xavier had told her. She had even remembered some of it, as much as she didn't want to. But it had seemed like a weird dream, some kind of funky horror movie that gave her nightmares but didn't really affect her, because it wasn't real life, how could it be? Amy realized that deep down, she had been sure it would turn out to be something else. Something sane, understandable, even if it was her own insanity.

And then he beat Shane to death. And then he looked at her wearing blood and brains for warpaint. *And then he flew down from the sky to get her.*

And just like that, everything she knew was wrong.

Amy looked over her shoulder at the nonexistent backseat for the dozenth time. She checked the floorboards. She looked at Louis. *Because he could be anywhere.*

Anywhere.

Anywhere.

When she thought about growing up with that secret, with him festering in her mind, buried in a shallow grave of forgetfulness, she wanted to scream. She wanted to puke. She wanted to crawl off somewhere and drink herself blind. *My whole life. My whole life was a playground built on a toxic waste dump.*

Her teeth were starting to chatter. Her head snapped around to look behind her again.

Again.

No.

No. I'm not going to lose my mind. Not over that fucking sludgepile. No. Fucking. Way.

So she started to drag herself back from the edge. It was hard. God, it was the hardest thing she'd ever done.

Louis was watching the road, not looking at her at all. She wondered if he knew. If he did, she silently thanked him for giving her the time to save herself.

Then Amy found she could talk again. She found she had to talk, as if the words would spin a silvery web between her and Louis and keep her from sliding back into the pit.

Amy cleared her throat. "What was that thing that got Rags? That water thing?" Her voice felt strange in her mouth, as if it belonged to someone else.

He sighed, not taking his eyes off the road. "I'm not sure, Amy. If I had to guess, I'd say it was Xavier's spirit."

Amy stared at him. "His spirit? Like astral projection? Louis, you don't mean that he died—"

"No, Amy, he didn't die. You saw him. He was alive."

The little car shuddered, following a rut in the road. Amy shuddered too. "But those horrible convulsions . . . " She lay her forehead on her knees and bit her lip. *I won't cry again. I won't.*

Louis glanced at her, and attempted an encouraging smile. "I think that was his spirit coming back in."

"Oh." Amy looked up at the gray morning sky. She giggled, and was hit by a sudden wave of nausea. *He is near, somewhere near.* "Oh shit. I'm losing it." She giggled again.

"No." Louis' voice was loud, angry, tough. "You're not. If you do, he'll have you."

She rubbed her eyes, fighting off another bout of hysterical laughter. "You don't have to get pissy. I'm not gonna start drooling or anything." *Not now, anyway. You don't know how close I got . . .*

"Good."

She wasn't certain, but she thought he was suppressing a smile. She suddenly decided that she liked his smile very much. *Still like it, don't you mean, babe? You still like it, after all these years.* Only it hadn't made her want to nibble his lips when she was six.

"Louis?"

"Mm-hmm?"

"So what did you do to Rags? How did you burn him?"

Louis did smile that time, a slightly fierce, slightly sad smile. "A vever. I cut a vever into my palm, and smacked him upside the head with it."

Okay, sure. Why not. Amy smiled back at him. "What's a vay-ver?"

"It's a sacred symbol. A sacred Vaudun symbol, to be exact. The one I hit him with was the symbol of Baron Samedi, Lord of the Cemetery." Louis flexed his bleeding hand. "He just can't stand things that are supposed to be dead, but won't lie down and be polite."

"Oh," said Amy, not liking the sound of that at all. She leaned her head back on the seat. "Um, no offense, Louis, but don't you Voodoo guys go around popping the heads off of chickens and sticking pins in dolls and cursing people and stuff?" She snack a glance at him. His face was immobile, almost stiff. "Hey," she said quickly, "Not like I'm criticizing or anything . . . " *Shut up, Amy, you idiot.* She blushed.

Louis let out a burst of laughter that startled her. "Amy, of course we do! No chicken is safe! Lock up your Barbie dolls and your sewing kits!" He laughed again. "We get a lot of bad press, Ame. Although it's true that we sometimes sacrifice to the loa. Our gods have to eat."

Amy shuddered. "What . . . exactly . . . do they eat?"

"That depends on the god. Erzulie, the goddess of dreams and romantic love, enjoys champagne, candy, jewelry, and the sacrifice of a white dove. Baron Samedi likes rum, cigars, and black goats. Some want chickens. Some want pigs. Some are content with corn cakes. Others demand a bull."

Amy stared at her hands, clenched together in her lap. She shuddered.

"Amy? You okay?" Louis touched her shoulder lightly. Before she could stop herself, she twisted away.

"You're afraid of me," he said. The pain in his voice made her turn and look at him. He was staring at the road, eyes narrowed with hurt.

"Louis, no, I'm not." He shot her a look, and Amy immediately wanted her words back.

Don't lie to him. He saved your life. He deserves better. Amy looked at her hands again. Her fingers were turning white. "Okay. Maybe a little bit. It's just the sacrifice thing. It's creepy. It just seems . . . wrong."

The corner of Louis's mouth turned up. "Why?"

A little surprised, Amy had to think. "Well, I don't know, it just seems so awful to kill some poor animal in a ritual. It seems cruel."

"Are you a vegetarian?" When Amy glanced over at Louis, she saw his dark eyes were sparkling.

"No, but—"

"Do you know how many thousands of animals are slaughtered in America every year? Thousands, hell, millions. Not killed to bring you closer to God, Amy. Killed to become prime rib and hot dogs and head cheese."

"I love prime rib," Amy mumbled, feeling slightly guilty.

"So do every one of the fire-breathing televangelists who call Vaudun blasphemy and devil worship. I'm not saying that I like to kill animals. It's just necessary. And it's certainly no worse than what goes on in factory farms all over this country."

Amy sighed. "Point taken. It's just so totally . . . I don't know, alien I guess."

Louis smiled, his eyes a little sad. "I know. It must seem completely strange to you. But Amy, Vaudun is not a cult or a superstition. It's a religion. It's not dark and negative. It's about healing, dancing, singing, creating."

Amy grinned. "You're starting to sound a little like a televangelist yourself."

A flush crept up Louis's cheeks. "Sorry. It's just that people think such godawful things about Vaudun. Sometimes I get a little defensive."

Amy reached out and squeezed his forearm. He looked at her, eyes shy and hopeful. Something about that look made Amy's stomach flutter. "I'm sorry, Louis. I didn't mean to hurt you."

"I know." For a moment, his fingers rested on hers. "I don't blame you at all."

"So, educate me." Amy smiled at him. "What did you mean about getting closer to God?"

Louis's whole body seemed to relax. "The Vaudun gods, called the loa, are very accessible to us. When we give them offerings and sacrifices, we make them strong. When they're strong, they can come to us during the ceremonies."

"You mean, they actually turn up in church?" *Well, why the hell not. Reality has turned out to be one big mind-fuck anyway.* Amy shoved the unpleasant thought aside.

"They do. At some point during the dancing and singing and drumming, the loa being honored will ride one of the congregation. Possess them."

Amy grimaced, remembering the twitching rats. "Oh, shit."

Louis laughed. "Not like in *The Exorcist.* It's an honor to be possessed by a god. The person doesn't get hurt, and the god can touch and talk to his followers. He can eat and drink and dance, answer questions, help people. It's a good deal for everybody."

"Wow. Have you ever been possessed?"

Louis nodded. "Many times. But I don't remember it. Nobody ever does."

Amy decided not to think about it too much. "So," she said, changing the subject, "If Voodoo's real, can't you just put a curse on Rags? I'll make the doll if you'll bring the pins." She was only half kidding.

Louis shook his head. "Dolls, curses, they're not Vaudun. They have as much to do with my religion as the implements of a black mass have to do with Catholicism. See, there are people who use the powers of Vaudun for their own reasons without practicing the religion. They're called bocors. Black magicians. They're the ones who curse people and leave pin-punctured dolls on their enemies' doorsteps. No houngan would ever do such a thing. Not ever."

A chill touched the back of Amy's neck, although the temperature of the car was rising with the sun. "Bocor. I've heard that word before. Rags said Mr. Iris was a bocor."

Louis nodded. "That's what Mama told me, too."

Amy rubbed her eyes. "What do you suppose he wanted with Rags, Louis?"

"My guess is that Rags' presence gave his rituals more power. He acted as a magic amplifier, so to speak."

Amy filled with sudden anger at the old man. "Magic for what? What was the twisted old fuck trying to accomplish?"

Louis snorted. "Oh, the usual, I'm sure. Wealth. Power. Life extension. Bocors are petrified of death."

"Aren't we all," Amy muttered.

"They have good reason to be. A bocor has selfishly used and usurped so much power, become so indebted to the loas without ever giving anything back—they have a lot to settle up at the end of their lives." Amy was surprised to see Louis shiver.

"I hope the Bad Karma Fairy gives it to him with both barrels," she said.

Louis laughed. "You have such a way with words, Amy."

She grinned back at him, wondering why he made her feel so good.

"But you houngans are chock full o' good karma, right?"

"Yup. Even us apprentice houngans."

Amy rolled her eyes. "Apprentice Voodoo priests. Dropout shamans. Where the hell's Van Helsing when I need him?"

"Peter Cushing's dead, Amy."

Somehow, it wasn't all that funny.

Xavier.

Her voice caught. "Do you think he'll be all right?" she whispered. She couldn't say his name; she would cry if she did. But Louis knew.

"I think so. I hope so. But he would have died if we'd tried to move him, Amy."

"I know." She bit her lip, thinking of Xavier's ash-gray skin. *And that security guard. He didn't look any older than me. She fought back the image of the young man's nose exploding in a spray of blood. And the nurse. Are they alive? Dead? Oh God, I drew him there. He wouldn't have hurt those people if I hadn't been in the hospital.* Amy bit her lip, hard. *And the old man. That poor old man, he was just there to enjoy the beauty of the sunrise, the wonder of the birds and the bats . . .*

Amy shivered, and wondered how the same world that held such beauty could hold a monster like Rags. She rested her cheek on her knees and looked out the window for a long while.

TWENTY-ONE

Rags lay perfectly still. He was curled up in the crawlspace beneath Amy's apartment building, and he was afraid. Afraid that the Brown Man would come back.

He hadn't felt such pain since Virginia nearly killed him, years before. The jaws of the spirit-dog had ripped chunk after chunk of his flesh away and then swallowed them. *Swallowed them, how fucking dare he!* The god damn coyote-thing seemed to absorb his flesh, getting bigger and stronger with each bite. Rags had been certain he was going to die.

His strength had failed him, and, still in the grip of the water coyote, he spiraled toward the earth. He hadn't feared the impact; he could reform himself. He had feared being on the ground with the thing that was ripping him to pieces. He imagined it planting impossible paws on his shoulders, and feasting on his face . . .

And then, a miracle. The coyote stopped rending him. Its head tossed back and forth, as if it were in pain. It let out a gurgling howl. Suddenly, it wasn't there any more.

The spirit-coyote broke up into a thousand shimmering drops of water, which whirled and danced and formed into a small, black thundercloud. Still falling, Rags watched it as it got farther and farther away. There was a blinding flash of lightening, and even the cloud was gone.

Then he hit the ground.

Messy, yes, painful, certainly, but really no big deal. He just stayed flat for awhile, creeping along the ground like a slime mold, hoping no humans saw him. He had the luck to have fallen into a park, one of the few green spots in this desolate, God-forsaken desert land. The grass lent him cover as he oozed along.

Rags wondered if anyone had seen him in the air with the Brown Man's spirit. If he'd had a mouth at the moment, he might have smiled. The idea was almost funny. They'd be telling the story for years, about how they saw a man-bat or a demon or an alien or whatever the fuck their puny human brains interpreted him to be. Probably the biggest thrill of their pathetic lives.

Just the same, he didn't want to be discovered. He sank into the cool, dark ground. It felt wonderful. He hated being out in the daylight. The sun burned his skin and made little pieces of him dry up and flake off. Underground he could liquefy and flow through the ancient layers of the Earth, where no one could find him, and no one could hurt him.

He hoped.

Why had the Brown Man let him go, he wondered? He knew that the shaman would have killed him if he could. If he had kept ripping Rags' flesh away, he certainly would have. The Brown Man's body must have started to fail, and his spirit was forced to return to it.

That's the only reason I'm alive.

The thought infuriated him.

I should go back there and kill him. But the truth was, he didn't want to. He didn't want to get anywhere near the Brown Man. For a few absurd moments, he wanted to run back home to the Irises, to slip inside his jar of glass, to view the world through its cold, familiar, utterly safe distortion. He wanted comfort. He wanted love. He wanted Amy.

And so he had flowed beneath the surface of the earth until he had reached her home, and here he was, cowering in the darkness like a frightened baby. Rags thrashed angrily. He formed himself into his manshape, and discovered that he was much smaller than he had been before. The spirit-dog had taken a great deal of his body. That upset him even more.

"Amy, Amy," he moaned, as he thrashed in the crawlspace like a worm on hot cement. He imagined her hair, her face, her delicious, curved body.

That's when he got the idea.

Becoming Amy was the sweetest, most erotic thing he had ever done. Ecstatic, he formed his hips into soft curves, caused breasts to bud from his chest. He made hair, soft and blond, sprout from his head in a golden cascade. Her eyes were even green, like his! Delighted, he ran his hands over his/Amy's body. It wasn't as good as touching her, but it was pretty damn good.

What would she think, he wondered? Surely she couldn't be scared of herself. He decided to go inside and wait for her.

He knew he had blown it at the hospital. He had frightened her, threatened her. *You were a total asshole.* He inwardly winced as he flowed up through the waterpipes toward her apartment. He never seemed to act the way he wanted to around her. His emotions overwhelmed him, and the hunger, the hunger . . .

Best not to think about that.

He came up from the sink in the bathroom in a green, burbling gush, and reformed his Amy-self lying on the dirty tiles.

He could smell the other one. Sarah. His eyes narrowed with jealousy. Amy loved her. Amy trusted her. Amy was never, ever afraid of Sarah. He suddenly feared Sarah had a part of Amy that he would never have, could never even get close to. An idea was forming in his mind.

Rags slipped from the bathroom in his naked-Amy form and quietly opened the door to Amy's room. For a moment he just stood there, breathing in her scent, bathing in her beautiful, utterly clean aura. He lay down in her bed and rolled, glorying in her presence. The whole room had a soft amethyst glow, it was so saturated with her.

He opened her dresser drawer and pulled out a pair of violet cotton panties. He stared at them for a moment, then rubbed his Amy-face on them. He giggled, wondering what Sarah would think if she saw.

"Oh, Sarah," he said quietly. The manvoice sounded ridiculous, bizarre, coming through his soft girl's lips.

Rags scowled and adjusted his vocal chords. "Amy," he said. It was still too deep, so he tried again. "Amy, Amy."

He stretched and pulled, thickened and thinned, but he couldn't get it right. Amy's sweet voice, its clear tones and merry lilt, were beyond him.

Oh well. I didn't really want to talk *to Sarah, anyway.*

Rags took a short, red cotton dress from Amy's closet and pulled it on. It was way too tight across the chest. He realized he had made her breasts too big, and pulled them in a bit. Perfect.

Rags walked out into the hall, trying to move like Amy did. It was impossible, of course, but he did a better job of walking than he did of talking. He paused in front of Sarah's door. He started to knock, but thought better of it. He quietly turned the knob, and slipped inside.

Sarah was sleeping, tangled in her faded red sheets, all alone.

Rags smiled hugely with Amy's face and crawled into bed with her. He snuggled up close, marveling over Sarah's warm, soft, voluptuous flesh. She murmured and rolled over, opening her brown eyes a slit.

Sarah smiled, not fully awake. "Ame! When did they release you?" She pushed a tangle of curls off of her forehead. "I would have picked you up, silly. How did you get here?"

Rags buried his face in her neck, glorying in her sweet girlsmell. Sarah wrapped her arms around him.

"It's all right, honey, it's all right," she whispered. She was stroking his Amy hair, patting his slim back. "I'm so sorry he hurt you. God, I'm sorry." Sarah's voice caught.

She feels guilty. She introduced that fucker Shane to my Amy. She should feel guilty. Rags held her tighter, his sensual feelings draining away, being replaced by something darker.

"Hey!" Sarah giggled, trying to pry his arms loose. "Don't squeeze me so hard, girlfriend. I'm not going anywhere. You're right here with me. You're safe." She pulled Rags' head away from her neck, looking into his eyes.

Sarah's brow knit, ever so slightly. "Your eyes look funny. Did they give you a trank or something?"

Rags seized her head and pressed his mouth to hers. Sarah's eyes widened in surprise. She giggled, caught totally off guard. "What are you doing, Ame?"

He kissed her harder, opening her mouth with his. He touched the roof of her mouth with his tongue, tickling, as his hand slid up to her breast.

Sarah abruptly pushed him away. Her face was a fascinating blend of confusion, worry, and just a little excitement. "Amy . . . honey, you've been through something awful. You don't know what you're doing. I love you to death, but—"

He grabbed her again, harder, jamming his hand down between her legs, feeling the silk of her panties. He began rippling with excitement. He was having trouble holding on to the Amyform.

Sarah gasped and grabbed his hand. "Amy, stop it!" She grasped his shoulder just as another ripple passed through him, making his flesh jump and twist.

Sarah screamed.

No longer even trying to hold the Amyform, Rags slapped a long, webbed hand over Sarah's mouth. The terror in her eyes was delicious. He knew how he must look—like a version of Amy from some late-night horror flick about mutant pod-people. He decided to play it up, causing green eruptions on his skin, making thrashing vines boil out of his mouth.

Beneath his hand, Sarah's muffled screams became shrill, mindless.

He heaved himself on top of her, loving the feel of her thrashing body. Rags caused something long and hard and lumpy to grow between his legs. It poked out from under the hem of Amy's dress as he rubbed it against Sarah, pressing it against her crotch, making sure she felt it too.

Her eyes rolled up, and her eyelids fluttered.

"Oh, no you don't," he muttered, and slapped her hard across the face.

Her eyes flew open and she sucked in air through her nose. She began to thrash and buck wildly beneath him.

This was going to be a lot more fun than he had bargained for.

TWENTY-TWO

Amy uncurled herself as Louis pulled the little car up to the curb in front of her apartment. He cut the engine, and turned slowly to Amy. "He could be in there, you know."

"I know. We have to warn Sarah."

Louis's eyes shone. "My God, you're strong, Amy."

"Which god?" She winked at him. He shook his head and mock-frowned at her, trying not to laugh.

Amy leaned her head against the seat, looking into his dark, warm eyes. "Listen, Louis. I'm sorry I gave you shit about the Voodoo thing. I didn't know any better. And I guess it's really none of my business anyway."

To her surprise, he took her hand. "Of course it's your business. I've just intruded into your life, Amy. You have a right to know everything about me." His gaze was steady and open.

Amy squeezed his hand gently. "Yeah, but it's got to hurt when people think your religion is some kind of psycho devil worship."

Louis's mouth quirked at the corners. "I'm used to it by now. It only bothers me when it's someone I care—someone whose opinion I care about." He released her hand and seemed suddenly interested in the dashboard.

"I'm sorry if I hurt you," she said. *And I'm not totally sure yet, but I think I care about you, too.*

"Nah. Let's go."

They climbed out of the Geo. Amy looked up at the pale, delicate eggshell blue of the early morning sky. She didn't want to go into that apartment. Not at all.

"Louis? One last question?"

"Anything."

"What about zombies? Are they for real, or what?"

He shut the driver's side door and looked at her over the top of the tiny car. "Do you really want to know?"

Amy thought about it.

"Nope."

They climbed the short flight of stairs in silence. Little tremors shot up and down Amy's spine. She shoved her hands in her pockets to keep them from shaking. Her stomach was filled with manic, twitching butterflies.

The complex was like a thousand others; two stories, long buildings like a cheap motel, patches of ratty, half-dead grass and a tiny swimming pool. *And right now, it feels like Dracula's fucking castle.*

Amy was fishing in her pocket for her keys when Louis cautiously put out his hand and touched the door. It swung open.

Amy's heart gave a painful kick and started pounding. She pushed the door open a little further.

The apartment was dim. The early morning light was barely filtering through the coarse, cheap curtains. "Sarah?" Amy called. Her voice was shaking. There was no answer.

"Louis?" she asked. Her voice sounded loud in her ears, although she was whispering. "Can you tell? Is he here?"

"I don't know. He's been here. He's left his . . . his trail all over the place. I can't get through it to find out. Amy—there's a lot of fear."

Amy nodded. She couldn't make anything come through her mouth but a shuddering sigh. She squinted, as if she were walking into a heavy duststorm, and went through the doorway.

Even in the gloom, it was obvious that the front room was trashed. Not one piece of furniture was standing upright. The posters had been ripped from the walls. The television was smashed, its screen a gaping, toothy hole.

Amy looked around, stunned. The room flashed with brilliant light, showing the damage in lurid detail. Did Louis have a camera? She turned to look at him. No, he was just standing there. Again, the room flooded with bright light. *No, it's just your rotten fucking brain.*

Amy heard herself start to cry. She grabbed Louis's hand and squeezed so hard it hurt her.

"Sarah?" she called. "Mick? Is anybody here? Sarah, please! Please . . . "

"Quiet." Louis was holding up his hand, his head cocked. "Listen."

Amy froze, trembling. She could only hear the hiss of air through her lungs, so she stopped breathing.

There it was. A whimper, tiny and lost.

"Sarah!" Amy called, Her sweaty palm slipped out of Louis', and she darted forward. In a frenzy, she threw open Sarah's bedroom door. Sarah was nowhere in sight.

"Sarah!" Amy screamed. "Sarah, answer me, god damn it!"

There was a muffled sob from behind the bed. Amy rushed over. *Oh god, oh please don't let her be dying, not Sarah, not my friend . . .*

Sarah sat on the floor with her back to the wall, cradling Mick's limp body in her arms. She screamed when she saw Amy.

"Sarah, Sarah, what's wrong? What happened?" Amy cried, squatting down next to her friend. Sarah pulled away from her.

"Sarah, it's me! It's Amy! Tell me what happened!" Sarah slowly turned her face to Amy. She stared at her, eyes huge and hurt.

"Amy?" she whispered. "Is it you? For real?" Fear flashed across her face like lightning. "Let me see your eyes! Now!"

She grasped Amy's face with both hands, staring. Amy smiled at her, wishing with all her heart that she could take the hurt away. After a moment, Sarah's face crumpled, and she started to cry.

"Of course, of course it's me, baby. It's Amy. It's your best friend." She slipped her arms around Sarah. Sarah rested her head on Amy's shoulder.

"What happened, Sarah? Tell me, you have to tell me."

Sarah blinked puffy eyes. "I . . . I was still asleep, 'cause Mick and I were up so late with you and stuff, and then I woke up, because you came in, and—" Sarah's voice ended in a constricted squeak.

Amy held her and waited. She looked down at Mick, afraid of what she would see. He was bruised and bloody, but the soft rise and fall of his chest made Amy weak with relief.

Sarah gulped in air. "And anyway, you came in and lay down next to me, and then you started kissing me, and I was laughing because I didn't know what to do but you were all lumpy and wrong and I screamed and then you changed into—into—Oh God it wasn't you Amy, I don't know what. You—it—tried to rape me. It hurt me . . . " She sniffed, wiping her eyes on the rumpled sleeve of her sweatshirt. "And anyway then Mick came in and started hitting it with the lamp, and it slapped him across the room, just like that . . . Oh God, that thing was coming for me, then it just stopped and screamed your name, and it flew, it flew Amy, it flew away . . . " Sarah stared into the gloom, eyes huge.

"Sarah, I don't know where to start, oh, no, I'm so sorry—"

Sarah screamed and started to scoot along the floor, trying to get out from under Mick.

Amy looked up and saw Louis standing in the doorway. "Sarah!" she shouted. "Sarah, it's all right. That's my friend. He saved me from the bad thing. He won't hurt you, I promise."

It took some time to quiet Sarah, but she finally allowed Louis into the room. She still stared at him with open suspicion, and protested when he hauled Mick onto the bed.

"No, no, it's OK," Amy reassured. "He can help him. He can heal people. Like Xavier."

"Xavier . . . " Sarah sat up straight, looking around, as if she had just awakened. "I went to the hospital to see you, but they wouldn't let me, and then Xavier called me, with his mind. I went to him, and he looked so terrible, and he started to tell me—tell me about that thing, and God, I didn't believe him . . . and then they threw me out. Amy, did you see Xavier? Is he—all right?"

"Yes," Amy lied. "He's OK. He saved my life tonight."

Mick groaned. Both women whirled around to see.

Sarah let out a little squeak. A soft blue light, barely visible, surrounded Mick's head. The light appeared to be suspended between

Louis' outstretched hands. Louis's brow was furrowed, his face rigid with concentration.

"What's he doing?" she whispered.

"Helping." Amy reached for her friend's hand.

Mick's eyes opened as the strange light faded. He sat bolt upright, nearly knocking Louis off the edge of the bed.

"Who the hell are you?" Mick raised his fist.

"No!" Amy and Sarah shouted. Mick stared at them with red, bleary eyes. His hand crept up to the cross around his neck, his fingers curling around it and clutching.

Amy sighed, feeling like she could sleep for days. "Okay. Sit down, Sarah. Be quiet, Mick. I have to tell you about this."

Louis touched her face, then got up and backed away. Amy was silently grateful. She knew it was going to be hard enough, and Mick was looking at Louis with a strange mixture of distrust and curiosity.

Amy pushed her hair out of her eyes. *This is harder than I thought.*

Sarah patted Amy's leg. "You can do it, blondie."

Amy was pierced through the heart by her friend's concern, especially after what she had just been through. *Let's go, Amy. You owe it to them.*

"That thing is my fault." There. I said it. "It followed me here. From Florida. I grew up with it." It sounded so ridiculous that she nearly laughed, but Sarah's trusting, worried face wouldn't let her. Amy shut her eyes and started from the beginning, when she was a little girl and rescued Peter Pan from a scummy swimming pool . . .

Amy wasn't sure how much time had passed, but the sunlight trickling through the mud-brown curtains was much stronger. Louis had fixed coffee and scrounged up some stale donuts, but they sat on Sarah's nighttable untouched. Mick and Sarah were staring at her in the suddenly oppressive silence.

"What are we going to do?" Sarah finally asked.

Amy shook her head. "What you're going to do is take Mick and leave town. It's only after me. And it's hurt you enough."

"You have to come with us!" Sarah's voice was high and strained. "You can't stay here, Amy. Don't be stupid." She turned to Mick for support. He was sitting bolt-upright on the bed, eyes a million miles away, still clutching the cross.

"I wish it were that simple." Amy took one of the donuts and began picking the rainbow sprinkles off of it. "That thing tracked me down from across the country. It has a—a link to me, Sarah. It'll find me wherever I go."

"We'll call the cops!" Sarah stood up and began pacing. "We'll tell them you're being stalked. It's the truth! We don't have to tell them—"

"Tell them what, Sarah?" Mick's voice was quiet, in a way that was somehow terrible. "Tell them her stalker is some kind of monster? A monster that can change into other people and has superhuman strength and can fucking FLY?" The last word was a strangled shout. Mick leapt up from the bed and stormed from the room. Amy heard him crunch through glass in the living room, kick something heavy with a strangled curse.

Sarah started to follow, then turned back to Amy. "I guess he's right." She tugged at her bangs, twisting the hair around her fingers. Her eyes were shiny, bright and glittering. "Okay, no cops. Besides, they wouldn't do anything even if he was human. What proof do we have? None!"

Amy watched Sarah pace like a trapped animal, wondering what was going on in her head. *You know what's going on. She's been mindfucked almost as thoroughly as you have. She's trying to keep from howling like a dog.* Amy turned to look at Louis. He was sitting on the floor by the dresser, watching Sarah closely. He looked worried. Amy was strangely touched.

"We have to find someone who'll believe us. Who'll believe us?" Sarah ran her hands through her hair, then did it again. "I know! I know! We'll go on a talk show!" She laughed, a shrill giggle.

Amy snorted. "C'mon, Sarah."

"No, really! They'll believe us. Ricki Lake will believe anything! And you'll be safe there! He wouldn't hurt you on national TV! Hah! Then some white supremacist group might kill him!" She shrieked with laughter.

"Shut up, Sarah! Shut the hell up!" Mick was standing in the doorway, fists clenched, trembling with rage.

She froze, a strand of dark hair twisted around her forefinger. Her eyes narrowed. "What is your fucking problem?"

"My fucking problem, Sarah, is that you're talking like a moron. My fucking problem is that some supernatural fucking freak tried to rip my head off, and you're babbling about fucking Ricki Lake!" He spun around and smashed his fist into the flimsy wall, leaving a bloody dent in the pale yellow wallpaper.

Louis stood up, took a step toward Mick.

"Get away from me," Mick snarled. He walked stiffly out of the room and slammed the door behind him.

"Oh, shit." Sarah flopped down on the bed. She started twisting strands of her hair again. Amy saw that her hands were shaking.

"There's no time for this," Louis said quietly. "Amy and I have a job to do. We have to go to Florida."

Amy knew what he was going to say. She knew it like she knew her own name, so she said it for him.

"We have to destroy it," she said. "Destroy its heart." She was surprised at the steadiness of her voice. Louis looked at her, eyes wide with surprise. And maybe a little admiration.

Amy took a deep breath. "We have to. Because if we don't, it'll never, ever leave me alone."

She sat on the bed next to Sarah, putting her arms around her very best friend. "You have to leave until it's over, Sarah. You and Mick. Because he'll go right through you to get me."

Sarah's head slipped down to rest on Amy's shoulder for a moment. Amy felt hot tears on the sleeve of her T-shirt. She brought her hand up to the back of Sarah's head, stroking the soft, curly hair. "It'll be okay," she whispered. "Go stay with Mick's folks in Washington State for a few days. They love you to pieces."

Sarah raised her head, red-rimmed eyes looking into Amy's.

"No."

Amy took Sarah's face in her hands. "You don't mean that," she said.

Sarah frowned. "The hell I don't. I—I want to come with you. I want to help."

Amy sighed. "I love you for offering, Sarah. But this isn't your fight."

Sarah pulled herself upright, eyes bright with anger. "How could you say that to me? We've been friends since we were in the fourth grade. We're practically sisters."

"Sarah—"

"Be quiet and listen to me, Amy. Do you think I could ever sleep again if I just let you go? That's not what—what sisters do." Sarah slipped her arms around Amy's neck. "Besides, I want to see it die. I'm terrified, Amy. But I don't think . . . I don't think I can live in a world where that thing exists, too."

Amy's eyes filled with tears as she looked at Sarah.

Mick opened the door. He stood and stared for a moment, then started clapping his hands. "That was beautiful, Sarah. Really. Just tell me one thing, okay? How are you going to kill it? How are you even gonna find it? It can change its fucking shape! Probably into anything! It could be above you, below you, behind you, *ladies,* and it could tear your goddam heart out of your chest before you even got a good look at it! For shit's sake, *grow up!*"

Sarah was across the room and in Mick's face in a heartbeat.

"Why are you being such an asshole, huh? I'm sorry the big nasty monster hurt you, Mick. But you know what? It hurt me too." She pushed up the sleeves of her T-shirt, showing livid purple finger marks. Hauled her shirt up under her breasts to show the scratches and deep bruises on her stomach.

"It didn't just hurt me, Mick, it tried to fuck me. It tried to ram this knotted, twisted, thing inside me. You wanna see what it did to the inside of my thighs?"

Her face was red with anger, hands clenched into fists. Mick took a step back.

"No, babe, I—"

"No. You don't. So just go back into the living room and sulk for awhile, or better yet, get the hell out. We have a job to do."

Mick retreated another step from Sarah's blazing stare. He sagged against the doorframe, and slowly sank down to the floor.

"I'm sorry." His voice was soft, strained from fighting back tears. "I'm being a fuck. I know. But Sarah . . . "

She knelt down in front of him, resting her hand on his knee. He looked up at her, cheeks streaked with tears.

"I know you thought the Catholic thing was weird. But it gave me a center. It made me steady. But now . . . now the rug's been pulled out from under me." He wiped his eyes with the backs of his hands like a little boy.

All the anger seemed to have drained away from Sarah, and she stroked Mick's hair. Amy watched them, feeling like an intruder. They were oblivious, lost in each other.

"Sarah, I thought I knew what things were about. I thought I knew about good and evil. But I don't know shit. I mean, how can that thing exist? How can God let it exist? Oh, Jesus. Oh, Jesus."

Mick hung his head. "What if I was wrong? About everything?"

Join the club, baby, Amy thought, then immediately felt guilty.

Louis moved over to stand by the bed next to Amy, sympathy etched on his finely-made features.

"Maybe it's a challenge, Mick. Maybe it's a test. Or maybe God just can't be concerned with problems as small as a creeping slime mold with a will to live. But if you lose your faith now, you'll never know."

"I'm scared," said Mick miserably. "I've never been so scared in my whole life." Sarah put her arms around him, and he clung to her.

"I know," said Louis. "So am I. But you have to decide what you're going to do, and soon. Nobody is safe here. Either come with us, or get out of town for awhile. Nobody will blame you if you do."

"Sarah," Mick murmured into her hair, "Please don't go with them. Please."

"I have to," she said, and kissed his cheek. "I have to help Amy. And I have to see that thing die. I have to, or I'll go nuts, Mick."

He let out a deep, shuddering sigh, almost a groan. "Then I have to." He stood up, pulling Sarah up with him. They clung to each other as if trying to weather a windstorm.

Amy felt something tear in her chest. *Oh God, I want them with me more than anything, but if something happens—*

She felt Louis's warmth right next to her, and silently took his hand.

If something happens to them, happens to Sarah, I'll die.

"Okay," said Mick, voice gruff, trying to regain his dignity. "Okay, fine, we're going to go kill this thing. Do we have the first goddam idea how to do that?"

"Yes, we do," Louis said, squeezing Amy's hand. "But let's talk about it later, okay? It could decide to come back any time. We have to be ready."

Sarah untangled herself from Mick and bounded over to Amy. "Let's pack!" Her eyes were fever-bright and danced with manic energy.

Part of Amy wanted to put her foot down, give Sarah an ultimatum, talk or threaten or plead her into going away with Mick, going somewhere safe.

But God help me, I don't have the strength.

I want her with me.

And I have to live with that.

The men cleaned up the living room in silence as Amy and Sarah threw clothes into Sarah's old floral suitcases, chatting about anything that would distract them.

They were packed, ready, Amy's hand reaching for the doorknob, when the doorbell rang.

TWENTY-THREE

Cool. Green, cool. Feels better. Better, yes.

He lay on his side beneath the surface of the water, curled up like the fetus he never really was. One of his knees rested against his savaged cheek, which had split open again after he fled Amy's apartment. The skin of his kneecap began to grow into his face, and he gently pulled it away. One of his hands was wrapped around his throat, the other held his crotch. He sighed. The unneeded air passed through his lips and broke the surface of the water. He looked up at the bubbles, shimmering against the green canopy of the vines that shrouded the ornamental pool where he lay.

He had run.

He was hiding like a spooked guppy in the fountain of an office complex.

But I did it for her. She loves me. I know she loves me.

Why doesn't she know it yet? I've showed her and showed her and showed her.

He shifted on the bottom of the pool, remembering a time not so very long ago, the second time he was a child. He remembered the pain, and the exhaustion, and the utter, utter despair. It was so hard, the coming back. He saw himself as a hunched, lumpy, sticky little creature, unformed and ugly, curled up in the corner of a big, fancy house, wishing himself dead.

"Amy," moaned the little creature. "Amy . . . "

Mrs. Iris bent over him, red-smeared mouth bowed up into a smile. "Oh, honey. What's wrong?"

"Want . . . Amy . . ." he forced the thick tongue to push the words from the ragged hole in his face.

"Oh, sweetheart!" Mrs. Iris clapped her hands and laughed. "You'll have her, my little Rag-bag. When you're big and strong and all-fixed-better, you'll go to her. Then you'll show that girl how much you love her. If you just show her, honey-bunny, really show her how much you care, well . . . " The red mouth pursed in coquettish amusement. "Well, then, she'll have to love you, too! Now won't she! Now won't she, oo big stwong boy!"

Then Mrs. Iris had scooped him up into her arms, placed him on the altar, and fed him sips of goat's blood. He smiled, remembering, and sucked water in a liquid sigh. Bits of algae slipped through his teeth like krill in the mouth of a baleen whale.

It had to be right, what she told me. Because I saw it on the TV, too. I saw it over and over again. I just have to show her some more. That's all.

But I keep messing up.

An emotion was burning him like acid, dripping into his guts, eating him from the inside out. He gradually recognized it as shame. He hadn't been able to finish it with Sarah. He wanted her, he wanted her in every way, but then—

But then you got scared, that's what. He winced, flesh contracting inward. The surface of the pond rippled, just a little. *You were afraid that if you did that to Sarah, Amy would hate you. Hate you forever.*

And I couldn't live if she hated me. I wouldn't want to.

That was noble, wasn't it? Then why did a little voice continue to nag him, calling him impotent, weak, pitiful?

It was all so confusing.

TWENTY-FOUR

Amy yanked her hand away from the doorknob like it was a snake. Louis took her upper arm protectively.

"What the fuck?" muttered Mick. Sarah clutched her suitcase to her chest, eyes wide.

Amy stood on her toes and looked through the peephole. All she could see was the glare of the sun, still creeping up from the horizon.

"Who is it?" Her voice was shaking.

"Police. Would you open the door, please, Miss?" The voice was gravelly and deep.

"No! Don't do it, Amy! It might be him!" Sarah's eyes were huge with fear.

Louis shook his head. "No. He wouldn't bother to knock."

"Make him show his badge," whispered Mick.

"Show me your I.D., please," Amy said to the door. her heart was hammering, her stomach an icy knot.

The glint of light from the peephole vanished. Amy looked through again. Bony fingers were holding up a badge and identification card in a black folder. Amy couldn't read the name, but it looked real enough.

"Just a second," she called.

Amy turned to her friends, shaking. "What do we do?" she whispered.

Louis leaned in close, voice soft, making the others lean in, too. "Take the suitcases into the bedroom. We don't want to deal with questions about that. Mick and Sarah, stay in the bedroom. If the cop realizes you're here, tell him you spent the night, Mick, and you and Sarah just woke up. I'll answer the questions about me and Amy. Okay?"

Mick started to say something, but Amy thrust her suitcase into his hands and gestured toward Sarah's room.

"Miss?" The policeman sounded worried, and maybe a little edgy. "Miss, open the door, please. We just want to make sure you're all right."

Mick and Sarah left the room. With Louis right behind her, Amy turned the doorknob.

The man at the door was tall and slim, in his mid fifties. He had thick black hair, buzzed short, and small, bright-blue eyes. His long face was lined, the skin thickened by years in the blasting sun.

He looked Amy and Louis up and down, then glanced around the apartment.

Thank God we cleaned it up, thought Amy. *I hope he doesn't see the damn TV.*

"Are you Amy Sullivan?" asked the cop, unsmiling.

"Yes," she said, wondering if she should have added a "sir."

"Detective Paul Blythe. May I come in?"

"Um, sure." Amy stepped aside. The detective walked in, eyes scanning like bird of prey's.

He stopped in the middle of the living room and turned back to her as she closed the door. His hand came up to his throat, and he adjusted the knot on his dark-blue tie. Amy wondered if he were hot in his blue pants and long-sleeved, starched, white shirt.

"Did you leave Desert Samaritan hospital this morning?" he asked, pinning Amy down with his stare.

"Yes," she said. *The less I say, the less chance I have to fuck up . . .*

"Why exactly did you leave? You weren't released."

Think think think think think

"I heard a big crash, and some screaming and stuff. I panicked. I had to get out of there." *Not bad, Amy, honey.*

"Uh-huh." Detective Blythe had produced a small notebook and was scribbling into it. "Sir, are you Louis Bouvier?"

"Yes, I am." Louis's gaze was firm and unwavering.

"Are you an employee of the hospital, Mr. Bouvier?"

"No, sir. I'm interning there as a crisis counselor."

The detective tapped his pen on the notepad. "Were you at the hospital with Miss Sullivan?"

"Yes."

"And is it hospital policy to allow non-staff interns to remove patients from the facility?" Blythe's stare was merciless.

Louis shook his head. "I didn't take Amy out of the hospital. I had finished my shift and stopped by to see her when she got scared. She was going to leave with or without me. I just gave her a ride home."

Damn, he's good, thought Amy.

"And what is your relationship to Miss Sullivan?"

"I'm a friend of the family. Our parents knew each other."

The raptor gaze was on Amy again. "Did you see anything unusual as you and Mr. Bouvier left the hospital, Miss Sullivan?"

"No. I just got out of there as fast as I could."

"Did either of you hear gunshots?"

"I— think so," said Amy. "I'm not sure. I was really scared."

"Yes," said Louis. "Four of them."

The detective paused to write. His head cocked up to look at Amy. For a moment, he said nothing. She found herself shifting from foot to foot. She was dying to ask about the victims of Rags' attack; the nurse, security guard and elderly patient, but she knew she couldn't. Not without opening a crack in her credibility that could never be sealed. She continued to fidget.

"Why were you in the hospital, Miss Sullivan."

She looked down at the grungy carpet. "I was assaulted."

"By whom?"

Amy's stomach tightened with anger. You must know that, asshole. "A guy I was going out with. Shane Matthews."

"Uh-huh. What exactly happened?"

Amy took a deep breath. *Shit, I don't want to talk about this.* "He tried to rape me. When I struggled, he hit me."

Blythe's eyes seemed to soften, just a little. "I know this is hard for you, Miss Sullivan. The rape kit that was run on you at the hospital turned up negative. What stopped the attack from being completed?"

Oh God, think fast—

"Some guys—some guys came and grabbed Shane. He—I'm not sure, but I think he was into, you know, drugs." *Oh, man. That sucked.*

"I see. Is there any particular reason you referred to Mr. Matthews in the past tense?" Blythe tapped the pen on his lower lip, one eyebrow raised.

Amy's heart froze.

"I told her he was dead. She was panicking, she thought he was coming to get her. I knew the guy was dead because I heard one of the doctors talking about it." Louis's face was earnest and a little worried. "Was that all right?"

Shit, he deserves an Oscar nomination.

Blythe looked a little irritated. "Um, yes, Mr. Bouvier. You did nothing wrong. Miss Sullivan, did you actually see any of Shane Matthews' attackers?"

Amy wrapped her arms around herself. "Oh, geez, not really. I was kind of, you know, freaking out. They were a bunch of white guys, I guess, about our age. One of them had on a Raiders T-shirt." Amy tried to look helpful.

Detective Blythe scowled, clearly not pleased. He put his notebook away and pulled a business card from his pants pocket.

"If you remember anything more, I'd appreciate it if you'd call me."

"Oh, sure," said Amy, taking it from him. She opened the door.

Detective Blythe gave her a long, intent stare that made her feel like she had ants under her skin.

"Good morning, Miss Sullivan. Mr. Bouvier."

He strode off down the concrete stairs, fishing for a cigarette.

Amy closed the door and leaned against it, eyes closed. "Holy shit," she breathed.

Sarah poked her head around the corner like a ruffled meerkat. "Is he gone?"

"Yes," said Louis, looking worried. "Let's get the hell out of here."

After locking up the apartment, the four crammed into Louis's Metro and swung by Mick's apartment so he could get some things together. Amy was suddenly curious to see Louis's place, but he already had a small bag, packed and ready, in the tiny trunk of the car. They headed for the airport. Less than three hours later, they were on the plane.

TWENTY-FIVE

Rags closed his eyes and concentrated on healing his face. He pulled a little of the water into his flesh, but rejected it. It was too lifeless. He slowly took his hand from his throat, and touched the lilies that grew on the surface of the fountain. No. They were too solid.

Rags slipped one finger into the water intake. The finger stretched, growing porous. His brow knitted as he produced cilia and began to scrape the alga from the walls of the tube.

It took a long time, but he filled in the missing flesh from his face. He rubbed it, feeling something that he was fairly certain was fear.

It wouldn't grow back. Why wouldn't it grow back?

The Voodoo Man and the Indian hurt him in a way he hadn't been hurt for many, many years. He was still missing mass from where the spirit-dog had ripped away his flesh.

Rags flattened out on the bottom of the fountain, stingray-like. He shifted his eyes to the top of his head. A fat orange and silver koi swam lazily above him. Rags extruded a long, funnel-shaped tube from his face, filling it with wicked spines like sharks' teeth. *Closer, closer . . .*

In a flash he sucked the koi into himself, grinding it, macerating it to pulp in his extended mouthparts. He savored its twitching to the very last, then swallowed.

He didn't think he was truly eating, not like humans and animals did, but if he chewed something well enough, practically liquefied it, he seemed to be able to absorb it in some way, to take mass and energy from it.

And I never have to shit. What a deal.

He ate several more koi, trying to immerse himself in the sensuality of killing, trying not to think of the coyote's jaws on his throat, or Virginia's torch on his face.

Rags winced, remembering. No, he wouldn't think about it. It hurt too much to think about it. he would think about her instead.

She loves me, but the bad ones are changing her mind. Changing her. I must take her away from them. I must save her.

Yeah.

Content, he went to work on his macerated throat, which didn't seemed helped at all by his fish meal. Rags found that disturbing frightening and frightening so he refused to think about it. Instead he extended himself into slender vines, flowing into the water intake, enjoying the feel of the slimy plastic plumbing against his flesh. He reached deeper and deeper into the pipes, scraping, gathering. It took even longer than his face.

No matter. I know what I must do.

Rags pulled down a water lily, imagining how it must look sinking beneath the surface all by itself. He smiled. Perhaps someone would be walking past, later, when the sun went down. A real estate lady, working late. He was certain that he had seen lights on in this complex at night before. Maybe she would come out—

Pain ripped through his body, making him thrash like a grounded carp. He opened his mouth to scream, but his air was all gone. Rags wrenched himself up out of the water.

She was leaving. He could feel her pulling away from his, second by second. It was like some vital organ was being torn from his body.

"Noooo!" he screamed. "Nooooooo!" He flailed wildly, splashing water, shredding plants. "You can't go!"

It was like he was being drained. Her presence fled from him. In his madness, he imagined himself to be a bottle knocked suddenly onto its side, precious fluid gushing out like blood from a severed artery. Soon, he would be empty of her. He reared up higher, shrieking.

"Amy, NO! You can't go! You can't leave me! NO!" He pounded at his newly formed face, knocking it out of shape, pulverizing his features.

The last drop of her was wrenched from him, nearly tearing him in half. Rags sank to his knees in the lapping water.

"Please?" he whispered. He sank down further and further, until he slid down the intake, and was gone.

He settled into the water circulation system, blocking it up. He could hear the pump whine, somewhere below him. Anguish washed over him in black, cold waves.

Amy . . .

He didn't hear the screams of the woman who had seen him from her office window. He felt them from within the comforting squeeze of the plastic piping. His anguish turned on him and bit. Rags was suddenly awash in red rage.

Shut up you bitch, shut up or I'll kill you. He pulsated, wormlike, in the confines of the tubes. Shut up, or I'll rip your fucking head off. Shut up, or I'll . . .

He fell very still.

I wonder . . .

If I can get to the drinking fountain in that building . . .

From here . . .

He decided it was worth a try.

TWENTY-SIX

Amelia clutched at her red velvet skirts in frustration, pacing back and forth across the opulent cabin like a beautiful captive lynx. Since Captain Tristan had taken her ship off the coast of Spain, she had been trying to devise a method of escape. But the design of her cabin was ingenious; it held all the comforts of a high-born lady's boudoir, without a single thing she could use as a weapon. It was almost as if he had designed it with her in mind . . .

But no, that was much too frightening to even consider. If he would go to so much trouble, he would never let her go. Amelia shook her head violently, her long red curls bouncing against her ample bosom. No, she thought, I will never give in to him.

Amelia started. There were heavy footsteps outside her cabin door. She quickly knelt down, and began unlacing her high kidskin boots.

The door burst open. The huge, lumpen form of Malvert, the First Mate, filled the doorway, and his malicious laughter filled her ears.

"The cap'ain would like to see ya in 'is cabin, little lady," he growled. "But I don't suppose 'e'd mind if I 'ad a go at ya first, ay?" Grinning like a broken-toothed shark, the horrid man advanced on her.

Amelia gasped for breath. At first, as her lip curled in disdain, she prepared to hurl insults and abuse at Malvert, to fight him to the last. But suddenly she knew what she must do.

Amelia lay her hand across her lush, heaving bosom, rolling her eyes at Malvert as if she were an unbroken filly. His grin grew wider.

"Oh!" she cried. "Oh, Malvert! I am quite overcome by you! Please, please do not take advantage of my weak woman's heart!" She fluttered her eyelashes at him.

Malvert rushed forward, reaching out to sweep her into his ape-like arms. With a ladylike war cry, Amelia simultaneously drove the heel of her boot into his groin like a dirk, and bent his forefinger back until it broke. Howling, Malvert fell to the floor.

Amelia rushed past him, up the stairs and onto the moonlit deck. Barefoot, she ran wildly for the ornate ship's railing, intending to plunge over the side to her death. "My fate is in the hands of my maker," she cried.

Strong arms seized her about the waist, sweeping her off her feet. Captain Tristan nuzzled at her neck and shoulder, his unshaven face making her shiver.

"No, my lovely one," he murmured, "Your fate is in my hands. The very hands that you will learn to love . . . " He was stroking her belly, reaching down for her thighs . . .

Amelia drove an elbow into Captain Tristan's stomach. He grunted, loosening his grip just enough for her to turn and face him.

He arched one perfect eyebrow and smiled. His skin was golden, and his ears pointed. His teeth, when he revealed them, were ever-so-slightly sharp, and—

No way this is way too scary he looks like a really young George Sanders instead. Yeah, that's good.

"My dear," he purred, in his rich, cultured voice, "You astonish me ever anew. But don't fear, you shall be mine, one way or another."

Amelia struggled, but he pinned both her tiny hands in one of his, and drew her near. He bent to kiss her, and she turned her head. She opened her eyes to look out into the night sky, to pretend she were at home, and gasped in astonishment.

A ship was coming from the East, and fast. Its sails swelled in the quickening breeze. It was lit like a wedding ship, but it looked like none she had ever seen before. Why did Captain Tristan not see it? Why had the lookout not warned him? Amelia didn't care. Her heart beat with wild hope.

"Ah, your body betrays you, little one. I can tell by your breath and your hummingbird heartbeat that you desire me as much as I desire you." Captain Tristan was attempting to loosen her bodice when the lookout fell from the crow's nest with a resounding thump. He had an arrow protruding from his neck.

The Captain strode across the deck, dragging Amelia behind him by one delicate wrist. With his other hand, he yanked the arrow from the throat of the dead crewman. Amelia winced and looked away.

"Moors!" He hissed. "What in the devil could they—"

One of the Moorish cannons roared, spouting flame like a furious dragon. The shot whistled over the Pirate Ship Slayer's bow—no not Slayer they suck—over the Pirate Ship Mettalica's bow, and hit the water like judgment day.

"Who dares?!" roared Tristan, drawing his sword.

"I, Captain Louis de Fenix!" came the bold reply. "Give me the woman you so cravenly took from her father's merchant ship, and I shall consider letting you live!"

Captain Louis! Amelia closed her eyes, imagining the handsome privateer's chocolate skin and fearless smile. She could hardly take her eyes from him when they had met in the marketplace in Toledo. But how had he known?

"Never!" was Captain Tristan's angry reply. "The woman is mine. I shall feed your black heart to the sharks!"

Captain Louis's laughter rang across the sea. "Nay, my skin is black, but my heart is as red as Cupid's lips, and beats only for the fair Lady Amelia. It is your heart, sir, that is as black as the pit itself! Prepare to be boarded!"

Pirates were swarming up from the decks below, drawing their cutlasses, manning the cannons.

Amelia gasped as Captain Louis, oblivious to the danger, boldly swung from the riggings of the elegant Moorish ship, and landed with the agility of a dancer not three feet away from Captain Tristan.

"Sir." Captain Louis spat the word as if it were a curse. He was as beautiful as she had remembered him—more so. His dark eyes flashed in the moonlight. A feral grin spread across his face. "Draw your sword!"

Captain Tristan tossed Amelia aside and drew his rapier in a heartbeat. He thrust for Louis' heart. In one blinding instant, Louis drew his own rapier and parried the blow as if it were a child's.

Amy cried out as Moorish cannonfire rocked the ship. Valiant Moorish sailors were boarding from all sides. The battle was suddenly raging around her.

"Salvatore!" cried Captain Louis. "Take Miss Amelia to the ship and put her safely below!"

A huge, dusky-hued, ruggedly handsome man with a golden earring cried, "Aye-aye, Captain!" and headed for Amelia. She held out her arms to him, only to see him cut down by the cutlass of one of Tristan's brutal outlaws.

Tristan's pirate turned to her, bloody and grinning. Amelia grabbed the dying Salvatore's cutlass, and holding it both hands, prepared to defend herself. The ship tossed wildly, like a frightened stallion . . .

⤝⤞

"Amy! Helloooo! Earth to Amy! Are you in there?"

Amy gasped. The plane bounced again. Turbulence. Louis was peering into Amy's face, looking half amused, half worried. Her heart gave a little kick at the sight of him.

This is ridiculous, Amy thought. *I'm flying out to the swamp to tango with my worst nightmare, not to mention destroying my credit rating and my GPA . . . and all I can do is have adolescent sexual fantasies about a man I've known less than a day?*

Louis smiled. "The windows are unfogging! There *is* someone in there! Hey, Amy, what were you thinking about so hard?" He brushed a lock of hair from her forehead.

Damn straight. Adolescent sex fantasies are good for you. God, he's beautiful . . .

"Oh, nothing, Louis. Just spacing out."

"Amy, I've gotta tell you, you space out with utter sincerity." He laughed.

Amy blushed, then turned to look at Sarah so Louis wouldn't see.

Sarah was rubbing her eyes. Mick was slumped against the little airline pillow, sound asleep.

"Hey, girlie," said Sarah, blinking like a possum in a flashlight beam. "What time is it?"

Amy looked at her wrist watch. "We'll be landing in less than an hour."

"Cool." Sarah fluffed up Mick's shoulder and snuggled in tight.

It had been a miserable flight. They had taken the cheapest airline possible, which meant no food, lousy air conditioning, and a three hour layover in Dallas. Amy had been burning to talk, talk about what they were getting into, about the thing they had to face. But she found she was ashamed. She was not afraid people would think she was crazy; that was so insignificant it barely crossed her mind. But Rags was, and had always been, her dirty little secret. To speak of him in the hearing of strangers would be unbearable. To speak his name in the mundane atmosphere of the airplane, where people were reading used copies of *Newsweek* and talking about their jobs and their kids and their hometowns, that would be the worst kind of juju.

Because it would be voicing what she knew, but could not bear to think about for long.

Monsters are real.

And if Rags is out there, walking, talking, moving through the world . . . what else is there? God, what else?

Amy fought the urge to rest her head on Louis, to press against him and take strength from his warmth. *You don't know him that well,* she told herself.

But when he smiled at her, she felt as if she had known him forever. She looked down, and tugged gently at Xavier's string bracelet around her wrist.

Without a word, Amy nestled her head against Louis's shoulder. She felt him rest his cheek against her hair.

Amy wasn't sure, but she thought she felt him kiss her head, softly as the brush of an angel's wing.

❧

The plane touched down with the usual squeal of landing gear, with the usual stuffy minutes before the door opened, with the usual zombie-like exit of the passengers.

Deplaning. Who ever thought of a lame-ass word like that? thought Amy as she shouldered her duffel bag and stepped out into the warm Florida night air. Her face felt greasy and her eyes puffy. *Goddam foul plane air. I probably just picked up three different viruses.*

"I can tell you're thinking cranky thoughts," said Sarah with a little grin. "I think we need to get some food into you."

"Nah," said Amy, slowly considering. "I'm not really hungry."

"That mystery-meat-on-a-bun probably killed your stomach," said Mick helpfully.

"I want to go to the hotel," Amy said, staring off into space. "Now."

"Great idea," said Sarah. "I could definitely use some freshening up, not to mention a nap."

"No," said Amy. "I mean the Martinique."

There was a flurry of words. We can't possibly. We're tired. We have no weapons. We have no idea what we're facing. You're crazy. You're crazy. Crazy crazy crazy

"I just want to look for now," said Amy, through the fog of voices and faces. Suddenly, the world came into cold, crisp focus, and the world consisted of the Hotel Martinique. "I have to look."

They picked up a rental car from Budget, adding it to Amy's already bloated credit card. The clerk was irritable, probably unhappy at having to work at a quarter to midnight. She didn't want to rent the car to someone under twenty-five, much less a group of four kids who looked underslept and ragged. A black look from Amy shut her up before she ever really got started.

As Amy pulled out of the parking lot, her lips quirked. Some darkened part of her loved the flicker of fear that passed through the Budget clerk's eyes. *Good job, Vampira, but what would you have done if the card hadn't gone through? You've probably got about three bucks credit left on the damn thing. What the hell. I'll just tell mom and dad that I maxed out the card because I needed a car to chase slime monsters through the Everglades. They'll understand.*

Her half-smile slipped away to nothing. A thin red streak of pain whipped through her mind at the thought of her parents. She wanted to call them more than anything in the world. She wanted to collapse into her mother's arms, to have her father stroke her hair and call her Mophead and tell her that everything would be all right, that there was nothing in her closet, that there were no such things as monsters. But stronger than her desire for the warm safety of her family was the biting fear that if she called them, if she breathed their names, if she even thought about them too hard, HE would know and HE would go looking for them. *No. Leave them out of it. Call them later, when it's all over, and cry and cry and blame it on a boy.*

"Do you know where you're going?" asked Mick from the back seat, sounding nervous, as Amy whipped the Taurus around the darkened streets just a little too fast.

"Oh, yes," she said, in a voice barely above a whisper. She could never forget. She could feel the weight of Louis's stare on her face, but she was afraid to look at him. Afraid that if she saw fear in his eyes, she would lose her nerve now and forever.

She drove the streets of Palm Beach as if she were being guided by some external force *(Maybe I am) (Shut up silly bitch)* pulling her closer and closer to the Martinique. As she turned onto the road it faced, still lined with coconut trees which had grown tall and gawky in her absence, her stomach contracted. She suddenly felt like she had swallowed a cold cannonball.

The car was silent. No talking, no laughing.

Where is the goddam thing. I should see it by now. I should see the ugly split white walls, the cracked red plastic sign on top. It must be around the corner—

Amy slammed on the brakes, sucking in air like she'd just surfaced from a dark, deep river. There was the stand of mango trees to the right of the Martinique. There was the tall, glittering condo, now faded down and looking 1970's ugly on the left. And in the middle . . .

In the middle was a parking lot.

Greenish lights drew moths and beetles as they shone down on the black, slick-looking asphalt. Crisp white lines marked space after space. A single car, an older BMW wagon, sat in the middle of the lot like the ship of the Lost Dutchman. All was quiet. All was calm.

"Ohmigod," whispered Amy. "It's gone."

"No shit," said Sarah.

Amy whipped around to look at her, a sharp spike of anger ramming through her brain before she had time to stop it. "Shut the fuck up," she snarled.

Sarah looked at her, first with hurt, then with understanding. She smiled. "You do need some food, Ame," she said. "Your head is spinning around. You'll be blowing pea soup next."

But Amy wasn't listening. She pulled the car slowly into the parking lot, and cut the engine. She stepped out into the sea of blackness.

Gone was the smell of mildew and old plaster, rats and algae. Now there was only the smell of tar and the faint afterimage of exhaust. Amy walked across the parking lot, the soles of her tennis shoes slightly warmed by the blacktop.

He's gone, she thought. *His heart is gone."*

"What now," said Louis, right next to her. For some reason, she had felt him there, and didn't start.

"I don't know," said Amy, as angels of despair sang hymns all around her.

TWENTY-SEVEN

It was Mick, pragmatic Mick, who suggested the next course of action.

"Let's get a hotel and flop. I'm fucking exhausted."

That did seem like the only thing to do. Picking the first fleabag that came along (the Whispering Palms Motel), the four hauled their luggage in, and tossed a dead roach (found in the sink, by Sarah) out.

Amy's head was buzzing. She felt like she was drunk. She felt like she was lost. She felt like she had no idea what she was doing. She sat on the edge of the bed and rubbed her temples.

They had put the room, a double, on Sarah's folks' American Express card. No one had said anything about getting two different rooms. No one wanted to be alone, even for a little while.

Sarah lay out flat on the bed with her arms and legs splayed out. "I'm never moving again," she announced.

"Move over," grumbled Mick, stretching his lanky form along the edge of the bed.

"I hope you don't mind sharing. I'll be a gentleman," said Louis, with a little smile.

I wish you wouldn't, thought Amy, *be a gentleman.* "No problem," said her mouth.

"Shit," said Sarah. "I'm hungry."

"Me too," said Mick, not moving.

"Let's go get food, then." Sarah sat up, fluffing her hair and rubbing her face.

"I—I have to think," said Amy. "I have to plan. You go, okay?"

"If you don't eat something, you're going to turn into such a bitch even I can't stand you." Sarah was smiling, but there was worry in her eyes.

"Why don't you bring me something? Take the car. I just need to lie down for a little while."

"I'm not leaving you alone," said Louis, in a voice like quiet steel.

"We'll bring you something too." Sarah was already heading for the door. "You take care of her, okay, Louie?"

"Bite me," said Amy, as the door slammed shut behind her best friend.

"Amy," said Louis.

"I know. I know." Her throat was aching. *Don't cry don't you dare.* "I have no idea what I'm doing."

He was stroking her hair, looking into her eyes, his face all sympathy and kindness.

"I got you all into this. It's not your problem. It's mine. It's mine, I pulled it out of the pool, and now we're all gonna die." A sob wrenched its way out of her.

Louis's expression had changed. There was just the slightest upward curve of his lips, a tiny twinkle in his eyes. *He's trying not to laugh,* thought Amy. Suddenly a giggle was bubbling up in her, too.

"We're all gonna die, huh?" said Louis. And then he did laugh; a chuckle without malice, sadness echoing behind it. Amy laughed too, laughed and cried, burying her face in his neck.

It wasn't clear to her when her sobs became kisses, or whether the salt she was tasting was her tears or his skin. She opened her mouth, running her lips as lightly as rose petals along the hollow of his throat, down toward his collarbone. Her tongue touched him, pressing into the pulse in his throat, feeling his life and warmth so close to the surface. Her mouth grazed the underside of his chin, up along the strong angle of his jaw, and finally rested on his lips. She kissed him, ever so softly. His scent, his own personal Louis-smell, was intoxicating.

What the hell am I doing? she thought, bringing her hands up to the short, curly hair on his head. *I don't know him, not really, not at all.*

Who gives a shit. It feels so good. So good . . .

And this could be my last chance.

But he was pulling away, taking her face in his hands. "Amy . . . Amy, are you sure this is what you want?"

She wanted to tell him yes, tell him how much she wanted him, how much she was drawn to him, to his beautiful dark eyes and his sweet curving mouth and the soft, delicious hollow under his jaw, but no words could come out and all she could do was nod. They locked eyes. He held her there for long moments that grew painful with need. At last he saw what he was evidently looking for; proof that she wanted him, that she really did.

"Yes," she managed to breathe as his mouth brushed against her cheek. "Yes," as his tongue flicked into the shell of her ear, giving her a shiver that started with the back of her neck and went straight to her crotch.

And then she was kissing him, their mouths sliding together, tongues touching, flicking, caressing. A low groan of desire vibrated through Amy's mouth and into Louis's. Her hands cupped his face, ran through the short, tight curls on his head, down the velvet stubble on the back of his neck. He caressed her back as her hands ran down his sides and up under his shirt, touching warm, muscular flesh. She rolled his nipple between her thumb and forefinger, and it was his turn to groan.

He kissed her fiercely, his hands in her hair. He was kissing her throat now, tracing a hot line down her neck and over her chest, kissing one breast through her T-shirt while his hand gently kneaded the other. Warmth spread from Amy's mouth and chest, across her face and down her body to the wet very wet place between her legs.

She could feel her juices flowing, flowing for him. A place deep inside her twitched, twitched again. Her clit began to throb, a deep, delicious pulse that tortured and delighted her almost to madness. She felt that if he were to touch her there, to just slide his hand between her legs, she would come so hard that the world would explode—

But he was pushing her away. A heated flash of want and anger whipped through her gut. *Why? Why doesn't he want me? What's wrong with—*

"Protection," Louis whispered, breath ragged. "Do you have anything?"

Amy stared at him for a moment, then laughed. She felt herself collapsing into helpless giggles. "N—no," she managed to squeak out. "It didn't occur to me to pack my rubbers. I—I didn't think the occasion would arise—" and then the giggles took over again.

Louis was laughing too, holding her in his arms. "I guess that was a silly question. Wait here. I'll go downstairs and get some."

"I'll go with you." Amy started to get up off the bed.

"I'd rather you didn't." Louis's eyes were suddenly serious, and sad in a way she couldn't quite comprehend. "It might not be a good idea."

What? Is he ashamed to be seen with me? "Why?" she asked, trying not to be hurt, trying not to be upset. "Don't you think we should stick together? I mean, I'll brush my hair . . . "

"Oh, Amy! Beautiful Amy. It isn't that." He cupped her face in his hands, smiling just for her. "This is the south. It might not be . . . prudent for us to go strolling into U-Totem together and buy contraceptives."

" . . . Oh." Amy stared at the garish purple-and-orange bedspread. It was so ridiculous she wanted to laugh, but so ugly she couldn't even smile.

"I'll wait here," said Amy softly.

Louis pressed his lips, firm and strong, against hers. "I won't be gone long. There's a market right on the corner." He scooped up the room key from the nightstand, and with a wink, he was gone.

Amy stood up, kicking off her running shoes. *I'm about to fuck the most gorgeous human being in the world. Maybe I should take a shower.*

With a wry grin, she padded over to the small, narrow bathroom.

Amy pulled off her T-shirt, slinging it over the back of the toilet. She wrinkled her nose, looking at herself in the mirror. Fluorescent lights make everyone look like a freakin' zombie. She cupped her breasts in her hands, eyeing them critically. Peach-sized, milky pale with airbrush-soft aureole and candy-pink tips. Not bad, not bad. Hope he likes 'em small but mighty. She plucked at her nipples, making them stand at attention, then held her arms over her head and struck a Theda Bara vamp pose. *Attack of the Fluorescent Zombie Babes from Hell!*

Giggling, she peeled off her jeans and panties, leaving them in a heap under the sink. She tugged the shower door, once, twice, before it popped open with a shuddering vibration.

The shower, like the rest of the bathroom, was a nasty rat-tooth yellow. Black tenacious mildew grew in the grout between the dulling tiles. Amy had the feeling that if she scraped it away, it would grow back before her eyes. She picked up one of the small, stiff towels and sniffed it. At least it smells clean, she thought. She turned on the shower.

After a series of minute, scientific adjustments to the temperature knob, the water spraying through the lime-encrusted nozzle was at least tolerable. It could have been a little warmer, but at least it wasn't going to boil off Amy's hide or flash-freeze her. She unwrapped a stinky little bar of lavender soap and stepped in.

It felt good. Amy could feel the muscles on the back of her neck and down her spine starting to relax as she allowed the water to run over her head and face. She washed her hair quickly, not trusting the water gods to stay benevolent.

Amy was languidly washing her leg, propping it up on the wall of the shower stall, when she saw the figure standing outside the Plexiglas.

Her heart kick-started. She backed up into the corner. *Calm down calm down it's not* him *it's only*

"Louis?" she asked, voice trembling just a little.

"No, it's the Avon lady," came his rich, humorous voice. She could see his outline, chocolate-brown, against the facets of the plastic. *Oh God he's naked. YES!*

She pushed the door, just a little, and it popped open. Louis stood there naked in the steam, looking like a god of heat and love. His body was long and sleek, muscles wiry, belly flat. His cock stood out from a dark, curling patch of hair, thick and hard and pointing at her heart.

They pressed together in the shower spray, kissing, biting, melting together. Amy could feel Louis's cock hard against her belly. She ran her hands down to his muscular ass, pulling him closer, tighter. He turned her in his arms so he faced her back. Amy leaned her head back on his shoulder as he nibbled her neck, arms wrapped tight around her waist. He licked her spine as he caressed her belly, then cupped her breasts. One hand

212

was sliding, sliding down her front, toward the patch of gold between her legs. Amy looked down at his long, artistic fingers, eyes glazed with pleasure, as he cupped her sex. *Our skin looks beautiful, she thought.*

And then she couldn't think any more, because his fingers slipped into her cleft, and he was rubbing her, gently stroking her clit in soft little circles, so slowly, *Oh God* and he was whispering in her ear, telling her how beautiful she was, *Yes* and his cock rubbed against the cheeks of her ass and the sensitive base of her spine *Oh yes* and he was stroking, stroking, and she could hear herself gasping, moaning, as she clutched at the back of his neck and reached behind her to grip his thigh and he was biting her shoulder, stubble of his jaw rough on her neck and his arm so tight around her waist and his fingers squeezing her nipple and it hit her, waves and waves of hot liquid pleasure; a super-nova starting in her crotch and shooting up her belly and down her legs and her back arched and she cried out, again and again, "Louis, Louis, Louis."

"Louis."

Kisses, warm and soft, and she laughed as she slumped against him because her legs were rubber bands, and she was so happy, and he made her feel so very good.

The water turned cold in a ferocious blast. Yelps and giggles as they jumped out of the shower, more kisses as they dried each other tenderly with the cat's tongue towels.

They fell into the narrow bed in a tangle of arms and legs, not wanting to let go. They explored each others' bodies with hands and lips and tongues, discovering with joy all the things that made the other gasp. Louis's hands slid across Amy's belly as he kissed the inside of her thigh, nipping softly, getting closer and closer. He buried his face in her crotch, breathing in her scent, eyes closed with pleasure. He looked into her eyes as his tongue slid between her lips.

A lightening-strike of pleasure hit her as he flicked her clit with his tongue. She squirmed, unable to keep still, whispering his name. He kissed her clit softly, then harder, sucking just a little. By the time he started licking her rhythmically, she was crying out, touching his face, grabbing the bedspread. Another massive, rolling wave of orgasm hit her and she was almost screaming, not caring who heard her.

Louis was over her now, kissing her, and she could taste herself on his mouth.

With a growl, Amy rolled him over onto his back. She straddled his thighs, looking down at his cock. She wrapped her fingers around him and squeezed gently. He closed his eyes, and she thought he looked like an angel. She began to stroke him. *Silk*, she thought. *Silk over steel.* She slid down lower, kissing the head of his cock. He groaned. Slowly, savoring the salty, musky taste of him, she slid her mouth down over his shaft. Up and down, now sucking, now licking, grabbing his ass with both hands. He had his hands in her hair and his spine was arched, head thrown back, and he looked like a young god, a forest god, *he looks like Pan.*

Unbelievably, Amy felt herself getting wetter, wanting still more. *More of* him.

She slipped him out of her mouth and lay on top of him. They kissed over and over. She could feel him, hot and ready, against her belly. Amy reached into the paper bag on the floor and pulled out the box of condoms. *Good ol' Sheik.* She unwrapped one, and rolled it slowly, sensually, down onto his cock. He was smiling at her, a grin so sweet but so lustful that she couldn't wait any more. She straddled him and, resting her hands on his chest, impaled herself on his cock.

Ooooooh yes.

Amy shivered, a shiver of pure delight that started inside her and went through her whole body.

"You feel so good," she whispered.

"You too." He was looking at her again, looking into her eyes, seeming to look into her soul. They began to rock together. She was so wet, so ready that he felt like silk inside her, smooth and deep and luscious. He touched her breasts and face and she rode him.

She wanted it to go on forever, to just keep up a soulful, slow rhythm for hours. She closed her eyes, lacing her fingers with his, when her orgasm started building inside her. Suddenly she just wanted to fuck. She thrust with him, harder and faster. Her head rolled back and she let out an animal groan before dropping down on top of him. He grabbed her ass, pulling her down onto him so hard as she slammed against him, biting his shoulders, sweating, crying out, and he felt so good between her legs and deep inside her was a hot coal and if she could just fuck him hard enough, she would explode into a thousand suns . . .

The orgasm caught her mid-stroke and she convulsed, rearing back, screaming. He hooked his legs over hers and cried out again and again as he came, one hand buried in the soft flesh of her ass, the other on the small of her back. They collapsed together in a wet, shivering heap.

Amy felt herself drifting off to sleep when Louis gently nudged her off of him. He held onto the rubber as he slid out of her. With a quick, deep kiss on the lips and a grin that nearly stopped her heart, he went into the bathroom.

Amy smiled and stretched, long and slow. *Oh my god. I think I'm in love,* said a little voice in her head. *Don't be stupid. It was just good sex,* she told the little voice, but she couldn't keep the grin off her face. *Okay, fucking incredible sex . . .*

Louis came back out of the bathroom and got back into bed. He pulled the covers up over the two of them, and kissed her on the nose.

"I guess we should get dressed," said Amy, not wanting to move.

That's when the door of the room swung open, and Sarah and Mick came in bearing bags of dim sum.

Amy felt herself turning red. She started to giggle as Louis hid his face on her shoulder, grinning.

"Hmm!" said Sarah. "Smells like sex in here!"

❧

Mick and Sarah were kind enough to wait in the hall while Louis and Amy threw on their clothes, but Sarah kept making rude remarks through the door. Finally Amy opened it up and dragged her in, threatening bodily harm.

They all munched on dumplings, channel-surfing and making jokes and trying not to think about why they were there.

"—One of the most shocking murders in Arizona's history," said the second-string CNN reporter.

"Hold it, hold it," Sarah said to Mick, who had just surfed past the news. "That's something about home!"

"And it sounds SO cheerful." Mick clicked the channel back and dropped the remote onto the bed.

The trim, bright-eyed female reporter stood in front of a white stucco-covered business complex, looking uncomfortably warm in her dark power suit.

"Oh God!" said Sarah "That's just down the street from our place!"

"Although the identity of the victim has not yet been released, we have learned that she was probably strangled."

Amy squinted. The tall, solemn figure of Detective Paul Blythe stood in the background, talking to someone off-camera.

"Police suspect that this crime may be connected with a vicious assault at Desert Samaritan hospital just last night." The reporter raised a knife-sharp blonde eyebrow incredulously, seeming to admonish the teleprompter. "There has also been an unconfirmed eye-witness report that the body of tonight's victim was, in addition to being mutilated, covered with some form of vegetable matter—"

Amy dove across the bed and grabbed the remote, clicking the power button with both her thumbs. Her forehead dropped to the bed as the device slipped from her fingers, landing on the faded green carpeting.

For a moment, no one said anything.

"You don't know it was him, Amy." Sarah's voice, soft and rational.

"Yes. I do." Amy's hands were shaking, so she clasped them together. "He killed somebody. Because of me. Because he was mad at me for leaving."

"Amy . . . " She felt Louis's hand on the small of her back, and the warmth of his palm was her whole world for a moment.

Her eyes flew open. "Oh God," she breathed, chest tight, stomach twisting. "Xavier."

Wild with manic energy and sickening fear, Amy grabbed the phone. First she called information, for the number of the hospital. Then she was dialing it, hands shaking, mouth dry. *Oh please, oh please let him be okay.*

"Xavier Arredondo's room," she told the cheerful receptionist.

"Please hold," then a click in her ear. Three pairs of eyes, watching her anxiously. Amy wished to God they'd look away.

"Hello, Ma'am?" It was a man's voice, not Xavier's.

"What happened?" Amy whispered, bitter pain filling her mouth.

"Mr. Arredondo's been transferred to the ICU. Are you a relative, Ma'am?"

"Yes." *He's still alive, thank you, God, thank you.*

An uncomfortable pause. "I'm sorry to tell you this, Ma'am, but he's slipped into a coma." Another pause. "You might want to come see him, if you can."

Because he'll probably die, Amy's brain finished for him.

"Yes," she said. "I understand. Thank you." She watched her hand drop the receiver back into its cradle.

"He's in a coma," she said, looking down, not wanting to meet their eyes.

"At least he's alive," she heard Sarah say. "Ame, do you think that thing's still there? In Phoenix? Or did it . . . "

Sarah's voice trailed off.

"Did it follow me here?" Amy was angry. *Not at Sarah. Not even at Rags. At me, for making friends with it, for—*

For ever loving it.

"I don't know. Maybe. Probably. It could be anywhere, Sarah. Anywhere." Amy looked at the waterstained ceiling, blinking tears away.

"Okay," said Mick, staring at the washed-out painting of dried flowers over the mirror, "Never mind where the rest of it is. How are we gonna find the heart?"

"We'll ask Mr. Iris," Amy murmured, not quite believing she just said it.

"No way!" Sarah squeaked. "Wasn't he the old satanic chicken-killer?"

"As a matter of fact," said Amy with a strange half-smile, "he was."

"Why would he help us kill it?" asked Mick. "I thought he loved the damn thing."

"He wouldn't." Amy felt suddenly distant. A chill passed through her, going straight for the bone. "I'll knock on the door and talk to him. You know, distract him. You guys can look for that—thing's heart. He's almost certainly got it in his house." She couldn't bring herself to say the name "Rags," and she didn't know why. She turned slowly to Mick. "And by the way, Mr. Iris doesn't love it. He doesn't love anything."

"But you think he's protecting the heart?" asked Louis, taking her hand in his.

"Yes, I do. It was his—his project." The cold was getting worse. Amy wanted to lean against Louis, but something inside wouldn't let her. Something that howled in her blood and told her to be strong, be strong, this is your fight. She twisted Xavier's bracelet around and around her wrist.

"He might not still be alive," said Sarah uncertainly. "I mean, he was pretty old, right?"

"He's too fucking nasty to die." The cold was heading for Amy's stomach now.

"Well, I guess that's a good idea." Mick was frowning, rubbing the back of his neck. "But how do we kill the heart once we find it?"

Amy rested her hand on her belly, on the knot of ice that had taken up residence there. She narrowed her eyes. "We'll go shopping in the morning."

"For what? Crosses and holy water?" Mick's tone was sarcastic, but his hand had crept up to his cross pendant.

"No," said Amy. "Fire. Propane torches, I guess. That's what Louis's mother used to trash Rags before."

"There's something else," Louis said. "Iron."

Sarah looked puzzled. "We're gonna burn him with an iron?"

Louis smiled, not unkindly. "Not an iron. Weapons made of iron. Fireplace pokers, gateposts, things like that."

Amy's eyes narrowed. She remembered Rags' howl as Virginia pierced his heart with a wrought iron rose.

"Why?" Mick was starting to sound belligerent. Sarah put her hand on his arm.

Louis's gaze was steady. "Because iron can hurt supernatural creatures. It's like they're allergic to it."

Mick pulled his arm away from Sarah. "According to who, Louis? What kind of weird shit is that?"

Amy looked at Mick, at his tense, trembling muscles and hot, angry stare. Don't lose it, buddy. Hold on. We've all got to hold on.

"Old time weird shit. People have known about it for thousands of years, Mick. It's why cemetery fences are traditionally made of iron. It's why casket latches and coffin nails were iron. To keep . . . things . . . inside."

Mick stared at Louis, eyes narrowed. "Uh-huh. Okay. I guess that's no weirder than the rest of this shit. But I'll tell you something, Louis. I'm having trouble with the Voodoo thing. To tell you the truth, it freaks me out. You freak me out."

Louis sighed. "I know. You don't have to like it. Just keep in mind that we're on the same team. We're all here to help Amy. I'll do it my way, you do it yours."

There was a long, long pause. "Yeah," said Mick, finally. "Okay."

"Great!" Sarah patted Mick on the back. "Now if you guys are done jawing, let's hit the sack already. I'm totaled."

After turns in the bathroom, fluffed pillows and a thorough cockroach inspection, everybody was in bed. Amy switched off the light (but left on the light in the bathroom, just because) and snuggled up next to Louis. Oh, you feel so good . . .

Five minutes passed, then ten. Sarah started to snore quietly, making Amy smile. Amy relaxed all over, felt herself drifting closer and closer to sleep. For once, it was a pleasant sensation.

"Mick?" Louis's voice, soft and husky in the warm darkness.

"Yeah?"

"Most Vaudun practitioners are Catholics as well."

There was a beat of silence. Then Mick started to laugh, waking Sarah and making her mumble in sleepy protest.

⌘

And so they slept, Mick curled protectively around Sarah's curving body, Amy and Louis tangled in each other's arms. Once in the night, Amy woke up, and felt Louis's warm breath on her neck. She snuggled closer, and all was silent.

TWENTY-EIGHT

And so he screamed. He thrashed, ripping chunks of earth and grass from the ground with his jaws. He pounded his fists into each other until they were pulp, and he had to form them all over again. He felt her pleasure. He felt her every gasp, her every cry. He felt it when that man that stinking disgusting human stuck himself inside her, and he felt her want him to. He felt her love. Amy's love. *She loves him. Not me. She loves him.*

He sucked at his teeth hoping for a last drop of the real estate woman's blood, hoping for a little comfort. He came up with nothing but bile and swampwater. He flattened out with misery and slithered along the ground. On the back of his head, his flatworm eyes rolled from side to side. *I can't live without her. I can't. I'm coming for you, Amy.*

I'm coming for you, because I can't live without you.

Because you can't live without me.

With a gurgle of pain, he sank into the ground.

TWENTY-NINE

Amy woke up in the dark, disoriented for a moment by the strange bed, and the strange body beside her. Louis had his arm around her waist, and his head was nestled against her shoulder. She stroked his cheek, enjoying the rough texture of the stubble along his jawline. He murmured something and nestled closer. Amy blinked, rubbed her eyes, looked around the little room.

There were cracks of sunlight under the heavy motel curtains.It was morning. For some reason that she couldn't quite pin down, relief flooded through Amy's whole body. She stretched, feeling strong.

Mick and Sarah were still curled up together, his long legs and her short ones tangled up beneath the starchy sheets. Sarah was snoring softly. Amy started to pull away from Louis, to get first dibs on the shower.

"Where you goin?" he asked, pulling her closer. His eyes were still closed, but his lips curved with a slight, sleepy smile. Amy kissed his nose, resting her forehead against his.

"Just to the bathroom."

"Kay. Amy?"

"Mm-hmm?"

"I love you. I always have."

His eyes opened, and she looked into the warmth of their depths, and felt love so strong it scared her.

An hour later, the four were pulling into a Burger King drive-through on their way to the hardware store. Amy in the driver's seat, Sarah beside her, Mick and Louis in the back.

Mick seemed to have made an unspoken truce with Louis, conversing with him, showing none of the suspicion and mistrust of the night before. Amy wasn't sure if it was a change of heart or an act for Sarah's benefit, but either way she was incredibly grateful.

Everyone was cheerful, everyone was laughing, refusing to think about what lay ahead. Mick and Louis had a lively debate on which version of *Cape Fear* was best, while Amy and Sarah sang with the radio. An old Oingo Boingo song came on; one of Amy's favorites. She and Sarah belted out the words around bites of Croissan'wich. *There's nothing to fear but fear itself, nothing to fear . . .*

Bullshit. The Radio God is totally yankin' my chain.

Amy fell silent as they pulled into the Wal-Mart parking lot. There was a quick pow-wow to determine who had the most money left on their credit card (Louis), and then they went shopping.

THIRTY

He travels fast, far below the surface of the Earth. He slides between Her layers of rock, through the black, cold water. He tastes the metal tang of minerals, the poisonous seepings of industry, and the compelling juices of rotting human beings made sour with embalming fluid. He stretches thinner and thinner still, becoming more liquid, more insubstantial. He slides through the layers of the Earth faster than he has ever moved before, with only one thought in his mind.

Amy.

THIRTY-ONE

"So, what now?" asked Mick, shifting the two propane torch boxes in his arms. They had been to R.E.I. and Home Depot after leaving Wal-Mart, and he looked slightly cranky and totally shopped out. "Should we go back to the hotel for a while?"

"Nah." Amy unlocked the trunk. *Smells like a whole bottle of Pine-Sol in there.* "I'm too amped. Let's find someplace to talk this through."

Louis dropped the iron fireplace pokers into the trunk with a clatter. They were followed by Sarah's armload of barbed iron gateposts. Mick set the propane torches on top, and Amy slammed the lid down.

"This is your town, babe. Where do people usually go to plot mayhem?" Sarah's smile was tense.

Amy considered for a moment, before visions of faux palm trees and tiki lanterns began to spin through her head. She grinned.

Lunch at the Forbidden Fruit; champagne, antipasto and big silly grins. Sarah had just boldly ordered snails.

"Garcon! Oh Garcon! Ess-car-go for the whole table, please!"

The sleepy-looking young waiter smiled, showing milk-white teeth against tanned, smooth skin. As he walked away, Amy and Mick let out a simultaneous, heart-felt "Eeeeeow!"

"I am not," said Mick, delicately peeling a piece of proscuitto from his plate, "eating a bug."

"Chicken," said Sarah. She drained half of her champagne with a toss of her head and a loud gulp.

"Chicken would be okay." Mick grinned at his plate. "Just not bugs."

"Gastropods," said Louis.

Sarah poured herself more champagne. "Sounds like a disease."

"Snails are gastropods, not bugs," Louis said around a mouthful of mozzarella and pesto. "It's Latin. It means 'stomach foot.'"

Sarah blew champagne through her nose. "OW! You made that up! Ow, ow!"

Before he could answer, the waiter had reappeared with the escargot. He set the plate in the center of the table. Round, whorled shells sitting in little hot-tubs of butter, fat, yellowish creatures poking out of them. A basket of bread on the side. Sarah stared, looking a little worried.

"It's easy," beamed the waiter, whose name tag said *Eduardo*. "Just use the little forks to scoop them out and set them on the bread. Dip the bread in the butter, and start munching, chica!"

"Yeah, start munching!" Mick's grin was less than charitable. Eduardo shook his head as he walked away.

All eyes were on Sarah as she boldly plucked one of the plump snails from its shell and plopped it onto a hunk of bread. She held it up to the light, regarding it. "Hmm." She poked at the snail with her fork. "It looks like a tiny little Jabba the Hutt lying there, doesn't it?"

"Is that an eye stalk?" said Mick, looking slightly green. Sarah glared at him as she dunked the bread in one of the buttery pools, and raised it to her lips.

"Sa-rah! Sa-rah!" chanted Amy. Mick covered his eyes. Sarah's lips peeled back, and she opened her mouth wide. Abruptly, it snapped shut.

"Nope," she said. "Can't do it."

Louis snagged the piece of bread from Sarah's hand and popped it into his mouth. Buttery juice ran down his chin. "Wuss," he said, mouth full, reaching for another. Sarah and Amy burst out laughing.

"Louis!" exclaimed Mick, eyes sparkling. You sophisticated son-of-a-bitch!"

And so the afternoon passed, with laughter and food, and the rare chemistry that can only be generated by a group of true friends. The time was golden, and Amy wished it would never end. But of course, it had to.

Now, over cannolli and espresso, the time had come to discuss what must be done next.

Madness. This is madness.

Amy sighed deeply and poked at the pastry with her fork. It cracked, spilling thick, yellowish-white ricotta cheese. Amy looked away from it.

"I'm almost certain Mr. Iris has it," she said. "We need to get into his house."

Sarah tapped the points of her fork on the table. "Amy, why does he have the heart? I mean, what did he want with Rags in the first place? I don't think I get that relationship at all."

Amy shook her head. "I've never known that."

"I think I do," said Louis. They all turned to look at him.

"See, Iris is a bocor—a sorcerer. Somebody who uses magic for his own personal gain. Bocors are always looking for sources of power, for anything that'll make them stronger. So far as I can tell, Rags is a creature born of pure magic. He's a power source. Iris was tapping into him like he was a car battery."

"Power for what?" Sarah asked. "What exactly do bocors do?"

"The same things that other corrupt, selfish people do. They try to get more power, more money. They help out their friends. They hurt their enemies." Louis took a deep drink of his water, as if trying to get a bad taste out of his mouth.

Mick looked faintly nauseated. "Okay, while we're on the subject, why did they want to, to join Rags' heart with Amy's? What the hell good would that do them?"

Louis bit his lower lip, thinking. "Well, the joining of a male and female is powerful stuff. It would create a specific type of magic that they could tap into. You could use magic like that for fertility, but that doesn't make any sense, because they're nine hundred years old . . . "

"Life extension," said Amy. She shuddered.

Louis's eyes widened. "Of course! They were trying to tack more years onto their lives. God, they could have done something like that before! There's no way of knowing how old they really are."

"You mean, they really might be nine hundred?" Sarah's face was horrified.

Louis laughed. "I sincerely doubt it. But they could be ninety, a hundred, a hundred and twenty, even. I've heard of such things before."

Sarah shook her head. "Shit, this is starting to sound like a mummy movie. And I guess we've gotta find a way into Iris-ra's tomb. Right, Ame?"

Amy nodded, trying to will the ice from her bones.

"Anybody know how to pick a lock?" asked Mick gloomily.

"I do." Sarah winked at him.

"No," said Amy, forcing herself to sound normal. "We can't do it that way. I know where he lives. Those houses go for millions, and they have alarm systems that go off if a mouse farts. I don't think any of us are quite up to that."

Sarah agreed, after humming the Mission Impossible theme.

"So, we just have to get ourselves invited in. Sarah and I will just—we'll just ring the bell, and tell him something. That we're lost tourists, or architecture students or something. Once we're in, we'll just look around until we find it."

"No way." Louis's eyes were fixed on the flamingo-and-palm-tree wallpaper. "It's too dangerous, Amy. What if he recognizes you? I'll go."

"We'll go," said Mick, looking at him.

"No offense guys, but yeah-fucking-right." Sarah sipped her espresso, looking at Mick and Louis. "There is no way that some rich old white codger is gonna open the door for a couple of young guys. Especially when one of them is—" she blushed.

"Black," said Louis, smiling. "You're right. We'll have to come up with a story. Tell him we're cable guys or something."

"Or pool guys. We can get some shorts, and—"

"No." Amy's voice was granite. "It has to be me. It just has to. I have to face this thing. And he won't recognize me. It's been thirteen years. I've changed. He's old. We'll go in and try to find it. Then we'll all come back together and figure out a way to get in and kill it." She stared at the ceiling, wondering how in the hell it got this far.

"But I have to go in first. It's something I have to do, okay?"

For a moment, no one said a word. When he spoke, Louis's voice was soft, and rough with emotion. "I understand, Amy. But we'll be nearby, okay? We'll sneak into the yard, and we'll be able to hear if anything goes wrong. At the first sign of trouble, you scream. Do you hear me? You *scream*."

Amy's smile was tight. "Sure. I've gotten pretty good at that lately."

For a minute or two, everyone was silent.

"Ame?" Sarah's eyes were round with worry.

"Yeah?"

"So . . . what happened after Virginia killed Rags? You must've been in rough shape after seeing all that stuff. What did you tell your parents?"

Amy licked her lips. With a horror she couldn't explain, she realized there was still a black, yawning gulf in her memory. "God, Sarah. I just don't know."

"I do." Louis drained the last of his water. "Amy was hysterical at first, then nearly catatonic. She withdrew into her own head and wouldn't come out. My mom carried her to her parents and told them that a strange man tried to abduct her. Mom said she saw him carry Amy into the Martinique, and when Mom started screaming at him, he ran."

Sarah stared. "And they believed it?"

Louis nodded. "When the police investigated, they found Marie's body in the old hotel. It was all over the news. Everybody thought Amy was incredibly lucky to be alive." He glanced over at Amy, squeezing her hand under the table. "Which, of course, you were."

Amy felt numb. Her food was a cold lump in her stomach.

Mick was frowning into his coffee. "But it was Mr. Iris who killed Marie, right? So why didn't your mom say he was the one who took Amy? She coulda killed two birds with one stone, so to speak."

Louis smiled. "I'm sure she thought about it. But Iris was a powerful man, both socially and supernaturally. She was probably afraid of retaliation. Against Amy. Or me, for that matter."

"So what happened? What happened with Amy and her folks?" Amy hated the pity in Sarah's eyes.

"They flew home from vacation early. Although she got intensive counseling, Amy wouldn't speak for the next two weeks. When she started talking again, she didn't remember anything about it. Her parents thought about keeping her in therapy, but they didn't want to make her remember something that might send her over the edge again. After awhile, everything went back to normal." Louis sounded so matter-of-fact that he might have been relating the plot of an *X-Files* episode.

Amy twisted her napkin until her fingers were white. "Jesus Christ, Louis, how do you know all that shit that happened after we got back to Arizona?" She shivered, feeling like something was crawling beneath her skin.

"Mama had her sources. Like I said, she loved you, Amy."

Maybe so, but this is still pretty fucking creepy. Amy's hand felt hot and sticky against Louis's. She gently pulled it away. "Did you know all this at the time? My God, Louis, you were only six, too."

"Hell, no. Mama told me years later. When she knew you were going to need my help." He leaned over and kissed her forehead.

Amy stared at him. She felt haunted, creeped-out, manipulated.

Louis smiled at her, almost sadly, as if he'd read her mind. "I'm sorry, Amy. I truly am."

Amy bit he lip. It *has to be enough. You can't afford to get freaked out by this. You have a lot worse to deal with, Amy-old-girl.* Louis was starting to look genuinely miserable. Amy suppressed a smile. *Besides, he really does look sorry.*

"Thank you," she whispered. She nudged his knee with hers, and a little of the weight lifted from her heart.

But just a little.

"Everything okay?" Eduardo was there with his sleepy eyes and handsome smile as he surveyed the table.

"Fine," said Amy. She put on a smile, and it made her face hurt. *Fucked, you mean, Amy-my-girl. Everything's fucked.*

THIRTY-TWO

Sarah was so excited her eyes were throwing sparks. Her grin was huge, and more than a little manic. "Okay, so we're history students. That's cool, since, y'know, I really am one. So. One of us specializes in the 1920s, so when we saw this house, we just couldn't resist knocking. Right?"

"Right, Secret Agent Girl. Now let's go, before I lose my nerve and barf all over this perfect lawn." Amy's intestines felt like a lump of cold oatmeal. Bad enough she was looking for Rags' heart, but the thought of having to see Mr. Iris again—she didn't realize how much the idea bothered her until she was here, standing on his doorstep wearing a pair of baggy Bermuda shorts and a cheese-eating grin. *I hope he doesn't notice what a wreck I am.*

She reached out with one forefinger for the doorbell, and noticed her hand was trembling. Sarah squeezed her quickly around the shoulders, and tousled Amy's hair. *My hair I should have dyed my hair and now it was too late, because her finger had just p*ressed the doorbell. It made a huge, hollow "ding-dong" sound that seemed to echo through endless rooms inside. The girls stood back and waited.

It really is a beautiful house. Massive and gleaming white, like the African plantation in that stupid old movie about migrating elephants. Amy vaguely wished that a herd of elephants would come along, right about now.

The arched oak door was swinging open.

❦

Louis and Mick, crouched in an enormous hibiscus bush along the side of the house, a huge duffel bag between them. Rags watches them from the rain gutter, his skin the mottled color and slimy texture of dead almond tree leaves. Amy's closeness is making him quiver, as if an electrical current ran through him. He is starving for her. He is amped, desperate, twitching. He looks at the human boys, and he is burning to kill them. Especially Louis. Especially him. He begins to flow, incredibly slowly, toward the drain.

⚜

It was Mrs. Iris, all right. Her blue eyes were still argon-clear and cold as a glacier. She regarded the two young women with a mixture of boredom and vague disgust. "Yes?" she asked, clearly meaning "Piss off," or whatever it was rich people said when they wanted you to leave.

"Uh . . . " Amy's tongue seemed to have glued itself to the roof of her mouth.

"Hi!" Sarah chirped, flashing her most charming smile, which was pretty fucking charming. Sarah to the rescue! "Hi, I'm Sarah Campbell, and this is Melanie Morgan. We're students—"

"Isn't it a little early for spring break?" asked Mrs. Iris, her eyes like ice chips.

"Oh, no, we're not here on vacation! We're history students, on a fellowship to the University of Southern Florida. I specialize in Victorian Literature, but Melanie here, her major is American culture of the 1920s. When we saw your beautiful house, we just had to stop. It's a gorgeous example of 1920s Palm Beach architecture, and we were just sure it would be as beautiful inside . . . "

Sarah's smile was enough to melt ice cream. And it seemed to be doing just that. Mrs. Iris's long face began to soften, just a little. *The old bitch always was a sucker for flattery.*

"Well," she said, rubbing her withered hands together with a sound like old paper being shuffled. "Well, that's different, isn't it. It's nice to see a couple of young ladies interested in something other than drinking and boys. Would you like to come in for a moment?"

"We'd love to, wouldn't we Melanie?" Sarah turned the hundred-watt grin on Sarah.

231

"Absolutely," she heard herself saying. *God, I wish I'd dyed my hair.*

They were greeted with a blast of cold air as they stepped through the doorway. Mr. Iris always did like to keep his house cold. Amy remembered shivering in her short little lacy dresses. She looked around at the patterned Art Deco ceilings, the retro-twenties wallpaper and furniture. They always said that places you had been as a child seemed smaller when you visited them as an adult, but the house still seemed cavernous and cold. Amy shuddered.

"I know, Teddy keeps it a little cool in here," Mrs. Iris was saying, as she picked a speck of dust from an Erté sculpture with one long, lavender fingernail. "He says it keeps him well-preserved." She let out a raspy laugh.

Sarah was bounding around the living room, exclaiming over everything noisily. "Oh my! This is an actual Maxfield Parrish print, isn't it? Oh, look at all the Erté!"

Taking the cue, Amy pulled a small notebook from her waist pouch and began to take notes. Mrs. Iris beamed approvingly. Amy felt her confidence grow, just a little. "Thank you so much for this opportunity, Mrs.—"

"Iris." Amy's spine stiffened. It wasn't the woman's voice. Mr. Iris stood at the top of the stairs, smiling down at her. "Mr. and Mrs. Iris. Welcome to our home, ladies."

Amy tried not to stare. He hadn't changed very much. He was older, but his shoulders were still square, his eyes bright. He still had the look of a fox about to close his jaws on the throat of a chicken. As his eyes met hers, Amy had the sickening feeling that he recognized her, recognized her the moment he saw her. But he didn't, because he was asking their names as he swept down the stairs in his corny red velvet smoking jacket.

"Melanie, is it? I've always liked that name." He was pressing her hand in both of his. *Lecherous old fuck.* "Let me give you the grand tour."

Sarah caught Amy's eye, and winked as if to say "Score!"

He flowed down the drainpipe in utter silence. If they were to look up, they would see a steady stream of dead, mottled leaves oozing down the wall, glistening like slug slime. But they didn't look up. They crouched there like the lumpen fools they were, faces sober with concentration, listening. Listening for her to call out to them. *But she won't, you bastard, you black, warm-blooded son-of-a-bitch. She won't have the chance. And even if she did, you won't be able to hear her—*

He froze. The young men froze. There was someone coming down the pebbled walkway. Someone so old she was bent at the waist. Her inch-high chunky heels ticking on the stones, her head shaking on its skinny stalk of a neck as if it would topple off at any moment. The shiny black wig she wore seemed ridiculously out of place hovering above her skull-like face. *Mrs. Lowell.* Rags recognized her, and started flowing down the wall once more. She raised a skinny hand, barely glancing at him. Seething, he stopped. He couldn't prevent himself from quivering. *Whatever you're doing, do it fast, old lady, or I'll rip their throats out, and they can watch each other bleed to death.*

The young humans looked up at her from their hiding place, their faces embarrassed and confused and stupid. The pale one, Mick, stood up and smiled idiotically. "Hello, Ma'am. We're from Foster Pool—"

The old woman's face split into a smile, revealing gleaming white dentures that looked far too large for her face. She pulled a small leather bag from her expensive blue silk dress. With a jerk of her arm, she threw the contents of the bag at the boys. Dust. Only green, glittering dust.

The dark one tried to cover his nose and mouth, but it was too late, because his eyes were already rolling back in his head. He collapsed onto the Hawaiian aggregate with a crunch. The other one was struggling to stand, clutching at the hibiscus plant. He crushed a blood-red flower between his fingers as his body spasmed, then went slack. He sprawled across Louis. Mrs. Lowell's smile grew larger.

Silently, in single file, people began to come around from the back of the house. First Mr. and Mrs. Josten. Then Mr. Tanner. Mrs. O'Neill. All of them. They were old, but there were many of them, and they wrapped their bony hands around the young humans' arms and legs.

Rags formed a face at the bottom of the rain gutter, because he felt like smiling as the old ones dragged the boys away. He knew they were taking them inside for him, for his pleasure. He would have plenty of time to deal with them. After he had dealt with Amy, of course. *Amy.* He could already taste her.

⌘

This is pure agony. What a pompous couple of rich-ass pukes. Mr. and Mrs. Iris had been showing Sarah and Amy their various historic treasures with a pride that bordered on arrogance. They went into long, boring detail about the history of each stick of furniture and object d'art. Amy's fear had receded, replaced by crushing boredom and general unease.

"Well! That just about does it!" Mrs. Iris exclaimed.

"Thank you so much." Amy chewed her lower lip. She had seen nothing that might be a clue to the location of Rags' heart. *This was a stupid idea.*

"Whatever do you mean, Estelle?" Mr. Iris beamed at his wife, then at the girls. "They haven't seen the basement yet."

Mrs. Iris froze for a moment, as if unsure of what to say. Then she smiled, just a little. "Oh, of course, dear. What was I thinking? We save our basement den for special company, which, of course, you young ladies are! Come right this way."

Amy was seized with equal parts of excitement and sudden fear. This could be it. *But what if they're serial killers? Weirder things have happened. My God, they killed Marie. What was I thinking? What if they did recognize me? We should have bought a gun! What if—*

"Come on, Mel! Let's not keep our hosts waiting." Sarah's look was sharp. Amy willed her feet to move. One step, then another, and she was following Sarah to the kitchen, through a door and down the stairs.

"Isn't it unusual for a house in Florida to have a basement? I mean, with the risk of flooding and all," she asked, trying to keep her voice steady. Mr. Iris looked over his shoulder, eyes twinkling.

"Oh, yes, it's very unusual. We had this one built. It's special, you see. It's watertight, and it has its own ventilation system."

"Like a bomb shelter?" Sarah asked as they reached the bottom.

Amy looked around nervously. *So far so good. No chains on the walls, no blood splatters. Just flamingo-pink carpeting, a tan leather couch, wood paneling and an oversized TV.*

"Indeed." Amy didn't like the look on Mr. Iris's face at all. Not at all. It was like when he used to tell her stories about executions and Medieval tortures. The old man's smile grew wider. "It's soundproof as well."

"Very interesting," said Sarah, backing toward the stairs, "but not very historic. I think we've taken up enough of your time, and so—"

Mrs. Iris picked up the TV remote and pressed a button. The door to the kitchen slammed shut.

"I think you'll stay awhile, girls," said Mr. Iris.

Sarah snarled. "Look, old man, I don't know what kind of pervert you are, but I'm inches away from kicking your wrinkled ass."

He turned on her so fast it was frightening. His bony fist caught Sarah in the temple. She made a kind of choking cough as she crumpled to the thick pile carpeting.

Amy's hands balled into fists. *I'll go down fighting.* She felt Xavier's bracelet tighten as her tendons flexed. But Mr. Iris made no move toward her. He just rubbed his knuckles, and smiled his chicken-eating grin.

"You never used to be stupid, Amelia. What happened? Did you really think I wouldn't recognize you?"

Amy wanted to scream, but her throat was constricted with rage and terror.

"He knew you were coming. He told me. He was so excited!"

"Let me go," Amy managed to whisper. "My friends know where I am."

"Oh, the two stupid boys in the garden? They don't know much of anything any more, do they, Estelle?" Mrs. Iris shook her head sadly. Amy's heart was gripped with ice. *Louis!*

"Oh, enough of this." Mr. Iris took the remote from his wife. "Let's meet the guest of honor!" He pressed a series of buttons, and an large section of the oak-paneled wall slid aside with an electrical hum.

And there he was, standing in the darkened room behind it, beautiful in Shane's now tattered leather jacket, a loose black silk shirt, tight black jeans and fashionably unlaced Doc Martens. Xavier's braid woven into his glossy black hair. Xavier's ring on one of his long, aesthetic fingers. Light glinted off his long canines and his green eyes burned like hellfire.

Amy opened her mouth and screamed.

THIRTY-THREE

He took a step forward, arms outstretched. "Amy," he whispered. His voice sounded clogged, like the gurgle of a half-blocked drain. His grin widened, impossibly huge, showing far too many teeth. Amy felt her mind slipping, slipping once again toward blackness and madness and sweet, comforting oblivion.

No. No. I'm not going to let the bastard win I'm NOT

"NO!" she shrieked, backing away. Mr. and Mrs. Iris had stepped aside, beaming like proud parents on their only son's prom night.

Figures stepped out of the gloom behind Rags. At first Amy's terrified mind thought they were monsters; shambling ghouls from a George Romero movie. But they were alive. Their shambling gait, shaking heads and trembling limbs were caused by age, not decay. Amy recognized one of them, a woman with shiny black hair and long, sharp fingernails. *Tongue Sandwich,* she thought, and almost laughed. But she was afraid that if she laughed, she would never stop. It was all so unbelievable, so outrageous, so fucking ridiculous.

Rags was reaching for her, his arms stretching like rubber, his fingers attenuating, wiggling as they got closer to her face.

Amy's lips peeled back from her teeth. Her heart was hammering so hard if felt like it might tear its way out of her chest. *This is it. He's gonna get me. The goddam boogeyman is gonna eat me all up. His smile was one of pure triumph, his eyes greedy.*

Suddenly, Amy's terror was replaced with something stronger, fiercer, hotter. She realized she was burning with rage. *How dare he. How dare this freak monster son-of-a-bitch step back into her life, terrorize her and her friends, act like she belonged to him, for Christ's sake.* Her stomach burned with furious anger. It boiled up her throat and into her mouth, breaking free with a shattering scream.

"Fuck you! Get away from me!"

Rags looked genuinely hurt. He retracted his fingers, just a little.

"Young people today are so foul-mouthed!" said Mrs. Iris in a stage whisper.

Amy snarled. "Shut up, you sick old bag! How dare you pack of freaks do this to me? How dare you?"

"Are you going to take that from her?" asked Mr. Iris, his voice pure poison. Rags looked at him quickly, like a child looking to a parent for approval.

"Take her," the old man whispered. "She's yours. She always has been." There was an approving murmur from the circle of worshippers in the darkened room.

"Mine," Rags whispered. His stretching-vine fingers brushed Amy's cheeks.

She slapped them away as if they were spiders. "You sick, deluded, pathetic monster! You can't even think for yourself. You let a vile, corrupt old man do it all for you. I'm not yours. Never will be. Not in a million fucking years."

Rags' mouth twitched. His eyes burned with anger. His lips began to curl, and behind them, his teeth had grown longer and sharper.

"You don't even know the difference between love and hate. You hate me right now. You want to kill me. That isn't love, Rags. You're not capable of love." Amy was shaking so hard she felt like her joints might come apart. But she wasn't going to just let him get her. Not this time.

"I AM!" he howled. "I love you, Amelia! My heart is yours!"

"Your heart," she snarled. "You're talking about a disgusting bunch of slime and fungus. What makes you think I'd want your heart? Where is it, anyway? At the bottom of somebody's swimming pool? In the back of a toilet, maybe?"

"It's here," he hissed. "Right here, you ungrateful bitch." He buried the fingers of both hands in his chest and pulled. His skin split with a gush of green fluid. He dug deeper, prying open the flesh, exposing woodlike ribs and slippery green muscles. Something moved, deep in his chest, squirming like a bucketful of worms. Amy recognized it immediately.

"Very nice," she said, with a nasty bravado she didn't feel. "You look like one of those gruesome paintings of Jesus they scare little Catholic kids with. Now fuck off and leave me alone. Show your ugly heart to the little old ladies. I'm sure they'll be overwhelmed." She started to turn her back on him.

Rags' hands curled into fists, or something like them. Heavy, knotted clubs of twisted wood. He raised them above his head with an inarticulate shriek. Mr. and Mrs. Iris watched hungrily as he advanced on Amy.

Sarah rolled over and groaned. Blood trickled from her forehead where it had struck the baseboard. Rags whirled on her, a dog smelling blood on a small, injured animal. He lunged.

"NO!" Amy screamed. She threw herself across Sarah's body as Rags hit her. One of his club-fists slammed into Amy's low back. She grunted, agony shooting up her spine and down her legs.

"Amy!" screamed Rags. "I didn't mean to! Amy!" He pulled her to her feet, embracing her, holding her close.

He thinks he's hurt me badly, she thought, turning her head away from his swampy smell. *Let's play it for what it's worth.* She sagged in his arms. "My legs . . . " she breathed. "Can't move . . . "

"WHAT HAVE YOU DONE?" Rags' voice was raw, shrieking metal, and Amy thought her ears would bleed. But he wasn't talking to her, he had turned to the Irises.

He laid Amy down gently on the couch, his fingers brushing the hair from her forehead. *I fooled him.* She tossed her head and groaned. She saw that Sarah had lifted herself up onto one elbow, and was watching the scene with stunned eyes.

"My dearest boy," purred Mr. Iris. "Why are you so unhappy? This is what you wanted. You wanted to posses her, body and soul. What does it matter if she's a little damaged? You'll end up destroying her eventually anyway. It's in your nature. So be strong. Get it over with."

"NO! I want to love her! I want—you perverted me! I hate you! I HATE YOU!"

It happened so fast that Amy didn't have time to turn away from the splash of blood. With a blinding motion, a sickening twist, Rags ripped Mr. Iris's head from his neck. Blood sprayed up in an unreal geyser, splashing the ceiling, the TV, the couch, everything.

His wife made a strange, choking noise and dropped to her knees.

Rags held Mr. Iris's head in one hand like a bowling ball, his long, vine-fingers sinking into the man's eyes, the soft flesh under his jaw. He brought the grisly trophy up high and smashed it down onto Mrs. Iris's perfectly coifed head. Her skull split with a sickening watermelon crunch.

The cultists were screaming, scrambling to get away. They poured from the hidden room like rats, clawing, knocking each other over, trampling. Rags roared, a predator in the grip of unstoppable blood-lust. He grabbed the nearest arm and crushed it in his grip. Before the man could start screaming, Rags smashed his head into the wall. The old woman with the shiny black wig was next. She was lucky: her throat was crushed in a single, vicious squeeze. The wig fell to the thick car-peting. *Looks like a dead rabbit,* thought Amy, fighting a crazy urge to laugh. Her stomach clamped down in a violent spasm, expelling her fancy lunch all over the floor.

Amy couldn't look away. She felt the hideous images burning them-selves through her eyes and into her brain, embedding themselves there in lurid, enhanced, superreal Technicolor detail. Words skipped through her head, bright and merciless. *Shell shock. Battle fatigue. Post-traumatic stress disorder. Fucked. In the head. For life.*

"Amy!"

Amy jumped. The voice came from the darkened room. *Louis!*

"Amy, get out of here! Run, if you can!"

Amy leapt from the couch, shoving through the bleeding cultists. Rags had his back to her, his arm down an old man's throat, and didn't see. Sarah was right behind her.

The hidden room was round, and tiled with deep red ceramic. The walls were red, as was the ceiling. *To hide the blood,* thought Amy, with a shudder. There was a stone slab in the middle of the room. Gutters ran from the slab, along the floor, to holes at the bottom of the curving wall. Brass candle holders protruded from the walls, thick black drippy candles perched in them unlit. *How fucking cliché. Looks like the set of a Peter Cushing movie.*

Peter Cushing's dead, Amy.

She pretended not to see the dark stains in the grout, or notice the faint slaughterhouse aroma that permeated the room. With the screams of the cultists ripping through the air, it could have been the outer lobby of Hell.

"Louis!" Amy shouted.

"Here! We're down here!" This time the voice was Mick's. Sarah shrieked in delight.

The men were in a shallow pit behind the altar, tied like a couple of spring hogs for the slaughter. A metal grille covered the hole, but it didn't appear to be locked. Amy and Sarah each grabbed the grate, and heaved. It came loose and they tossed it aside. Amy winced at the resounding clatter. *He had to have heard that. We're out of time.*

"Mick!" Sarah's eyes were streaming. He sat up, and she crouched down and tugged at his ropes.

"Super Sarah to the rescue," he said, and there was a love in his eyes like Amy had never before seen in him. But then Louis was sitting up, smiling at her, and he became her whole world. She wanted to kiss him, hold him, but there was no time.

"The bag!" he said.

"What?"

"The arrogant bastards threw the duffel bag in with us. I think they planned to use this stuff on us later. I'm lying on top of the damn thing!"

Amy helped him heave himself out of the pit. "Excellent," she breathed, pulling the huge skinning knife from the bag. *Just one of the little goodies we have in store for you, Rags. God bless Wal-Mart.*

She quickly cut Louis's ropes, then handed the knife to him so he could free Mick. Then she began pulling things from the bag.

❧

How overjoyed he had been when the door slid open, and there she was! Amy! His Amy! He knew she might be afraid of him, after their last few encounters. He was ready for that. Fear and love often seemed to go hand in hand. But he was not prepared for the anger. *How could she*, he thought, snapping an ancient spine over his knee. *How could she say those things to me?* He knew he had done things wrong. He could have approached this all much better. But he didn't deserve that. Pain shot through him as he thought of her face. That look. So furious. Disgusted. Almost . . . he couldn't bring himself to think the word, but it crept into his brain anyway. Almost hatred.

No. Amy can't hate me. Not when I love her. She just can't. He dropped the woman whose arms he had just twisted off, and looked over at the couch. Amy was gone. He felt the roar rising in his throat, and suddenly feared himself. He feared what he might do to her.

THIRTY-FOUR

They spun around, facing the doorway. The sound was so loud, so terrible, that Amy thought her eardrums might burst like overfilled balloons. It overpowered the shrieks and wails of the dying outside, filling her ears, so shrill it was like tearing metal, so deep it vibrated in her breastbone.

Amy clutched a hand-held propane torch before her like a magic talisman. Mick had an iron gatepost in each hand. His eyes were narrowed, feral. Louis held a fireplace poker up over one shoulder like a baseball bat, face hard and expressionless. Sarah had the other propane torch, which she was holding far away from her body, as if it might bite her. She was breathing hard, eyes wide and bright with fear. Amy felt her lips skin back in a snarl. *Come on, you bastard. Come on in.*

But when he did, nothing could have prepared her for the sight of him. He looked like some red demon from a Japanese Hell, green eyes burning from his crimson face. Particles of tissue slid down his blood-slick cheeks like meaty tears. His broken-glass fangs dripped blood. Amy saw hair and flesh caught in that nightmarish mouth, and felt her stomach lurch, her head go light. Blind, screaming panic tried to claw its way up out of her, but she savagely pushed it down. She heard her own breathing in her ears, loud as a steam engine. For a moment, everything in the room was hyper-real, crystal clear, from the drop of sweat on Mick's temple to the slight quiver of Sarah's lower lip.

And then he was in the air. He leapt flat-footed, his legs attenuating as he lunged for Amy, hands twisted into squirming, thorn-studded claws. "Traitor!" he screamed through his mouthful of knives.

She couldn't possibly get out of the way. He was coming way too fast. Amy held up the torch and screamed.

Louis swung the poker. It smashed into Rags' face with a repulsive squishy crunch, flipping him backwards.

Mick was ready with the iron gateposts. He brought one up in a vicious underhand jab, aiming for the center of Rags' back. It would have been a direct hit, but the creature twisted as he fell, and the gatepost scraped a deep trench across his ribs instead of impaling him. He whirled on Mick, and as he turned, Amy could see his face, smashed in like a pumpkin the week after Halloween. Thick green slime oozed from his mouth, and the furrow in his back. He made a horrible gurgling sound as he lunged.

Stretching his arm a good five feet, Rags wrenched one of the gateposts from Mick. He brought it high and swung it down directly at the top of Mick's head with horrifying force. Mick managed to block the blow with the other gatepost, but the impact brought him to his knees, and Rags was moving in for the kill.

Mick tore the cross from around his neck and held it up in front of his face. Rags let out a phlegmy, barking laugh and drew his gatepost back like a sledge hammer.

Mick flung the cross into Rags' face. It hit him in just below the eye. To Amy's amazement, it stuck and started smoking.

The look on Mick's face, the wonder, the triumph, the ferocious joy, was something reserved for saints in divine epiphany.

Rags shrieked and clawed the cross from his face. It stuck to his fingers for a moment, burning into his flesh, before he flung it against the wall.

Still kneeling, Mick swung his gatepost at Rags' ankles. Rags brought his boot down on it faster than the strike of a rattlesnake. Hissing, he drove the point of his gatepost toward Mick's face in a vicious jab.

That's when Sarah turned up her blowtorch and started toasting the back of Rags' neck.

He had managed to reform his face and he screamed in earnest. He dropped the gatepost and clawed at his neck, shrieking. Louis landed another blow with the poker, this time to the side of Rags' head. Mick hauled back with his gatepost, the point aimed at Rags' heart.

A knotted tentacle exploded from Rags' chest and smashed into Mick's forehead, knocking him backwards onto the cold tile floor. His head bounced when he hit, and then he was still.

With a wild scream, Sarah dove at Rags, pushing the propane torch at his face. He snaked sideways, stretching his neck like a cobra. He knocked the torch from her hands as Louis landed a blow on his lower back. Rags fell forward, and Sarah, barehanded, leapt onto his back.

"Bastard! Fucker!" she screamed. She dug her fingers into his face, ripping at his eyes.

"Sarah, no!" Amy screamed. Rags had extended his mouth into a ridged beak, like a snapping turtle, and Sarah's hands were way too close. He began to spin around with her on his back, cackling in a high-pitched voice.

Louis lowered the poker, face sick with frustration. He couldn't swing it without hitting Sarah.

Amy was frozen with terror, pinned to the spot like a butterfly on a corkboard.

"What should I do with her, Amy?" Rags shouted, still laughing. His words were hollow, distorted by the grotesque beak. "Should I fling her into the wall like a blob of dough? Should I smash her against the ceiling?" He abruptly stretched his entire body straight up, slamming Sarah's head and shoulders on the soundproof tile. She grunted, but held on. "Or, should I just bite her apart, a piece at a time?" He grabbed Sarah's forearm in both his hands, like an ear of corn. Slowly, deliberately, he brought it toward his mouth. But it wasn't a beak any more. It was a pair of glistening, jagged mandibles, surrounded by greedy, thrashing pedapalps. Smaller bug jaws gnashed and whirred and clicked beneath the fangs. The face of a spider in a junkie's nightmare.

Rags was still spinning, and every time he whirled past Amy saw Sarah's arm getting closer to his hideous jaws. Sarah looked over his shoulders and saw what was happening and she was screaming,

screaming, and Louis was trying to get a clear shot but it was happening too fast. Amy wrapped her arms around herself and started to scream and she felt the little string bracelet roll against the skin of her wrist—

And just like that, her mind cleared. Amy twisted the knob on the propane torch, making the little blue flame shoot out almost a foot. She threw herself to the ground and torched Rags' lower legs.

He let go of Sarah with a deafening squeal. She flew from his back and landed heavily on the floor, her head missing the stone altar by inches. She lay there gasping, the air knocked from her lungs.

Rags skittered backwards away from Amy. Louis began savagely hammering at Rags' head and shoulders with the iron fireplace poker.

Amy could smell burning leaves. The cloth of Rags' black jeans and the flesh underneath it were smoking. Louis was jabbing with the poker now, trying to crack Rags' chest and pierce his heart. Rags had both arms crossed over his chest, trying to protect himself, thrashing, twisting away, looking frightened and defeated.

That's probably why Louis didn't see it coming.

Balling both hands into fists, Rags shot his arms forward like unnatural pistons, like a character in a Warner Brothers cartoon from Hell, and knocked Louis across the room. The poker clattered to the floor.

Amy's breath caught, but Louis was immediately up again. This time he had one of Mick's gateposts. He threw it like a javelin, and it skewered Rags through the belly. The creature howled and grabbed at the post.

Louis began chanting something that Amy couldn't hear over Rags' screams. Louis was drawing something on the floor in chalk; some kind of design. She had never seen the pattern before, but Amy recognized what it was. A vever. Like in the hospital.

Rags fell to the floor and began to thrash. Amy crept up to him, torch in hand. *I have to finish it. I have to.*

He turned toward her, gasping, sobbing. His face was no longer that of a spider. It was smooth, unlined, beautiful. The pointed chin and ears, the full, expressive lips. Peter Pan. The Rags from her childhood, all grown up. The Rags she once loved.

"Amy," he said, his face streaked with tears. "Amy, help me. He's killing me." Rags pulled at the gatepost, but it was barbed, and held fast. Louis's singsong voice grew louder, and Rags let out a miserable howl.

Incredibly, Amy felt her eyes welling with tears. "I have to finish it," she said, out loud. She brought the torch toward his chest.

"Amy, please. I love you, I love you." He touched her hand with his, and it was just a hand, smooth-skinned and golden. "Amy, don't." His whole body shuddered. The post quivered in a way that made Amy sick to her stomach. Rags' eyes were huge, green, filled with tears, filled with love. Amy felt herself faltering. She hesitated. Her hand was releasing its grip on the torch no reaching for him *oh no* brushing his cheek *Rags my Rags*

And that was all he needed, because he was ripping the gatepost from his belly. It came loose with a nasty pop and a chunk of green flesh, and he reared back and flung it at Louis. The spinning post slammed into the side of Louis's head and dropped him to the floor with a thump and a spatter of blood.

Amy shoved the torch into Rags' face, but he took it away from her as easily as if she were a child, as if she were six years old again. He threw it aside and scooped Amy up with one arm. She kicked and pounded on him and screamed, but his arm was like a steel band around her waist.

Sarah leapt up with a cry and grabbed onto Amy's feet, but Rags was already moving, moving so fast, and Amy's tennis shoes came off in Sarah's hands.

Rags was running with her, carrying her out of the room, and Mick was unconscious on the floor and Louis was in a pool of blood and Rags was running up the stairs with her, stepping on corpses. His boots crunched on flesh and bone, his free hand tossed aside bodies that only occasionally groaned or shrieked or gurgled. He was pounding the door at the top of the stairs with a fist like a burl in an oak tree, not knocking but battering, smashing. The door came down.

He was carrying her through the house. They were out the back door. Rags was changing, holding her close to him as his body got lighter, and something sprouted from the back of him and grew and grew.

Wings.

He ran, his wings beating the warm, golden air, and suddenly they were aloft.

Amy was dizzy, short of breath, and he was squeezing her so tightly, too tight. Amy saw spots in her vision as she looked down at the house and watched it shrink into the distance.

"I love you, Amy," said Rags, laughing into the wind, and then everything went black.

THIRTY-FIVE

He was hurting. *Amy's band of thugs did some damage,* he thought, as he picked another piece of dead, hardened tissue from his neck and threw it into the swamp. The blows from the iron weapons had left exquisitely sore spots all over his body, although they had left no permanent marks. He put his hand over his chest, where his heart was untouched and strong, despite their best efforts. *Despite Amy's best efforts.* But he couldn't think about that too much. He didn't want to get too angry with her. Not when they were all alone together. *Amy. My love.* He smiled, and waited for her to wake up.

Amy stirred. She took in a deep breath and tried to roll over. She couldn't move. Her head was hanging at an uncomfortable angle and her neck was on fire with pins and needles. She slowly realized she was upright. She raised her head and opened her eyes, eyelids sticky and heavy. *What in God's name happened to me . . . ?* When she looked down and saw the thin, ropy vines wrapped around her chest, her belly, her arms and legs, she remembered it all. And wished she hadn't.

God, she was so beautiful. She looked like an exotic butterfly as she struggled in the center of the web. At first she seemed calm, pulling at her bonds as if to test their strength. But she had quickly become angry, and now she was thrashing, cursing. Her hair danced around her face like flames. Beads of sweat flew from her skin, sparkling gemlike in the air. He was very, very excited. He made himself grow hard, since that seemed like the best response. It was all too delicious. He started to laugh.

⤙⤚

"God DAMN you! Let me down from here, you fucking bastard!" Amy threw her entire weight into the struggle, although she somehow knew it was no use. It just seemed to make more of the sticky vines cling to her flesh. They were repulsive, slimy against her bare legs, and her belly where her shirt had ridden up. They stuck to her like slug slime, and seemed to be as unbreakable as steel. She yanked at them again, and heard him laughing. Anger blazed white-hot behind her eyes.

"Fuck you!" she screamed at him. Again, he laughed.

"You used to have a better vocabulary, Amy. Calm down. You're only tangling yourself up worse."

She struggled another few moments, not wanting to seem like she was obeying him, then sagged. She was exhausted.

For the first time, she took a good look at her surroundings. There were trees everywhere, twisted trees dripping with moss and vines. There was almost no land, only sluggish green water interrupted by occasional rises of mud, swamp grass, and tangled, thick roots like the tentacles of half-submerged octopi. She was suspended between two trees, in the center of a giant circular web. She saw her feet dangling in their purple socks a good two feet above a twisted platform of roots, some as thick as her thigh. She smelled brackish water and the wild, green scent of plantlife growing out of control. Mosquitoes buzzed around her head in a halo.

"Where are we?" she asked between gritted teeth.

"That should be perfectly obvious, darling. We're in the Everglades." He smiled at her winningly. He was once again his handsome, elfin self. His jacket and silk shirt were gone, and he wore only the black jeans and boots. His chest was smooth and hairless, golden as a sunset. Sections of the jeans were burned away near the calves, she noticed with some satisfaction.

Her heart was slowly wrapped in ice as she looked at him, the clouded green eyes, the charming, remorseless smile. *The Everglades.*

250

We may as well be on the fucking moon. No one's going to hear me. No matter how loud I scream.

She forced her mouth into a nasty smile. "It looks like you've won, Rags. Go ahead. Do whatever it is you're planning to. I don't give a shit."

"Really?" He slid up next to her, seeming to glide over the water. She shivered, although the air was warm and sultry. He ran a finger along her throat. "You really don't give a shit?" She turned her head away from him, teeth clenched. *He's gonna kill you anyway.*

"Get it over with," she said. "I'm getting bored."

He laughed into her neck. "You're so brave, Amy. That's just one of the things I love about you. And you're right. I could do anything I want with you, but I won't. Not yet." He moved his head snakelike to meet her averted eyes. "You see, I want you to want me, too."

She snorted. "In your dreams, wormboy."

"Yes. In my dreams, for years and years and years." He brushed his lips along her jawbone. They were cold and smooth as glass. She felt his tongue flick into the hollow of her jaw. *Oh Jesus Christ no*

"So how come you're alive?" she said, voice harsh, wildly hoping to distract him.

"You and your band of desperadoes weren't *that* deadly, my love. You didn't even scratch the surface." His grin was overly toothy.

"That's not what I meant. I thought Virginia had killed you. Why are you still here?"

He abruptly pulled back from her, eyes narrowed. "I don't want to talk about it."

"Oh, you don't want to talk about being nearly killed by petite middle-aged woman? I guess I can understand that. It's pretty embarrassing, huh." Amy stared him down.

"I was a child," he muttered. "It wasn't my fault."

"Nothing's ever your fault, is it, Rags."

He turned his back to her, his boots squelching in the mud. "Mr. Iris came looking for me. He found me. Found my heart, I mean. There was nothing left of . . . of me."

Amy remembered his shriek as Virginia brought the torch to his face, and winced. *I will not feel sorry for him. I will not.*

251

"Anyway, my heart was still alive. Barely. Mr. Iris took what was left of it home with him. He put it—put me in a jar and filled it with swampwater. Then he sacrificed for me. Over and over. I remember all the blood . . . "

Rags' face was dreamy. "Mr. Iris would leave me in front of the TV all day, and then he and his friends would bring me in for ceremonies at night. After a while, I started to grow."

"Left you in front of the TV all day? No wonder you're fucked up," Amy sneered.

"You're funny, Ame. You always were. But you can't make me mad at you right now. I had to grow up all over again, did you know that? My heart finally healed, and I started to grow a body again. It took me thirteen years to come back all the way." He was staring out into the swamp, eyes melancholy. "Mr. Iris raised me. He brought me back. And I killed him. Jesus, Amy, I killed him."

Amy tossed her head in a vain attempt to drive off the mosquitoes. "He was a bastard, Rags. He didn't care about you. He just wanted to use you in his ugly rituals. You were just a power source for him. A wall outlet he could plug into whenever he wanted. He didn't love you." She scowled, wondering why she had told him that. *Why she had just tried to make him feel better?*

He looked thoughtful. "I suppose you're right. I wish he had . . . maybe I'd have a better grasp on things now. Oh well." He grinned. "He's dead now, right?"

A chill ran down the back of Amy's neck. "Yeah, Rags. He's dead. And so are all the rest."

He chuckled. "What a mess! Gee, maybe they'll think your friends did it. That'd be funny."

Amy felt anger rising in her, but she felt too defeated to unleash it. She closed her eyes. "Why don't you just shut up, okay?"

His demeanor was unchanged. "Sure, I'll shut up. In fact, I'll just leave you alone for awhile. You can think about me while I'm gone. Absence makes the heart grow fonder, don't-cha know!"

And just like that, he was gone. He seemed to melt into the swamp. Amy stared after him, relieved he was gone, afraid to be alone. She struggled against the web for a little while, although she realized it was futile. She watched swamp rats scurry through the trees. She tried to keep the mosquitoes off her face. She tried to ignore the growing pressure in her bladder. Finally, she hung her head, and slept.

THIRTY-SIX

He lay in the moss-lined branches of a tree, far enough away that she couldn't see him, but not so far that he couldn't smell her. Night was falling, and the swamp was filled with the voices of bullfrogs and insects. He closed his eyes, and remembered things he'd rather forget. The searing, agonizing pain when Virginia brought her torch to his face. The sensation of dying, or the closest he could come to it; being reduced down to his most elemental level. Feeling his consciousness burn away until there was nothing left but his wounded heart, and all he could feel was hunger and ripping agony.

There was a blank in his memory after that, and he was abstractly grateful. The next time he regained awareness, he was in a glass jar, in Ted Iris's den.

"Hello, Rags," he remembered Iris saying, beaming down at him. The man's face was stretched and distorted by the thick, uneven, curved glass of the antique vinegar jar. "What a fine trick! You have eyes! Would you like to see?"

He thinks *no, please,* but it is too late, the man is holding up a mirror, and he sees himself. A twisted mass of pulsing green floating in murky fluid, like a repulsive sideshow exhibit, something kept in the back room with a sign that says "The Thing." Vestigial eyes on stalks, like those of a crab, stare back at him. "Where is my body?" he wants to shout. But he has no mouth.

"You're very lucky, my boy," says Iris. "That black bitch nearly killed you. But you're stronger than she is, aren't you. Yes, you are.

254

Aren't oo, widdle boy." In his mouth, the baby talk sounds obscene, insulting. Rags wants to strike out, but he has nothing left. Nothing but the pain.

Iris reaches for him, wrapping his big white hands around the jar, and Rags feels the queasy sensation of being lifted. Iris carries him through the hidden door and into the round back room that would become so familiar over the next decade, but today, the first time, it is terrifying. He is suddenly surrounded by humans in black robes, chanting, shouting, bending over him and looking with their watery, distorted eyes. They are grotesque in the flickering candlelight. Rags shrinks down to the bottom of the jar like a salted slug and cowers.

They are holding something over his jar, something black and horrible that screams and flaps spastic wings. A flash of silver, and the jar is coated with red. The room, the people, Iris and his wife, all seen through a bloody lens, and he quivers half from fear and half from hunger. Then they are opening the jar, shaking the rooster's carcass, blood falling into the filthy water. He sucks it into himself greedily, and the pain gets just a little better.

Time goes by, although he doesn't know how much. There are more ceremonies, more sacrifices. More chickens. A goat. A skinny black man. A young Cuban woman. He grows stronger, and eventually, the pain fades away.

Mr. Iris leaves him in the den during the day, with the television as his companion. He watches, watches, and learns everything he should know. He learns that the strongest wins, that love prevails, that everything is made right at the end of the show, that the woman loves the one she hated at the start of the movie. He watches, and takes heart.

In the evenings, Iris brings him a bowl filled with swampwater and algae. He begins to form a new body. It is tiny at first, curled up like a shrimp, a mutant fetus with tentacles and a lobster tail. It is hard, hard work, but he builds it up each night, making it stronger and bigger, because he has a purpose. He has a true love. *Amy,* he thinks, *Amy.* She is his whole world, his whole reason for being.

The body grows bigger. It outgrows the bowl, and Iris moves it to the bathtub. Rags watches as it splashes and mewls for food. He does not yet occupy it; it is merely an eating machine. He is disgusted as its tiny, razored jaws close on the head of a mouse. Iris laughs as it snaps at his fingers.

Soon the body is included in the sacrifices. It seems to take delight as it thrashes and wallows in blood and flesh, but Rags knows that is impossible. It has no soul, not yet. He wonders what makes it seek out death. He looks at Iris through the jar, at the quivering grin on the man's face as he eviscerates a goat.

The day comes when he is ready to merge with the body. It is roughly the size of a three-year-old child, lumpen and ungraceful. It has legs now instead of gills, and a face instead of a clump of tentacles.

Iris holds the thrashing thing down as Heart-Rags slides inside its skinny chest. He stretches his tendrils, veinlike, through the creature's arms, its legs, its head, and takes possession. It feels incredibly good. He opens the creature's eyes, and looks out through them. For the first time in years, he sees the world unhampered by glass and dirty fluid. Iris and his wife are grinning down at him. He stands, unsteadily. They cheer and clap their hands as if he were their baby son taking his first step. Unwillingly, he feels a surge of love for them.

It is no more than a month later when they press the knife into his hands, and help him slit the throat of a crying, pleading junkie.

Rags' eyes opened with a start. He had been dreaming, or something like it. He slid down the tree, unsettled, agitated. He needed Amy to make it better.

THIRTY-SEVEN

Amy awoke in darkness. She felt arms around her waist, a face pressed to her belly. Terror started to surge through her, then she remembered where she was. *It's only Rags.* She frowned at the strange thought, and grew angry. "Get off me," she snapped. She could barely see the top of his head in the gloom.

He looked up at her, face streaked with tears. "Stop it," she said. "You told me once that you can't cry. Don't jerk me around."

"I learned how," he said, releasing her. He left his hands resting lightly on her hips as he knelt before her. "I love you, Amy."

She fought back a wave of pity. "Well, I don't love you. Do you know what I did when you first showed up on campus? I puked. I puked every time you got near me."

She was amazed at his smile. "I know you did. Do you know why?"

"Because you make me sick?"

"Not exactly, Amy. Your blood was remembering me. I'm a part of you. You have me in your veins. You didn't forget, did you? That part of you was waking up, reacting to me." He kissed her belly, and this time his lips were warm. "I'm not offended. I'm just sorry you were sick."

She tried to twist away from him, but the web held fast. "Let me go, Rags. I'm tired. My neck hurts. I'm hungry. If you loved me, you wouldn't do this to me."

He looked at her for a moment, green eyes unreadable, opaque, then scampered up the nearest tree with unnerving speed. He perched in the very top like a vulture, smiling down at her.

"I'm so sorry you're uncomfortable, my love. But people have . . . have told you bad things about me. You've been brainwashed against me. See, I think if you stay here awhile, you'll remember that you love me too. You did love me, Amy. You can't deny that."

He was right. There was a time, when she was just a child, that Rags was her whole world. A tear slid down her dirty cheek. She couldn't think of anything to say, so she turned away from him and tried to sleep.

"Don't worry," she heard him say. "I'll protect you. I'll watch over you. Always."

THIRTY-EIGHT

The pirate ship bucked and tossed on a sea gone mad. Blood drenched the decks, washing warm over Amelia's bare feet, touching the hem of her dress and creeping up the white satin like red lace. Death was all around her, inescapable. She looked around wildly. Captain Louis was nowhere in sight. The body of Salvatore, the noble sailor, lay at her feet, a brutal, meaty gash across his chest exposing his once-fearless heart. The dying crawled over the dead, trying to escape the slaughter.

And there were so many dead. Old women and men, scattered like crimson autumn leaves across the ship. *Old? Why are they old? Pirates aren't old.*

Screams rose and fell in a horrible symphony that seemed to get louder and louder, until Amelia thought she might lose her mind. *No it isn't like this why is it like this?* The smell of blood and gunpowder made her feel faint. Captain Tristan's thug advanced on her, grinning like a rabid hyena. She grasped the cutlass harder, harder, until her fingers where white as bone.

"C'mere, you little bit 'o crumpet," the man laughed, showing broken, jagged teeth. Amelia willed herself to swing the cutlass, to separate his offensive head from his body, but her arms would not obey. He was almost upon her.

The man's chest exploded into a red, juicy orchid of bone and flesh. He had time to look surprised before he gurgled blood through his nose and fell heavily to the blood-slicked deck.

Captain Tristan rose up behind him in the haze, pistol smoking, green eyes narrowed and glowing like witchfire. His black silk shirt billowed like the cannon smoke that swirled around him. His pointed ears and long, sharp canines made him look like the Devil Himself. Amelia wanted to look away, but found she could not. He was as beautiful as he was terrible. No no I don't want to do this

Tristan kicked the body of the ugly pirate aside, and Amelia saw that his boots were bloody to the ankle.

He shoved the pistol into his belt and cocked his head at her, smiling.

She raised the cutlass higher. "Come no closer, sir, or I'll be forced to harm you." She tossed her head, her fiery hair dancing like the mane of a wild horse. Her emerald eyes sparkled with fierce anger. Anger she didn't feel any more, all she felt was tired, just let this be over, please?

With a wicked laugh, Tristan plucked the sword from her hand as easily as picking a flower from the vine. He tossed it aside and swept her into his arms.

"I apologize for the behavior of my man. I felt he was being a bit too forward, so I took it upon myself to discipline him. He will not bother you again." He busied himself with nuzzling in her neck.

She turned her face away. "You are a brute, sir, and a coward. When Captain Louis comes for me, he will deal with you like the criminal you are."

"Captain Louis?" Tristan laughed again, roughly, lips brushing Amelia's cheek. "Do you see Captain Louis? He is not here, Amelia. He cannot save you. No one can save you."

She felt his tongue flick into her ear, and shivered.

"Would it be so terrible to love me, Amelia? Would it?"

"Yes!" she cried, struggling against him, tiny fists raining blows on his chest. But he was strong, so very strong. His words echoed over and over in her ears.

"Would it be so terrible to love me?" Would it? It would be so easy to say yes, so easy, and then he'd let you down from there . . .

Spent, Amelia sagged against Captain Tristan's broad chest, and awaited her fate.

THIRTY-NINE

When she awoke this time, the sun was high above the trees. Thirst clawed at her throat as she opened her sticky eyes and looked around. Her neck and shoulders were tortured with countless, white-hot muscle spasms. To her utter humiliation, Amy realized her bladder had let go in her sleep.

How long have I been here? Two days? Three? Her stomach ached with hunger and sorrow. Wincing as she turned her head, she saw Rags crouched in the tree, a plastic bag in his hand. His eyes were wide with worry.

He slid down the tree like a snake and was at her side in a moment, taking her face in his hands.

"How are you?" he whispered.

"How do you think I am?" She didn't recognize the rasping voice that came over her lips.

"Poor Amy." He took a plastic bottle from the bag and twisted off the cap, raised it to her lips. Water. She drank greedily.

When she was finished, he took a cloth from the bag and wet it down with the bottled water. He began to wash her face, ever so gently.

She sighed as he smoothed her eyes, her forehead, her neck, the cool cloth feeling like heaven. "Thank you," she whispered. He only smiled at her. With another cloth, he washed her legs, where urine had left trails on her sweaty skin. She couldn't look at him. It was too embarrassing. But he didn't say anything, just washed her, and now he was taking off her socks and washing her feet. It felt so good she nearly groaned.

He set the cloth aside and began to massage her feet. "Amy," he said, not looking up, "This is ridiculous. It doesn't have to be like this. All you need to do is tell me."

Her eyes were closed, and she didn't seem to have the strength to open them. He was rubbing her calves now, and it just felt so good. "Tell you what," she murmured.

"You know what." His hands were strong on her thighs. "Tell me you love me. That's all."

"Rags—" she wanted to say something, but she didn't know what. Somehow he had slid back up the tree and was behind her in the branches. His hands closed on the back of her neck, and began to knead. This time, she did groan.

"Hush. Hush my angel, my precious. Just think about it. All you have to do is tell me, and I'll take you down from here. We'll go into town, to the most expensive hotel in Miami. I'll draw you a bath. We'll order room service. You can have anything you want."

Amy's stomach grumbled, and Rags chuckled. "Steak, lobster, name it my darling one, and it's yours. And then we'll love each other. All night. Every night. We'll love each other for the rest of our lives, Amy. What's so terrible about that?"

The muscles in her shoulders slowly relaxed under his touch. Tears of relief slid from the corners of her eyes. It just felt so impossibly delicious.

He was working the muscles at the base of her skull as he spoke quietly into her ear. "I'm sorry about all this ugliness, Amy. I never meant it to be like this."

Little shocks of pleasure spread down the back of her neck. She wanted to be angry, to scream and fight, but that seemed so hard right now, as impossible a task as making water flow uphill. *Would it be so bad? Would it really?*

He spoke as if he had read her mind. "I can be anyone you want me to, Amy. I can look any way, I can feel any way. I'm yours. Yours to command."

She tried not to cry out as he rubbed the muscles along either side of her spine, giving her a lot of pleasure along with just a little pain. "Then let me go," she gasped.

"Of course, of course. All you have to do is say that you're mine, too. Just say it, Amy."

He slid around the web like a liquid, kneeling before her on the tangle of roots. His hands rested on the curves of her hips, his eyes gazing upward like a saint pleading for mercy from God. "Say it," he whispered, like a lover. "Say it."

Amy licked her cracked lips and gazed into his eyes. They were the greenest things she had ever seen, and deep, like the waters of a shimmering lagoon. *But hadn't they been cloudy before? No, of course not. Rags has beautiful eyes. Beautiful.* They seemed to reflect nothing but love, perfect, undying love. She feared that she would become lost, would drift through the green forever, so she let her heavy eyelids close.

I could say it. It would be easy. And it wouldn't be so bad, not really, because he's beautiful, and he loves me, and he'll take care of me . . .

She felt her lips starting to open, her mouth starting to form a word. She still did not dare open her eyes.

"Come on, Amy," came his voice in a husky whisper. "Come on, love. Don't be angry with me. I'm sorry about all this. But it had to be this way. You made me do it, that's all. But it'll soon be over, and we'll be together."

You made me do it.

Amy's eyelids flew open, but all she could see was white-hot rage.

"You bastard!" she screamed. "How dare you tell me I made you do this! You did it yourself! You did it all!"

"Amy, Amy . . . "

"Shut up! Just shut the fuck up! How dare you blame me for what you did. You sick fuck!"

His eyes had changed from limpid green to a hot, blazing jungle-cat emerald. Emerald—with a muddy, dirty film somewhere beneath, a film that had never really gone away. His mouth twisted into a petulant frown.

"You don't know what you're saying. You—"

"The hell I don't! You kidnapped me! You slaughtered all those people! You hurt my friends, maybe killed them! If you killed them—if you killed Louis, I'll hate you forever, you piece of shit!"

He was snarling now, his teeth lengthening. "Don't say his name! I'm warning you, Amy, don't say it!"

She looked down at him, and he seemed to be coiled tightly, a cornered animal ready to spring. *He could kill me,* she thought, and realized she didn't care. *It has to end now. Now.*

Amy grinned, a nasty, sardonic snarl that hurt her face. "Don't say Louis's name? Why not, Rags? I've said it hundreds of times already. I've whispered it, I've moaned it, I've even screamed—"

The blow caught her totally by surprise, snapping her head sideways so hard she thought her neck would break. The pain followed, blossoming in her cheek and spreading into her skull in nasty little spikes.

Tears in her eyes, she forced her grin wider. "Good boy, Rags. I knew you'd show your true face to me before this was over. I remember it, you know. That squirming, wriggling monstrosity of yours. That's who you really are—a pathetic monstrosity."

He was rippling all over. Thorns and spikes blossomed on his skin and shrank back again in waves. His face was contorted into a mask of murderous rage. His clenched fists were ironwood clubs. Amy's stomach cramped with fear, but it was too late to stop.

It has to end.

"Go ahead," she hissed. "Kill me. It's what you really want, isn't it. Underneath all that sweet talk about love, all you really want is my blood in your mouth. You really are the big bad wolf, Rags."

She laughed, a harsh, rasping chuckle that was ugly and unfamiliar in her ears.

"No," he said, tears spilling from his narrowed eyes. "I'll show you."

"Oh, you already have." With deadly accuracy, she spit a bloody glob in his face.

Seeing it run down his cheek was the last thing she remembered before his fist lashed out and the world exploded into white light.

FORTY

"Oh God, I didn't mean to, I didn't mean to." Rags curled his arms around his belly and sobbed. He looked up at her, Amy, his love, hanging from the web so limp and bloody, and he wanted to die.

He threw back his head and screamed as his fingers dug into his chest, green fluid gushing from his body and mixing with the fetid water of the swamp. Howling, weeping, he tore his heart from his body.

It hurt. Oh, how it hurt. Nothing had ever felt like that, not even when Virginia had torched his face, not even when she had plunged the iron through his heart. He felt as if he were ripping in two. White-hot pain screamed from the center of his chest and into his arms and legs as he pulled the tendrils of his heart free.

He dropped to his knees, the world spinning around him. He crawled across the roots to Amy, reaching for her with his free hand, grasping her foot.

He pulled himself up her body with desperate grabs, like a man pulling himself from a pool of quicksand. He stared into her slack face.

Tenderly, he licked the blood from her mouth and chin. She didn't stir. Her head swung heavily, like a sack of sand.

"Don't be dead," he whispered. "You can't be dead. Here's my heart. Take my heart."

And he wrapped it around her chest, a pulsing, living green octopus that clutched at her and snaked its tendrils into her clothes, seeking her bare flesh, squeezing, squeezing.

Rags dropped from her body like a satiated tick, landing in a heap at her feet.

He lay there for the longest time, forming and reforming, squirming slowly, like molten metal in the crucible. Still she didn't move. When his guilt became too much to bear, he slithered into the stinking water and vanished, leaving his heart behind.

FORTY-ONE

Amelia brought her hands up to Captain Tristan's chest. He chuckled as he bent his head to kiss her.

Violently, she shoved him away.

He sprawled on the bloody deck, eyes wide with surprise.

"How dare you?" roared Amelia. Roared? Amelia doesn't roar. *"HOW DARE YOU!"*

She raised her hands over her head, jabbing her fists at the heavens. Black clouds started to form above the ship, roiling like a cauldron of molten lead. The pirates from both vessels ceased to fight, lowered their cutlasses, and looked to the sky. The clouds were a living thing, angry, vindictive and murderous.

"Come on!" screamed Amelia to the heavens. "Strike! STRIKE!"

Her scream was lost in a deafening blast of thunder. For a split-second, the world was silent, and then the lightning came. It forked down from the sky like Satan's pitchfork, exploding the Mettalica's mast in a rain of splinters and flame. Burning shreds of the sail floated down like autumn leaves, spreading fire to the body of the ship. Somewhere, a keg of gunpowder exploded.

Amelia whirled around and around, laughing wildly. Captain Tristan was scuttling across the deck on his back like a crab, trying to escape the flames, trying to escape her.

The captain's cabin caught fire, the windows exploding out in a glittering shower of glass. Tristan covered his head and wailed.

Amelia seized a long, jagged section of the mast that had landed near her feet. It was already soaked in blood as she raised it over her head, hellfire dancing around her, making her look like an avenging angel.

Tristan screamed like a girl as she plunged it into his black heart, pinning him to the deck like a bug.

He squirmed and thrashed as she danced around him through the flames, a goddess gone mad with vengeance, drunk on the scent of blood. Her laughter soared to the sky, and it roared back its thunderous approval.

FORTY-TWO

The first thing she felt was the pain in her jaw. It was total and inescapable, pounding in her head, making her eyes water. Her mouth was hanging slack, and she couldn't close it. Her efforts brought her only grating agony and dry heaves. The side of her face was hot and swollen. Her right eye ran constantly, torturing her with the itch of tears running under her chin and down her shirt. Her chest felt hot and tight.

Amy raised her head, and nearly passed out. She breathed deeply until the pain and throbbing subsided, then opened her eyes. Her eye, anyway. The right one was swollen to a puffy slit.

The sun had set, and Rags was nowhere in sight. She remembered his fist flashing toward her, and once again her rage boiled over. She struggled against the sticky web like an animal caught in a leghold trap, screaming, snarling. Bloody spit ran down her chin.

It was no use. If anything, she was more embedded than she had been before. *Amy the tarbaby. Amy the fly. Why was it so tight around her chest?* She dropped her chin to her breastbone and tried to see.

The scream ripped out of her with a will of its own, tearing at her throat, stretching her mouth and sending a sickening wave of pain through her jaw.

His heart embraced her like a lover, its tendrils creeping under her clothes and squirming against her skin. It was cool and slightly clammy and it was squeezing her so tightly that her breath came in shallow pants.

She thrashed. She screamed. She knew, *knew,* that if she didn't get it off of her, she'd lose her mind. Eyes rolling, she stared into the darkness, and it seemed to close in on her. Hot, muggy, like the breath of a giant beast.

Flash. The vines and moss and trees, illuminated flashbulb bright. Amy stopped struggling for a moment.

Flash. The roots below her.

Flash. The sky above, lit strangely, like a nighttime filter in a sixties horror movie.

This is what it feels like. This is what it feels like when your mind cracks wide open.

A cloud of mosquitoes, perhaps drawn to her sweat and the crust of blood around her nostrils, encircled her head in a squealing halo.

Amy tossed her head, causing deep throbs of pain, but they still buzzed in her ear. They still crawled across her cheeks, and bit her tender lips. One crept across her swollen eyelids, tiny feet touching her eyeball. It was unbearable. Had her hands been free, she would have clawed her own face off to make it stop.

"Get off 'ee!" Amy shrieked, her words slurred and thick, her lips unable to meet.

"DIE!"

And they did. Just like that. The mosquitoes jumped away from her skin and dropped into the swamp, as if Amy were a human bug zapper.

For a moment, she was perfectly still.

I'm a part of you . . . You didn't forget, did you?

Amy's head cleared, slowly, like a clouded pane of glass being wiped clean. The pain in her body, the grip of Rags' heart, receded into the distance. She became aware of the sounds of the swamp. The distant, shrill cry of a nighthawk, the ripple of a watersnake passing by, a swamp rat rustling in the trees. Her eyes narrowed. She concentrated. The night became lighter, lighter still, as if God had turned up a giant rheostat.

I'm not crazy. It's his blood.

In my eyes.

Amy's head snapped around to look at the rat. It was crouched in the fork of a branch, nibbling at something. It finished its snack and began to wash its paws with a tiny pink tongue.

"Stah," Amy said. *Stop.*

The rat froze. Not as if it had been startled by a predator, but literally froze, tongue out, mid-lick.

Come here.

This time Amy used only her mind, but the rat heard her just the same. Slowly, it crossed the branches, trembling. It leapt from its tree to one of the two which supported the web, and continued closer, closer. Amy could see the terrified glaze of its eyes as it approached her.

Stop.

Again, the animal froze, just short of the sticky green vines that imprisoned Amy.

Chew through it. Set me free.

Trembling harder and harder, the rat reached forward, opening its mouth to reveal chisel-like upper and lower teeth. It closed its jaws on the nearest strand of web, and gnawed.

Amy reached her mind out into the swamp, ever-expanding concentric circles of thought, and called. Rats began to creep from the surrounding trees and roots, vibrating with terror.

She looked at their twitching whiskers, their miserable eyes, their heaving flanks, and pitied them. They were innocent victims, victims of circumstance, in the wrong place at the wrong time. Like Xavier. Like Rosie.

Like me.

She pitied them, but still, she called them. Tens, dozens, hundreds of them. And they came.

FORTY-THREE

He came slithering back to her on his belly, as he knew he deserved. He swam below the surface of the swamp, wriggling through the mud, his body long and tapered. *She'll forgive me,* he told himself, over and over again. *She has to.*

Because if she doesn't, you're nothing. Nothing at all.

He would apologize, would fall on his face before her and beg her forgiveness. He would cry, and promise her it would never, never happen again.

A lie.

He winced, causing a little splash in the water. *Not a lie. I won't hurt her again. I won't, I won't, I won't.*

She would forgive him. Of course she would, and then they'd leave this place. He imagined giving her a bath, washing her alabaster skin, worshipping her. He would brush her golden hair, placing the tiniest kiss on the back of her neck when he was done. He would take her hands in his and rub them with the finest lotion, kissing each finger as he did. He would—

Rags emerged from the mud, eyes still flat and reptilian, and he couldn't believe what he saw. It just couldn't be.

Amy was free. Bits of the web still clung to her, wrapped around her arms and legs like bracelets. She stood on the roots, hands dangling at her sides, head cocked, perfectly motionless. *Waiting for me.* Her mouth was puffy and twisted, face distorted with swelling, discolored with bruises. Her right eye was a black, shiny, slitted plum. Her left blazed hot, feral green, cutting him to the core. A legion of rats crouched around her, quivering. His heart was still wrapped around her chest.

He emerged fully from the swamp, taking his manshape as he did. Naked, he stood before her. His mouth opened and closed. "No," he whispered.

"Yes," she said through her swollen, bloody lips, and she tore his heart from her chest.

She threw it down onto the roots and stepped on it.

He screamed, unsure if the pain that ripped through him was physical or mental.

Her molten stare never wavered as she crouched down and grasped two of his heart's tendrils in her hands. The heart was thrashing like a bug beneath her foot, wracking him with agony, but he couldn't move, couldn't do anything.

She won't hurt me, not really, she can't. But it wasn't true, and he knew it.

—*Kill him*—

He heard her thought as clearly as if she had spoken it. Tears poured from his eyes as the rats sprang at him, sinking their tiny, vicious teeth and claws into his flesh.

He looked at her face, at her sweet, beloved face, battered almost beyond recognition. He saw her sweet mouth, crooked and bloody, and knew he deserved to die.

Knew he wanted to die.

That didn't stop him from screaming when she began to rend his heart with her hands and teeth.

His last thought:

To savage me with broken jaws.

How much she must hate me.

❧

Amy didn't remember wandering into the swamp. She didn't remember being sick with fever, or the pain in her face and head. She didn't remember passing out in the cradle of a banyan tree's roots. She didn't remember the airboat tour guide who found her, gently loaded her into his boat, and took her to safety. But she did remember the rats.

Lying in her hospital bed she saw them, over and over in her head, ripping Rags into pieces, pulling chunks of his flesh away and burrowing in for more. She heard his shrieks. She saw him standing there, then lying there when he couldn't stand any more, not fighting them. She didn't really recall everything she did to the heart, to *his* heart, and for that she was grateful.

She did remember releasing the rats, telling them they could go, apologizing to them for what she had done. They had run from her like they were on fire.

Holding her parents' hands, she lied to them. She told them she was abducted by a crazy man, who later shot himself in the swamp.

There was a half-hearted attempt to find a body. Of course, there was no body to find.

Weeping, Mandy told her daughter that the authorities suspected the same man who had raped Rosie, who had killed a real estate woman and a hospital security guard back home. They suspected he had been stalking Amy for a long time; maybe since she was a child. Tom and Mandy exchanged a strange, horror-sick, guilty look that Amy wasn't supposed to understand. Mandy told her daughter she was lucky to be alive. Amy nodded, eyes filled with tears.

She could barely bring herself to ask about Louis, Sarah, and Mick. Not knowing was torture, but if they were dead, if *Louis* were dead, she was sure her heart would stop.

"Are they okay?" she heard herself whisper, and then her breath caught, and wouldn't go in or out.

Tom and Mandy exchanged worried looks. Amy's heart seized up.

"They're fine," Mandy said, voice hesitant. Whoosh, Amy's breath let out. Her whole body went limp.

"But honey, something horrible happened. There was a—a massacre. They're questioning your friends about it."

"They can't think they did it—"

"Of course not, Mophead" said Tom, patting her hand. He hadn't called her that in years. "It was just something really awful, really, well . . . kind of unbelievable. They think it was the same guy. Amy, do you remember Mr. Iris?"

"Yeah?" Amy feigned surprise, interest. She fingered Xavier's bracelet, stained with her blood and sweat. Her father glanced at it, his face registering faint distaste before he spoke again.

"Well . . . he was one of the people killed, honey. Him and his wife, and some of the other folks we used to know around here. Mrs. Lowell. Mr. Jasper."

"My God." She looked away from him, as if it were too horrible to bear, because she didn't want him to see the lie in her eyes. The slaughter she had seen was distant, insignificant, like the throb of the wires in her jaw below the cool surface of the morphine in her blood.

Her father brushed the hair from her forehead, like he used to do when she was a little girl. "Amy?"

"Mm-hmm?" She was incredibly tired all of a sudden.

His brow was knit. He couldn't meet her eyes. "What were you doing here? In Florida? What were your friends doing at Mr. Iris's house?"

"I'm tired, Daddy."

"Of course you are, baby. Go to sleep." He kissed her forehead. Her mother bent down and kissed her cheek. Amy breathed in her clean, sane scent as she sank into darkness.

Amy awakened, hours later, to find Detective Paul Blythe in her room, along with a moon-faced woman from the FBI. She cried and sobbed and deflected their questions with an ease that almost alarmed her. Amy watched them leave, and took some satisfaction in knowing that they were more confused than when they entered.

My reality is trashed, boys and girls. Here, have a little taste.

EPILOGUE

One Year Later

Laughter rang through the apartment, and Amy drank it in like sweet cool water. She leaned back in the big double papa-san chair, snuggling up against Louis. He wrapped his arm around her shoulders and kissed her head.

"Careful, you two!" warned Sarah. "Those things fall over if you look at 'em funny!" She was sprawled across Amy's blue plaid Goodwill-special couch, her feet in Mick's lap, munching M&Ms from a plastic cereal bowl.

"Thud," added Mick.

"Wouldn't be the first time," said Louis with a wicked smile. Amy smacked him on the arm.

Sarah looked at Xavier, sitting cross-legged on the floor. "Hey, you! There's plenty of room up here for you too, you know." When he didn't respond, Sarah bounced a peanut M&M off his head.

He looked up and grinned. "Sorry. I was totally absorbed in Amy's CD collection. You have a lot of cool stuff here. I love the blues."

"Most of them are Louis's. I, on the other hand, contributed most of the Taco Bell superhero glasses." Amy stretched, smiling. The chair creaked.

Sarah rubbed her fingers through her newly short-cropped curls. The tiny diamond on her left hand glittered, and she held it up to inspect it for what Amy figured to be the eight millionth time. "A match made in heaven. And I really like your new place, Ame. You guys did a good job decorating it."

Amy looked around at the mismatched furniture, the cheaply matted movie posters and Art Nouveau prints, the blue paisley curtains. "You're too kind."

"Or possibly visually impaired," said Louis. Sarah whipped an M&M at him with deadly accuracy.

I love this, thought Amy. *I love it so much.*

"What're these?" Xavier scooted across the floor to examine a set of big heavy old encyclopedias lined up against the wall.

Amy sat up so fast that Louis had to lean sideways to avoid being pitched out of the chair. "My folks sent 'em. They used to be mine, they were in the basement or something. Don't touch 'em, they're all dusty and gross."

Amy jumped out of the chair and Louis dove for the center as it started to rock backwards. It steadied. Mick and Sarah clapped appreciatively.

"Good show! Good show!"

Amy held out her hands to Xavier. He took them, smiling, and she helped him up off the floor. She had long ago become used to the sight of his missing finger.

"So how're the wedding plans coming?" Amy asked Sarah, who was playing with her engagement ring yet again.

"T-minus four months!" Sarah grinned. "Everything's cool. Mick's mom and dad have really been doing most of the work."

"Yep. They're just thrilled to death that we're getting married in the church." Mick tickled Sarah's feet, making her squirm.

Xavier plopped down onto the couch next to Sarah and grinned down at her. "So how are those Catholic lessons coming, you little heathen? Have you at least stopped smoking when you walk through the church doors?"

"I wear sunblock. And they're going just fine, thank you. I really like Father McKenna. He's pretty cool." Sarah held her ring up to the light. "And he's really cute!"

"Sicko!" Mick gave her a mock-scowl and pushed her feet off his lap. She gave him puppy eyes and crawled across the couch to snuggle.

"Eeeeow!" shouted Xavier. "Breeders in heat!"

Amy walked around to the back of the papa-san chair and put her hands on Louis's shoulders. She watched Mick and Sarah get mushy. *Sarah, Catholic. Who woulda thunk it?* She rubbed Louis's solid muscles, making him sigh. *Oh well. They cope in their way. I cope in mine.*

"How'd your folks take you guys moving in together?" Sarah was now sitting in Mick's lap, eyes sparkling.

Amy laughed. "Oh, they went through the usual 'not my baby girl' spasms, but they got over it. Mostly due to Louis. He totally charmed them."

"How'd you manage that? Voodoo?" Mick's smile was wicked.

Louis raised an eyebrow. "Well, I took these little dolls, see . . . "

Everybody cracked up.

Sarah stood up and stretched. "So Amy tells me you're going home for a week, Louis."

"Yup," he said. "Back to Florida."

Sarah and Louis locked eyes for a moment. Amy knew what she was thinking;

Don't bring it up. Don't talk about it. Don't even mention it.

Amy knew what Sarah was thinking, because she was thinking the same thing.

Not that Amy and Sarah had never discussed it. In the first few weeks after it happened, Sarah had pressed Amy for the full story of Rags' death, for every detail. And Amy had told her. Not once, but over and over again. It hurt her. Oh God, how it hurt. But it was what Sarah needed to survive, to get over it and get on with it. Amy knew she owed her that much, and more. Then there finally came a day when Sarah didn't ask to hear the story, and by mutual, unspoken agreement they never spoke of it again. Amy hoped they never would.

Louis wasn't about to, either. "Just to see my family for awhile. My— my friends."

He almost said 'congregation,' thought Amy, amused. Then not so amused, *He's given up so much for me. And I love him so much for it.*

Sarah nodded. "That's cool. Listen, Ame, if you want to stay with us while Louie's out of town, you're welcome to." Sarah was smiling, but her eyes were grave and worried.

"Nah, that's okay. I don't mind being alone." It was almost true.

Xavier glanced at the clock on the stereo and stood up. "Yikes, I've gotta run, boys and girls."

"Awww!" shouted Amy and Sarah.

"So early?" Sarah complained. "It's only ten! We've only watched two Peter Jackson movies! We've only killed three sixpacks of Fat Weasel Ale!"

"True," said Xavier, "But I have a date."

"Oooooh!" howled the girls.

"So why didn't you bring him along tonight, medicine man?" asked Louis. "We could have checked him out for you. You know, inspected his teeth, checked his hooves and withers . . . "

Xavier's smile was sly. "Because I want him to go out with me again."

He fled in a hail of peanut M&Ms.

Sarah went to the kitchen for another six-pack. Mick stretched out on the couch with a triumphant laugh. "Mine! All mine!"

Amy vaulted over the back of the papa-san chair and landed next to Louis. She threw up her hands like an Olympic gymnast. "A perfect ten!" she cried.

The chair fell over backwards.

❧

Hours later, and Amy is lying on her back next to the sleeping Louis, head pleasantly buzzing with alcohol. He is snoring softly, and she loves the sound.

She holds her hand up to the pool of light cast by her bedside lamp, and regards Xavier's string bracelet around her wrist. She twists it like Sarah did her engagement ring, and to Amy, it is as beautiful as a diamond. Rust-colored stains and all.

She lowers her hand and looks at the battered nightstand, where a little silver desert fox sits in the glow of the reading lamp. Another gift from Xavier, to replace her gecko. The fox is strong, and carries away most of Amy's bad dreams.

Most of them.

Amy fights off an urge to call her parents. It wouldn't be the first time she called them at two in the morning. It used to happen a lot, especially right after it happened. They were so kind, so strong for her. And they never pressed her for details. They knew she wasn't ready to talk about it. They accepted that maybe she never would be.

Or maybe they just didn't want to know.

But she has no reason to call them tonight, other than a sudden, aching loneliness.

She cuddles up to Louis's warm, bare back, wrapping her arms around him, kissing his spine. He murmurs pleasantly in his sleep. Amy presses her forehead against his shoulder and feels herself drifting.

The apartment's tempermental swamp cooler starts up with a shudder and a groan. As she falls asleep, Amy hopes that the faint smell of mildew from the vents doesn't sour her dreams. She wills Xavier's fox to do its job.

✦

It doesn't.

She awakens with a gasp, rolling over, grabbing for Louis. He is there, of course, sleeping soundly, still snoring just a little.

She kisses his cheek, and slips out of bed.

Naked, she opens the bedroom door, pads down the hallway to the living room. She doesn't bother to turn on the light.

✦

Amy approaches the stereo, reaches to the back of a stack of cassette tapes, and pulls one out. She puts it into the cassette player, turns down the volume, turns on the power. A low, soulful song flows from the speakers like honey.

> . . . Whatever he'd offer, I'd be happy to take
> for the big empty promises you used to make,
> for the memories of you that are no longer sweet
> I wish he could haul them all down the street
> Rags and old iron, rags and old iron . . .

She shoves the stack of encyclopedias aside, moving them from the corner, and peels back the rug.

> When love doesn't last, then how much is it worth?
> It was once my most precious possession on Earth . . .

She lifts a loose board from the floor, and reaches into the hole it leaves behind.

Now I asked that old ragman if he'd like to buy . . .

She holds the jar up before her face. It glows slightly, with a soft green light.

But he just shook his head and continued to cry . . .

She pulls it close to her chest, the jar, and the tiny thing it contains.

Rags and old iron, rags and old iron . . .

The tiny piece of Rags' heart she had clutched in her hand when the airboat man found her.
She holds it to her chest, and weeps.
It pulses only for her.

All he was buyin' was just rags and old iron . . .